A one-time legal secretary a[...] charitable foundation, **Susar[...]** bliss when she became a full-time novelist for Mills & Boon. She's visited ski lodges and candy factories for 'research', and works in her pyjamas. But the real joy of her job is creating stories about women for women. With over eighty published novels, she's tackled issues like infertility, losing a child and becoming widowed, and worked through them with her characters.

Kate Hardy has always loved books, and could read before she went to school. She discovered Mills & Boon books when she was twelve and decided that this was what she wanted to do. When she isn't writing Kate enjoys reading, cinema, ballroom dancing and the gym. You can contact her via her website: katehardy.com.

SECRET FLING WITH THE KING

SUSAN MEIER

HIS STRICTLY OFF-LIMITS BALLERINA

KATE HARDY

MILLS & BOON

First published in Great Britain 2025
by Mills & Boon, an imprint of HarperCollins*Publishers* Ltd,
1 London Bridge Street, London, SE1 9GF

www.harpercollins.co.uk

HarperCollins*Publishers*, Macken House, 39/40 Mayor Street Upper,
Dublin 1, D01 C9W8, Ireland

Secret Fling with the King © 2025 Linda Susan Meier

His Strictly Off-Limits Ballerina © 2025 Pamela Brooks

ISBN: 978-0-263-39674-4

03/25

SECRET FLING WITH THE KING

SUSAN MEIER

MILLS & BOON

For my crazy grandsons who are bundles of love.

CHAPTER ONE

"WE HAVE A SITUATION, SIRE."

King Mateo Stepanov adjusted the knot of his gold tie in the full-length mirror, frowning at Leon Novak's reflection directly behind his. The short bespectacled man could have been a lawyer or an accountant. Instead, he headed the human resources department for the Eastern European kingdom of Pocetak. He was good enough at his job that everyone ignored his whining.

"And what's that, Leon?"

"You know Arthur Dragan is on leave."

He checked his thick black hair in the mirror before he gave his vest a quick tug to make sure it was in place. "Emergency gallbladder surgery. Yes. I know. I got the report. And I'm assuming that's why you're here. Someone needs to replace him for the few weeks he's out."

"He's actually requested two months' leave of absence."

Mateo turned to face Leon directly. Because he towered over him, he modulated his voice to keep from sounding threatening. "Two months? I thought that surgery was easy now. One or two weeks of recovery time."

Leon winced. "He wants to relax a bit with his family."

"I see." He thought for a second. "And the reason you're here instead of his replacement is that you're preparing me for that replacement." He frowned. "It's someone I'm not going to like."

"Honestly, I think you'll like her."

"Her? My *personal* assistant is a woman?"

"You have two problems here, sire. First, she's next in line seniority wise, and your position on gender equality is strong. You can't prevent a woman from taking a job she's entitled to."

"Artie and I go over my schedule while I'm dressing. Just like you and I are talking now. In my dressing room."

"That's because he was your nanny before he was your personal assistant. That was a very convenient shift of jobs for him and you."

"When I was thirteen, I no longer needed a nanny and did need an assistant."

"And it worked out beautifully," Leon agreed.

"Yes. It did."

Leon waited a second, then carefully said, "Are you saying you can't work with a woman?"

"Of course, I can work with a woman! There are women in my security team, and I have a cabinet and a hierarchy of royals who aren't all men!" He took a breath, then grabbed his jacket from the valet stand and slid into it. Though it was mid-April and the trees had begun to get leaves, temperatures could still be cool enough to warrant a jacket. "It'll cut an hour off our time together, but I'll be fully dressed before she enters my quarters. But that's all the compromise I'm making. She'll meet me in the dining room when I'm eating breakfast, and we'll go over my schedule then."

Leon breathed an obvious sigh of relief. "Very good, sire."

"And I'm not so difficult that you had to fear telling me. I might like things a certain way, but I'm not obstinate."

"No, you're not. But nonetheless let me suggest you relax before I tell you issue number two."

"Issue number two?"

"I told you there were two problems with Arthur's replacement. The second one is that she is Eleanore Smith's mother."

"Who's Eleanore Smith—Wait! Isn't she the woman who testified against that American politician who was found guilty of drugging and sexually assaulting her? What was it? Ten years ago?"

"Yes."

He fell to the Queen Anne chair beside the small desk in his dressing room. "Ouch."

"If you give her mother the position—for a mere two months while Arthur is on sabbatical this spring—you won't go against your very public fight for gender equality. But if the press discovers she's Jessica Smith, Eleanore Smith's mother, there might be…*conversations*. Articles. Podcasts. Still, if you don't give her the job and the press discovers that you blocked her from a promotion she deserves, that opens the original can of worms."

"So, we're damned if we don't but only potentially damned if we do."

"Yes."

Mateo shook his head. "That situation was ten years ago."

"Doesn't matter to the press."

"And the subject of all the publicity wasn't Jessica herself. It was her daughter. Plus, nothing about that case affects me. Not personally. Not politically."

"The press won't care. There will be publicity. Questions. It will disrupt our days and the palace privacy. There will be reporters at the gates. Rabid reporters hoping to make it into a story."

He thought that through. He remembered the days after his wife died. How reporters scrambled to get pictures of him or his kids. There was nothing worse than scrutiny from the press when you were suffering.

Still, no one knew how to keep a secret better than royalty.

"If you take this to its logical conclusion, the problem revolves around the press finding out that she's Eleanore Smith's mother. Meaning the chance exists that they won't find out."

Leon winced. "Typically, we put out a press release when there's a staff change."

"Seriously? For every darned position?"

"Yes. People like their jobs here so much that it's usually a list of lower-level or entry-level positions, or employees who are being promoted to the next rung on the ladder. And because it's usually maids, gardeners, motor pool workers, I doubt anyone reads it. She was on that list when she was hired. No one investigated."

"But this position interacts with me. Someone will look into her. All it takes is one zealous reporter, desperate to make a mark, for our secret to be out." He thought for a second. "Give her the job, but don't announce it."

"The press is accustomed to—"

"Did Arthur do a press release about having gallbladder surgery?"

"It was an emergency surgery. I doubt he had time. But we should—"

"We *should* nothing. The woman deserves the job. That's the end of the matter as far as I'm concerned. You, on the other hand, would like to put out a press release. As your king I'm telling you not to. See? Problem solved."

Jessica Smith sat in the waiting room for the king's suite of offices, not sure if she should be excited or fearful. An opportunity to work directly with the king was almost unheard-of. The steno pool might type, line edit or proofread his documents, but they never interacted with him. Their work was delivered by Pete Franklin, the security guard who acted as receptionist/gatekeeper for the king's private office or Arthur Dragan, the king's assistant.

When King Mateo turned thirteen, Arthur—his nanny— became his personal assistant, and the man never left the job. Technically, seventy-four wasn't too old to be working. But the unintended consequence of employing the same staff for at least two decades was that the king would be expecting things to be done a certain way. He was probably so accustomed to his routine that she'd be jumping to keep up with him.

She wanted the job anyway.

With a deep breath for courage, she looked around at the sedate reception area. White woodwork. Shiny floor tiles. Medallion light fixture. An antique mahogany desk where pretty red-haired Molly, the receptionist for this part of the building, sat focused on a report she was reading.

The silence of the place made her nerves jangle. There were enough receptionists and guards that no one stood a chance of getting to the king unnoticed—not that she was trying to sneak in. She'd been invited. But she'd never been beyond her own section of the palace offices. *No one* entered the executive suite except the king's direct staff and esteemed visitors. Only cabinet and in-person meetings were held in his private conference room. The king himself didn't roam the halls. He didn't pace, thinking through sticky diplomatic situations. He stayed secluded.

An office employee for over five years, she'd never met the big boss. She simply did the technical work on his decrees, memos, letters and sometimes treaties and agreements.

The door opened. Molly glanced over.

Leon said, "The king will see Ms. Smith now."

Her heart tumbled. She'd been a legal assistant most of her adult life. A fluke had gotten her a job in the palace and three or four unexpected moves had put her in a position to replace Arthur.

She was about to meet *a king*.

She rose from her seat, straightened her simple sheath dress and walked toward Leon.

He stepped away from the door, motioning for her to go down the forbidden hall. "Right this way."

She left the segment of the building that was the original palace built in the seventeen hundreds and entered the long corridor leading to the new wing. Gone were the woodwork and shiny tiles, replaced by elegant hardwood floors and walls of arched windows that displayed leafy green trees and colorful flower gardens outside.

Three steps took them up to the next level. They turned right, then left, then right again. Leon opened a door and stepped aside for her to enter first.

Tall, muscular Pete Franklin rose. "Good morning, Leon." He nodded at Jessica. "Jessica." He motioned to the door behind him. "The king is expecting you."

Leon said, "Thank you," as he opened the door.

She took a silent breath to steady her nerves and followed him into the huge office. She anticipated bookshelves and dark paneling with heavy velvet drapes. Instead, the room had a pale sofa and chair, a simple modern desk with two chairs for visitors, and two walls of glass, again displaying the grounds outside. White drapes had been opened and stood bunched in the corners. He probably needed them for the afternoon sun. But mornings were perfect for sitting in the big, almost empty room, and communing with nature.

The chair behind the desk swiveled to face them. The king, tall, gorgeous, dark-haired Mateo Stepanov, rose.

She knew better than to curtsey—palace employees had a special dispensation to keep the level of bowing and curtseying from interrupting work—though she desperately wanted to. In a black suit with a gold tie and vest, King Mateo went beyond imposing to magnificent.

"King Mateo, this is Jessica Smith." Leon faced Jessica. "Jessica Smith, this is your king, Mateo Stepanov."

He bowed slightly. "Ms. Smith."

The urge to curtsey was so strong that she had to fight it. But because he'd bowed slightly, she let herself mimic the move. "Your Majesty."

"Please have a seat."

She sat on one of the two chairs in front of his desk. Leon

sat on the other and the king lowered himself to his seat behind the desk.

"You are the one in line to replace Arthur while he is on leave. But we have an issue."

Her muscles tightened. Her breath froze. Anger rippled through her. Not anger with the king, anger with her daughter's situation. Like a certain White House intern who lost all chance for a normal life after an incident with the US president, Eleanore's life had changed completely. She'd been drugged, raped and held at an estate until she was "debriefed" and allowed to leave, but questions still swirled around the incident. Even after the perpetrator was convicted and sentenced to twenty years in prison, Eleanore's account of the events was doubted. She had been twenty, old enough to consent, and the beloved politician swore she'd consented. After he was convicted, she'd had to change her name and leave her country to find any peace.

Yet even after all these years, somehow that incident managed to find its way into Jessica's life. She'd stopped using her first name and began using her middle name, but apparently the scandal had found her.

Again.

"Arthur and I had certain routines and rituals that we'll have to change for you."

Shocked when King Mateo began talking about the job, not her daughter's troubles, she said, "I don't see why. I'm as capable as Arthur."

"Arthur and I ran over the day's schedule while I was dressing in the morning." He winced. "If a day was particularly busy, we'd do it while I was showering. I'm sure you'd prefer me fully clothed."

"Fully clothed would be better." Her cheeks pinkened. A shadowy vision of her going over the king's schedule while he was naked under the spray of his shower popped into her head. He was tall and fit. Everyone knew he worked out three days a week and jogged in the evenings after most of the staff was gone.

The shadowy vision sharpened and became more real. She envisioned his well-defined muscles with rivulets of water sliding along smooth skin. Her mouth went dry.

She shook herself back to reality. Blaming her weird thoughts on the pressure of meeting a king, she pulled herself together. She was a fifty-two-year-old woman who had gone through every second of her daughter's trauma with her. She'd divorced Eleanore's father when he'd hedged questions with the press, making things worse. She worked to support herself, always paid her own way. She never got flummoxed. She wouldn't start today just because the guy she was talking to was a handsome king, who went over his schedule while dressing. He'd already said some things would change. This was probably one of them. That was undoubtedly why he'd brought it up.

She straightened in her chair.

He laughed. "Relax, please, Ms. Smith. I wanted to give you an idea of how we'll both be adjusting to our situation, not just you."

She nodded. "Okay."

"You and I will meet while I'm eating breakfast. Meaning, you will come into my dining room. Though there are times I will require assistance with the choice of clothing for specific meetings or events, those moments we will be in my dressing room. Additionally, there are documents we can consult about what should be worn where. Arthur kept copious notes."

She nodded, finally understanding that a personal assistant's job was quite different than an office assistant. There was no dividing line between his life and his work. He lived at his job. He *was* his job. What he wore, what he ate, where he went—everything meant something.

That's what she would be dealing with. That was the shift in her thinking that had to be made. She might not have to read his schedule to him while he showered but it was her job to keep him on track. Both professionally and personally. No more typing, editing or proofreading documents.

Leon rose. "If there's nothing else, sire…"

The king rose and Jessica scrambled to her feet.

"That's all, Leon." He faced Jessica. "You and I have a schedule to go over."

Her chest froze. She displayed her empty hands. "I don't have anything."

Leon said, "The king's schedule has been emailed to you, along with his calendar and all appropriate phone numbers. You will also receive an access code to a spreadsheet with confidential phone numbers and emails."

With that, Leon turned and left. Her gaze followed him until the door closed on him, then she faced the king.

The king.

He smiled. "Leon never says a spare word."

She took a breath. "No. He doesn't."

"And he can be a bit stuffy."

She fought a laugh. "Yes."

"I'm not stuffy." He motioned for her to sit again. "Out of necessity, the office atmosphere is sedate." He glanced around. "Honestly, sometimes the place is weirdly quiet."

She looked around the way he had. "I see that."

"But there will also be times when my family arrives unannounced." He winced. "When they were kids, they'd sometimes barge in fighting."

She laughed.

"As a personal assistant, you might be required to help with that. Sometimes to divert their attention." He pointed outside. "Oh, look, it's warm out. Why don't you go swimming?"

She snickered.

"You laugh, but that one worked with my kids until they became teenagers. Now, it's more things like fighting over who gets the Bentley."

"Yes, Your Majesty."

"You'll get a feel for when you should intervene and when you should step back and let them rant. There'll also be times when they want to come in and lounge around. If my schedule allows it," his voice softened, "I like having them here."

She smiled at the affection in his tone. His wife had died several years ago when his oldest daughter was about eighteen. Technically, he'd raised his kids through the hardest part of their lives alone.

"I imagine it's difficult being a single dad when you're a king."

"I think anyone who works from home has the same problems."

She considered that. "It sounds the same but it's not."

He relaxed in his chair. "That's probably true. But I want you to get comfortable with the fact that you're allowed to shoo them out, as long as you do it tactfully. Also, if you observe something, like if one of the kids seems moody and I'm not catching it, you're allowed to speak up." He smiled. "You simply might have to wait until the child in question isn't in the room."

"Got it. I know all about raising kids. I have a daughter."

The word *daughter* fell into the room like a brick. If he noticed, he didn't mention it or bring up Eleanore's situation. Probably because he had troubles of his own and work to do and her daughter was irrelevant.

Her brain froze. Had she found a place where her daughter's troubles really were old news?

Lord, she hoped so.

He smiled again and her breath stalled. With his dark hair and dark eyes, and a face that was just a bit rugged, he was about the sexiest man she'd ever met. And he wasn't a bully or a tyrant. He seemed like a nice guy.

It was going to be a struggle not to stutter in his presence, let alone to keep herself one step ahead of him so that he was always prepared.

But she'd never had a chance like this and probably wouldn't get one again.

She had to make it work.

CHAPTER TWO

MATEO CAUGHT HIMSELF staring at the woman sitting in front of his desk and shook his head to clear it. Gorgeous women weren't uncommon in the world of royalty, but this woman wasn't painted and primped. Her dark hair fell to her shoulders and was nicely shaped around her face. Her clear blue eyes seemed to see everything at once, a good quality for someone who had to adjust to this busy environment and help him get through his days. But there was also a softness in those pale blue orbs that intrigued him. The simple dress she wore might have been designed to play down her figure, but sometimes there was no hiding gentle curves.

He handed her an electronic tablet. "This is mine. You can use it to go over the schedule."

She looked at it as if she thought it would bite her. "Yours? Are you sure I should be touching that. Aren't there state secrets in there or something?"

He laughed. "No. The only things in this particular tablet are addresses, phone numbers and schedules. You'll actually be using Arthur's tablet, which is at his desk, but for now, we'll go over the schedule with mine."

She nodded and slowly lowered her gaze to the tablet. "Okay."

"So, this morning I have two phone calls, followed by an in-office meeting."

She tapped the tablet a few times.

The schedule appeared on the screen, as it was programmed to do. He swore he saw her sigh with relief.

"The phone numbers for both of this morning's calls are beside the names."

She slowly looked up from the screen. "Got it. Thank you."

Their gazes caught and he watched her cheeks turn red. She couldn't be embarrassed. Nothing embarrassing had happened—

But she might be attracted to him.

He almost snorted. That was wishful thinking. Only a certain kind of woman was attracted to a man in power, a man whose whole life was fodder for the press. After experiencing the pressure of the media in her daughter's situation, she probably was not that kind of woman.

Which was too bad. She was so pretty and seemed so normal. Especially for a person who'd gone through a crisis with her daughter the way she had.

All of which was none of his business. Though she was allowed to step into his life and maneuver things around, including his children, her private life was off-limits to him.

He pointed to the right. "Arthur's office is through that door. You place the calls the way you would for any boss. Then buzz me and I'll pick up."

"Yes. Good. I did this all the time when I worked for lawyers."

"That's why you're here."

She rose from the chair and walked into Arthur's office. Then stopped, turned and walked the tablet back to him. "Sorry. You know, for future reference you might want to let Leon explain these kinds of things to new employees."

"What would the fun be in that?"

She blinked, then laughed.

"I used these little tasks to help you get accustomed to me. I know it's weird to work with a king."

She smiled. Her entire face softened. Her pretty blue eyes met his. "I guess that's smart."

He leaned toward her and whispered, "Trust me. It is. I am a king. I know things."

She chuckled, turned and left his office.

He sat back in his chair abundantly pleased with himself. Showing new employees the ropes wasn't his normal way of getting them comfortable working with him. But because Jessica would be working with him for so long, he'd wanted to meet her and talk to her before promises were made. Just in case her situation with her daughter had soured her. Now, he was glad he had. She was nice. Pretty. She also didn't scare easily.

He was extremely pleased with Jessica Smith—

Maybe too pleased. It might be because of her age, but he felt unexpectedly comfortable with her. The kind of comfortable a man feels with a friend—

Or a woman he was interested in.

He held back a wince. That was actually the problem. There was something about her that made him want to flirt. And that was wrong. A smart boss—even a king—knew that getting romantically involved with an employee was nothing but trouble.

But, boy, she was tempting.

When his phone rang, he assumed it was Jessica with one of his two calls on the line. "Yes?"

"I'm sorry, Your Majesty," Jessica said. "But Molly just called me. Your son is on the way back to your office."

"I told you they come by unannounced."

"Should I open the door and eavesdrop?"

He laughed. "No. Joshua is still in law school, but he also works in the government. He might simply have a question. Get those calls for me. If he's here to chat, I can use that to ease him out. Besides, my schedule's tight with the ambassador coming. Can't let him dillydally."

"Yes, Your Majesty."

He hung up the phone just as the main door to his office swung open and his son strode in.

"We have a problem." Tall and dark-haired, Joshua began to pace. "Sabrina's been drinking and clubbing again."

Mateo knew his eighteen-year-old daughter was going through a fun phase, just as Olivia—his oldest daughter and heir to the throne—and Joshua had when they entered university.

"I know your sister's underage, Joshua, but let's not panic."

Joshua spun to face his desk. "Panic? There's a picture of her flashing her breasts in a club." He combed his fingers through his hair. "She is turned away from the camera. But it's clear what she's doing. Especially since her shirt is halfway up her back."

Mateo barely controlled his anger. "Damn it." He now understood why Joshua was so upset. She'd crossed "the" line.

"In her defense," Josh said, "cameras aren't allowed in that club. She had a reasonable expectation of privacy."

Mateo tossed his pen to his desk. "We *never* have an expectation of privacy." He sighed. "You've seen the picture?"

"No. A friend called to tell me about it. It only went out to a select group of friends—people Mike Conrad knows," he said, referring to one of the friends in his social group. "And because it doesn't show anything, it probably won't go any further. But I think it illustrates a pattern of behavior."

Mateo took a second to wonder about his decision to send his son to law school because everything turned into a legal matter to him, then said, "Get her down here." He sucked in a breath. Remembering he had an ambassador arriving within the hour, he changed his mind. "No. I'll go up to her."

He rose from his seat and walked to Jessica Smith's door. Opening it a crack, he said, "Don't place those calls. I have to go upstairs to the family quarters. I'll let you know when I return."

She nodded.

He strode to Sabrina's room. He didn't even knock, just opened the door and walked in. "What in the name of all that is holy do you think you were doing flashing at a club!"

She winced. Average height with black hair like his and her mother's green eyes, she blinked innocently. "I had no idea someone had a camera."

"We've had this conversation before. It doesn't matter if there's a camera or not. You *never* do anything like that. If the press gets ahold of that shot, it will take you *years* to fix your reputation, if we can even fix it at all! You better pray that picture stays private."

The innocent blink became puppy-dog eyes. "Or you could make sure that it does. I know the security department has sources who could find out who took it, and you could get it back."

"It's digital! It's almost impossible to simply take it back like a print photo. Besides, I shouldn't have to get it back."

"You're right. Cameras aren't allowed in that club." She pursed her lips. "Maybe we can have the person who took it banned from the club, so we'll know it will never happen again."

Though his anger subsided a bit, frustration began to replace it. "You are missing the point."

"Or maybe *you're* missing the point. You never take my side. Never defend me. Everything is always my fault!"

"Your behavior is supposed to be above reproach."

She sighed and shook her head. "That's right. It's always me."

His frustration grew. He couldn't tell if she was being deliberately obtuse or if she genuinely didn't understand that her life was different. Her brother and sister didn't fully appreciate it until they hit their twenties. But they also weren't as uninhibited as she seemed to be.

The phone in his jacket pocket rang. He reached for it. "What!"

"I'm sorry, Your Majesty," Jessica Smith said. "But the French ambassador is here early."

He took a breath, working to get himself into a better frame of mind. He could not greet an ambassador while he was angry. "I'll be right down."

"Would you like me to get him set up in the conference room?"

He took another breath. "Yes. He loves coffee. The kitchen would have prepared his favorite. By the time he's in the conference room, his coffee will be there. That'll amuse him for a while."

"Thank you, sir."

"I'll be right down."

He disconnected the call and looked at his daughter. If she really was confused, somewhere along the way he'd missed teaching her something. He had to fix that. "This isn't resolved. We'll talk again tonight."

"I have plans for tonight."

He headed for the door. "Cancel them."

When the king walked through Jessica's office to go into the conference room where the French ambassador awaited him, his behavior had gone from congenial to almost silent with overtones of anger. He tried to hide that when he greeted the ambassador, but she saw it.

After closing the door on the conference room, she returned to her desk and took out the policies and procedures manual that Arthur must have created thirty years ago because the pages were tattered and dry. She'd looked for an updated copy in his computer and tablet but there wasn't one. Probably because the guy knew his job so well, he didn't need it.

Still, she did. She'd worked in offices most of her life, but she'd never been a *personal* assistant. The easy way King Mateo had mentioned her helping choose clothes for events and shooing his kids out of his office showed her she didn't fully understand the scope of this job. Old or not, this was the only guide she had. Specifics might have changed but the big things probably remained the same.

Flipping through the pages, she found the dress code section with details of which of his uniforms were to be worn when. But there were also line items about making sure he had a clean and pressed tux for formal affairs and affording him a choice of shirt. Housecleaning would provide soaps, shampoos, clean towels, and do his laundry, but it was up to her to make sure the clothes he needed were ready to wear when he needed them.

She looked up from the book. She supposed that made sense.

There were pages of birthdays of dignitaries and holidays of other countries so she could help the king send greetings to the appropriate people on the correct day. In the back were lists of his favorite dishes, things he liked to eat for lunch and even recipes in case the cook left and sabotaged the recipe bank by stealing the instructions for making the king's favorite foods.

That made her snicker. Arthur was one suspicious old man.

But she got the picture. While the king was in meetings like this, she could sneak away with the tablet containing his schedule and take a look at his closet, his clothes, to assure the suit or uniform he needed was ready when he needed it. The man had visitors every day. It shouldn't be too difficult to find a few minutes to check his wardrobe.

The group broke for lunch, which Mateo and the French ambassador ate in the king's dining room. She took advantage of that time to slide into his enormous closet.

Dark and formal with cherrywood shelving between rows of suits and uniforms, shirts, sweaters and trousers, the place reminded her of a dungeon. Ignoring that, she looked at uniforms and formal wear that dated back a century and decided that at some point she would catalog them. He also had at least a hundred pairs of shoes.

Aside from a ball over the weekend—for which there were several clean tuxes—he didn't really have any outside-the-office events, so she scurried downstairs and was at her desk when they returned from their break.

They spent another four hours behind the closed doors of

the conference room. After the French ambassador left, King Mateo asked her to come into his office to get instructions for some work she would be doing the next day. All the laughter was gone from his voice. It was as if their pleasant beginnings that morning hadn't happened.

When he was done explaining the two projects, he said, "That's all for the day. I'll see you tomorrow."

She headed to her office, but a weird sense hit her two seconds before she would have walked over the threshold. He'd gotten angry after his son had come into his office and raced up to the family suite. He'd said his son wouldn't be a problem, but what if he had been?

She stopped and turned around, retracing her steps to his desk. "Is everything okay?"

He glanced up. His deep brown eyes caught her gaze. Attraction zinged through her. In pictures he was impressive. In person, he was breathtaking. Serious, yet sexy. Ruggedly handsome. Everybody he came into contact with was probably attracted to him. Accepting that made it easier to ignore the little fizzles that raced along her skin.

"Everything's fine."

His eyes said the opposite.

He'd said she could interfere if one of his kids needed to be eased out of his office or if she noticed one of the kids was moody. Right now, he was the one who was moody. From the open way he'd spoken that morning, it was clear he would be honest if he wanted or needed her help. Since he'd told her everything was fine, she would take that as his way of telling her not to probe any further.

She smiled, said, "Good night," and left, the way a good assistant is supposed to.

The next morning, she arrived at the palace, ready to go to work. During his after-lunch session with the ambassador the day before, she had played with Arthur's tablet and laptop, and knew how to get to everything from the king's schedule to lists of phone numbers and names of foreign dignitaries. She hadn't forgotten the two calls she was supposed to place the day before but couldn't because the ambassador arrived early. That would be the first thing she'd remind him.

Coat in her office closet, tablet in hand, she made her way to the king's quarters. A maid greeted her and led her to the dining room, which was as formal and stuffy as his dressing room had been. A long cherrywood table sat in the middle of the room in front of a matching buffet. A silver tea service which she suspected held coffee sat on the corner nearest to the king. Pale blue floral wallpaper covered the space above the wainscoting. A huge chandelier dripped elegant crystals.

He rose as she entered. "Good morning, Ms. Smith." He motioned to the chair kitty-corner to his. "Have a seat."

Much to her relief, his voice let her know that the mood from the evening before had improved.

"Good morning, Your Majesty."

"Have you eaten?"

"Yes."

"Well, tomorrow, save your appetite. I've asked the cook to make blueberry pancakes. You won't want to miss that."

She laughed and he smiled at her. The wonderful ripples of attraction she always felt around him spiraled through her. Because they were wrong and pointless, she forced her thoughts onto the work they needed to do.

Though she was becoming troubled by them. Usually, when she told herself something was wrong or off-limits, her feelings fell in line. But she could not seem to stop her attraction or even minimize it.

Still, this was only her second day. Surely, it would soon begin to shrink until it disappeared into nothing.

They put the two calls he'd missed the day before on the top of his to-do list for the day. Then they went through his schedule. That sorted, he reminded her of the work he'd given her to do before she'd gone home the day before.

When she would have risen and left him to finish his breakfast, his eighteen-year-old daughter burst into the dining room. Wearing jeans, a T-shirt and flip-flops, she glared at her father. "You've suspended my motor pool privileges?"

He set his napkin on his plate. "I told you to stay in last night so we could have a discussion. You went against a direct order."

"A direct order! I'm not one of your subjects."

He sighed. "Actually, you are. You are also my daughter. Your privileges are suspended until we have that talk."

She rolled her eyes and sighed heavily. "Whatever!" Then she stormed out of the room.

Mateo shook his head. "That was my youngest."

She knew that from pictures in the press. But their conversation the day before about his family suddenly took meaning and she understood why he had warned her. If his daughter had done this in the king's office, she'd have first closed the doors so no one could hear her. Then she would have started timing. After five minutes, she would have interrupted with a phone call.

"Sabrina, right? I've seen pictures."

"She is turning out to be more of a handful than my other two kids put together."

Jessica pressed her lips together to keep from laughing. He didn't look forlorn or angry. He appeared to be out of his element. "I've heard that happens with the baby of the family."

"Her mother would have been infuriated. Instead of losing motor pool privileges, Princess Sabrina probably would have been grounded for a month."

"Why don't you do that?"

"Ground her for a month?" He winced. "She would be like a bear with a thorn in its paw! That would be punishment for me, not her."

"Okay. Make it two weeks…or a week." She shrugged. "Punishment has to hurt, but also if she's hanging around the palace that gives you time to talk to her." She smiled. "I can fix your schedule so that you could have lunch with her or TV time at night…or riding time. I know you both go out riding. Maybe do that together?"

He smiled. "I see what you're doing."

"What? Giving you time to chitchat with her and not lecture?"

He chuckled. "That's pretty smart."

Lifting her tablet, she rose from the table. "I'll look at your schedule and talk to the people in the stables."

"Thank you."

She nodded. "You're welcome."

Her job suddenly fell into place. Giving him a little advice now and again wouldn't be difficult. She didn't have to probe or overstep. She simply had to make a suggestion or two. She could choose his clothes, keep his wardrobe clean and ready to wear, remind him of appointments, birthdays and anything he needed to know.

Piece of cake.

Unfortunately, considering her attraction, she worried that assuming so many personal roles in his life might cause it to grow. But she dismissed that thought. She was a *personal* assistant. Not just help in the office. Plus, she knew her attraction stemmed from the fact that the king was attractive and normal—

Well, darn. That *was* why it wasn't going away. He was normal. Likeable. If he were stuffy, the way he sometimes appeared in public, or arrogant, the way a lot of royals could be, or pretentious, she could have easily dismissed him.

But he was likable.

Good-looking and likable.

And if she didn't get control of this she would be in big trouble.

CHAPTER THREE

SHE LEFT THE dining room and Mateo forced his attention to his breakfast.

Arthur probably would have told him to lock Sabrina in her quarters for a month and only let her out for dinner. Jessica had given him a usable suggestion. His appreciation for her as an assistant grew, even as something personal inside him shimmied with understanding. He liked her. He liked that she wasn't afraid of him or hesitant. He liked that she gave him suggestions without being overbearing.

He also liked that she was extremely pretty and appeared to be very soft.

That observation forced him back to reality. He didn't get involved at all with staff. Except his assistant. In that case, they had to be somewhat personal. She saw everything in his life. Even in a short two months she would get to know his children, his likes and dislikes and pick out his clothes and help him plan menus.

If he didn't figure out a way to stop noticing how pretty she was and how they sort of fit as people, it wouldn't affect his life as much as it would hers. After his disastrous first marriage to a pampered princess who liked being a queen more than she liked him, he had vowed never to marry again. Anything he might have with Jessica wouldn't go beyond a romance. And she seemed to be the kind of person who wanted more—who might need more—meaning anything between them would hurt her because it would end.

Not to mention what getting romantically involved would do to their work. He needed her as an assistant, and she probably needed this job.

He would keep his distance.

After his Wednesday morning ride with Sabrina provided him with the perfect opportunity to talk to her in a pleasant atmosphere, he saw even more the value of Jessica Smith. With the state Sabrina was in, and his responsibility to lead his daughter into her next phase of life, he couldn't afford to lose an assistant who seemed to have really good ideas about addressing his daughter's behavior.

He returned to his office all business. Thursday, he could have been the Pope, he was so respectful and professional. Friday morning, they did most of their communicating at breakfast before he had a long list of meetings.

Friday evening, she poked her head into his office, he thought, to say good-night. Before she spoke, he looked up and smiled. "Thank you. We had a good first week. Enjoy your weekend."

"I will. But I'm told you need to go down to the ballroom and sign off on everything for the ball tomorrow night for your son's twenty-second birthday."

Signing off on the ballroom setup was something his deceased wife had put into play when the staff inadvertently used the wrong silverware. He hadn't believed anyone had noticed. She'd had a hissy fit.

He rose. "We're going to have to change that rule."

"I'll put it on your calendar."

"Thank you. And by the way, you come with me on this final inspection."

"I do?" Her face contorted with confusion. "Why?"

"I don't know. Arthur always did. I think he used his eagle eyes to look for things I'd miss." He motioned to the door. "Which means, your job is to look around too. See if there's a goblet that doesn't match the china."

She snickered, then she frowned. "Oh, you're serious."

"My mother always said, two heads are better than one." He directed her to the door again. "Shall we?"

She shrugged. "If it's part of the job, I'm ready."

They walked down the hall to the huge ballroom. "This is another thing we added on when we renovated the palace," he said, opening a side door into the room, ushering her into the enormous space with high ceilings and rows of chandeliers, sufficient round tables to seat five hundred guests and an empty space for dancing in front of a section for a band.

She looked around in awe. "It always amazes me when you open a door."

He felt the pleasure of how she didn't monitor her reactions. She made him feel like a person, not a role. "Really? Do you think I should have minions who go before me and do that kind of stuff?"

"Yes."

He snorted. "Seriously?"

She shrugged. "What do you expect we'd think? You never interact with staff. You never even walk through that section of the building. You're so aloof sometimes our imaginations run wild."

He guffawed. "I can only imagine the rumors."

She looked around again. "This is amazing."

"And you've *never* seen it?"

They eased through the rows of round tables, glancing at silver and china. "No, Your Majesty." She peered over at him. "Do we have to measure the distance between the silverware and the plates?"

"The staff do that. They also measure the distance of each tablecloth to the floor." He grinned. "My mother taught me that."

"I think she knew the day would come when you'd be signing off on the setup."

"No. She simply liked me to understand that things didn't

magically appear. The rule came about not because my late wife wanted to check everything out, but because she wanted staff to know she was watching. I trust the staff."

"Humph. So, all this is a formality?"

"I think my wife believed if they knew she was coming down to check their work they'd check it first."

She bobbed her head. "I guess it makes sense."

"It makes no sense and once we get it on my calendar, we will be getting rid of it."

They reached the end of the tables, and he turned to get a perspective of the entire dining area. "It looks perfect to me."

She sighed with appreciation. "Grand and elegant." She turned. "And I suppose this is the dance floor."

Watching her, he smiled. "Yes. It amazes me that you work in a palace that you've never seen."

"We're told that's *your* doing."

He laughed. "Again, that was my late wife. She liked the line between us and staff. Mostly because of privacy. That I understood."

"I do too. But that's why palace employees don't ever see certain things." She looked around again. "Like this gorgeous room."

"Maybe it's another rule we should reconsider when I get the king-must-approve-ballroom rule off the roster."

She laughed, but twirled around, looking at the ceiling, as if fascinated by all the sparkle and glitter. "Just trying to en-vision what dancing here must feel like."

He ambled over to her. "Really?"

"Every little girl imagines being Cinderella, dancing with a prince in a glamorous room like this."

He took her hand and pulled her into a dance hold. "Then, let's give you the real feeling."

He saw her breath stutter and all but felt the warm wave of her attraction to him. She'd hid it well all week, but with her hand in his and his other hand on her waist, it was so plain he wondered how he'd missed it.

"You're not a prince."

"One better," he said, studying her eyes. "I'm your king."

The way he said it was possessive and primal enough to send a zing of electricity through her. Struggling with the urge to lean into him, she didn't know what she thought she was doing, moving around a ballroom floor as if she was dancing. "There's no music."

He laughed. "Okay." He began to sing the music of "The Blue Danube" waltz. "Da Da Da Da Da... Da Da, Da Da."

Their slight moves became the wide swirling motions of a waltz.

And it felt wonderful. Before she could stop herself, she wished for a full skirt to bell out when they twirled. She wished for real music and the noise of a crowd celebrating in this wonderful room.

He reached the end of the song and when his humming stopped, he stopped dancing. She caught his gaze. Expecting to see laughter there, she smiled. But he didn't. His dark eyes searched hers. A shower of tingles rained through her. Her chest tightened.

They were close enough that they could kiss. The temptation of it rose in her, stealing her breath with fear, even as she wished for it.

But then what? The man was a king. She wasn't a pauper, but she was a commoner. An employee of his palace. Someone who existed in his world only to make his life easier.

She took a step back.

He released her from the dance hold. "I'll phone the ballroom staff and give my approval."

"Yes, Your Majesty."

She said the title slowly, deliberately. Not just for her own benefit, but for his. There was a distance between them that couldn't be breached. Not merely because he was royal but because her life came with problems that would cause him more grief than he could imagine.

Of course, none of that would matter if they simply had a fling, nothing serious. Something no one would ever hear about.

But looking into the dark eyes of Pocetak's king, she knew this was not a frivolous man. Everything he did, he did with passion and sincerity.

She took another step back. "I'll see you on Monday."

She turned and began to walk away from him. For the first time since she'd gotten a job in the palace, she wished she hadn't. Some temptations weren't to be missed. Some were simply too delicious to walk away from. And she had a feeling this was one of them.

But he was a king, who, technically, was still raising a child—

She stopped abruptly as her brain kicked in. She pivoted to face him. "Are phones allowed in the ballroom for your parties?"

He took a few steps toward her. "Those things are confiscated at the door, so most people know not to bring them."

She glanced around the big room. "Make sure security checks everyone. I know you think that incident with Sabrina was just kids' stuff. But what if it wasn't? What if someone is either trying to undermine you or blackmail you? Has security considered that someone might have nudged Sabrina into flashing her friends at that club?"

Mateo blinked to bring himself fully into the moment. The longing to kiss her drifted away as reality forced him to be a king again. "Yes. Every possibility is discussed when something like this happens. My son is comparing the guest list for the ball to the people who were at the club."

"Your son sounds very much in control."

Mateo snorted and motioned for her to walk to the door and up the corridor. "He will run parliament when his sister is queen. They will be very effective." His nerve endings jangled from the shift of almost kissing her one minute to discussing his kids the next.

"And his sister? Olivia who will be queen? Is she ready?"

He worked to hide a smile of fatherly pride. "She's the epitome of a future ruler. She's smart, forward-thinking, and totally in control—"

He finally saw that she'd kept talking about his kids to completely end the almost-kiss moment. Not merely as a distraction, but a reminder of their different stations in life. Except what she didn't understand was that he was well aware of the uniqueness of what was happening between them. He'd never been instantly comfortable with someone the way he was with her. People had to work their way into his good graces to gain trust. Her past had made her into someone special, and even as it made him curious, the attraction added a layer of something that made the comfort level risky.

Not because he should be afraid of her. Because she would never want this life. Anything they had would go nowhere.

He stopped walking. "You go on ahead. I'm taking the stairs to my quarters. Have a lovely weekend."

She smiled at him. "Enjoy your son's birthday."

He took a step backward, reminding himself that limiting his time with her was for her benefit and a good king looked after his subjects. "I'm sure we will."

With that she turned and walked away.

He didn't damn his station in life. He didn't wish to be someone else. But he did wonder what it would be like to be in a relationship with someone like her. Someone authentic. Someone as soft as silk—having held her as they danced, he knew that now. Someone who made his heart skip a beat.

CHAPTER FOUR

WALKING UP THE stairs to her fourth-floor apartment, Jessica scolded herself, annoyed that she'd let things go a little too far when they danced in the ballroom. Gazing into each other's eyes? Feeling a connection, a rightness?

She winced. That might actually have been more than a little too far.

Of course, he'd started it.

She fought the urge to roll her eyes at the silly, primary-school comeback. Her brain wanted to be happy and frivolous. It didn't want logic and reality disturbing the memory, the moment. She'd felt young and free when she'd danced with the king, more like herself than she had in years. She'd lost a chunk of her life fighting alongside her daughter. Then she'd more or less gone into hiding. It felt good to just be herself again.

She carted her groceries up the last flight of stairs and dug out her apartment key. Feeling young and free or not, a king was still a king—not someone she should be dancing with. She'd successfully gotten them out of the situation when her brain had switched on and made the connection between the picture taken of his daughter and the ball occurring the following night and she'd reminded him that security had to be aware.

But for ten minutes or so, they'd fallen into something that was pure joy. A private conversation. A short dance. And a wonderful longing to kiss.

The kiss hadn't happened, but hadn't someone once said that anticipation was better than actually getting what you wanted?

Opening her door, she frowned. Anticipation might be fun but kissing Mateo would have been better.

She grimaced at her use of his first name and reminded herself of her life goals. Retiring to a quiet cottage in the country. Privacy. Gardening. Flying to Brazil to visit her grandkids once her daughter gave her some. That was her endgame. Flirting with a king could derail that if she wasn't careful.

Walking her groceries to her kitchen island, she heard the sound of someone climbing up the steps, and knew it was probably the guy who lived across the hall, Bob Greenburg. He was a transplant from the States. Nice guy. Always considerate. Never once asked her about her daughter or her job. Not a nosy bone in his body.

Of course, she was an expert at keeping people at bay. Everyone knew she worked in the palace, but she never told them about her promotions up the ranks of the assistant pool to the point that she was now the king's personal assistant, albeit temporarily. She always told people the least she had to tell them to satisfy their curiosity because she didn't want her daughter's name to enter into things. She never knew when a tabloid or even legitimate press would start poking around, looking for her daughter for an update. So she was careful. And it didn't hurt. It didn't even matter. She loved her privacy.

As she took two cans of soup out of her shopping bag, her phone rang. Setting them on the counter, she turned to get her purse and picked up her phone to see the caller was her daughter.

She hit the screen to answer. "Speak of the devil."

Eleanore, now Ellie, said, "You were talking about me?"

"No. I was thinking how my lifestyle lends itself to privacy, which protects you…but also, how I like being alone." The temptation rose to tell her about the king—a guy she seemed to be able to talk to easily, if only because she and Ellie both had issues with men after being betrayed. But she remembered the almost kiss and the simple joy of it. Maybe she'd tell Eleanore after the assignment was over, when the conversation could be whimsical fun about what it was like to work for a king. After all, Mateo deserved his privacy too—

Darn it! She'd done it again. Thought of him as his first name rather than His Majesty.

"Honestly, that whole privacy thing is something I don't have to worry about here. I love Brazil."

"From what I've seen when I visited, I loved it too." With her phone on speaker, she took an apple out of a bag, rinsed it off to eat and said, "So what's up?"

"Nothing. Just checking in. Though I have to admit I did wonder why you were late getting home tonight. I've been calling since six o'clock."

Once again, the urge to tell Ellie about her new position and the gorgeous king stole through her. Like a schoolgirl who'd been noticed by the popular guy, she wanted to gush.

Ridiculous.

"Really? I never heard it ring. Plus, I had to stop at the store for groceries…" Not a lie, but the easy way she hedged the truth that she'd been inspecting a ballroom with a king made her realize how often she did that. She didn't have a boatload of friends, and those friends she did have didn't know everything about her. Only what they needed to know. Because she was an expert at keeping things to herself—which made it even more odd that she was so open with the king. *A king.* For God's sake. What was she doing getting close to this guy?

She got out of the conversation without talking about the waltz by promising herself she'd give Ellie every wonderful detail when the job was over. By the time her two months as his assistant were finished, she'd surely be beyond her unusual feelings around him. Familiarity bred contempt and while she didn't want to dislike him, it would be great not to want to swoon around him.

Saturday night, though, he crept into her thoughts again and she wondered what was going on at the ball. It might be his son's birthday party, but certain dignitaries had been invited. There would be unattached women all around Mateo, hitting on him because he was gorgeous and eligible. She wondered how he'd managed to stay single for the six years since his wife's death, then suddenly realized his daughter Sabrina would have been twelve when her mother died.

Though it was none of her business, thinking through Sabrina's situation was a smarter thing to ponder than Mateo's love life or lack thereof. Talking about his kids was a safe subject. Not just because it eased those times when her attraction was so tempting, but because he'd said he wanted help with his kids, meaning it was part of her job to see things he might not.

She tried to imagine how Ellie would have reacted if Jessica had died suddenly but the vision was distorted by her father's potential behavior. Would he have brought women to the house? Would he have cared for his daughter or ignored her? He probably would have ignored her. He was so self-centered that it sometimes floored her that she hadn't really understood it until he'd left their daughter twisting in the wind during the trial.

Luckily, Mateo wasn't like that. Extremely strong and powerful, he nonetheless had a sensitive side when it came to his kids.

She squeezed her eyes shut. Here she was again. Back to thinking about him. He might need her to step in or notice things, but she couldn't use that as an excuse to think about him all the time.

In fact, there was a novel on her bedside table that she should be reading. That was her point of contact with *her* future. She'd be gardening, reading, communing with nature. *That's* what she wanted.

The idyllic vision in her brain shimmied and shifted. She suddenly saw herself as an old crone with her hair in a bun and wrapped in a shawl, bent over her roses, someone with regrets because her life was incomplete.

She shook her head to get rid of the image. She'd been married, had a child, gone through a major life crisis with her daughter. Now she was working for a king. She'd seen and done plenty.

She had no reason for regrets or to think something was missing.

She read for two hours then went to bed reminding herself that she'd seen and done enough for one lifetime, which ushered in thoughts of Mateo again.

That was probably why she'd dreamed about him.

Monday morning, Jessica woke grouchy. She wasn't sure which bothered her the most: the fact that the wonderful future she'd imagined suddenly seemed quiet and made for a gnarled old woman, or the way she couldn't stop thinking about the *king* she was working for.

Annoyed with herself, she entered Mateo's quarters for their start-of-the-day meeting. She straightened her shoulders, forcing herself to be professional. She could not believe that the vision of the future that had kept her sane during the trial now seemed dull. Worse was the way her nerves jangled when she thought of Mateo dancing with women at the ball. She shouldn't care. She *didn't* care. That wasn't her. And from here on out she'd behave like her normal self. Not a wannabe Cinderella. Not a woman flummoxed by an unexpected attraction. But a worker bee. The king's assistant. The person who kept him on track and helped him run his life. The person he could count on.

That was who she was.

Period.

As she walked into the dining room, Mateo rose. "Good morning."

He looked magnificent in his dark suit and white shirt, definitely like one of the men who ruled the world. His good looks acknowledged, she let those thoughts slide away.

"Good morning." All business, she set her tablet on the table beside her plate. "You know, it dawned on me that with an official event being held in the palace, I probably should have asked if you wanted me to work the weekend."

He motioned for her to sit, as he lowered himself to his chair, just as he had every other morning.

"Actually, I spent Saturday and Sunday clearing up paperwork that didn't require your help. Honestly, if there is ever a reason why I need you on a non-workday, you will be called."

She nodded, closing the subject, very relieved their dealings were back to boss and assistant.

Nevil, the butler, brought two plates of eggs, bacon and fried potatoes and set one in front of each of them. She just looked at hers as Nevil walked away.

He winced. "I'm sorry. They're so accustomed to catering to me that they brought you the same thing I'm having."

"It's fine. I love bacon and eggs." She grimaced. "But I don't usually eat this much. I'm going to have to start skipping lunch."

"Or you could walk the grounds a couple times a day. Working in this part of the palace, you have access to my track."

Access to his track felt like a perk she didn't deserve, but maybe that was part of her problem? Instead of accepting the benefits of her assignment, she was making a big deal out of them—when they weren't. Technically, working for a king should come with some advantages. A track was a simple, harmless, wonderful thing.

"Thank you. I'll bring yoga pants and a T-shirt tomorrow."

"We also have a shower in the locker room."

Her skin prickled.

It shouldn't have. A shower in a locker room was ordinary, expected. Not an invitation. Not a chance to be around each other in various stages of undress. Her silly brain was going off the deep end again.

"Since you'll be here two months, we'll assign you a locker

and you can put in whatever you need." He thought for a second, then added, "Given that you will have been in this part of the palace for months... I'll talk with HR about allowing you to keep it." He smiled at her. "As a thank-you of a sort for stepping in for Arthur."

"That's very kind of you."

He opened his napkin. She opened hers. They picked up their forks. Each dug into their breakfast.

The table got quiet and stayed quiet. After a few minutes, she wondered why he hadn't jumped into a discussion of his schedule. Normally, that was what he did.

She was just about to bring it up herself when he said, "Don't you want to ask about the ball?"

She desperately did, but she was working to suppress her interest because what she was most interested in was the ladies he'd danced with, the ones he'd spoken to. Opening that can of worms when her brain was finally on track seemed risky. "I'm sure you all had a great time."

"We did! It was spectacular." He leaned forward conspiratorially. His dark eyes brightened with joy, and she suddenly saw the reason it was so difficult to keep her own feelings in check. He was excited to tell her, to share with her.

They were kindred spirits.

"Some balls are more fun than others. My son's friends are a particularly happy group. They danced every song and groaned when the band took a break."

She let the kindred spirits idea sink in. It certainly explained why they'd gotten so close so quickly. "They do sound fun."

"I danced the first song with Sabrina to more or less open the dancing, then I did some schmoozing... There were people in attendance that I needed private time with."

She carefully met his gaze. "You worked?"

"Things like balls are great opportunities. Everybody's happy." His voice was matter-of-fact, confirming that what she sensed was correct. He didn't worry about confiding in her because he knew she would keep anything he said to herself. Even if she hadn't signed a confidentiality agreement, their conversations were private. "Everybody's in the mood to let bygones be bygones or maybe accept something they might have had reservations about."

She should have let the subject die, but the instinct to converse went both ways. He was such a nice guy, a good father, a determined leader that thinking about him working at a ball struck her as wrong. "So, you didn't have fun?"

"It was fun. It was great fun watching my son and his friends celebrate. And Sabrina was particularly well-behaved." He chuckled at what she was sure had to have been the look of concern on her face. "Being a king is not what everybody thinks it is. Especially if you're a *ruling* king."

She looked around the dining room of his quarters as if seeing it for the first time. All the while she'd been imagining him dancing and laughing with female guests, he'd been wheeling and dealing in dark corners.

He was right. Most people probably had no idea what it was like being a king. He was his job and his job was his life. She'd realized this before. But knowing him a full week now, having had a peek behind the curtain, it took on new meaning.

She met his gaze again. "Do you ever have fun?"

The question rolled around in Mateo's brain for a few seconds. He could take his answer in a very personal direction and talk with someone who wouldn't judge. But she would be a part of his life for another seven weeks. It was more important for her to understand his work than for him to enjoy being able to speak freely with someone...to be himself.

He answered slowly, but truthfully. "It's as much fun for me to jump on diplomatic opportunities as it is to dance."

"You think striking a deal is fun?"

"Yes. I know my life is weird and honestly, it's good that you're seeing the truth of it. The more you see, the more you'll understand why I'm concerned about Sabrina's behavior. I don't want her to say or do something that could haunt her forever. But I'm also her dad. I worry that I missed teaching her something."

She nodded.

Seeing the concern in her eyes, he sighed. "The way our private lives and work lives intertwine seems like an albatross but it's also a privilege. It doesn't make sense until you understand how much of an honor it is to be charged with keeping our people employed, safe, happy. I'm failing at finding the way to help Sabrina understand that."

He waited a few seconds while Jessica absorbed what he'd said.

He wasn't surprised when she spoke openly with him. "I don't think you give yourself enough credit. Even with a spouse and a normal life, I had some issues raising my daughter. I can't imagine how you do it, as a royal…and alone. When my husband backed out of Ellie's situation, I got a taste of being a single parent. It's not easy."

Her understanding and grasp of his life was like a soothing balm. Not that he needed anyone's approval or for anyone to really comprehend what his life had been like. But having her understand his fears about raising Sabrina meant something. And though he knew it was wrong, he let himself enjoy it.

Jessica continued on. "Kids in middle school can be mean. Kids in high school are always trying things. Ellie wanted to go to an American beach for spring break her final year of secondary school. We didn't let her go but when she was at university, she didn't need our permission…"

She stopped.

His heart thudded. She'd accidentally stepped into the story of when her daughter had been drugged. Just as he found it so easy to talk to her, it seemed she also let her guard down enough with him that something she undoubtedly wanted to keep private had slipped out.

The room stilled, the air filled with anticipation. Of what, he wasn't sure. He didn't think she'd intended to tell him about her daughter's situation, but now that she had opened the door, he wished she would trust him.

When a full minute of silence went by, he decided to give her a nudge, hoping she'd open up.

"You blame yourself for what happened to your daughter?"

She sucked in a breath and carefully said, "We should have at least tried to stop her. Not been so accepting."

The butler came in with a fresh pot of coffee, Joshua on his heels.

"Good morning!" Always cheerful at the start of the day, Mateo's son took a seat at the dining room table. "Ah. Bacon."

"Jessica, this is my son Joshua. Joshua, this is Jessica Smith, Arthur's temporary replacement."

"Nice to meet you. Am I here in time for the review of the schedule?"

"We didn't get to it yet," Mateo said. He faced Jessica. While he battled disappointment that such an important conversation had been abruptly ended, she seemed relieved.

She picked up her tablet. Joshua told Nevil he'd have the same breakfast the king was having. As Nevil scurried out, Jessica began listing his appointments for the day. The meal went on like business as usual.

But he couldn't stop thinking about Jessica and her daughter. He didn't merely want to hear the story. He knew she needed to talk about it. The same way he longed to talk with someone who would understand, not judge, she needed someone in the public eye, someone who'd faced down the press and his critics, to understand her.

But that would mean creating a true confidence. The things she saw in his palace, the things she overheard, the things he would tell her might have national security implications. Her keeping that information to herself was a part of her job.

Her story was of a broken heart. Getting her to tell him that story created a connection. A genuine, personal connection—

Longing for exactly that rippled through him.

Still, as much as it tempted him... Was it the right thing to do? She was a temporary employee. He was ruler of a kingdom, a man who out of necessity put his country before himself. He wasn't supposed to get close to an employee.

Somedays, he genuinely believed he wasn't supposed to be close to anyone.

That usually didn't bother him, but today it seemed wrong. Or maybe off-sync. As if he'd misinterpreted his entire life.

And in a way, Jessica paid the price because he sensed more than ever that he should return the favor and let her get her story off her chest.

To tell him—someone who really would understand.

And he couldn't let her.

CHAPTER FIVE

DISCUSSING A BORING trade agreement most of the morning, Mateo let his gaze drift to the door between his office and Jessica's. If he wanted to know the details of her daughter's troubles, he could probably find everything somewhere on the internet. But information wasn't what stole his focus.

It haunted him that Jessica was so hard on herself. He tried to imagine how he would feel if someone drugged Olivia or Sabrina and the desire for blood swelled in him as a hot wave.

The dignitary left and as Mateo ate lunch, he pulled out his phone. He searched Eleanore Smith—not Ellie. He'd noticed Jessica had used a shortened version of her name and knew that was because Eleanore Smith was immediately recognizable. Article after article popped up. He didn't read the text, only studied the pictures.

Eleanore walking into the courthouse with Jessica by her side.

Eleanore in the courtroom at the politician's trial, her mother sitting beside her.

Jessica was in every picture. Except her name was Pennelope. Pennelope Smith. The Smith might be common, but Pennelope wasn't. Just like her daughter, she now used another name to at least give herself a modicum of privacy.

The more important thing, though, was that she'd never left her daughter's side.

He returned to his office to find Jessica wasn't at her desk.

Before he had a chance to question that, his office door opened. Pete walked in with billionaire CEO Allen Risk.

Risk extended his hand to shake Mateo's. "Thank you for seeing me, Your Majesty."

"It's my pleasure." He motioned for Allen Risk to sit on the chair kitty-corner to his comfortable sofa. "I understand you want to set up shop in Pocetak."

Tall, slender, confident, Allen grinned. "Yes."

"To do what exactly?" The billionaire had only gotten an audience because he was well-known for being on the cutting edge of technology. The right project could shift Pocetak from mediocracy to relevance in the next decade.

"I want a space program."

Positive he'd heard wrong, Mateo laughed. "What?"

"The US has NASA and Elon Musk. There's no room for me."

"And you think there is here?"

Allen sat forward, putting his forearms on his knees and caught Mateo's gaze as if confiding. "Picture it. Long-distance travel using space. A trip to Australia would be a few hours. Japan would be a hop, skip and a jump." He grinned again. "Let me set up here, and I'll employ some of your best and brightest who might not feel like they have opportunities in your current labor pool. I'll need everything from lawyers and engineers to blue-collar workers for assembly. Plus, your country will get a name for being on the forefront of the involved technologies."

And his best and brightest would have reason to stay in Mateo's country. Allen didn't have to say it. They both knew people with advanced degrees weren't afraid to relocate, some even leaving their countries for greener pastures.

He sat back. "I'd be willing to see a prospectus. At least a ten-year plan."

Allen sniffed. "How about a five-year plan?"

Mateo smiled. "I want ten. I want to see that you won't come in here and get everyone all excited and then desert us."

He sat back. "I'm committed."

Mateo rose. "Good. Then it should be easy for you to write a ten-year plan."

Allen rolled his eyes but rose too. "I want to know that you are more than considering this."

"Having you run that kind of program here would be a boon to our economy and our people in general. We're solid. We're not going anywhere. You're the wild card. I look forward to you showing us that you're serious and committed."

Allen held out his hand for shaking. Grinning again, his self-confidence back full force, he said, "Okay."

He left through the office door and within seconds Jessica walked in. He had no idea how she knew Allen had gone, but she'd popped in at exactly the right time.

"You have two more appointments. Molly's sending General Wojak down now," she said without looking at him. "This is just a briefing before the big meeting you have tomorrow with the heads of all branches of the military. The second meeting is with a union rep looking for your support. Files for that are on your desk."

She said it efficiently and turned to walk out of his office.

A weird feeling shuffled through him. She needed to talk and he was probably exactly the kind of person she needed to talk to, but he was holding back. He simply didn't think it wise to cross that line with an employee.

But while the general went on for an hour about border control and two treaties that were expiring, Mateo thought about Jessica, knowing her cool efficiency was either the result of her not wanting to discuss her daughter or the guilt she'd inadvertently admitted.

He decided it was the guilt. The upset about unintentionally mentioning her daughter would have easily melted away because Joshua's appearance stopped the conversation from going any further than a few sentences. So it couldn't be that. It had to be guilt.

He could talk to her about guilt…couldn't he?

The general left. Ten minutes later, the union guy entered.

Mateo always knew that his life was busy, but back-to-back meetings were killing him that day. With the hours that had gone by, he now knew he didn't want Jessica to bare her soul. He simply wanted to tell her that she shouldn't feel guilty, and talking about that was not a big deal. It was not the start of an inappropriate personal relationship. It was simply finishing a conversation. Letting her know he understood. One human being to another.

Unfortunately, the union rep talked for hours.

When he finally left, Jessica walked into Mateo's office. "Are there notes or anything you want to dictate for me to type up?"

"No. I make notes on my tablet, then beef them up myself. It's my way of reviewing the meeting." He paused, getting ready to shift the discussion back to where it had been at breakfast before Joshua arrived.

But she quickly said, "Thank you, Your Majesty," turned and headed out the door. "Good night."

All right. That was a sign. A signal. She did not want to talk about her daughter with him.

Which was probably for the best.

He glanced at his watch, saw it was after seven o'clock, and realized why she'd gone so quickly. Discomfort rumbled through him. He kept her late on a day when she probably wanted to get home and forget everything she'd said—

Maybe. But he couldn't get rid of the awful itchy feeling that they needed to finish that conversation. That she needed to talk, or he needed to help her to see that she shouldn't feel guilty. *Something.*

He ate dinner with Sabrina and Olivia, but as soon as the

girls left, he called the motor pool. Ten minutes later, he was in a car and headed for town.

He'd changed clothes and now wore jeans and a nondescript shirt. He also had a cap pulled down over his forehead, more or less altering the look of his face. Plus, it was a bit after nine. Only a smattering of people still milled on the streets. Most of them were probably headed home.

When they neared her building, he leaned forward and spoke to the driver. "Pull over and let me out here." They'd taken a black sedan, not a limo, but he still didn't want the car to stop in front of her home.

"Yes, sire." His driver frowned. "But are you sure?"

"We're a block away. I'll be fine. My detail is only a few feet behind us. They've been instructed to blend in, but they are there."

Shoulders hunched and head down, he walked to her building. He opened the door and looked for an elevator. There was none. He wasn't sure if he should gripe or laugh. Luckily, he jogged every day, and four flights of steps was simply additional cardio.

When a knock sounded on her door, Jessica's head snapped up. She never got visitors—especially not this late—but if someone from the building needed something, she liked being a friendly neighbor. She jumped up and walked to the door, taking a second to look through the peephole.

Seeing the king dressed like a normal guy, she yanked open the door.

"What are you doing?" She grabbed his arm and pulled him inside her small apartment.

He shoved his hands in his jean pockets. The sight of him, looking so normal, sent jolts of confusion and attraction through her.

The man knew how to wear a pair of jeans.

"I…um…felt uncomfortable with the way we left our discussion at breakfast when Joshua joined us. We never finished it."

He took in her oversize T-shirt and black yoga pants, then her bare feet, looking at her the way a man looks at a woman, not like a king. Just a guy.

Her nerve endings sparked to life. She couldn't believe she'd made that slip about Ellie. But having him worry about her— enough that he had put on jeans and a knit cap and sneaked out of the palace to check on her—sent the warmth of pleasure spiraling through her, even as the kindness of it touched her heart.

Still, this was a king. The conversation had started because he had been concerned about his own child. Telling him about her situation with Ellie had been a way to show him that all parents second-guessed themselves, but she'd gone on too long. She'd actually been glad they were interrupted.

"That's because the conversation was over."

"But you blame yourself for what happened to your daughter."

She took a breath, then walked over to the sofa to move her book so she could offer him a seat. But really, she needed a minute. Not one other person in her life had noticed that she blamed herself. Nobody else had ever cared. Of course, she was secretive with everyone—

Except him. Her openness with him was so uncharacteristic that it scared her. She liked this job. She *needed* this job. And allowing things to get personal could ruin that. Worse, it was wrong for her to get involved with a king. Any boss for that matter. But a king was someone of note and reputation and recognition. She shouldn't burden him with her life.

Unfortunately, she could also see from the look on his face as he sat on her comfortable, but worn sofa, that he wasn't going to let her pretend everything was fine.

She sat on the chair across from him. "Yes, I blame myself…" She could admit that because he clearly saw it. Now, she would steer him away from worry. "But millions of kids go on vacation alone without incident. She was twenty. Old enough to make her own choices. I have come to terms with that."

"Not if you still blame yourself."

She took a breath and looked at the ceiling. "All right. Sometimes I wonder if there was something I missed teaching her. Then I remind myself that all she had to do was turn her head away from her drink for two seconds for someone to drop some powder into it."

"So, what bothers you, then, is just that it happened."

"That Ellie was the unlucky woman in the wrong place at the wrong time with the wrong person?" She shrugged. "Something like that. The arbitrariness of it. In a way, no one is safe."

"That's not really a good way to live your life." He looked around. "Is that why you're here? In an apartment? Because no one would expect you to be here? Your ex was a well-known lawyer. I'm sure your divorce settlement would have allowed you to afford more than this."

She didn't question his knowledge of her finances. She was sure HR thoroughly vetted her before she was hired.

Instead, she laughed. "Are you calling my apartment a dive?"

"Not a dive as much as a hidden place."

"That's part of it, but it's more about saving for retirement."

His eyes narrowed. "Seriously? You're living simply so you can save for retirement?"

Glad for the shift of topic, she said, "I want to retire early. I envision myself buying a really cute cottage in the country, and gardening and reading."

He shook his head. "Wow. You really do want to check out, don't you?"

"Check out?"

"Live separate. Ignore the world."

Of course she did. She'd learned a lot about people during

her daughter's trial. But she wouldn't tell him that. He still seemed to be worried about her. And he needn't be. She was very good at taking care of herself.

"Nope. Just saving for retirement."

"Humph. Retirement." He pondered that. "It's something I've never considered."

"You have responsibilities."

"Big ones," he agreed. "I'm the person who keeps war at bay so you can retire in your cottage and forget the rest of us exist."

She laughed again then inclined her head slightly in acceptance of that. "Thank you."

"Are you kidding me? That's all I get? Thanks for keeping the world safe so you can check out." He rolled his eyes. "I came here because I was worried about you but you're very comfortably hiding."

"I wouldn't say I was hiding."

"Oh, you are hiding."

"It's not a sin."

"No. It's not. It's just not a luxury afforded to all of us."

She gaped at him. "Are you jealous?"

"Maybe a little."

She laughed. "Come on. Don't pout."

"I'm not pouting. Just thinking things through."

She rose from the chair and sat beside him on the sofa, bridging the physical distance between them as a way to sort of comfort him. "I'd trade places with you any day of the week."

He snorted. "No, you wouldn't."

"All right. I wouldn't. But can we just agree that both of our lives come with some quirks and restrictions?"

He took a breath. "Yes." His voice softened. "But I don't like thinking of you as guilt-ridden."

She smiled. "I'm not. I helped Ellie recover by teaching her to focus on the future. Because that was what helped me. All through the trial, I pondered what our future would hold and how our lives needed to change so that when the trial was over, we were ready." She motioned around the room. "Believe it or not, living like this, saving, makes my future seem real."

He studied her eyes. "You're a remarkable woman."

Mesmerized by his soft voice, she suddenly realized how close they were sitting. But she didn't move. "Don't give me too much credit. It was a learn-as-you-go situation."

He leaned toward her, whispering. "And it looks like you aced it."

Their gazes caught and clung. Her voice soft as a feather, she said, "I did."

Once again, they were close enough to kiss. This time she wasn't letting her brain tell her that anticipation was better than the actual kiss. She wanted the kiss. He did too or he would have moved away.

Still, she wouldn't make the move. He had to do it.

He negated the final few inches between them, his lips touching hers ever so slightly. When she didn't protest, he caught her upper arms to pull her closer and kissed her completely.

Everything inside her shimmered. Curiosity and need tightened her chest. His soft lips applied just enough pressure to send tingles of delight through her. But it was closeness, the rightness that made it perfect. Kissing him was like coming home. She'd dated a few men since her divorce but hadn't ever felt this. Actually, she'd never even felt this for her ex.

She stretched forward the slightest bit. He deepened the kiss. Even as she clung to the reality that reminded her that she did not want this particular fairy tale, she let herself fall into it. Allowed herself to feel all the sensations of being kissed and held. Somehow his arms had gone around her, and a warm, protected feeling enveloped her. Not because he was kissing her, but because he wanted to kiss her. The same way she wanted to kiss him. It was a powerful, tempting thought.

He eased back, stared into her eyes for a few seconds, then said, "That was amazing."

She whispered, "I know."

He took a breath, pulled his arms away from her and rose from the sofa. "I should…" He rubbed his hand across the back of his neck. "I should go. But I'm not sorry I came. I just couldn't get that conversation out of my head. I needed to know you were okay. Really okay with everything. Not just okay with the fact that you slipped an important piece of information to me."

She rose too, slowly. The impulsiveness of kissing had been unexpected, but wonderful.

"I've made mistakes with my kids, blamed myself because I'm the parent who is supposed to be guiding them, but your situation is different." He sighed. "As you said, arbitrary. There was something inside me that rebelled at thinking you blamed yourself for the actions of someone who was the dregs of society."

She sniffed. "Well, now he's got a prison number, so we at least get the satisfaction of knowing he couldn't fool anyone else."

He took a step closer. "That's really the bottom line, isn't it? That he might have been doing this for a while, but someone finally stopped him."

"That was Eleanore's crusade. What kept her strong. The knowledge that if she pushed through this and he was convicted, she wasn't a victim anymore but a fighter. Not a crusader. Simply someone who was wronged and she got justice."

"That's a very good way to look at it."

She nodded. "Yes."

"So, no more guilt?"

"I'll probably forever have my moments when I say I wish I had argued, stopped her, been there…"

He slid his hand to the curve of her jaw. "But?"

She swallowed. He was going to kiss her again. They both knew it. Even after pulling away and standing up, intending to leave, they'd extended the conversation just long enough that he seemed to have forgotten he shouldn't have kissed her—

Why the hell did this all feel so right?

"But I promise. I will now banish those thoughts and remind myself that she is strong and smart."

"Like her mother."

His whispered words danced on her skin. A compliment to be sure, but a connection. He saw her. The real her. While everyone else saw a good worker, a quiet but reliable neighbor, he saw *her*. That's why all this felt so right. She'd already realized they were kindred spirits, but right now they were tiptoeing toward destiny.

He slid his hands to her shoulders and bent his head. He paused right before their lips would meet, holding her gaze, giving her a chance to stop him. She didn't. As much as her heart was thinking foolish things like destiny, her brain knew there was no such thing as people who were meant to be together. Everyone's life was a series of actions, reactions and decisions. Things that tumbled into each other. When he returned home, to his palace, he would look around and realize nothing could come of the feelings they had for each other, and he would decide that a couple kisses was all the destiny they would get.

Which was all the more reason to enjoy what would probably be their final kiss.

Their lips met softly again, but this time she decided to be the aggressor. She touched his lips with her tongue and the floodgates of need opened. He pulled her close and she wrapped her arms around his neck as the kiss went on and on, warm and delicious.

Once again, he pulled back. His hands slid from her biceps, down her forearms to her fingertips before he finally broke contact.

Regret filled the air. It was the poignant end of anything personal between them. The next morning, he would be a working king, someone who carried the weight of his little corner of the world on his shoulders, and she would be the assistant who helped him reach his goals.

Nothing more.

"I'll see you in the morning."

Emptiness filled her. "See you in the morning."

Walking to her door, he retrieved the knit cap from his pocket and smoothed it on his head, reminding her of the great lengths he'd gone to to see her.

Her breath caught, but she remembered the way he'd eased away from her. The finality of it.

He opened the door and left.

And that was the end of her fairy tale.

Because the very thing that brought him to her that night, his worry about her past, was the thing that destroyed even a wisp of hope they could follow what they felt. The press would love to find her with a king. Not only would they salivate over the sensational stories they could print—

But her daughter would be exposed again.

She would never deliberately do anything that would hurt her daughter.

CHAPTER SIX

THE NEXT MORNING Jessica arrived in the dining room for breakfast, wearing her professional face. He would have laughed, except all this was very serious. For as much as it might cause turmoil in *his* life if the press discovered their interest in each other, it would cause a hundred times more problems for her.

Not to mention troubles for her daughter. A story that had been closed for years would be reopened, along with the old wounds that accompanied it.

He needed to assure her that she had nothing to worry about. He wouldn't ever again show up at her apartment uninvited. He wouldn't pursue her. He'd tried to say that the night before, but he'd been so gobsmacked by their kiss that he'd given mixed messages.

He would rectify that now.

"Good morning, Ms. Smith."

She set her tablet on the table. "Good morning, Your Majesty."

Joshua and Olivia picked that exact second to enter the dining room. "I'm telling you that he's not the innocent you think he is."

Both walked to the table. Olivia smiled and said, "Jessica Smith, right? We never got a chance to meet but I'm Olivia..." She bobbed her head and grinned. "The one who will take over when Dad decides to retire."

"She's such a braggart," Joshua said, pulling out his chair. "You're just jealous because it's not you."

He snorted. "It's no great feat to be born first. You had nothing to do with it. So don't act like it's an accomplishment."

"It will be an accomplishment if she can handle the job," Mateo said. He wasn't happy his kids had shown up. But it was good for Olivia to meet Jessica. "And I'm sorry you haven't yet met Ms. Smith. She'll be doing everything Arthur did."

Olivia brightened. "Oh, I hope you tossed out those old notes he had about what Dad should wear to certain events." She grimaced and shuddered. "I swear I want to burn that one military uniform."

He sighed. "It's tradition. Like it or not, you'll be following those same rules, or the press will want to know why."

The mention of the press gave him a squeezy feeling and his gaze shot to Jessica. She immediately looked down at her coffee cup, which Nevil was currently filling.

Nevil moved to pour Olivia's coffee, and she said, "You haven't seen me because last week wasn't my week to meet with Dad. This week is." She smiled at Nevil as he shifted away. "It's not like we have actual meetings where he explains how to rule. But we do deconstruct some of the things happening in parliament."

Jessica smiled at his daughter. "Right now, you're serving in parliament, right?"

Olivia angled her thumb at Joshua. "Under *him*."

"Because he's second in command in parliament," Mateo said to Jessica. "He won't take over completely until he's twenty-five."

"And done with school," Joshua said. "If Dad reigns another twenty years that's a lot of years that I get to torment her before she's my boss."

Olivia rolled her eyes. "You'd best remember that because if you push too far, I'll have a hundred ways to get revenge."

The teasing continued as Nevil took breakfast orders. When

he left, the conversation shifted to actual business. Jessica quietly took in what was being said, but Mateo could also see her absorbing the family dynamic. She would be the perfect replacement for Arthur if he ever decided to retire. She was good at her job, but she also knew how to move from his professional life to his personal life and back again without so much as hiccup.

Which was another reason to get time alone with her to have that discussion where he would very clearly promise her that he wouldn't upend her life by pursuing her. Arthur had never before asked for a leave of absence and Mateo had to consider that he was testing out the idea of retiring. If he decided it was time, Jessica would be the perfect replacement. Telling her that would prove his desire to keep their relationship professional.

When their food was served, Jessica activated her tablet and began the discussion of his schedule. Olivia and Joshua paid close attention. They might love to squabble and tease, but they were both dedicated leaders. No matter what Joshua said, he was committed to their country and his sister. Plus, he liked being next in line to head parliament. It was hands-on politics and he was good at it.

They were going to be an amazing team.

Jessica made entries on his schedule as his children added events to his calendar, then she left to get things organized. He walked up to her desk twenty minutes later.

"Jessica, could you come into my office for a few minutes?"

Grabbing her tablet, she said, "Absolutely."

He would take the first five minutes to give her his reassurances, then that would be out of the way, and they could get down to work.

But before they even sat down, Pete arrived with one of the two union representatives from the day before.

He just looked at them. "George?"

George walked into the office, his hand extended for shaking. "It's our regular meeting the morning after the meeting." When Mateo was certain he must have looked confused, George added, "We always meet the day after talking with all the representatives so I can clear things up—explain how we came to certain decisions. That kind of thing."

Jessica scrambled for her tablet again, hitting the screen a few times.

She peeked up. "You're not on the schedule."

"I'm never 'on the schedule.' It's not a secret meeting, but it's not something we want advertised."

She turned to Mateo apologetically. "I should have realized an hour of blank space on your calendar meant something. I take full responsibility."

He motioned for George to have a seat. "No harm done, Ms. Smith."

She nodded and left the room from the right, as Pete exited from the main office door.

George took a seat. Kitchen staff brought in coffee. He and George talked for an hour and then Pete brought in a group of kids who'd won that year's Geography Bee for pictures. George said his goodbyes and left.

A huge encourager of education, Mateo posed with the group, then each one individually. As he gave them a short talk on the value of learning and hinted that great opportunities might be coming to their country and they needed to be ready, Pete watched over the scene like a proud papa. When Mateo stopped talking, Pete herded the kids out. Even before Mateo could get organized enough to call Jessica in, Pete returned with a stack of documents.

"I'm leaving at noon," he explained with his usual sunny smile. "Dentist. Otherwise, I would have waited until three o'clock to bring these in."

Mateo nodded, sitting at his desk in front of the big stack he would be expected to read before he signed.

He took a breath, as Pete left his office, then paged Jessica who arrived with her tablet. She eyed the big stack of correspondence and reports.

"What are your plans for lunch?"

"I have none," she said, still taking in the big stack of papers. "If you need help with that," she said, and nudged her head toward the documents on his desk, "we can get started now."

"Oh, I'm going to need help with that, but we'll tackle it this afternoon. I want to steal a few minutes alone for one final discussion between us."

She caught his gaze. "I thought we didn't have anything to talk about."

"Just maybe some reassurances."

Though she looked like she wanted to argue, she said, "I'll meet you in the dining room."

"Actually, let's meet in the stables."

She frowned and glanced down at her dress.

"Did you bring things for your locker as I suggested?"

She nodded.

"Hopefully, you'll have trousers in there."

"How about yoga pants?"

"Good enough. And you ride?"

She winced. "A little."

He smiled. "You'll be fine. We'll get you the gentlest horse."

A few minutes before noon, she strode into the stables, wearing yoga pants and a sweatshirt. He smiled when he saw her, but she grimaced. "I don't run the track in finery."

"No one does." He displayed a picnic basket, and she realized the stables were empty. No one would see the basket or realize they were going out riding together. She didn't know if that was because it was normal for the stable to be empty at lunchtime or if he had arranged this. But either way, no one saw them.

"Are we ready?"

Remembering just how long it had been since she'd been on a horse, she said, "I hope so."

As promised, the stable staff had provided her with an extremely gentle, smaller-than-average horse. She remembered how to mount and within seconds they were easing out of the stable.

They rode slowly through a huge, slightly sloped grassy area with just enough trees to provide a bit of cover, until they came to a fence. He opened a hidden gate, and they continued on through tall grass that swayed in the almost-May breeze.

She glanced around in awe. The palace was now so far back it was growing smaller and smaller. "How big is this estate?"

"A thousand acres."

She gaped at him. "We're going to ride a thousand acres?"

"No. We're actually on the short side of the property. There's a lot more land to the left of the palace. But either way, we keep the land extremely private. There are four fences. The very edge of the property doesn't have a fence, so no one realizes it's royal land. It just looks like a grassy field. The area borders a forest where people regularly hike, so the trees on the edge are peppered with hidden cameras and motion detectors. Nothing happens if someone accidentally steps into our land. Especially if they simply leave."

"Everything they do is recorded?"

"Everything they do on *royal land* is recorded. The first fence is actually fairly far into the property, at another strip of trees. There is nothing about it that says this is royal land. It's just a wooden fence. Again, that area is monitored with cameras. On the other side of those trees is another fence with sporadic cameras." He motioned beyond them to the grassy area. "That's where we're going."

"So there are two fences and hundreds of cameras beyond that grassy area?"

He winced. "I wouldn't say hundreds."

"Wow. You really do want privacy, don't you?"

"Do you want someone to see us?"

She thought about her life and his life and Ellie's somewhat quiet life and said, "Oh, my goodness. No."

"I never realized how congested my schedule is until this week." He snorted. "Then, today, trying to get two minutes alone with you?" He shook his head. "We had to come out here to get even thirty seconds of peace and privacy."

"On the bright side, you brought lunch."

He laughed. "That's what I like about you. You find the good in everything."

"Ellie's troubles made me an expert that that."

"Well, it's a good trait. Don't lose it."

He stopped his horse in a small cove of trees and dismounted.

She stopped hers. Then she frowned. "I forget how to get down."

He laughed and walked over. "Bring your right leg across the horse, and turn toward me."

She did. He caught her by the waist and swung her to the grassy field.

Batting her eyelashes, she purred at him. "Oh, you're so strong."

He rolled his eyes. "Stop. Even pretend flirting has to be off the table."

Though she agreed, she said nothing, glancing around, as he removed the picnic hamper from his horse and dug out a blanket.

"It's really nice out here."

"This is that privacy you're saving up for."

She looked around again. "Hey! It is!"

He motioned for her to sit on the blanket and pulled a few containers from the hamper. "Just sandwiches. I didn't want the staff to start wondering."

"Good plan." She took the sandwich he offered her, unwrapped it and took a bite. "Mmmm. Good."

"Our kitchen staff is the best."

"I still remember the blueberry pancakes." She waited a second, then said, "So why are we out here?"

He took a second. Once again, when he was alone with her, everything got confused. Or slowed down. Or something. He didn't feel the weight of his obligations. He didn't feel happy or sad or have a sense of expectation. He just felt comfortable. And that in and of itself was like a gift from heaven.

"My original intent had been to get a few minutes alone so that I could reassure you that the kisses from the night before were the end of my confusion about our relationship."

One of her eyebrows rose. "Original intent?"

He looked around, absorbing the peace and quiet of the area. "It was a busy morning. It's kind of nice being out here. Not thinking. Not doing. Just being. I want to soak that in for a minute before we have a depressing conversation."

"You know what's happening, don't you? You're seeing my point about the cottage in the woods."

He snorted. "Maybe, but, honestly, sitting on a blanket, outside in the fresh air, everything feels different."

"You're relaxed."

"No." He sucked in a breath. "I haven't figured it all out yet, but I think it has more to do with being alone with you."

"We're crossing over into that wrong territory again."

He motioned around them. "But it's okay. No one can see us."

"No cameras?"

"Not here." He smirked. "I checked." He pointed behind them. "Plus, see that fence back there."

She nodded.

"It's razor wire."

"What!"

"Don't worry. It's marked. And by the time anyone gets to that fence, all those cameras I told you about would have alerted staff, and they'd be there to greet the intruder before they got any further. But if they don't get here before the intruder, that wire's hard to climb or cut, trying to do either one keeps them at the fence long enough for my people to get out here, guns drawn."

"Now, I think you're just showing off."

"Give me that today. I don't get a chance to show off because people think it comes across as arrogant."

She chuckled.

"Seriously, I did want peace and quiet to tell you that I will behave. Watching you with Olivia and Josh this morning, I realized you'd be a perfect replacement for Arthur if he's testing out retirement in this leave of absence."

Her breath caught. "I would love that. Thank you."

"But the behaving doesn't start till we get back to the palace."

She looked at him.

"Come on. It's a beautiful day. We are totally alone. And this is it for us. Our last chance to just be us."

"You said that last night."

"It's not polite to argue with your king."

Her sandwich gone, she stuffed the wrapping into the hamper.

He finished his sandwich and stretched out on his side, his elbow supporting his upper body, his head resting on his closed fist.

"Being drawn to someone like I am to you has never happened to me before."

"You've never been in love?"

"My marriage was arranged."

"So, you've never had that feeling of free-falling down a well?"

He laughed. "That does not sound fun."

"Honestly? At first, falling in love is kind of confusing. My ex was a partner at a law firm where I worked. He was handsome. He was smart. He was funny. When I realized he was interested in me, everything seemed to happen at once. It was confusing and out of control. Maybe chaotic is the best word. And yeah. I felt like I was falling."

Distaste filled him. "Falling for *him?*" The husband who'd deserted her and her daughter. The very idea was revolting.

"Yes. But it was smoke and mirrors. He wasn't the guy he pretended to be. After we were married, I started noticing little things, like how his needs always came first. But because we lived an extremely comfortable life, that didn't matter. I could always work around it. Then Ellie was raped, and he reacted weirdly."

"He wanted to kill the guy?"

"No. It was more that he saw the whole thing as an inconvenience."

Confused, he stared at her. "What?"

"Her trip, the aftermath, the trial…that was about three years. At first, he pretended to be a concerned parent. Then he got angry that it was interfering in his life. Though he didn't come right out and say it, I recognized the signs. Then one day, toward the end of the trial, he out-and-out belittled our daughter when a reporter asked him for a comment."

"What did he say?"

"He said this is nonsense and he wanted it over."

"Could it have just been a bad day?"

She shook her head. "Nope. He really was angry that Ellie wanted justice. He thought she should suck it up and get on with her life."

"That's when you left him."

"I kicked him out that night after a blowout argument."

"And you had another day in court the next morning."

"Yeah. I stood by Ellie, and he happily let us go alone."

"So, that love feeling you had didn't pan out?"

"It didn't. I mean I loved him, but maybe blindly. I should have seen sooner that he wasn't who he pretended to be. While

I was free-falling, he was just fulfilling his life plan. I was like item number seven: Find a good woman and marry her." She paused a second, then said, "What about you? You never got the sense of free-falling with your wife? Not even after having kids? Or one Christmas morning?"

"My wife didn't want that."

"Really?"

"Like your husband, she didn't want to be bothered with anything she believed was beyond the scope of what she perceived her job as my wife to be. She did her duties with children and public appearances—oh, she loved public appearances. And she made it look like we were a happy couple."

"Weren't you?"

"We were a team. Not a couple. And, honestly, I was raised to believe that was a good thing. I wasn't disappointed in her. I wasn't disappointed in our marriage. I thought that was the way things should be. But as the kids got older, I saw that she didn't like being part of their lives."

Her face fell, as if what he'd said was incomprehensible. "Really? She didn't like being a mom?"

"I don't think so. I mean, she loved the kids. She just wanted them to be self-sufficient. When Sabrina turned ten, she started going on long trips with friends. I don't believe she was ever unfaithful, but she loved Fashion Week and film festivals and safaris…anything to get out of the palace and away from the kids."

She stared at him. "That's weird."

"No. It was very telling. She liked the person she had been, the life she'd had, before we were married and once the kids hit a certain age where she believed her work was done, she drifted back to that life."

"That was hard on you?"

"It was hard on the kids, which made it hard on me. I had no illusions about her. But I hated watching the kids lose theirs. I hated that there was an emptiness in their lives. I worked double time, loving them, doing things like movie nights and going on vacations as a family, while technically she left us. Until she got sick, then she came back. Used us again for a state funeral."

"Wow. She really soured you on marriage."

"Like your husband didn't sour you?"

"Oh, he did. I might date but it would be a cold frosty day in hell before I got married again." She leaned back on her elbows, stretching her legs in front of her. "Don't you think enough time's gone by that someone's going to miss us?"

"I've been watching. I'd say we have another fifteen minutes. Then I'll let you go back to the stables before me. I'll wait a half hour and dare anyone to ask me where I've been when I get back from lunch late."

She laughed, the sound drifted away on the breeze.

The romance of it rippled through him. Peace. Quiet. Privacy. With someone he liked very much.

"You know, everyone would love it if we'd start dating. They'd love a royal romance. Widowed king smitten."

Obviously confused at the change of subject, she peered at him, but answered honestly. "They might love it if you started dating, but no one would want you dating me."

"Oh, it would be great until they dug into your past. But it wouldn't hurt me as much as it would hurt you…and your daughter." He shook his head. "But right now, none of that matters. No one knows. No one is digging for anything. We could come out here every day and no one would even suspect if we found a way to get out here separately. We couldn't use the stables every day—" He let the thought hang in the air, not sure where his brain was going.

"Are you suggesting that we regularly sneak onto the one part of your property that doesn't have a camera?"

She laughed, but he sat up, his thoughts coalescing. "We are sort of the perfect candidates for an affair. You have to be careful to protect your daughter's privacy. And I'm too much in the public eye for you to get involved with me." He motioned around again. "Yet here we are. Perfectly happy, almost giddy, because we like being together."

She grimaced. "Someone would figure it out."

He leaned back again, stopping his rushing thoughts before the idea could go any further. Technically, he'd known her a little over a week. He shouldn't even be thinking about an affair, let alone suggesting one. The intensity of his feelings around her baffled him, until he thought about her description of falling in love. The confusion. The chaos.

But falling in love was an even worse idea than an affair.

Whatever was happening, he needed to stop it. Not just for his own sanity but for hers.

"You're right. Nothing ever stays a secret."

She rose. "What do you say? Is it time for me to go back to the stables?"

He sucked in a long breath then got to his feet. "Do you know the way?"

"It was pretty much a straight line."

He shoved his hands in his jeans pockets and glanced around. "Yeah."

Even he heard the disappointment in his voice. She walked over and pressed her hands to his chest before she rose to her tiptoes and kissed him. "My King Charming and I can't even keep you."

The way she'd so casually kissed him sent arousal fluttering through him. He bent and kissed her back. The arousal ramped up exponentially. He'd gone from conspiring romantic to desperate lover in about twenty seconds. Because she was right. She could not keep him. He couldn't keep her.

He broke the kiss, stepping back.

"I'll see you in the office."

She smiled and inched away from him. Then she turned and walked to her horse, which she mounted with only slight difficulty. In another ride or two, she'd be skilled at getting on and off the horse.

But there'd be no more rides, and he would suggest she be seen on the track tomorrow at lunch, so no one started questioning where she might have been on her lunch hour today.

Because as wonderful as an affair sounded, even that came with problems.

CHAPTER SEVEN

THE FOLLOWING MONDAY, Jessica settled the king in with his first visitor and grabbed her tablet to head upstairs to his closet. It amazed her that she could so easily move around the palace that had formerly been forbidden to her. Depending upon which route she took, she sometimes came across a member of palace security, but after checking her credentials the first time, they now waved her on.

That morning when she flipped through the suits and shirts in Mateo's closet, an odd wistfulness flitted through her. There was a certain intimacy to touching the things he would wear. But that wasn't it. She missed him. Not the guy who dictated letters or offered her the cream for her coffee at breakfast. She missed the person she could really talk to. After their picnic the week before, he'd almost become someone else, but so had she. Their sense of decorum stood strong.

They should be proud.

Should be.

And maybe someday she would be, but right now, she missed what they'd had in their few private encounters. She'd never really been herself like this before. Open. Honest. She'd learned quickly in her marriage that topics or needs that caused arguments usually weren't worth mentioning, until the scales of their relationship had tipped so far in her husband's favor there was no bringing them back.

She hadn't minded. Their life together had been fine. Good usually. But vanilla.

She winced.

After a decade of being divorced, looking at her marriage objectively, she had to admit there had been no passion. No excitement. Just day-to-day taking care of business. At the time, she'd felt lucky that her relationship was so calm. Now, knowing she'd held back to keep him from yelling at her, she recognized she'd sacrificed herself, her wistfulness, her dreams, her passion.

Things were not like that with Mateo. He was strong enough to handle an opinion different than his. He was strong enough to handle *her*. If they ever got the chance to make love, it would be explosive.

The closet door opened, and she just barely held back a gasp as she spun around to see who it was. When she saw Mateo, she clutched her chest. "Your Majesty! Is everything all right?"

He displayed the cuff of a white shirt that was currently coffee colored. "I spilled my drink."

Their gazes met as the door closed behind him. The last time they were alone, they'd spoken honestly about having an affair. After the thoughts she'd been having about him—about them—seeing him brought ripples of arousal.

She swallowed and pointed at a row of shirts in the closet. "You have plenty of shirts you can change into."

"Yes. Thank you."

The appropriate thing to do right at that moment would have been to leave. But her heart rate had ticked upward as a million possibilities raced through her brain. They were alone at certain points every day, but never alone like this. Where the chance that someone could burst in was almost nil.

He slipped out of his jacket and reality stole her breath. She could not be in this room when he removed his shirt. She was about to head for the door, but she stopped her foot when it wanted to move. She'd have to walk by him. Might brush against him.

Meaning, she should take a circuitous route around the cen-

ter island and bench for putting on shoes. It would walk her
so far away there be no risk that they'd accidentally touch.

She headed that way.

"Stop!"

She froze.

"Seriously, you're going to walk twenty feet out of your
way just so you don't have to get close to me?"

"It seemed prudent."

He tossed his jacket to a bench. "Oh, the hell with prudent."
Quick strides brought him to her. He said, "I miss talking to
you," then he kissed her.

The words might have been correct, but the kiss was the truth.

Warm and desperate enough to border on wild, the kiss
stole her breath and sent need careening through her. Whatever they had, it was strong and forceful. And unpredictable.
And wonderful.

But she wasn't the kind of woman to daydream about someone she couldn't have, and he wasn't the kind to kiss someone
he wasn't *allowed* to have.

He broke the kiss and stared into her eyes. "What's the
matter with us?"

She laughed. "You mean because we can't keep our hands
off each other when we know anything between us would be
wrong?"

"It *can't* be wrong. Inappropriate maybe, but something this
strong can't be wrong."

"Attractions are wrong all the time."

"This isn't just attraction."

She stepped away, shaking her head. "No. There's something here."

"Something I've never felt before."

She caught his gaze. "Something I've never felt before. And
I was sure I was in love at one point."

"Maybe it's just like one of those fluke things that is excit-
ing then runs its course and fizzles?"

She hated to even consider that. "Maybe."

He looked at the ceiling, then back at her. "But even if it is…aren't you curious?"

Waves of relief billowed out on the laugh that escaped her. "Oh, absolutely."

"I mean, even if it's not forever, it's certainly a once-in-a-lifetime thing."

"Yes." She paused and frowned. "Actually, that might be the problem. What we feel hasn't happened before to either one of us, and it won't happen again."

"In a way, that's nice to think about." He blew his breath out on a sigh. "You know… I never even considered something like this existed, but I like it. Which makes it seem like a mistake to ignore it."

"Yes. I feel that too."

They stood there, in his huge dressing room closet, both contemplative. Or maybe both thinking the same thing and afraid to mention it.

She swallowed. "I'm guessing this is why people have affairs."

He groaned. "Don't make it sound sordid. I *like* you."

She cautiously stepped toward him. "I like you too." Pressing her hands against his shirtfront, she said, "Who would have ever thought a king could be so normal."

He snorted. "I was a bad kid, a mischievous teenager… and let's not even talk about my years at university. I've been normal."

"Which is probably why you're so understanding with your kids."

He said, "Probably," but the feeling of her hands on his chest, even through a shirt, were driving him crazy. He wanted to scoop her off the floor and carry her to his bed and make passionate love. But he had people waiting for him.

Anger and the unfairness of the situation made him pull away. "I better go downstairs."

"Yes. Me too."

But their gazes clung.

He squeezed his eyes shut. "You know, we're not going to get rid of these feelings unless we act on them."

She smiled. "Maybe I don't want to get rid of these feelings."

"You're saying you'd spend your life pining for me?" He frowned. "That would be fun?"

"It's better to have loved and lost…"

"In order for that to be true, we'd have to have loved—which means act on this."

She laughed, grabbed her tablet from the big island and headed for the door. "You overthink. Just enjoy the warm, fuzzy feelings. That's more than a lot of people get."

He watched her walk to the door. The warm, fuzzy feelings did something totally different to his body than they did to hers because he would need a few minutes before he'd be able to go downstairs. He slipped out of the soiled shirt and into another, but as he was buttoning his fingers froze.

What if they *were* overthinking? He was a smart guy. He'd already planned one private picnic. He owned properties. She had an apartment—

He also had a security detail.

A driver.

Children who came looking for him when he least expected—

He groaned. Damn it! He would figure this out.

Because her friendship mattered to him as much as the romance. He liked talking to her, being genuine with someone. He could not believe he was supposed to ignore this.

Maybe that was the point? The romantic part of their relationship might be wrong, but their friendship wasn't. Maybe what his instincts were telling him was that he should be happy for the friendship and not lose it by reaching for something that couldn't be.

At the end of the day, when his meetings were over and guests were gone, he pulled up the schedules of all three of his children. All three had dinner plans.

He walked into Jessica's office. "Ms. Smith?"

Her head snapped up. Her eyes held the sincerity and determination of an assistant focused on seeing to his every official need.

"I was wondering if you played chess."

"Chess?"

"Yes." He motioned for her to join him in his office and walked over to the sofa. He'd set up a board on the table in front of it.

She laughed gaily. "I love chess. I just don't have anyone to play with."

He spread his hands. "Well, here I am. With my kids growing older I find myself without players too."

She inched toward the table, as if confused. He'd moved the chair closer to the chessboard for convenience of play. She slowly made her way to it, as if still not sure what was going on.

He returned to the door between their offices and closed it. "I was thinking about us today and realized we might not be able to have anything romantic, but I didn't want to lose our friendship."

Understanding filled her blue eyes. "I agree."

He removed his suit jacket, hung it on the back of the sofa and sat in front of the chessboard. "I'll be black. Give you the advantage."

"Going first doesn't automatically give me an advantage."

"Recent stats show that white wins fifty-six percent of the time. If that holds true today, the next time we play we'll flip for it."

She laughed. "Okay." She took her seat. "This feels weird."

"The chair is uncomfortable? Or the situation feels weird?"

"The situation. I'm playing chess with a king."

"No. You're playing chess with a guy who likes your company and your friendship. Chess gives us a chance to talk. If anybody walks in, they'll think we're getting to know each other...which is also true."

"Makes sense..." She eased her pawn to a new position. "And is very diplomatic of you, Your Majesty."

He studied the board. She'd made the classic King's Pawn opening.

He countered.

Focused on the board, she said nothing.

Neither said anything for three moves.

But in a way that was good. They really were playing the game. But he liked talking to her more. "Have you been looking at next week's schedule?"

Studying the board for her next move, she said, "Yes. I always try to get a jump on things."

"Good. And you noticed there were still empty afternoons?"

She nodded. "Three. I figured they'd fill up in the last minute."

"Sometimes they do. Sometimes they don't. Keep your eye on those. Try to save at least one so I can schedule some riding time."

She looked over at him. "Okay."

"I always consider the afternoons off, when I can sneak away, as making up for the times I work around the clock."

"During big crises?"

"We might be a quiet, simple country but we still have union walkout threats, border nudges, terrorist threats."

"I've never heard of anything like that."

"That's because we keep it under control. We don't hide things from the press but if a threat doesn't materialize because we neutralized it, there's no reason to tell anyone."

She looked like she might disagree but said, "Okay."

"I've also spent late nights walking the floor hoping Olivia and Joshua choose good mates."

She laughed heartily. "That I understand. I've done that myself."

"Olivia is aware that whoever she marries will live in a spotlight."

Jessica didn't answer for a second as she pondered her next play. She moved her game piece then said, "Do you ever consider arranging a marriage for her?"

He winced and moved his bishop, ending the game. "My arranged marriage was fine, but empty. I'm not sure I'd want to do that to her."

She gaped at him.

"Are you surprised that I beat you so quickly or confused about me not wanting to arrange a marriage for Olivia?"

"I'm not happy you beat me so quickly. I agree about Olivia."

He reset the board. "Wanna be black?"

She snorted. "I'll stay with the white. And before you get too proud, it's been years since I played. I'll be looking for chess online when I get home so I can practice and be ready for the next session."

During the second game, they shifted easily from discussing Olivia finding a mate to Josh being one of the smartest people Mateo had ever met. "And I've met a lot of people."

She lifted her gaze from the board. "Do you wish he was your successor?"

"Not even a little bit. He's perfect where he is. He's the detail guy. Olivia has heart. She likes the details, the numbers, the logic, but then she considers the human side of things and some of her decisions are interesting."

She smiled at him for a second, then she said, "You know what else is interesting? All this time we've been talking about

Josh and Oliva, and their futures and you've never once mentioned Sabrina."

He sucked in a big breath. "I don't eliminate her from conversations deliberately. Josh and Olivia are already on their career paths and talking about them is basically talking about work. But I also think that's part of why it's my fault that Sabrina is an attention seeker. I've inadvertently made her feel like there is no place for her. But there is. If you look at the big picture, Olivia as queen and Josh as head of parliament... Sabrina could be our 'presence' outside the country."

"Like an ambassador?"

"A royal visiting a country is more than an ambassador. There's a power to the position of being part of a royal family. Plus, if you consider her personality, she has the qualities of someone who has a heart like her older sister and a brain like her brother...with the personality that wins people over."

"From what I've seen of her, yes, she would be very good at that. Have you told her yet?"

He took a breath. "I'm facing some delicate timing. If I tell her too soon, she could get cocky and arrogant."

"Your other two kids knew their positions when they were in grammar school, and they did just fine."

He inclined his head. "Yes. They did. But Sabrina is different from her brother and sister. I'm not sure how I missed teaching her this, but she hasn't yet learned that we serve the people of our country. She still sees people as serving her."

"I know how you missed it. You didn't have to teach Olivia and Josh that they served the kingdom because they knew they had a position they were stepping into and they knew service was part of it. Without looking at a future in the government, Sabrina didn't have that sensibility."

"Huh. I never thought of that." He smiled. "That's how I missed teaching her that."

Jessica shrugged. "I think so." She peeked over at him. "So, what you need to do now is watch for opportunities to tell her there's a place for her. Once she sees herself having a position, you'll be able to help her shift the way she looks at things. Especially, the idea that she serves her people."

During game three, they talked some more about their country, his job and the cottage she hoped to someday buy. He even teased that she could find land on the outer edge of the royal estate and build her cottage there.

"Didn't you say that was a natural park or something?"

"It's a forest. People use it like a national park, but really, it's nothing because we keep it that way."

"So, you'd have to sell me the land?"

"No. We don't own it…we just keep track of it."

She laughed, but her laugh turned into a yawn. "Oh, my goodness. I'm so sorry."

He rose. "No. You're tired." Glancing at his watch, he said, "I shouldn't have kept you so long." He walked to his desk and pressed a button on his phone. "Philip, have someone bring Ms. Smith's car to the front entry. We worked a little late tonight."

With the office staff gone, the motor pool wasn't surprised to hear from him directly. Philip said, "Yes, Your Majesty."

He faced her again. "Can I see you out?"

"No. I'm fine. I appreciate not having to walk across the parking lot though."

He sniffed. "Arthur snagged that perk years ago. When he arrives, he actually pulls his car up to the front entrance and has one of the guards park it, then he has the car brought back to him when he leaves."

"I would really like that."

"Consider it done."

She walked to the door separating their offices and he followed her. "Tonight was fun. The next time, I promise I won't bore you with talk about my kids."

She laughed. "I could tell you about my crocheting… Oh, or the book I'm reading."

She gave the title, and he nodded. "I'll read it too."

"We'll be a book club!"

He stepped closer and gave in to the irresistible urge to run his hand along her back. "A private book club."

She smiled at him. "Yes."

His other hand went to her waist of its own volition. He didn't see a battle taking place in her eyes. She was too busy smiling, drifting closer to him.

He swore he could feel the chemistry he'd been fighting all evening rising like mist over a lake. Subtle, but so natural there was no stopping it.

Knowing this part of the palace was empty, he gave in to his instinct to kiss her, even though this was only supposed to be a friendship evening together. His hands on her waist itched to drift lower, but she broke their kiss.

"My car's waiting for me."

He bent to kiss her again. "No. It'll take a minute for Philip to send someone to take that walk you now won't have to make and get your car."

She laughed but kissed him back. What started simple and easy ramped up and became a passionate exchange. Their tongues twined. His hands roved. Her hands slid from his shoulders down his back, igniting little fires everywhere they went.

The thought that they couldn't go any further sent fury screaming through him. Nothing had ever seemed so natural or so right. Yet it wasn't to be.

He attempted to break the kiss, but impulse had taken over and kept coming up with new ideas for how to kiss her, where to touch her. He'd made love before, many times, but he'd never felt the guttural instinct that rolled through him, almost demanding that he take what he wanted.

The intercom on his phone buzzed. "Your Majesty?"

He stopped; confusion froze him for a few seconds, then he raced to the other side of the desk and pressed the button. "Yes, Philip?"

"The car is here. I'm about to clock out. Dale is replacing me."

He sucked in some air and looked over at Jessica, who was running her fingers through her hair, straightening it. Because he'd messed it up. And he wanted to do it again…and more.

The injustice of it spiraled through him, but he said, "She is on her way now."

"Thank you, Your Majesty."

"Good night, Philip. We'll see you tomorrow."

He disconnected the call and glanced at Jessica. Their eyes met. He could see the same regret in hers that he knew filled his. She wasn't upset that he'd kissed her. She was as upset as he was that they'd had to stop, and she had to leave.

It tore him apart to watch her walk out the door.

CHAPTER EIGHT

THE FOLLOWING MORNING, Jessica stepped out of the shower and looked at herself in her full-length mirror. She'd always been average sized, but exercise kept her tummy from being overly squishy, her butt tight and her breasts from sagging. She wouldn't mind if Mateo saw her naked.

She took a quick breath, pushed that thought out of her brain and strode out of her bathroom to get herself dressed for the day.

Her work clothes were laid out on the bed, but when she picked up her bra, she grimaced. She'd always considered herself young at heart. Yet here she was about to put on a sensible bra and granny panties.

She carried them back to her dresser and rummaged for the pink bra and panties she'd bought on her last internet shopping trip. She couldn't remember why she'd bought them—they were probably on sale—but she was glad she had. Just as her cottage in the woods was beginning to feel like she was giving up on life, her old lady underwear made her feel frumpy, so it would now be replaced. All of it. In fact, she might just burn it because it reminded her of a time in her life where she'd clung to anything sensible that she could find, desperate for normalcy. But things were changing. *She* was changing. She would follow the impulses wherever they led.

Happy with that plan, she slid a light blue sweater and black skirt over her pink undies and all but bounced into her kitchen.

She wouldn't let her brain tiptoe toward the idea that her feelings for Mateo were giving her a youthful glow and causing her to focus on how she was still young, still vital—

And could be happy.

Her hand paused over the coffeemaker. For heaven's sake. That's what this weird feeling was. Happiness. The kind of joy she believed she'd never find again. What they had might not go anywhere permanently, but even the flirting and kissing were changing her, reminding her that there was a lot of life left to be *lived*. Not just endured.

Even if she never had a full-blown romance with Mateo, he'd pulled her out of that funk. She could at least admit that.

When she reached the palace guard station, Franco greeted her. "I hear you have new parking accommodations."

"You know Arthur's out for two months, right?"

"Gallbladder surgery."

"Well, I'm his replacement."

He laughed. "Yeah, Arthur finagled parking privileges a few years ago."

She smiled at Franco. "Now, they're a thing."

And just like that she was over her fear of people knowing she worked for the king and her distaste for getting privilege. She knew she'd held back on a lot of things because she didn't like being seen or being recognized. But inside the gates of this palace no one was looking at her as Eleanore Smith's mom. Here, she was the king's personal assistant.

When she entered her office, Mateo was already there. "Ms. Smith. You're early."

She shrugged out of her coat, ready to dive into work. "Is there anything I can help you with? Find for you?"

He told her about an old treaty with a country that no longer existed. "I need to refresh my memory about the terms of the agreement."

"Really? With a country that hasn't existed for ten years?"

He laughed as she sat at her desk and started typing on her

computer keyboard. She'd quickly learned that the old physical filing system was antiquated, and it would take a compass and sherpa to help her find anything in that mess. But it didn't matter because everything existed somewhere digitally. Those files were sleek and elegant and more easily navigated.

"The land still exists. The boundaries are the same. The government is just different. And let's just say they're a little full of themselves. I want to remind their president of the terms his predecessor agreed to and hope he realizes I won't be bullied. But first I need to show it to my cabinet, see if they still agree with what we'd penned ten years ago."

"Ah. Found it." She twisted around to face him. "Do you want it printed?"

"Email it to me." He smiled. "Ready for breakfast?"

She rose from her desk. "Yes. I'm starving. I didn't eat dinner last night."

He winced. "Sorry about that."

She nearly stretched up to kiss him but caught herself just in time. When they were working, those impulses were out of place. And she would control them.

She laughed. "It was worth it. But now I'm super hungry for whatever the chef has in mind."

He motioned for her to precede him to the door. He didn't make any references to her saying it was worth it. His eyes didn't even ask if she'd actually been talking about their make-out session being worth missing a meal or the chess games. With the exception of her near-miss with wanting to stretch up and kiss him, in this minute they were nothing but a boss and his personal assistant.

And it didn't feel odd. This felt as right as kissing him had the night before. It wasn't as if she were two people but more like they had a professional relationship and a personal one and they were growing accustomed to separating those roles.

They walked up the stairs together and down the hallway

to a side entrance to the royal king's quarters, the one she'd been instructed to use when she needed to go into his closet.

He pointed to the left to a hall she'd never walked down. "There's a really fancy foyer at the end of that corridor. In case you're ever asked to escort someone up here to see me, that's the entry you would use. The elevator will take you right to it."

"Do you think I should get a tour of this place, so I'll always know where to go?"

He frowned. "We've used up two and a half weeks of Arthur's leave of absence. If he doesn't retire, you probably don't need an official tour."

She heard the bit of sadness in his voice and felt a corresponding sadness in the pit of her stomach. Working for him had been so much fun and so good for her that she hated to see it end—

But that wasn't the reason her chest tightened. She'd never had feelings like these for another person. Never felt so connected. Never felt so sexy and beautiful. Never longed to make love with someone the way she did him.

It didn't matter. That was a consideration for another day. Right now, she was a personal assistant about to have breakfast and go over her king's schedule.

They eased into the dining room to find Sabrina and Olivia already there.

Olivia stood. "Good morning, Your Majesty."

He pulled out Jessica's chair for her. She hesitated. He'd never done that before. Still, this was the first time they had entered together.

He sighed. "Olivia, right now, I'm your dad. Not your king."

Olivia took her seat again. "I know, but some days it's fun to go overboard with the pomp and circumstance."

He shook his head as he sat at the head of the table. "And good morning to you, too, Sabrina."

She mumbled, "Morning, Dad," into her oatmeal.

"You're eating oatmeal?"

"I'm not really hungry and I thought this was the most inconsequential thing to waste."

Mateo laughed. Olivia rolled her eyes. Jessica didn't react at all. She was at the table only as an employee.

Nevil came in and took the king's breakfast order, then Jessica's. As soon as he was gone, Olivia said, "I'm actually here because I want to hear your schedule. If you have nothing going on tonight, my oversight committee is meeting. It's been about six months since you attended one of our meetings and I just thought it was time for you to sit in. You know...let us see we're not forgotten."

"No one is ever forgotten."

"I know that, and you know that," Olivia said. "But an appearance from you always reignites a committee's fire."

He shrugged. "Sure. What time's the meeting?"

"Seven. We typically work about three hours."

"Okay."

"Thanks."

A few minutes later, Nevil returned with their breakfast. Jessica dug into her eggs and bacon like the starving woman that she was. When she reached for her coffee, she noticed Sabrina staring at her, studying her.

With the youngest royal child at the table, the mood of the meal was considerably more casual. She couldn't believe Sabrina disliked the relaxed atmosphere, but she might dislike an outsider eating with them.

The easiest way to make herself look like she had a purpose at this table was to bring out the schedule. Olivia had asked about it and received an answer without actually having to go over the day's events. But her purpose at breakfast with this family was to go over the schedule.

She lifted the tablet from the chair beside her and tapped the screen. "So? Ready to hear the day's schedule?"

Mateo pointed at her half-eaten meal. "Finish. We have plenty of time."

"No. I'm fine."

She began with that morning's meetings and while Olivia perked up, Sabrina sighed and pulled her spoon through the oatmeal she wasn't eating. Occasionally, Olivia would begin a short discussion of a meeting or a visitor, and Jessica would use that time to eat more of her food.

It was a very smooth operation. They went over the schedule. Everyone ate in between line items and the meal was both delicious and productive.

With the schedule read, Olivia left.

Sabrina sighed.

Jessica wanted to ask if she was okay, but that wasn't her place. Besides, Mateo had said if she noticed one of the kids behaving strangely, she should be discreet.

Plus, looking at Sabrina's red eyes, she wondered if she had a hangover...or if she'd come in late and gotten up too early.

Mateo glanced at her. "I know we don't go over my weekend schedule until Friday, but could you check to see if I have an event for Eliminate Hunger?"

She picked up her tablet again. Eliminate Hunger was a European charity and she'd seen it on the schedule on Saturday. Still, she double-checked.

"Yes. On Saturday."

"Is it in their facility—the warehouse?"

"Yes." She hit the line item to access the details. "You are to go to their warehouse for a tour, then present a check as a gift from Pocetak."

He sat back. "The last time I went, I wore a suit and felt like a stuffy old man. Can you put together something like a cashmere sweater and...not jeans."

"How about kakis?"

"Yes. Or something like gray trousers. Maybe put two or three options together for me. I don't want to look like a stodgy old man. I want to look like a king who is involved—aware of things. Not just a guy who comes in once a year and pretends."

"Okay."

As she made notes on her tablet, Mateo turned to Sabrina. "I'd love for you to come with me to that event."

She gaped at him. "It's on a Saturday!"

"I know, but I've been thinking about your place in the kingdom, and I have to admit that I've always seen you as our ambassador."

Her face scrunched with distaste. "You want me to be an ambassador?"

"No. I want you to be *the* ambassador. Not for one country, but our point of contact with all charities and humanitarian efforts. You'd be the face of the family's philanthropy."

Sabrina still gaped at him. "You and Olivia and Joshua already do those things."

"We fold it into our schedules. But with you spearheading that part of our rule, you could turn it into a cohesive effort."

For a few seconds, Sabrina said nothing. She glanced from her father to Jessica. Then she looked at her uneaten oatmeal.

"Sabrina," Mateo said, bringing her attention to him again. "This could be the best job in the palace. You could do so much good, but you could also bring hope. I'm telling you now before you go to university, so you can think it through and consider the kinds of classes that would assist you."

"Okay."

Mateo laughed. "I thought you would be happier."

She took a breath and peered at Jessica again, before turning her attention to her oatmeal. "I'm just a little tired still. Late night last night."

Jessica wished she could fade into the wallpaper or disappear at will. The second glance from Sabrina had been extremely uncomfortable. Even if the late night and lack of sleep explained her sour mood, Mateo's youngest did not like Jessica at the table.

Knowing this was the perfect time to make an easy exit, she rose.

"I will see you in the office, Your Majesty."

Mateo rose. "Thank you, Ms. Smith."

As she walked out of the dining room, she heard Mateo say, "So you will go with me on Saturday?"

She didn't stick around to hear Sabrina's reply. If Mateo needed help or advice, he would ask. But she had the feeling that once she left, Sabrina would be honest with her dad, and they would work this out.

Because, truth be told, if someone offered her the chance to be a goodwill ambassador, handing out checks, giving hope… she would call it her dream job and she was fairly certain Sabrina would see that too.

She continued walking down the stairway and would have considered the breakfast a successful first step to Mateo getting Sabrina on the road to her place in the monarchy—

Except for the looks Sabrina had given her, the way she'd studied her, as if she were looking for something.

Or trying to figure something out.

Oh, Lord. What if she'd searched her on the internet and found Ellie's high-profile troubles? What if she'd figured out Jessica had begun using her middle name to throw people off track?

No. Even if she figured that out, there were so many Smiths in every corner of the internet that it would take a while to make the connection.

At the bottom of the steps, she took a long breath and reminded herself that Sabrina was tired, and the king's youngest daughter could simply be curious about the person who'd replaced Arthur.

At eighteen, she was still a kid. Her concern would be about her dad's staff—not who Jessica was personally, only who she was in terms of her position in the palace.

Actually, it made more sense to think Sabrina was trying to figure out how to deal with her dad's temporary assistant, if she could trick Jessica, fool her if she needed a favor.

That she would watch out for.

CHAPTER NINE

WHEN THE KING was in his third meeting of the afternoon, Jessica slipped out of the office and up to his closet. She entered his quarters through a side door that opened on the same foyer they'd used that morning to get to the dining room.

Instead of racing to get to his closet door as she usually did, she paused and looked down the corridors to the right and left.

She knew the back way to the dining room, but now she also knew that the family quarters had a main entrance. It was also obvious this side entrance was a private entrance for Mateo's quarters that also led to the main living space. She wondered if there were side entrances like this one for his kids' living spaces. If there were, that would make personal quarters something like apartments. Meaning, people could come and go as they pleased.

Though the family lived together, they could stay in their own quarters if they wanted privacy or alone time.

She walked down the silent corridor to the door that led to the closet. The fact that she could enter the king's closet without going into his quarters also did not surprise her. She supposed he had a front door of a sort that probably opened onto a sitting room. He might even have a small kitchen. But with this side door, his assistant didn't have to traipse through his private space to get to the place she needed to go to put together outfits for him when he needed her help.

She didn't mind being kept out of his private space, but curiosity about the way he lived filled her as she stepped into his dressing room/closet. Especially when she saw that the door to his bathroom had been left open.

She tiptoed over and sighed when she saw the elegant room. A huge walk-in shower. A stand-alone claw-foot tub with a tray for tea or books or even reading a document if that was what he wanted to do while relaxing in the huge tub.

Shiny white tile covered the floor, and four mirrors were strategically placed. Two above the sinks of the bleached wood double vanity and two full-length mirrors.

The main light was a chandelier, but each mirror had lights above it. Pale blue towels were rolled into cylinders and stored in an open shelf for easy access.

She walked inside and twirled around. It was huge, bright, clean and probably had every convenience known to mankind tucked away in the drawers and shelves. But more than anything else, it was peaceful, tranquil…like a spa.

She stopped twirling when she noticed the door on the other end of the bathroom. This one wasn't open, but one little flick of a doorknob would fix that.

Temptation rose. Nine chances out of ten his bedroom was just beyond that door. Even more curiosity flitted through her. It would be so easy to open the door and take a quick peek—

No. That wasn't right. Technically, his private space wasn't her business. She would behave.

She turned to leave but pivoted to face the door again. No. This was not the time for behaving. She might never get this chance again. She just wanted to see his room. It was no big deal. Normal curiosity.

Though she was alone, she tiptoed to the door and opened it only a crack to look inside.

"Find anything you like, Ms. Smith?"

Her heart about exploded out of her chest. She spun around. "You scared me!"

He chuckled. "I probably should have done something, so

you'd hear me, but it was just funny catching you." He sighed. "I know you're curious. *Everybody* is." He motioned to the opened door. "Go ahead. I have nothing to hide."

Guilt stopped her from moving. "I'm sorry. I above everybody else should respect your privacy. I know what it's like to have everybody wonder about everything in your life."

"I don't look at it that way. I think everybody's curious about how *everybody* else lives. Not just royals or people in the news. Have you ever used somebody's bathroom and opened their medicine cabinet?"

She pressed her hand to her chest. "No!"

"Sixty percent of people do."

"Sixty percent, really? Did you take a poll?"

He laughed. "I get a lot of information sent to me. Some of it is valuable... Some of it's about nosy visitors and weird statistics." He motioned to the door again. "But it's natural to be curious. Besides, I'm glad you're up here. We can choose my sweater for Saturday."

It finally hit her that he was supposed to be in a meeting. And even if he wasn't, he didn't go to his quarters willy-nilly. "What are you doing up here?"

"Meeting ended early. I'm a firm believer in stopping things when I've gotten my way... No sense continuing to talk and giving people a chance to change their minds."

She snickered. "I get that."

"Besides, I was hoping to find you up here. You know...to take a look at those sweaters...and maybe entice you into another make-out session."

The easy way he said it sent warmth fluttering through her, stopping in her heart that sort of melted with happiness. She loved that he liked her.

She stepped over and flattened her hands on his chest. "So all that stuff about medicine cabinets was a lie?"

He caught her fingers, then brought them to his lips to kiss. "Nope. That's true. But when I got up here and saw you so close to the privacy of my bedroom, I realized we'd never get another chance like this. Right now, everybody in my office suite assumes I'm in a meeting. And your job requires that you move around. No one looks for you."

"Unless they're trying to find you."

"No one is looking for me."

"That's true." She stood on tiptoes and kissed him. He shifted his hands to her back, letting them roam as he brought her closer and kissed her deeply. Everything inside her blossomed to life. It seemed impossible that they weren't meant to be together. Then she remembered that not being able to have something permanent didn't mean they couldn't have anything at all.

And he was right. They might never have a chance like this again.

When he broke the kiss, she took his hand and guided him into the bedroom. With the drapes drawn, the room was dark. She stopped at the foot of his bed, then laughed. "Really? A black comforter?"

"I didn't like the flowery stuff housecleaning kept putting on the bed. So I asked for black."

"You are such a guy." She stepped close, sliding her hands up his shirtfront until they eased under his jacket, and she could nudge it off.

Seeing her intention, he let his suit coat fall far enough that he could remove it. "I am a guy." And right now, he was feeling that more than he had in decades. The sensation of her hands on him coupled with the knowledge that she was seducing him, nearly rendered him speechless.

She paused and caught his gaze. "Your Majesty, I think I should tell you I wore my matching pink bra and panties."

Desire ratcheted through him, but so did a horrible fear. Was all this too easy? Too wonderful? Was he being played? "You planned this?"

"No. But I want it. I think I knew that this morning when I got dressed."

He studied her eyes. As much as he yearned to make love with her, he had to remind her of the truth. "This won't go anywhere—can't go anywhere."

She began unbuttoning his shirt. "Doesn't matter. I think you and I are meant for the moment." She met his gaze. "You know. We're meant to enjoy what we have while we have it. We can't plan for tomorrow, and we can't take this out in public," she said, motioning around his bedroom. "But maybe that's what makes what we have so special. It's ours. No one else's."

The idea of having something private, special, was breathlessly tempting to a man who'd shared his entire life with the world. He'd never had anything that was just his. And now, here she was. Just his. Not something to be shared or analyzed. Simply enjoyed.

He lifted her chin with his index finger to kiss her deeply and was rewarded with her sigh of pleasure. Then his hands slid down to the bottom of her sweater and began to ease it upward.

"Let's see what the pink bra looks like."

She laughed. "You know if you tease me too long, I could return that favor."

He pulled the sweater over her head, examined the pretty pink lace garment. "I like it."

She kissed him. "Sweet talker, but as I said, turnabout is fair play."

"I'm not worried. We only have a half an hour before we're missed. One of us is going to have to go downstairs before the other to throw everybody off our trail, cutting another five minutes off. I can tease and you can't retaliate."

She laughed, and he kissed her, pulling her close to enjoy the feel of her. But he still wore his shirt. With a quick curse, he pulled back and rid himself of the unwanted garment. Just as quickly, he found the zipper on her skirt and got rid of that too.

While he worked on that, she undid all the connections for his trousers, and they fell to the floor. Not about to argue with efficiency, he stepped out of them.

"Twenty minutes, you say?" She gave him a swift nudge that caused him to fall on the bed. "We don't have any time to waste."

He caught her hand and yanked her to the bed with him. She fell willingly into his arms. Nothing had ever felt like this. Free. Spontaneous. So oddly different than his role as a royal, a king, that the sensation of being himself, only himself, flooded him with ridiculous need for her. For everything about her. Her laugh. Her sighs. The way she talked. The way she felt so right. The way she hadn't been afraid to kiss him. From the very beginning there'd been something wonderful between them.

The smoothness of her skin shot a burst of fire through him. He told himself to go slow, to remember everything, but when his lips met her smooth flesh, the temptation to quickly taste every inch of her was too much to ignore. Her soft sighs let him know she enjoyed it as much as he did and something inside him exploded with the need to give her pleasure.

But when he brought them face-to-face again, aligning their bodies so he could absorb the feeling of her skin against his, she turned the tables. Running her tongue from his neck to his navel, she teased and tempted him until he rolled her over and reversed their roles.

He loved the spontaneity of it, the way need dictated action. He rained kisses from her neck to her breasts, stopping to savor their taste while she ran her hands down his back.

But their game became very serious as arousal and instincts he didn't even know he had roared through him igniting his blood. He joined them in a rush of adrenaline-fueled hunger that took over and wouldn't stop until he was inside her.

Then the unexpected happened. They both stopped.

She took a long, pleasure-filled breath.

He simply lost himself in the moment. He didn't know if

they'd ever be able to do this again. Savoring the feeling of her warmth wrapped around him and the wonder of their connection, was part of his need. The thing he'd remember forever, if only because it was a wonderful, but passing gift.

They began to move, slower this time, at a pace laden with enjoyment and awe. He didn't want to think she'd ever felt this arousal-filled bliss with another man because he'd certainly never felt it with another woman. He shoved the jealousy out of his mind and gave as much as he took.

When they reached the peak, intense pleasure exploded in every cell of his body. Her cry of delight told him she felt the same.

After a few seconds absorbing the unexpected wonder of it all, they broke apart and he rolled her to his side of the bed with him, their heads on the same pillow.

"I don't know where I'd protest, but if we don't get the chance to do that again, I will find someone to complain to."

She laughed. "It was pretty amazing."

He shifted to his side so he could look at her face. "*You* are amazing. You make me feel so different. It's as if I spent my whole life as a role…heir to the throne, then king…and everything sort of bowed to that. With you, I'm just me."

She smiled and twined their bare legs. "With you, I'm just me too."

Need for her spiraled through him again. He would have cursed it because their time was melting away, but it was all so new, so intense, so wonderful, he let himself enjoy it. "Why did we have to get to fifty before we found this?"

She shrugged. "Maybe we had some life to live before we could appreciate it."

He took her hand and kissed her fingers. He loved the philosopher in her—the smart person who could counsel him with his kids and keep him grounded—as much as he loved her smooth skin, her delicate hands, the sheer femininity that seemed to reach out and pull him to her.

"Maybe." He ran his hand along her thigh and her belly. Savoring again. Not just the reality of being with her, but the mood, the moment.

"We're going to have to figure out a way to find some more time together before Arthur comes back."

And just like that she broke the mood and brought sadness to his joy when she gave them a timetable.

The unfairness of it shot through him, but he understood what she was saying. There were too many hurdles to maneuver around for them to even daydream about having this relationship forever.

They had to make the best of the here and now.

CHAPTER TEN

THEY DRESSED QUICKLY with Mateo leaving first by way of a back balcony so that when he entered his office, he could make it appear he'd been in the garden thinking. She redressed then shuffled through his closet looking for three sweaters, shirts and trousers to lay out on the table. If anybody missed her, she could talk about searching for clothing for the king's Saturday outing.

Walking out of the closet into the hall, then the foyer, then the staircase, the joy of making love with him almost overwhelmed her. She loved touching him and having him touch her, but there was more. Making love intensified the heart connection she'd always felt with him. The sense that they belonged together. She knew that would grow every time they were together like that. Still, his schedule was so busy, and everybody wanted to know where he was every minute of the day, that she honestly despaired that they'd ever get to do it again—

But maybe that was a good thing. In spite of her suggestion that they try to find more times to be alone, the thought of someone catching them and potentially thrusting her into the news cycle again tightened her chest. She remembered not being able to pull into her own driveway because it was filled with people from the press. She remembered staying in a hotel with her daughter to avoid them then waking to find the lobby teeming with people who peppered them with questions.

Being with Mateo might be delicious but a real relationship with him came at a price. And not just for her. His sedate, quiet palace would explode with speculation. From reporters, yes. But he also had kids and a dedicated staff—

How would they see this?

Would she be a gold digger and he be a foolish man falling for a woman whose daughter might have also seduced a man in power?

That's how the press had painted Eleanore, a gold digger looking to blackmail the politician and when he wouldn't pay, she trumped up the rape. Would they paint Jessica with the same brush? Would Eleanore's life be torn apart again?

Mateo entered his office trying not to grin. But something about the atmosphere of his workspace brought his mood in line almost automatically, as if his brain instantly made the separation of his private life and his work.

Which was good.

The last thing either he or Jessica wanted was for their behavior to cause people to question things. They needed to conduct themselves as they normally would so no one suspected or guessed they'd become lovers.

The reality of someone finding out they were lovers came tumbling down on him like an avalanche of cold snow. The press would want details. Her identity would come out. Her life would become fodder for speculation. Her daughter's life would be shoved into the limelight again.

He squeezed his eyes shut and sat back in his chair.

And all of that would impact his life, his kids, his *rule.*

This had to stay private. Or maybe stop. Because the ramifications of it becoming public were too horrible to contemplate. If he only had himself to worry about, he might risk it. But throwing Jessica into the public eye again? Or her daughter who'd worked so hard to have a normal life? No. He would not do that to either one of them.

She returned to her office, and he glanced up from his desk, into her room. Their gazes caught. He could see from the seriousness in hers that she'd come to the same conclusions he had. Making love might have been the most wonderful experience of his life, but none of their problems had gone away. None of their reservations had even shrunk. There was no future for them.

They didn't play chess that night. Because he would be going to Olivia's committee meeting, he sent Jessica home at a normal hour. With the motor pool employees seeing her arrivals and her departures, he enjoyed a minute of relief. They were a built-in alibi that Jessica came and went like a normal employee.

His constant stream of visitors also saw nothing but a ruler and his personal assistant. Their breakfast on Thursday was a working breakfast with Olivia and Josh joining them, but Sabrina strolled in on Friday morning.

Jessica went over that day's schedule. Mateo added tidbits. Joshua reminded him of a few points to raise in meetings with certain officials. Olivia simply listened intently. He told them about Sabrina going with him to the Eliminate Hunger event and her potential new position.

Everything had gone back to normal. So normal, his heart sank. His day bored him. His life bored him.

He missed Jessica so much that his focus wobbled.

He considered inviting her up to his closet to choose clothes for the next day—but they'd already done that. He had no reason to ask her to meet him. And he didn't want to make up one.

He said goodbye to her at five, letting her go at a normal quitting time so she could have a nice evening. But his night dragged on and on. His kids had plans, so he told the chef he'd make a sandwich, then sent her and the evening butler home early too.

Then he rattled around in his too-empty palace. If Jessica

really did live in a cottage that bordered royal property, he could ride a horse there and no one would be any the wiser.

He frowned. He didn't really need a horse to make that work. He usually didn't give his security detail the slip, but there was a car at his disposal. It was a little something his parents had instituted. They called it their getaway car. They rarely used it. But they'd said that without the availability of that vehicle, they would be prisoners.

He finally understood.

Right now, he felt like a prisoner. There was somewhere he wanted to go. It might not be innocent, but it wasn't illegal. And it was necessary for his sanity.

He changed into jeans and a sweatshirt and took the back way to the garage. Using an old key, he unlocked a side door. He didn't flick on the light. Too much chance someone would see him. He ran his hand along the front fender of the old car, laughing softly as he found his way to the door and hopped inside. After he started the engine, he pulled the hat down his forehead so no one would suspect it was him driving the old relic.

The garage door rattled as it opened, but all three of the on-duty drivers were out with his kids. Even if there was someone in the motor pool, the huge building would absorb the sound.

He was literally sneaking out and no one knew.

The joy of it nearly overwhelmed him. He took the road behind the garage to a back gate. He stopped at the keypad and input the password and just like that he was on the road, by himself.

He found a parking space in front of Jessica's building, pulled the knit cap even farther down his forehead and walked inside. The four flights of stairs didn't bother him. Freedom rushed through his veins like a drug.

He knocked on her door and when she opened it, he hauled her to him and kissed her.

* * *

Jessica was so dazzled, she didn't even consider that they were standing in a public hall, kissing.

When he finally pulled back, he quietly said, "I missed you."

She laughed, but reality suddenly flooded her, and she yanked him into her apartment, quietly closing the door behind him.

"What are you doing!"

"I had to see you." He took off the knit cap and ran his fingers through his hair. "Don't worry. No one knows I left. The kids are all out for the evening. And I ditched my detail by taking my dad's old mental health car."

"Mental health car?"

"I never understood it until tonight. It wasn't that the pressure of the job made him feel he needed a car at his disposal that no one knew about. He just liked getting away sometimes."

"You needed to get away?"

He shrugged out of his hoodie and tossed it to a chair. "I think I got a taste of what normal feels like, and my life suddenly seems like an old camel-hair coat. Restrictive and itchy."

He sat on the sofa.

She sat on the chair. "I'm sorry."

He snorted a laugh. "Why? For making me happy?"

She winced. "Yeah. People don't usually complain about that."

He ran his hands down his face. "I will figure out how to handle this."

She rose and slipped over to the sofa to sit beside him. "Maybe we can figure it out together." She nestled against him and laid her head on his shoulder. "Because since I met you, the life I was planning suddenly seems empty. And I don't want it anymore."

"We are a pair."

"I think we're a matched set. Unfortunately, we don't live in the same china cabinet."

"And we can't."

"No. We can't."

"So how do we handle this?"

"Well, I like that you're here now."

He chuckled. "I like that I'm here too."

"We could spend the time commiserating about how unjust our situation is or we could…you know…make the best of the time."

"Why, Ms. Smith. Are you going to seduce me again?"

She gasped and pushed away so she could look at him. "Again?"

"Well, you did sort of take the lead on Monday. First, you led me into the bedroom." He paused and pretended to ponder. "Then if I remember correctly, you shoved me onto the bed."

"You weren't exactly fighting."

He sobered. "No. I wasn't." He leaned in and kissed her quickly. "But I didn't just come here for sex. I really missed you."

"We saw each other every day this week."

"We worked together every day." He sighed. "I like talking to you. I like being with you."

"I'll tell you what." Too happy to let reality ruin their evening, she rose and took his hand, nudging him to stand too. "We can do all the pillow-talk you want."

"So, you are seducing me."

She sighed. "Oh, you royals. You want everything spelled out."

He laughed, following her into her bedroom.

At the foot of her bed in her extremely frilly bedroom, she slid her hands under his T-shirt and sighed with contentment when she touched his warm skin. Trim and toned his body quivered under even her slightest touch. Answering need whispered inside her, making her bold enough to ease his T-shirt over his head and toss it behind her.

He laughed, caught her by the waist and kissed her greedily. She savored the sensations of his mouth on hers, their tongues mating, their bodies brushing. Then he stepped back a bit to remove her sweater. Even as they kissed, they removed each other's clothes in a frenzy of need that filled her with as much joy as the idea that he'd sneaked away to see her.

She shoved her comforter aside so they could lie on the one indulgence she allowed herself, silk sheets. He sighed as he pulled her to him.

"Interesting expense for a woman saving for retirement."

She laughed. "It's the little things."

He laughed, rolled her to her back and kissed her until neither one of them cared about bedclothes. All she knew at that moment was that he was warm and naked, wrapped around her like someone who couldn't get enough of the feel of her.

They made love slowly, as if being in her apartment—away from the demands of his life—was the real luxury. Inhaling the scent of him as he kissed her neck, she realized it was. She'd never felt the physical longing she did with him, and she ran her leg along his to appreciate it. Making love with her husband had been a sort of paint-by-numbers game. With Mateo the yearning to kiss him and touch him and feel him inside her was so intense her breath fluttered away on a sigh of need. As he kissed his way down her belly, she couldn't stop her hands from coasting along his shoulder muscles, feeling them tremble from her touch.

He kissed his way to her neck again. Warmth and need expanded in her middle and she inched to the right, trying to reposition their bodies to where she wanted them. He read the movement correctly and shifted to enter her, filling her, satisfying one kind of need only to create another.

Every inch of her body prickled with arousal, and she moved with him, intensifying the sensations inside her. Greedy for the feel of him, she let her hands roam as his body did amazing things to her.

When the world exploded with a white-hot light, both groaned with pleasure. She couldn't seem to move. Neither could he.

Eventually he rolled over to the pillow beside hers. Silence surrounded them. She knew why. Every time they made love, they knew it could be the last.

She refused to give voice to that and instead eased over to nestle against him. "You're really kind of wonderful…you know that?"

Sliding his hand down her upper arm, he laughed. "I was just going to tell you the same thing."

She swallowed back the almost automatic reply that it was too bad they didn't belong together, but she refused to allow that into their conversation tonight.

"I've been rethinking the whole cabin in the woods."

He slid up to lean against the headboard. "So you said."

"Yeah, I'm thinking it's out."

"Where would you go?"

"Maybe a city."

"A city? That's like the opposite of what you had planned."

"After meeting you, working with you, I want to be part of things again. You said my cabin plan sounded like I wanted to hide from the world. And maybe I did. But now I don't. I feel like I'm coming back to my normal, energetic self."

"There's no need to move. You are very much a part of things at the palace."

She said, "I try to be," even as she realized their affair might change that. It was another thing she had to think about. Could she stay working for him, feeling things for him, but never seeing him. Never touching him. Never knowing that he felt the same longing for her—

Deciding this wasn't the time for that either, she shifted the conversation to Sabrina.

Nestled together, they talked a bit about his daughter and that slid into discussing the unexpected joy of parenting. Then the unexpected disappointment of a frustrating spouse, and finally, the peace of being single again.

"Not that it doesn't have its problems," Mateo said, stroking her hair. "I mean, I am dateless most of the time."

She laughed. "You became an eligible bachelor. I somehow became a burden on society."

He chuckled at the same time that his stomach rumbled.

She sat up. "Didn't you eat?"

"I had the chef make me a sandwich."

She rolled to get out of bed. "Good as her sandwiches are, it appears it wasn't enough."

He sat up. "Where are you going?"

"I have some homemade vegetable soup. I'm not even going to try to compete with your chef. But I bought a loaf of crusty bread that pairs very well with homemade soup."

He laughed. They both found their clothes and kissed happily as they redressed. Finished first, she raced into the kitchen and by the time he got there the bread was cut and the soup was warming. She served it on her little two-person table by a bay window with a breakfast nook. But before he sat down, she closed the blinds.

"Too bad," he said, taking his seat. "I'll bet your street is fun to watch at night."

"Coffee shop on that side," she said, pointing across the street. "And tavern down that way." She angled her thumb behind her. "Both places attract unique customers." She shrugged. "Sometimes I watch."

The simple sentence tugged at his heart. She was as lonely as he was. They might both have busy lives, but in spite of their children, they were alone.

He caught her hand. "Thank you for this."

She smiled. "I love to cook."

He picked up his spoon and tasted his soup. "And you're very good at it. This is delicious."

"It's kind of my specialty. If you'd popped in last week, I'd have had to make French toast because I was eating cereal for supper every day."

He laughed but thinking of her coming home to an apartment as quiet as his palace and eating alone—cereal no less—squeezed his heart.

She changed the subject to the book she was reading and he told her that he'd bought his copy and would be starting it that night. "No spoilers."

"Seems to me you're not going to be starting it tonight if you're here."

"Oh, much as I'd love to stay, I have to go."

"Now?"

"I have about twenty minutes."

She laughed. "Let's not waste them."

After making love again, he returned to the palace, sneaking in the hidden back entry, parking the car in the private garage, easing through the darkness behind it and into the quiet entrance in the back of the palace.

But there, at the security desk, sat Marty Goodwin, the head of security for the palace and the entire royal family. A former military man who'd gone into public relations after his last tour of duty and eventually became a fixer for public figures, he could examine palace security from angles most security guards wouldn't even consider. Which was why he had been hired to lead palace security and manage the details of all the royals. He frequently worked nights, at this desk, monitoring the overnight shift, but also evaluating everything they had in place.

Unfortunately, tonight, it didn't feel like a coincidence that he was working the desk when Mateo had decided to sneak out.

"Good evening, Your Majesty… Have a nice drive?"

He hadn't really believed he could sneak out of his palace without his detail noticing. He simply hadn't expected to be confronted so soon. And he wouldn't apologize. He knew his parents had gone for Sunday drives and long rides to the beach—alone—while they ruled. He might not have done it before, but maybe it was time.

"I took the car I'm allowed to sneak away in."

Marty peered up at him. "You know it has a GPS locator, right?"

He stopped halfway to the back stairs, facing Marty. "No. I did not."

"Interesting thing about GPS locators, though, is that information doesn't always get checked and even if it does, there's rarely any reason to publicize it."

Realizing Marty was telling him he knew Mateo had gone to see Jessica, he took the few steps back to the desk. "No. There is not."

Marty sucked in a breath. "Your Majesty, your detail isn't charged with questioning you or judging you or even caring where you go and what you do, as long as it isn't dangerous. I would think by now you would know you can trust us and would have let us go with you."

"I'm entering new territory."

Marty laughed. "I get that and I'm sort of glad. The people you usually date seem a little phony."

"She's not phony."

Marty shook his head. "No. *She's* not. Most of us like her."

He noticed the careful way Marty avoided her name, her position at the palace or even that she worked there. "So, I have your blessing?"

"And we have your back." He returned his attention to his computer screen. "Remember that. If there's anybody you can trust, it's us. You can go anywhere you want, any time you want. We will be discreet and keep your secrets."

He knew that, of course. He'd simply never been in a situation before where he wasn't the one who would suffer if a secret leaked or the press found out. He wasn't sure Marty understood that they might be protecting him physically, but emotionally, personally, they were protecting Jessica.

"Okay. Thank you."

"You're welcome."

He walked up the stairs, torn. He absolutely trusted his security. But if push came to shove, they'd protect him, not Jessica...not her daughter.

CHAPTER ELEVEN

JESSICA WOKE SLOWLY the next morning, savoring the scent of Mateo that lingered on her pillow.

Then she realized the ringing of her phone had awakened her. Concerned that it was Ellie, she grabbed it from the nightstand and answered frantically. "Hello?"

"Did I wake you?"

Mateo.

She smiled. "No...well, maybe. I kind of drifted awake and then heard the phone. But it could have been the ring that woke me." She sat up. "What's going on?"

"I'm sorry to call you, but I am still your boss, and I need you this morning."

She eased her legs to the side of the bed, smiling at the fact that she was naked. She hadn't slept without pajamas in ages. "And I'm happy to do my job. What do you need?"

"Remember those clothes you put out for me for this afternoon's event?"

"Yes."

"Apparently, after they spent a few days on the island dresser in my closet, housecleaning thought they were dirty and took them."

She groaned. She'd pulled them too early and left them out to justify her being gone so long on Monday morning. "I'm on my way."

"Thank you. It isn't that I can't find clothes myself. It's just that I trust everybody's opinion over my own."

She laughed. "You have enough to worry about without trying to keep up with fashion. Get breakfast. By the time you're done eating I'll be there."

"It's already ten thirty."

Her gaze leaped to her clock. "It is!"

His voice dropped seductively. "Sleep in?"

"Yes. And it was wonderful. My pillow smells like you."

He took a quick breath, and she laughed. "Hang up. I'll be there in a few minutes."

She dressed hastily and almost left her apartment without makeup. In the end, she decided to at least put on lipstick and mascara before she raced down her four flights of stairs and out into the street. Coffee would have been great, but she ignored the scent coming from the coffee shop across the street and hurried to the back of her building where her car sat.

Philip was at the palace entry when she pulled up. "Good morning, Ms. Smith."

"Good morning."

He opened her car door. "Working extra this week?"

She got out of her car. "Fashion emergency."

He laughed. "Don't let me delay you."

As Philip drove away with her car, she headed into the palace and directly to the elevator. It stopped in front of the main entry to the family's private quarters as Mateo had told her it would. But she turned right and headed down the hall to the closet/dressing room and the door through which she typically entered.

She stepped into the closet and Mateo walked in from the other side. Dressed in jeans and a sweatshirt that he'd probably worn to breakfast, he didn't say hello. He just ambled over, pulled her to him and kissed her.

She laughed. "Stop. We have serious business here. I chose your three best outfits. If housecleaning didn't bring them back, I've got to start all over again."

"I have plenty of sweaters and trousers. Arthur purged my closet and refilled it twice a year."

She opened his deep sweater drawer. "I'm guessing he was a seasonal shopper."

He leaned on the big island dresser. "If he retires, that job would fall to you too."

She looked over at him. He'd spoken of this before. Told her she would be the perfect replacement for Arthur, but after her thoughts the night before, it suddenly felt odd. Like she didn't need to worry about losing him. They could be together forever. Or at least the remainder of his reign.

She pictured them being together like this, happy, for decades and her heart swelled—until she realized they would be sneaking around. Never out in public.

In some respects, it sounded dreamy and romantic. A secret, forbidden love was better than being the old crone in the woods, wrapped in a shawl, feeding birds—

Wasn't it?

Or was there something equally sad and desperate about being his dirty little secret? Never going to the parties he held, never having a holiday together.

"Ms. Smith?"

She shook herself back to the present. "Sorry." She pulled out a gray sweater, then walked to the closet for a blue dress shirt to wear under it. She held them against him. "Gray keeps you conservative. And the blue will look stunning with your hair."

"You know, Arthur never talks to me like this."

She laughed. "Arthur is probably very formal with you."

"In spite of being together since I was a kid, yes. He's still formal. He got worse after my coronation."

She handed him the sweater and shirt, then went searching for charcoal-gray trousers. "I think it's nice. Respectful." She glanced at him over her shoulder. "Plus, you've earned that respect."

"Thank you."

She handed him the trousers. "Should I stay and watch you dress the way Arthur does?"

He snorted. "No. But it wouldn't hurt if you chose another outfit in case this one doesn't work for me."

"Okay. Go into the bedroom and put that on while I look for something else."

"Seriously? You want me to go into the bedroom?"

"Yes! We're running out of time, and I don't want to be distracted."

He thought about that. "I like being a distraction."

She turned him in the direction of his bathroom door. "Go."

He left the room with a hoot of laughter, and she returned to the sweater drawer. She found a beautiful pale beige cashmere sweater that would probably look great on somebody with brown or red hair, but it would look plain on him.

She dug a little deeper and found a white sweater. She pulled a blue-and-white striped shirt from the closet. But she also had second thoughts about him not wearing a jacket. He was a king. A sweater might make him look casual, but she meant what she'd said about Arthur's formality being a good thing. A navy-blue blazer over his sweater really would be appropriate.

The closet door suddenly popped open. "Hey, Dad!"

Jessica froze. "Sabrina!"

"Ms. Smith?"

Mateo came walking in from the bathroom, fastening cuff links. "Hey, Sabrina. What's up?"

Sabrina looked from her dad to Jessica and back again. "I tried calling you, but you didn't answer."

The chastising tone didn't escape Jessica.

Mateo took it in stride, apparently accustomed to his daughter's moods. "You probably called while I was in the shower..."

He displayed the gray sweater with the blue shirt underneath. "What do you think?"

Jessica said, "Good. But I've decided you have to put a jacket over that."

Sabrina groaned. "You might as well have 'old man' printed on your chest."

Mateo looked at himself in one of the full-length mirrors. "I think it looks good."

Jessica presented the white sweater with the blue-and-white striped shirt. "This might be a little fresher."

Sabrina made gagging noises.

"What would you suggest?" Mateo said. "A sweatshirt and jeans?"

His daughter brightened. "I think your subjects would love it if you dressed down."

"This *is* dressing down." He glanced in the mirror again. "Besides, you're probably saying that because you want to wear jeans," he added, walking over to Sabrina.

"Yes! I'm young. I'm always on trend. You said I'm supposed to be something like an ambassador. I think dressing normally makes people relate to me."

Mateo's mouth shifted slightly in distaste.

Jessica rushed to fill the awkward moment. "Actually, I think you might have a point. It sounds like this job could be whatever you want it to be. And this seems to be your first outing…like an introduction to the position. If you dress the same way as the people you're going to see, it shows a connection."

Mateo frowned, then said, "Maybe." He took a breath. "Actually, you know what? Jessica's right. You're looking to make a connection. I *want* you to connect with the people. Not always being a formal princess, but instead dressing like a people's princess sounds like a very good idea."

Sabrina glanced at Jessica, then back at her father. "Really? You changed your mind because your *assistant* thinks it's a good idea?"

Jessica could have been insulted, but she was more concerned about Mateo's reaction. He'd said Sabrina hadn't yet grasped the concept that they served the people not the other way around. He might not take kindly to the way she referred to Jessica so condescendingly.

"I changed my mind because I realized this is your job and you're very good with people. Meaning, I should butt out. Let you define the job."

Sabrina pursed her lips, not buying one word of that. Though Jessica believed her father was being honest, Sabrina did not.

But she pasted a sunny smile on her face and said, "Thanks, Dad." She made one final scrutiny of Jessica and Mateo, her eyes narrowing, before she headed for the door. But she stopped. "Sorry. The whole reason I came in here was to find out what time we were leaving, and I got distracted." She looked at Jessica again.

Jessica combined the calculating look along with Sabrina's phrasing of being distracted and her mind hopped to a bad conclusion. She was here, on a Saturday, in Mateo's closet, as he tried on clothes and Sabrina was jumping to conclusions she shouldn't.

Glad she'd had Mateo dress in his bedroom, she eased away from him over to the closet, looking for an appropriate navy-blue blazer, getting some of the focus off herself.

Mateo smiled at his daughter. "We're leaving at noon."

"Fine." Sabrina sighed. "Wear the white sweater and blue-and-white striped shirt." With that she left, all but slamming the door behind her.

Mateo gaped at the door. "What the hell was that? I agreed with her!"

"I'm starting to get the feeling it's me she objects to."

"You?"

"I'm a woman in your closet."

"You're my *personal* assistant! Besides, I changed in my bedroom!" He drew a quick breath. "You know what? It's an hour drive to the charity. I'll have a talk with her in the car."

"Don't! I mean, you can slide in something about what a

great assistant I am, making comments that are focused on my ability to do my job. But don't bring up anything else. It'll just look like we're scrambling to cover something." She winced. "Which is bad considering we do have a secret."

"Yeah, I guess." He sighed, then laughed unexpectedly. "We have a secret."

She shook her head. "Stop."

He walked over and pulled her close. "I like having a secret with you."

"In a way, I do too. But secrets can sometimes turn on a person." She caught his gaze. "We have to remember that and be careful."

CHAPTER TWELVE

ONCE MATEO WAS happily attired, Jessica left. Instead of heading directly to her apartment to clean or read, she drove to a farmer's market and chose some fruit before browsing the work of local artists displayed in booths along with baked goods and produce.

She couldn't believe what a difference a few weeks had made in her life. Getting to know Mateo, falling for him, sharing things with him, had brought her back to herself. If nothing else came of her remaining time with him, she would be eternally grateful that he'd helped give her real life back to her.

In fact, now that she was considering moving to a city, she was pondering the idea of moving to one in Brazil. She wasn't foolish enough to think that leaving Mateo would be easy—but once she wasn't his assistant anymore, their affair would be over. Rather than mope, she needed to focus on herself. Maybe restart her life. And why not move to the city where her daughter lived? In the ten years that had passed, they had pretty much become anonymous, if only because they lived simply, quietly and carefully. It wouldn't hurt to test the waters to see if they could live near each other again.

She drove home, smiling. It wasn't the perfect plan for her future, but she finally felt like she was getting closer. The crone had served her well for a decade, but she knew she needed more. She wouldn't rush to make a decision. She had weeks until Arthur returned—or didn't. Meaning, she would remain Mateo's assistant. There was plenty of time to ponder all the angles.

Right before she would have fallen asleep, her phone pinged with a text.

What are you wearing?

Mateo.
She laughed and typed, Is this your attempt at sexting?
She swore she could see him chuckle after reading that.

How am I doing?

I think we should stick to what we know. In-person contact.

Want me to come over?

She thought for a second. She wanted nothing more than for him to come over. But something tweaked in her brain. Not quite a warning, it was more of a reminder that this relationship didn't work if they went overboard. Worse, every time they met was an opportunity for someone to catch them if they weren't careful.

Sorry. Long day. I'm already in bed.

Okay.

Maybe we should discuss this on Monday? Figure some things out. Maybe make some loose plans.

That sounds good.

We'll make it good.

He sent her an LOL then texted, Okay... Goodnight.

Goodnight.

She waited a few seconds in case he had something more to say, but the light on her phone went out indicating no more texts.

She took a breath and snuggled into her pillow. Tonight, if she dreamed of him, it would be a very good dream. She would spend the next day trying to figure out places they could meet or ways he could come to her apartment. Because she really did want to take advantage of the few weeks they had left.

After that, her life would be very different. If Arthur returned, she would probably be leaving the country. If he didn't, she would be his permanent replacement, and that opened a whole new can of worms.

Sunday morning, she woke to three hard knocks on her door. Worried it might be Mateo impulsively visiting, she jumped out of bed and slid into her robe. On her way through the living room, she heard the sounds of a crowd on the street below her apartment. The coffee shop was busy, but never *that* busy. Still, she didn't have time to check.

At the door, she looked through the peephole and saw Marty Goodwin, head of palace security, with two of Mateo's regular team at his side. Confused, she quickly unlocked the dead bolt and then the simple doorknob lock.

Marty all but pushed her inside as he rushed in. "Pack a bag. We have to get you somewhere else."

"Somewhere else?"

"Our first stop will be the palace so His Majesty can explain this to you." He pointed at the window. "But until we get rid of them, you can't stay here."

Confused and a little scared, she walked to the window and saw the crowd of people in front of her building. Reporters. Some held microphones. Others notebooks. Cameramen stood at the ready, as the reporters craned their necks, trying to get a glimpse inside the glass of the building's front door.

They had figured out who she was.

Judging by the size of the crowd, it appeared they also knew she worked directly with the king.

Marty said, "This building has a basement and there's an exit that leads to your parking lot."

She faced him, heartbroken and speechless.

Marty quietly said, "We have to get going. The sooner we leave the better."

Confused, she asked, "You want me to take my car?"

"Oh, heavens no. You ride with me. I'll have someone else drive your car so it will be at the palace." He nudged his head toward the hallway that led to her bedroom. "Go pack your bag."

She gathered enough clothes for a week. At first, she thought she'd only need a weekend's worth, but the possibility existed that it might be days before this mess died down. And in that time, she'd have to resign her position. She'd have to stop working for the palace in any capacity and start looking for another job—

In another city.

Maybe even another country.

Except after this, it couldn't be Brazil.

She could not live by her daughter.

Her heart shattered. She'd been so happy. Everything had been going so well.

Maybe too well?

She would never get to live near her daughter again. Not unless she wanted to expose Eleanore to this mess. And she did not. Her own whereabouts might have been exposed. But as far as she knew Ellie was still safe.

In the car, sitting in the back seat with Marty as one of his men drove, she said, "So what happened?"

A train of cars followed them. Which was foolish. There was no way they'd get on the palace grounds.

"I've had two guards watching your apartment since you took over for Arthur. I'd been the one to vet you, so I knew your past and I recognized the possibility that some zealous reporter would dig too deep. About six o'clock this morning, my guys called in to let me know that people were gathering at the entrance to your building. Didn't take long to verify they were reporters."

"Because I'm Eleanore Smith's mother."

"That would be our guess."

"But you don't know for sure?"

"Not yet. After all, you do work directly with the king. If only one reporter was at your building, we'd assume that person had gone digging and found you. Because it's *everybody,* we know something happened."

She took a breath, saying nothing. What was there to say? Her happy life was over. She would go back into hiding, not contacting Ellie until this died down. She wouldn't bring this to her daughter's door.

They arrived at the palace and drove to the entrance Jessica always used to go to work. Marty and his team hustled her back to Mateo's office.

He rose as she entered. The look he gave her broke her heart. She couldn't let him take the blame for this.

He dismissed Marty and his guards who closed the door behind them when they left.

She immediately apologized. "I am so sorry."

He shook his head. "Don't. This isn't on you."

"But I—"

"Didn't Marty show you the video?"

"Video?" She blinked. "No. He only said that something had to have happened and that you would explain it."

"Because he's good at his job. He never oversteps."

He motioned for her to take the seat in front of his desk as he picked up his tablet and angled it so they both could see it. He hit a few buttons and a video of his daughter Sabrina popped up on the screen.

"Hey, peeps. It's me. Local princess." She smiled prettily for the camera. "It's not official yet, but I'm being groomed for a new position. The whole thing is totally bogus. Made up. Just my dad trying to make it appear that I belong, when we all know there's no real place for me in this royal family. And where did he get this idea?" She snorted. "Probably from his temporary assistant—the woman replacing his usual assistant, Arthur. When he told me about this position, she butted in. Gave an opinion that my father took. If you asked me, the woman is up to something."

Jessica's heart about stopped. Her gaze flew to Mateo. "Oh, my God."

"Keep listening."

"Seriously, not only is she overbearing but there's something weird about her." Sabrina leaned into the camera. "Like she has a secret. So, I had some hacker friends do some digging and found that her name used to be Pennelope. Pennelope Smith. Now why does that sound familiar?" She snorted in derision. "Didn't anybody vet her?"

Jessica flopped back on her chair. "Oh, my God." Shock rendered her both frozen and speechless.

"I'm so sorry."

"I'm already somewhat packed." She rose from her chair. "I'll clean out my desk."

"No! I won't let you run from this. You'll stay in one of the guest quarters of the palace until the story dies down."

She sighed and sagged into her chair. "It never dies down. Every time I think it's going to, something like this happens. I have to leave. Find somewhere else to hide. It's easier for me. I'm not the person they want. I'm merely the trail to Eleanore. But I won't have them finding her through me."

"Again, no. I won't let you leave. My daughter did this. I will handle it."

"You can't handle this! People love this story. The facts are plain as day. Why would the senator's staff have kept Eleanore at his mansion for two days except to get the drugs out of her system? Yet everybody likes to twist the story, speculate, and say what if…"

"Maybe it's time they stopped."

Her eyes filled with tears as she slumped in the chair, her body worn, tired. "I'm sorry. I shouldn't have taken this job. I should have seen what would happen when I started working directly with you. I should have realized someone somewhere would dig a little too deep—"

"And thanks to my daughter they did. But if you and your daughter were as careful as I think you were there's no connection to Ellie. There are millions of Smiths in the world. If we don't cower, don't give them anything else, they might not find her."

"I don't know… It seems risky."

"Let me put it to you this way, if you stay or you go, they have the same information. If you disappear, they can look up your airline tickets, or scan flight manifests, hoping to find times you've visited your daughter. But if you don't run away, stay here, in your little apartment, quietly working for your country, there's no connection. Hopefully, no way to narrow things down enough to find her.

"And—" He leaned across his desk. "Just once, wouldn't you like a swipe at them? The chance to tell them to get lost… with the power of a king behind you?"

When she didn't answer, he picked up the receiver of his phone and hit a button. "Pete, I want a press conference set up for noon. Those reporters want to print something? I'm going to give them something to print."

He hung up the phone and Jessica said, "I know you think you can fix this, but you can't."

"Oh, yeah? I might not fix it, but I won't let anyone tell me who I can or can't employ." He picked up the phone again. "Marty, escort Ms. Smith to the first guest quarters."

She heard Marty say, "Yes." Then Mateo hung up the phone again.

"I hope you brought something suitable for a press conference because you're coming too."

They walked into his press room to pandemonium. Every seat was filled, and cameramen lined the walls. As soon as he stepped up to the podium, the room became silent.

Mateo sighed. "Shame on you."

The hand of every reporter in the room shot up.

"Your Majesty!"

"Your Majesty!"

"Your Majesty!"

"No! You will let me have my say. First, the situation with Eleanore Smith has absolutely nothing to do with this country or my reign. So why you're concerned about her mother working for me is beyond me. Jessica was and is a normal mother. Second, Eleanore Smith was the victim. If you question that, if you fall for the innuendo that she tried to blackmail that politician and when he refused to pay she had him arrested—Answer this: Why did they keep her at that mansion for two days? That in and of itself was false imprisonment. But it also assured that the drugs used on her were out of her system.

"You're supposedly smart people. Figure some of this stuff out and stop revictimizing a woman who has been through enough."

Fifty hands shot up again.

"Your Majesty!"

"Your Majesty!"

"Your Majesty!"

"No! Stop! I won't encourage this! And Ms. Smith will not

be leaving palace employ. When Arthur returns, she will go back to her usual job, and you will stop harassing her. Any outlet that pursues a story that should have been dead long ago will lose palace privileges."

He turned to walk away from the podium, motioning for Jessica to leave with him. The hands of the reporters shot up again. A few reporters yelled, "Ms. Smith! Ms. Smith! Don't you have anything to say for yourself?"

She stopped. Mateo stiffened. He had handled that situation very well, but he'd also asked her if she wouldn't want a chance to take a swipe at them. He couldn't yank that away from her. But he wished he'd thought to warn her not to make matters worse.

"Why would I need to have something to say for myself? I'm a normal person supporting herself honestly. What is wrong with you people? Are there not enough problems in the world that you have to make news out of something that isn't news? Do your jobs. Your real jobs."

She turned and led Mateo out of the press briefing room and down the hall to his office. When they were behind the closed door, he caught her to him and hugged her fiercely.

"You were a star."

She took a breath. "Only because you paved the way."

He pulled back. "But you got the chance to have your say. That was important."

"Yes."

"Now, we have to deal with Sabrina."

She shook her head. "No. *You* have to deal with Sabrina."

"You can't run from this either. It's a power thing. If she believes she intimidated you, she'll use it. I watched both Olivia and Josh go through it. Hell, I did it myself. Testing out my power as a royal. She hasn't yet learned that ruling by fear makes everyone an enemy."

"That's probably exactly what you should tell her."

He laughed. "Agreed. Then I'm going to ground her. The

way I should have when she flashed at the club. I'm also going to make her shadow Josh and Olivia for a week."

"Oh, I'll bet they're going to love that."

"I don't care. I might have created this problem with her by letting her get away with things or not being around enough. But I intend to fix that while she's grounded. She'll be at *my* side too. She'll eat most meals with me. Play chess with me. Go riding with me. Until we find that common ground where we can talk for real and get to the bottom of this."

CHAPTER THIRTEEN

BECAUSE IT WAS SATURDAY, Mateo's kids all had plans for dinner. Except for Sabrina, who had received the lecture of her life from her father and was grounded. In an attempt to protest, she refused to come down to dinner and he sent her a note that said, "Fine."

Knowing he'd be alone with Jessica, he'd had the chef make steak Florentine with Brussels sprouts, roasted potatoes and red peppers because he knew it was one of her favorites.

He knew a lot about her now. Silly, frivolous things like her love of pancakes, warm, cozy blankets, and antiques, furniture and accent pieces that had meaning. But tonight, she looked forlorn after their long day, especially since she could not call Ellie. He had to cheer her up.

"When we're done with dinner, I can give you a tour of the palace."

She sighed. "Thanks, but I'm tired."

"You're not curious about the paintings or vases that date back to the seventeenth century or even the gifts given to us by dignitaries from other countries. We have a whole room full of those things."

She laughed softly. "Are you about to show me that you live in a museum?"

"No. With the exception of artworks of note, all those things are in one big room." He frowned. "I guess that *room* is like a museum."

"And I guess I might like to see it."

He snorted. "Might?"

"All right. I really would."

"You know with your love of things from the past, wonderful paintings, and furniture used by dignitaries, you should have been the royal."

She peeked up at him. "No. You're doing just fine. You were like a school principal with a bunch of bad kids with those reporters this morning. You didn't try to defend me. You told them they were off base rehashing old news."

"No, you were the one who reminded them it was old news." He chuckled. "I think the guy in the third row peed himself."

"Don't even!"

"Ech. He's new. The other reporters probably went back to their offices, weighed the pros and cons of opening up a story that really is ten years old and decided it wasn't worth their credentials at the palace...and he followed suit."

"With a sigh of relief."

Mateo nodded. "With a sigh of relief."

Nevil served dessert—chocolate cake with chocolate frosting and whipped cream. To his credit, he didn't miss a beat or change his expression while serving the entire meal, but Mateo saw the sympathy in his gray eyes. Nevil had been around almost as long as Arthur and he knew working for the royals wasn't all peaches and cream.

But the sympathy in his eyes also showed how much Nevil liked Jessica. He saw her nearly every morning at breakfast and knew that she worked hard. Like Mateo, he appeared to see the injustice in the way Jessica had been treated.

Tossing his napkin to the table, he said, "Ready for that tour."

"Considering that I'm staying here for a while, how about if we save the tour for someday when I'm less tired."

"Okay... Then I'll just walk you to your room."

"No need. Marty took me there this afternoon, along with my luggage."

He pulled out her chair, took her hand and nudged her to stand. "I'm walking you to your room anyway."

"But—"

He put a finger to her lips to stop her. "My home. My rules. Plus, the staff you see here today are very loyal. No one will say anything."

"I guess there's no law against walking a woman to her room."

He snorted. "Exactly. But I thought maybe we'd watch a movie."

Her gaze flew to his. "Really?"

"It's my daughter's fault that you're upset. Therefore, it's my responsibility to entertain you enough that you can fall asleep."

They found a movie they both wanted to see and sat together on the sofa in the sitting room of her suite. She nestled against his side, and he put his arm around her. Memories of Sabrina's mean-spirited video drifted off into nothing, along with the press conference and her worries about her daughter. She didn't have to say it. He could feel it in the way she relaxed against him and laughed at the silly movie they'd chosen.

He wasn't happy that she'd endured what she had that day, but he was unbelievably touched that she turned to him, trusted him. He wasn't surprised. They had a genuine emotional connection. But he'd also never felt this with another person. The honor of her trust.

This time when they made love it cemented something. The thought that he would lose that something rent his heart. Without even knowing, he'd waited his entire life for her and in a few weeks, she'd be leaving him.

The following morning, he awakened in her bed and groaned.

She sniffed as if slowly pulling herself out of her slumber, then her eyes opened, and she bolted up in bed. "Oh my God! We slept in."

He winced. "And with each other."

He expected her to commiserate. When she started laughing, he gaped at her. "What part of this is funny?"

She stole a quick peek at the clock on the bedside table. "If you want to make it to breakfast on time, you're going to have to do the walk of shame."

"The what?"

"Walk of shame. You know, a person stays out all night with a lover and then somehow they have to get back in their house. Or pull their car into their driveway without the neighbor seeing them. Or climb up the stairs of their apartment building before the guy next door comes out to go to work. Or in this case, sneak back to your quarters without anyone seeing you in the same clothes you wore yesterday."

"You're lying there all smug, but this doesn't reflect well on you either."

"Why? I slept with a really handsome, extremely sexy guy last night."

"Yeah, well I slept with a gorgeous woman—"

"Not the same. I get a lot more street cred for sleeping with you than you get for sleeping with me." She stretched up off her pillow to kiss him. "Clock's ticking, Your Majesty. The longer you stay in this room, the more chance someone will see you. Or that you'll be extremely late for breakfast…when one or all of your children could ask why."

Disgruntled and just wanting to stay with her, not have to race around starting his day, he eased out of bed and began yanking clothes off the floor.

Jessica said, "If it's any consolation, I thought last night was worth it."

"Probably because you're not about to be caught."

"There is that. But I meant what I said about you being handsome and sexy."

He paused, enjoying the full force of her compliment as it rolled over him. She always knew the right thing to say at the exact moment it would have maximum effect, mostly because he knew she meant what she said.

He remembered his thoughts from the night before, when he'd felt something cementing between them. Not just a click of connection or a sense of rightness. More like forever.

After the unified front they had to present the day before, the thought didn't surprise him as it usually did. But he decided that was because they were getting close. Closer than he'd ever been to another person. Yet he hadn't forgotten their relationship wouldn't last. Realistically, with Sabrina's latest stunt in the disastrous video, it was clear just how eager the press would be to find Eleanore Smith, while Jessica wanted her to stay hidden. He knew she would move heaven and earth to keep her daughter safe if they began getting close to finding her.

Even if she didn't have to disappear for her daughter's sake, Arthur could decide to come back, and she would return to the assistant pool, where seeing her would be next to impossible and personal time together would be nonexistent.

So, no. He and Jessica did not have a future.

He looked at her, still snuggled in the ornate bed of one of his glamorous guest suites and his heart shimmied. He loved seeing her in his home. He thought of dancing with her the night before the ball for Josh's birthday and knew she had loved getting a taste of his life.

He wanted to give her all of it. But he couldn't. He could only make the best of the time they had.

"What would you think about me hosting a ball for the employees?"

She blinked. "A ball just for employees?"

"Considering there are at least two hundred including security, office staff, maids, cooks, motor pools, groundskeepers, I think it would be fun."

Holding the sheet against her chest, she sat up. "It would be wonderful."

"We wouldn't be giving tours of the palace. But everybody would see that corner of it." He sat on the edge of the bed. "I could mingle, meet everyone." He frowned. "You'd probably have to give me a study sheet, so I'd know who everyone was and where they worked."

"But they'd get to meet you." Her face shifted from surprised to pleased. "I think everyone would love it."

He squeezed her toes beneath the thick floral comforter, undoubtedly one of the ones he'd nixed for his own room. "And we could have a dance."

She gasped. "Are you sure that's a good idea?"

"I will dance with as many people as I can so that my dance with you blends in."

"I could wear a gown with a big skirt that would swish when we waltzed."

He got up from the bed. "Sounds like a plan."

She smiled. "It does."

"And you're in charge."

She pressed her hand to her chest. "Me?"

"You'll get plenty of help from the kitchen and waitstaff." He bent down and kissed her. "Plus, I think you'll have fun doing it."

He took his clothes into the bathroom to dress. When he emerged, she was up and dressing too. He caught her around the waist and kissed her, happy with his plan of hosting a ball for her. But misery quickly filled him. No matter how many things he squeezed into the next few weeks, his happy affair with the most wonderful person he'd ever met would end. She'd be gone from his life. And he'd be lonelier than he'd ever been because he now knew what he was missing.

She pulled back and grinned at him. "Good luck getting to your quarters." She turned to go into the bathroom but faced him again. "Oh, and some people don't put on their shoes when they sneak out so they can be stealthier."

He looked at her, studying her face, memorizing the color of her eyes, the way her hair looked disheveled from making love with him the night before. "Now, I think you're just pulling things out of thin air."

She laughed. "Go ahead and think that but if a board creaks when you step on it and somebody hears you, don't blame me."

She walked into the bathroom, closing the door behind her and his heart actually ached. Still, he had work to do and a breakfast he couldn't be late for. He glanced at his shoes. If a person had to make the walk of shame shoeless that might be part of why it was so shameful.

He carried his shoes anyway and was relieved when he saw no one in any of the corridors. He also had the advantage of the entry through his closet, which cut down the amount of time he was in public areas. All pitfalls navigated, he made it without being discovered.

He showered and dressed and arrived at the breakfast table to find Olivia and Josh.

Pulling out his chair, he said, "No Sabrina?"

Josh winced. "She's pretty angry with you."

He gaped at him. "She's angry with *me*?"

His daughter and son looked at each other. Olivia clearly spoke for both of them when she said, "Honestly, Dad, we're a bit confused. Was Ms. Smith not vetted?"

"Of course, she was vetted. Of course, we knew who she was. But..." He glanced from his son to his daughter. "Think it through. Did she really *not* deserve a job because of something that happened to *her daughter*? And when Arthur took his leave, were we supposed to overlook her when she was next in line for the position?"

"I understand what you're saying," Josh put in. "But you have to admit she is a lightning rod for controversy."

"Which is confusing since her daughter's situation was ten

years ago," Mateo said reasonably. "No one would have even known who she was had your sister not decided to use her hacker friends to investigate her. In a roundabout way, she's the one who broke the law."

"Oh, really?" Sabrina said, sashaying into the dining room. "Eleanore Smith's mother might not have broken any laws, but she obviously has your ear. You take her advice. And that's dangerous."

"No, it isn't! I took Arthur's advice too. A personal assistant is supposed to offer observations and advice about family, about what I wear, about what should be served at state dinners... There's a lot of things I need her advice for."

Sabrina took a seat. "She went too far."

Mateo just stared at her. "She always saw your side of things and that made you angry?"

"The two of you were just a little too chummy."

"Clearly, you forget how close Arthur and I are. Do you know he's called me three times a week on this sabbatical he's taken?"

Sabrina mumbled, "No."

Josh winced. "He's called me too, checking up on you."

Mateo pointed at his son. "See? A personal assistant is more like a friend than an office mate."

Sabrina said, "Whatever. I still don't trust her."

"Then you're in for a world of trouble because if Arthur resigns, we're offering her the job." He glanced at Olivia. "Do *you* have a problem with her?"

Olivia sighed. "No. Honestly, she does the job as well as Arthur. She caught on as if it was second nature to her. There wasn't as much as a ripple in the way you handled your days."

"Josh?"

He shrugged. "I saw the same thing. She's smart. She stays quiet."

Sabrina snorted.

Josh glared at her. "She does! I think part of your problem

might be that you're the one who forgets decorum. You barge into Dad's office. You barge into his quarters—"

"He is my father."

"She's right, Josh." He looked at Sabrina. "I don't mind you coming into my quarters or my office. But you do have to respect my systems. Having an assistant who is with me in my office and at breakfast…who chooses my clothing…buys gifts for dignitaries…reminds me to drink water and runs interference with staff…is a huge help to me. And she's doing a great job."

Sabrina rolled her eyes. "If you overlook the fact that her daughter is questionable."

"Sabrina, her daughter is not questionable."

"How do you know! My God, Dad! No one even knows where Eleanore Smith is. Innocent people do not hide."

"Innocent people who don't want to be hounded by the press have no choice but to hide."

Sabrina threw her arms in the air. "There is no talking to you! You don't simply take everyone's side but mine; you also ignore my advice…which, in this case, might be extremely valuable."

Bouncing up from her seat, she stormed out of the room.

Silence reigned for thirty seconds. Mateo took a breath. "If you two agree with her about Jessica's daughter being some sort of security risk, there is no time like this minute for you to say so."

Olivia quietly said, "I understand why her daughter hides. One misconstrued comment can live in the press forever."

"Actually, Olivia, Eleanore simply wants a normal life. It isn't just the press that questions her, it's bosses, neighbors… She's had to change her name."

Josh said, "And you know this because?"

"Because Jessica and I spend from eight to twelve hours together every day. We talk. Just as I knew everything about Arthur's family, I know about Jessica's daughter. There is no more story there. And, if anything, working for *us* potentially hurts Jessica more than she could ever hurt our family."

Josh winced. "That's true. Sabrina investigating her might revive her story and send reporters looking for her."

Olivia shook her head. "We are the trouble here."

Mateo took a breath. "Yes. We are. That's why Jessica is staying in the palace for a few days. And God only knows what will happen after that." He said words that stuck in his throat, hurt his chest, as a horrible realization hit him. "She might leave us. She might have to walk away from everything that's in her apartment and disappear so she'll be gone before anyone even misses her. Before the press has a chance to realize she's on the move."

Olivia dropped her head to her hands. "Ugh. We're terrible."

"Not us. The life we live. We are the lightning rods. Not her."

Josh said, "Do you think she's just going to leave one night... Not tell anyone?"

The thought went through him like an arrow, and he realized that what he'd felt while they made love might not have been a cementing of their connection as much as desperation. Passion that shot through them because they both knew they didn't have forever. "I'm hoping not. I'm also trying to think of ways to fix this."

Olivia pondered that. "We could give her that little guesthouse behind the vegetable garden."

He thought of how Jessica had wanted to live in a cottage in the woods and almost smiled. She'd never leave before the employee ball, if only because she had a responsibility to plan it. But the house behind the vegetable garden would be a good way to keep her protected, and yet give her some space until then. But he couldn't say what would happen after that.

"We could make the offer."

"If she can't ever leave the property," Josh said, "wouldn't that be a little bit like a prison?"

"Maybe she could stay there until the noise dies down?" Olivia suggested.

Mateo gave voice to the horrible thought that had been on his mind since Jessica had said it. "If the noise ever dies down. With us being part of the story, it gets new life." He picked up his napkin as Nevil entered the room. He quickly asked for eggs and bacon and Nevil scurried to the kitchen. "Until it fritters away, I'm keeping Jessica preoccupied planning a party for the palace employees."

"A ball?"

"When we had to inspect the ballroom for Josh's birthday party, Jessica told me she had never been in that part of the palace. She told me no one she worked with ever had."

Olivia and Josh looked at him expectantly. "And?"

"And we don't know any of the people who work for us—who serve us—beyond their jobs. They are all extremely competent people who are loyal, and we vet them, make them sign confidentiality agreements, want their undivided loyalty, then all but ignore them."

Josh frowned. "That's true."

"While Jessica is living here, rather than have her focus on hiding out, I suggested we hold a ball for employees that she planned. That way she won't have time to worry or over-think things."

Olivia caught his gaze. "You've certainly thought this through."

"It is our fault she can't go home."

Josh said, "Agreed."

Olivia said, "I'm all for it." Finished with her breakfast, she rose and kissed her dad's cheek. "You have a very soft heart." She smiled at him. "A good heart."

He caught her hand and squeezed. "You do too. You'll make a wonderful queen."

Josh rose too. "Well, my *pragmatic* heart and I are going to work. I'll see you both later."

   Mateo waited for Jessica in the dining room for fifteen minutes after he'd finished eating. When she didn't show up, he made his way to his office where he found her at her desk. "You didn't come to breakfast."

   She winced. "Sorry. Was I missed?"

   "We talked about you."

   She sighed. "That can't be good."

   "It wasn't really bad either. I got to ask Josh and Olivia the obvious questions. They support you. Sabrina does not. But, honestly, the bottom line to her ranting was that she wants me to hear her opinions. She thinks I don't pay attention to her because I never do what she wants. Which is ridiculous. She left breakfast in a huff, but she's grounded, so I'll have a talk with her tonight. I'll explain that the two of you aren't competing. That you fit into certain roles, and she fits into other roles. But when it comes to what clothes I wear or what I send to foreign dignitaries as gifts...your opinion rules. And when it comes to philanthropic things, her opinion will rule."

   Jessica thought about that for a second. "That sounds good."

   He sighed with relief. "Thanks. Actually, after her performance at breakfast this morning, I finally saw where I went wrong with her." He ambled into the room. "Her brother and sister are so much older than she is that I forgot that they've been easing into their duties for years. They've been attending meetings, conferences and negotiations as observers since they were eighteen, and now they look perfect for their positions. But I sort of dumped Sabrina into her role the day that we visited the Eliminate Hunger warehouse. I need to find a way to ease Sabrina in too. Maybe take her to more of my charity events, introduce her to people...with her knowing that someday she will be in charge of this end of our duties, the way Josh and Olivia knew they would someday run parliament and the kingdom."

   "That sounds perfect!"

"I hope so." He paused for a second then said, "Olivia also had an interesting idea."

"She did?"

"Yes, she suggested we give you the cottage behind our vegetable garden to live in while you're staying with us. We can't let you go back home until at least some of this dies down but the cottage would give you a sense that you aren't living at work."

"It does feel a bit strange to be here all the time."

"I can take you back there but before I do, I think we should meet with the master of the household and at least pick a date for the ball."

"That would be great."

They designated Friday four weeks out for the ball. Jessica was thrilled to be planning it, but a wisp of melancholy wove through her as she and Mateo met with the master of the household and made a skeleton outline of the night's events. Arthur should be returning the Monday after the ball. In a way, that night would be like her Cinderella moment. She'd get to dance with her handsome king, but her time with him would be over.

With the bare-bones idea for the ball sketched out, Mateo rose. After he dismissed the master of the household, he faced Jessica. "Let's go look at the cabin. We won't take any of your things over until we're sure you like it."

She nodded. "How could I not like a cabin behind a garden. It sounds perfect."

"Yes, but if you've never actually lived in a house that is behind a huge garden and in front of a forest…it might surprise you. Especially the wildlife."

She winced. "I've actually only ever lived in cities."

He laughed. "This should be interesting."

He led her down a corridor, then another that took them to a sunroom. Plants filled every available space where there wasn't a sofa or a chair.

"This is beautiful."

He opened the back door. "Let's hope you feel the same way about the cabin."

They walked down a cobblestone path that wound through flower gardens filled with buds and blossoms that had been started in a greenhouse and now filled the space with color. That morphed into vegetable gardens where young plants were beginning to flourish.

She looked around in awe. "This is huge."

"We like our fresh vegetables."

Beyond the vegetable garden was a patch of grass like a front yard and beyond that was a cozy little house. She approached cautiously. "It's pretty."

"And I called ahead to have housekeeping come in and give it a quick dust and change the linens while we talked about the ball."

She faced him, knowing her eyes probably shimmered with happiness. "Thank you."

"I know how hard it is to work where you live...so—" He shrugged.

"You came up with this idea?"

"Olivia did."

She laughed, fighting the urge to take his hand and lead him up the wide front porch with two wicker chairs and a small table...a good place to have morning coffee.

When they stepped inside the house, it was as charming as the vision that she'd had for the cottage she'd believed would be her sanctuary. A thick sofa and matching chair were angled toward a stone fireplace. Hardwood floors were partially covered by fluffy rugs. Vases of flowers were everywhere.

"It's lovely."

"I'd offer it to you forever, so you'd always have the protection of the royal family. But Josh reminded me that after a while it could seem like a prison."

She faced him. "You know that the three of you are quite a team, right?"

"Yes."

"And now you're going to add Sabrina to that mix."

"Slowly."

She laughed. "Every time you take her to an event is a chance to talk to her, draw her in." She smiled, realizing he'd probably planned it that way. "Damn. You really did think this through."

"She's my daughter. I want her to be happy and to fit in."

"I feel the same way about Ellie. I just want her to fit in. It isn't that she hides, but she does look over her shoulder. Keep her past to herself. She'll never have a normal life…not completely. She was offered the job as head of public relations for the real estate company where she works but she had to turn it down…even though her degree is in PR."

"Why'd she have to turn it down?"

"It involved going to events, doing interviews with the local paper when the company was expanding, being in ads that were televised. That kind of thing. Though she desperately wanted it, it was too much exposure. So she stayed an agent."

"She still has to meet people, be around people."

"Yeah. But it's local people, one-on-one. Her name's never in the papers. She doesn't do television commercials." She sighed. "She still talks about how she hated not being able to take that opportunity."

"The unexpected consequence."

"Of someone else's actions," Jessica agreed. "That one night totally changed her life."

He glanced around the small cabin. "So do you think you could be happy here for a few weeks?"

She nodded. The reminder of their limited time brought her back to their own problems. Mateo might not understand that these could be their last weeks together. She didn't know if he realized Arthur could be returning the Monday after the ball.

But she knew Arthur hadn't filed papers to officially retire or even discussed it with human resources. True, he might make a last-minute announcement, but Arthur wasn't a last-minute kind of guy. He was a planner. The way things looked to her, he would be coming back to his job—

And she would be ready. She wouldn't pout or be sad, but she would miss this. Their casual conversations. Their easy connection. She knew she'd never find this with another person. And when the time came, she'd be even lonelier than she'd been when she'd lucked into this job.

Because now she knew what she was giving up.

CHAPTER FOURTEEN

THE DAY OF the ball arrived with the palace buzzing with excitement. Given that it was a party for the employees, including the kitchen and waitstaff, the event had been catered. Security was being handled in rotating shifts so that all the guards would get to attend the ball for a few hours with their spouses or dates.

Jessica decided to dress for the event in the guest suite in the palace so she wouldn't have to walk up a cobblestone path in a gown. A member of palace security had gone to her apartment to retrieve the red gown she had worn to her ex-husband's Christmas parties. She brought her makeup and toiletries with her to work that morning and set them up in the guest suite bathroom before she went to breakfast.

By late afternoon, everything in the palace sparkled and glittered from a recent cleaning. The scent of good beef, roasted potatoes and sugary baked goods filled the air.

She made her last inspection of the ballroom then headed to the guest suite to dress. The security guard had been instructed to lay her gown on the bed and she went directly to the bedroom to make sure it was there. But when she walked in the room, her red dress was not on the bed. Instead, a big white box with a huge yellow ribbon sat on the floral comforter.

Seeing a card under the bow, she walked over and retrieved it.

This is your night. I bought you the dress you'd told me you wished you had.

Mateo

She slid the ribbon off the box and opened it to find a purple satin dress. When she lifted it out, it swelled around her, and she realized it was the dress she'd said would fan out when they twirled while waltzing.

Her heart squeezed and tears filled her eyes. For thirty seconds, she asked the universe why she'd met him, why she'd been allowed to fall in love with him, when there could be nothing permanent between them.

Then she realized that she'd so very casually admitted to herself that she loved him, and she fell to the bed.

She loved him.

She loved him.

Not in the "I'm content" way she'd loved her husband, but with passion and hope. Commitment. She'd do anything for him, and she knew from the gown sitting on her bed, he'd do anything for her too. She wasn't simply a convenience to him or a number on a to-do list or someone he sneaked to the cottage to sleep with every night. He saw her. He respected her opinion.

They were a perfect match. If her life and her daughter's life were different, she would leave everything for him. With him, she could face the life of being his queen, if only because they would be in it together. She longed to be the one who could support him, advise him. She longed to be the one who could keep him sane when there was trouble. She longed to be the one who filled the needs no one else knew he had.

She just wanted the chance to love him. Everything he was. For real.

The futility of all these wonderful feelings closed her eyes in despair, but she popped them open. She refused to wallow or wonder why. They might not be able to be together forever, but this time with him had been a remarkable gift and she intended to enjoy this night.

She showered, put on makeup, did her hair, then slid into

the gorgeous gown. She didn't know how he'd figured out her size or even where he'd gotten the dress, but she didn't care. She knew security was aware of their affair, but every damned employee in this palace could wonder about their relationship. It didn't matter. In another day or two, she'd be gone.

Mateo might think she was going back to the assistant pool, but she couldn't. She could not work in his palace and pretend there was nothing between them when she loved him enough that she'd give up her plans and be his queen.

Every day would be torture. She would have to leave.

A knock sounded on her door, and she lifted the full skirt of her gown to race to answer it. When she saw Mateo, she caught his arm and dragged him into her room the way she had the first time he'd visited her apartment.

"What are you doing! Anyone could see you out in that hall!"

He closed the door with his foot, then pulled her to him and kissed her. "You look amazing. I knew you would…and I didn't want my first glimpse of you to be in front of everyone where I couldn't enjoy it."

She fanned out the big skirt of the gown. "It is beautiful." She caught his gaze. "Thank you. I will remember this forever."

Mateo loved her thanks, but he hated the finality of her words. Saying she'd remember the dress forever was the first piece of admitting their time together was coming to an end.

"This is a night for fun. Not a night for thinking." He kissed her. "Let's go downstairs."

She raised her eyes to meet his gaze. "Together?"

He winced. "We can walk together so far. Then my arrival has to be announced with trumpets. I'd love to have you walk in with me, but I'm pretty sure you don't want any part of that."

She could picture it. Because they belonged together. But

it wasn't to be. So, she faked a laugh and answered the way he expected her to. "No. I do not."

"Fine. I'll walk in with Sabrina or Olivia the way I always do." They headed for the door, but he stopped her. "You do remember that you're hostess for this, right?"

"I thought I only planned it."

"That makes you hostess. You're like the liaison between the royal family and the guests. They'll be more comfortable with you anyway, so it's up to you to make them feel welcome. You should stand at the main entrance and greet them. If you want a receiving line of a sort, get Pete and Molly to join you. They are also well-known and liked by staff."

"That would be really nice. Thank you."

The urge to kiss her was so strong that he had to fight it. But he looked at it as practice. For the rest of the night, they would have to behave the way they did in the office. Not the casual, comfortable way they were in her cottage. Two lovers who wanted nothing more than to spend precious time together.

They took the stairs to a common area, where Jessica veered to the left and he headed down a hallway to a small room where the royals gathered before all major events in order to enter together.

Josh had brought a date. "Dad, this is Irene Corsicovia." He turned to his date. "Irene, this is my father, His Majesty Mateo Stepanov."

Wearing a strapless peach gown that acknowledged the warm weather, and looked perfect with her red hair, Irene curtsied. "It's a pleasure to meet you, Your Majesty."

He bowed slightly. "It's a pleasure to meet you too." He frowned. "I think I know your father."

"You do, Your Majesty. He owns several vineyards throughout Europe."

Mateo smiled. "I am acquainted with him and his wine. I hope he and your mother are well."

"They are, Your Majesty."

Olivia arrived, also with a date. Glittering in a white gown covered in crystals, she said, "Dad, this is Raymond Daher. Raymond, this is my father. His Majesty Mateo Stepanov."

Raymond bowed. "It's a pleasure to meet you, Your Majesty."

"The pleasure is mine," Mateo said. His heart warmed at the way Raymond and Olivia held hands like people in a serious relationship and Josh stared adoringly at Irene. His children were growing up, but more than that, he could picture Jessica fitting into the intimate family scene. A scene where he, Olivia and Josh were simply people, not royals. Just a dad meeting the love interests of his two adult children.

Sabrina arrived alone, but for once she wasn't angry. With her dark hair piled on top of her head in fat curls and sparkling green eyes, she looked so pretty Mateo began to realize just how beautiful she was. But sometimes beautiful and reckless spelled trouble. She'd spent the past four weeks grounded for outing Jessica in the video, but he'd been drawing her into his charitable duties, hoping she'd begin to see her role and some of her anger would dissipate. While she did very well meeting people and understanding the place of philanthropy in their kingdom, she continued to be grumpy and moody. Still, he blamed that on the boredom of being grounded.

They entered the ballroom as three couples. Olivia and Raymond were announced first. Josh and Irene were second. He and Sabrina were third. He'd asked Olivia, Josh and Sabrina to prepare remarks acknowledging and thanking the staff. Olivia's thank-you became a toast that nearly brought down the house with applause. Josh's was a little more sedate and also showed that he very clearly knew who worked where and that he appreciated them.

When he faced Sabrina, she shook her head slightly, indicating that she had not prepared anything. Not surprised, Mateo simply rose and went to the podium.

"Well, this party is certainly long overdue."

The crowd applauded. Someone whistled.

"I know that my life is busy, and the loss of my beloved queen made my private life difficult…but these past few weeks, working with Jessica Smith has shown me that in a lot of ways, you are my family."

The applause erupted again. More people whistled.

He quieted them with a motion of his hand. "I've always known just how much you do for me, but these past weeks talking with Jessica, I've realized you might not know how much I appreciate all that you do.

"I'm not going to give you the it's-lonely-at-the-top speech because I know I am blessed. But I'm also blessed to have each one of you. I'd like to make this appreciation ball a yearly thing."

The applause began again, but this time he raised his champagne glass in toast. "I could not be as efficient of a leader as I am without you. Salud."

With that, he motioned for the band to begin the dancing. As always, he danced the first dance with Sabrina. It was a tradition begun after her mother's death that continued on as she grew up. And now, here she was, a young lady. Suddenly, he could see a bright future for her, and he knew instinctively that the day would come when she'd see it too.

"Thank you for the dance."

She smiled. "It's tradition now."

He laughed. "Yes, it is."

"Until you find someone."

He searched the statement for a double meaning, or a hint that she knew about him and Jessica, but found none. "It might be a while given how busy I am."

She giggled and patted his arm. "Poor Daddy."

The words hit him right in the heart. They transported him back in time to when she was a very happy little girl. His heart swelled with love.

"Anyway, I think the ball was a great idea and I'm looking forward to meeting the staff."

That took him by surprise, but he didn't let that show in his expression. Her steps might be shaky and inconsistent, but she was growing up. He said simply, "As am I."

The music stopped. She curtsied and he kissed her cheek, then she blended into the crowd.

For the first time in weeks, he had the sense that he didn't have to worry about her. Then he glanced around the room, looking for Jessica. But remembering that he was supposed to be dancing with other women to take the attention off them when he danced with Jessica, he tried to find likely candidates to dance with.

Having memorized the spreadsheet Jessica had created for him, complete with employee pictures, he moved into the crowd. The first person he found was the executive suite receptionist, Molly. Glad that the first person he ran into was someone he knew, he happily invited her to dance, and she accepted.

After that dance, he joined a group of his security detail, who were hanging out at the bar. The people who would be taking the next shift and the one after that were abstaining from alcohol, but the group that had just gotten off duty had ordered beers.

He drank a beer with them, then found the head of housekeeping and asked her to dance. After the dance, he mingled with people who were still seated at tables.

Half a row in, he ran into Jessica. Literally.

She laughed. "Pardon me, Your Majesty."

He instinctively caught her hand. "No. It was my mistake. Not looking where I was going."

He fought the instinct to kiss her knuckles. "Since we're already here…how about a dance?"

"That would be lovely."

He guided her to the dance floor, but the band played a fast song that prevented him from really dancing with her and didn't allow for the flare of the skirt of her ball gown.

When the song was over, she curtsied and scurried away.

Disappointment shuffled through him. But he continued his plan of dancing and mingling.

After the band's first break, Arthur and his wife approached him.

A tall, slender man with white hair, his former nanny, current personal assistant, caught him in a huge hug. His wife curtsied, but Mateo laughed and hugged her.

"We're like family."

"As you said in your speech."

"Yes," he agreed, "but the three of us were family before that."

Arthur looked down at his champagne glass then up at Mateo. "Thank you for this."

Mateo tilted his head in question. "For the ball?"

"Yes. You have the most dedicated staff in the world. They appreciate being acknowledged."

"I'm sorry it took me this long to figure that out."

"Rumor has it that your temporary assistant Jessica might have instigated this."

He snorted. "We were here, doing the Friday night inspection for the ball for Josh's birthday, and she mentioned that most of the staff hadn't ever seen the ballroom, and some hadn't ever even been on the executive side of the palace."

"That's true."

"It hit me that it shouldn't be that way."

"I'm happy you saw…and I think Jessica does get the credit."

Mateo chuckled. "She moved into your job remarkably well."

"I'm so glad. It was good to be able to recover in peace." He glanced around. "But I'm fine now. Not just recovered but rested and ready to take my job back."

Mateo was surprised. But Arthur was very good at what he did and probably the most loyal employee in the palace, which was saying a lot. The job was his and he was well enough to return to it.

"It will be good to have you back."

"Monday morning, the usual time?"

Mateo reached out and shook his hand. He said, "The usual time," happily but his chest tightened. Jessica would go back to the assistant pool, and now that a month had gone by since Sabrina's disastrous social media post he also suspected she would move back to her apartment.

Arthur and his wife drifted away, and Mateo stood on the sidelines, disappointed that his one shot at dancing with her had been a dismal failure, until it finally dawned on him that he could ask the band to play a waltz. He walked up to the lead singer and made his request then went back to mingling again.

When the band played the familiar chords of the waltz, he found Jessica in the crowd, and she found him. Too far away to hear each other, he didn't say a word. He simply smiled at her.

They walked across the dance floor and met in the middle. Enthusiastic couples joined them, and they blended in like the other attendees. Just two people enjoying the dance.

Their gazes caught and held as the music swept them away, the huge skirt of her gown flaring out behind her.

When the music stopped, his heart hurt. He had finally fallen in love. It was so much deeper and richer than he ever imagined but it was wrong. Pointless. Again, he was struck by the injustice of it. Worse, they were in public. He couldn't kiss her, tell her he loved her—

He couldn't say or do anything.

They drifted apart slowly, with Jessica smiling like the perfect employee. He smiled like a happy boss. No one would ever guess there was anything between them.

It was a foretaste of what his life would be without her. With

Arthur coming back, even if he ventured into the assistant pool, this cool, efficient version of Jessica was all he'd ever see.

Marty Goodwin scurried through the crowd and caught Mateo's arm. "Your Majesty! Sabrina has been in an accident. She's at the hospital." He twirled Mateo in the direction of the door. "We need to take you there now."

Jessica ran over in time to hear Marty say, "We need to take you there now," and followed them, saying, "I'm going too."

Swiftly moving through the crowd, Marty said, "There's no reason—"

Mateo stopped dead. He might not be able to kiss her or tell her he loved her, but right in this minute, he needed her. "She's going."

Marty said, "Of course, sire," and hustled him and Jessica through the crowd which had stopped dancing and stood in a weird, suspended animation.

From the corner of his eye, Mateo caught Josh taking the microphone from the band's lead singer. Clearly having been briefed, he told the attendees to continue dancing. "Sabrina's been in an accident, but she's fine. Everything will be fine."

From the slight shimmy in Josh's voice, Mateo didn't believe that.

CHAPTER FIFTEEN

THEY WERE RUSHED through a private entry of the hospital and whisked up to a private floor with security at every corner. The guards didn't surprise Jessica; neither did the secure entry, or the entire floor being designated for the royal family. What shocked her was the décor. The nurse's station looked like a small office. The floors were gorgeous hardwood. There were no numbers or markings on the doors. The place looked like the bedroom area of the palace.

A man in green scrubs met them halfway down the hall. "I'm Doctor Ford, Your Majesty, the physician who saw Sabrina when she was first brought here by ambulance. Your daughter was in an automobile accident and her left leg was broken. She's being taken to surgery and is expected to make a full recovery."

Jessica pressed her hand to her chest, grateful it wasn't as bad as it could have been.

Mateo said, "Thank God."

Dr. Ford motioned them to walk into a room with sofas, chairs and a television. Jessica glanced around again. Everything was so perfect, it could have been a sitting room in the palace. Quietly luxurious.

"I'm sorry, Your Majesty, but you'll have to wait here."

The doctor left and Marty entered the room slowly as Jessica and Mateo lowered themselves to one of the sofas.

"Details are sketchy, but we've been told that Sabrina was riding with a friend who was driving drunk."

Mateo shook his head. "She was at the ball."

Marty took a long breath. "We think she must have taken advantage of one of the times when the guards at the gate were changing shifts." He sucked in another breath. "If you'll pardon my forwardness, Your Majesty, nothing gets by Sabrina. Knowing she wouldn't have a detail assigned to her at the ball, she could have had this planned or simply seen an opportunity and taken it. The gentleman she was riding with was also at the ball. His injuries were less severe and he's fine."

"Thank you, Marty."

He bowed slightly. "If that's all, sire, I'd like to check on the security downstairs and then return to the palace."

"Yes. Thank you, Marty."

The door closed behind him and the waiting room became quiet. She caught Mateo's hand. "I'm so sorry."

"The doctor said she's expected to make a full recovery."

"Yes. But it's still hard."

He blew his breath out on a sigh and rose to pace. "Where did I go wrong with her?"

"You didn't. She's eighteen. She's been grounded for weeks. She's probably bored silly. She saw an opportunity and took it."

"With a guy who was drunk?"

"Maybe he didn't look drunk? Maybe she didn't think far enough ahead to even wonder if he'd had too much to drink." She shrugged. "You told me that you had your share of 'normal' moments when you were young. Didn't you ever take a foolish risk?"

He looked at the ceiling. "Yes."

She rose and walked to him. "I know this is upsetting. But you have to keep your wits about you. Technically, she's going to be stuck at home for months because of this. You could tell her that she extended her own grounding by sneaking out. You could also tell her that Fate isn't always kind...or fair. That she's been lucky until now, but things won't always break her way." She paused long enough to be sure he was paying attention. "But that's a talk for when she's feeling a bit better."

He squeezed his eyes shut. "Yes."

She took his hand and led him to the soft couch again. "Now that we're clear on that, I'm going to give you permission to be a normal dad. To pace. To worry. To get all your confusion out while you're alone with me. So no one has to see it. Especially not Sabrina." She winced. "At least not yet."

He sat. "Okay."

She sat beside him. "For the next couple of hours just be a dad."

He nodded.

Her heart went out to him, but she was overwhelmingly glad she was there. Not just to support him but to help him respond correctly with Sabrina. This was the role she was born to play. His helpmate. It couldn't be forever. But she was here now, and she would be whatever he needed.

She took a breath, looked at the solid door that separated them from the rest of the world and laid her head on his shoulder.

He'd been there for her. She was here for him.

Hours later the surgeon came in and explained the procedure they had performed to realign the broken pieces of the bone. The prognosis was good, but he intended to keep Sabrina in the hospital for at least a week, maybe longer, depending on how she was healing. Full recovery would be four to six months.

"She'll be out of post and in a private room shortly. You can see her then." He glanced at the king's tux and Jessica's ball gown but didn't mention their attire. He simply said, "I'll be in my office for another hour or two, Your Majesty, in case you have questions."

When he left, Mateo felt his first relief in hours. She really would be fine, and she was about to be trapped at home, to heal, for months.

He turned to Jessica. "You're right. She certainly extended her grounding. There's a lesson there."

"Something you can use when she's well enough to have the discussion about her behavior," Jessica agreed, pulling out her phone. She went to contacts and he heard the beeps of the phone dialing.

"Marty? This is Jessica. Would it be possible for you to have someone from your team get jeans and a sweater for His Majesty?"

Mateo said, "Have them get something for you too."

"Have them go into the cottage and grab jeans and a sweater for me too."

She disconnected the call and smiled at him. "I have a feeling you're not going to leave. This way we're good until late tomorrow."

He ran his hand down his face. "Thank you."

"That's my job, remember?"

He did. But the things she did didn't feel like obligations or even thinking ahead to help him the way an assistant would. They felt personal. Like this is how the person in his life would be a partner. They'd think of things for each other, do things for each other. Not just perform roles, and handle mandatory tasks, the way he'd spent his entire life.

Except with his kids. He'd always been real with his kids. Jessica had seen that and stepped in with good advice so he could keep it that way.

His heart began to mourn her loss again, but he stopped it. She was here. Now. And he was beginning to understand why people lived in the moment. Sometimes it was all they had.

The following afternoon, Sabrina was recovering well enough that Jessica and Mateo returned to the palace. When the driver pulled up to the entryway, he faced Jessica.

"There are a few things we need to handle in the office, if you don't mind."

"Of course, not, Your Majesty."

They exited the limo and the guard at the door opened it for them. At first, they went in the direction of the office, but he took the quick left that led to the back stairway to his quarters.

Climbing the steps, he caught her hand. Her heart bumped against her chest. They were holding hands in a common area. Of course, Sabrina was in the hospital. Josh now had a girlfriend he spent time with, and Olivia rarely came over this way.

And security knew about their relationship.

There wasn't any reason to panic.

He led her into his quarters through the closet and she laughed. "I know you've been under a lot of pressure, but you're going to get us caught."

"Nope. I made that up about having to work so no one would be expecting you to leave and after a while they'd forget you were here. You're going to do the walk of shame in the morning."

Another laugh escaped. "Not if I don't fall asleep!"

He stopped, faced her. "Yeah. That's a better plan."

"I still have to walk outside to get to the cottage."

"Not if you stay in the guest quarters one more night. No one would question that."

"Huh. You're right." They walked through the bathroom into his bedroom and when he stopped by the bed, she said, "You've been planning this."

"A king doesn't host a ball for the woman he loves without wanting the chance to show her that he loves her."

Her heart shimmied. "Don't say that."

"It's my country. I'm pretty much allowed to say what I want."

With that he kissed her and every nerve ending in her body melted. He was the love she'd waited her whole life to find even though she didn't know she'd been waiting.

They undressed each other slowly, as if they had all the time in the world, and she understood why. They didn't have all the time in the world, so they had to memorize every important second. This time right now might be the most important memory they'd make because he'd told her he loved her.

She didn't just love him. He loved her too.

They fell to the silky sheets beneath the comforter. Their gazes caught and held as he ran his palms along the curve of her torso. Her breasts nestled against his chest. Their legs tangled.

"Have I ever told you you're beautiful."

"You might have mentioned it a time or two."

He laughed. "You are."

She didn't want them talking. There was too much chance they'd slide over into forbidden territory. She'd spoken to Arthur at the ball, knew he was returning on Monday and she didn't want to get stuck on how awful it would be to lose each other. She wanted the raw, earthy passion of two people desperately in love.

Her hands cruised down his chest, as she eased up enough to kiss him. She put everything she had into the kiss. Not just to keep him too busy to talk but to ignite the kind of fires he always lit in her. She loved the feel of him, strong muscles under smooth skin, peppered with dark hair, and wouldn't let herself think any further than the moment.

He rolled her to her back, kissing her greedily, igniting burning sensations deep within her. Then he eased his lips from her mouth to her breasts, fanning the flames until every inch of her tingled with need. As if feeling the same things she was, he separated her thighs with his knee, and they came together in a storm of passion that left them both breathless.

Afterward, they whispered in the dark, though she doubted anyone could hear them even if they shouted. She wouldn't let him slip over into the conversation that haunted them both.

Not only had the weekend been difficult for him, but there was no point to discussing their future.

They had none.

When he fell asleep, she redressed, then picked up her shoes and laughed.

It seriously would not be the walk of shame if she wasn't carrying her shoes.

Laughing through tears, she headed into the bathroom, then the closet, then the extremely quiet corridor. She walked down the hall to another set of steps and quietly climbed them to the floor with the guest quarters.

She almost took a shower but didn't want to risk ruining the warm glow that filled her. He loved her. No thought, no words, had ever been so wonderful.

After a good night's sleep, she showered and dressed to return to the hospital. Right before she would have texted Mateo for instructions, he told her he would be at the limo waiting for her. They would eat breakfast at the hospital.

When they arrived, Sabrina was asleep, so Mateo went to the nurse's station to make sure they had alerted her doctors that he was there and ready for an update on his daughter's condition.

Phone in hand, Jessica took a seat on one of the chairs of Sabrina's quiet room.

"I really screwed up this time, didn't I?"

She carefully glanced over to the bed where Mateo's youngest child lay, her leg in traction.

"That's not for me to say."

Sabrina snorted. "You never hesitated to give your opinion before."

"I don't counsel you. I counsel your dad. If he were here and you said that, and he looked to me…then I would give my opinion. That's my job."

She grimaced. "That's what my dad said. But I know he's probably furious with me. And I might need help."

Jessica said nothing.

Sabrina groaned. "Come on. Throw me a bone. Tell me what to say to him."

"Ohhhh…no! This is all on you."

She sighed. "Yeah. I get that."

Jessica turned her attention to her phone, but curiosity got the better of her and she glanced at Sabrina again. "Let me ask you something. Was sneaking out of that ball all about needing to be out? Or was this a power trip? You know…showing your dad that no matter what he said or did, you'd find a way to do what you want."

"I'd been cooped up for weeks! I needed to get out!"

"Oh, poor you. Cooped up with a chef and swimming pool and a gym and tennis courts and horses and beautiful gardens."

"It's all boring!"

"Is it really?"

"Yes!"

"What do you do when you go out that's not boring?"

Sabrina shrugged. "I don't know. Talk. Dress up. Take rides. Dance. Have fun."

"You could have danced at the ball."

"Maybe."

Jessica suddenly saw what was going on. "You *were* proving a point."

Sabrina said nothing.

"You know that ball was in appreciation for all the people who work in your palace, and you left. Your actions said that you could not care less about the people who serve you. Did you even talk to anyone?"

When Sabrina stayed silent, Jessica shook her head. "Your dad adores you. He'd give you the moon, yet you always find ways to rebel like nothing you have is good enough. Have you ever once said thank you or that you were sorry when you pulled one of your stunts?"

The door swung open, and Mateo walked in. "Hey, you're awake."

Sabrina shifted on the bed. "Yeah."

He walked over and kissed her forehead. "Feeling better today?"

"A bit."

He turned to go to a chair, but Sabrina caught his hand. "I'm sorry."

He smiled at her. "We'll talk about that later."

"No. Really, Dad. I'm sorry. I didn't think about anything but the fact that there'd be a chance I could escape. I didn't think about anybody but myself."

"You know, the friend you talked into driving you to freedom was arrested."

She squeezed her eyes shut. "No."

"Things you do have consequences, Sabrina. Being a princess doesn't protect you from life or promise you anything. You have to grow up. Maybe even faster than a normal kid does. Because that guy's life is forever changed. You can walk away from this. He can't."

Her eyes filled with tears. "I'm so, so sorry."

"And you have four to six months of recovery time to think through how you need to change."

Several of Sabrina's friends asked for permission to visit her. Mateo did not grant it. First, she wasn't recovered enough to have friends. Second, she was on enough pain meds to believe she could get out of bed and try to escape…again.

He and Jessica stayed all day Sunday, and Sabrina slept on and off, proving she wasn't yet ready for company. At nine o'clock that night, she was so sound asleep that Mateo decided it was time to go home.

They walked down the hall holding hands and he didn't even realize it, until they met the security detail that walked them to the door to the private area of the parking garage. If either one of his guards noticed, they said nothing. It wasn't their job to comment or criticize. Their job was to protect him. They escorted him to the sedan, opened the back doors for him and Jessica, then slid into the front seat to drive them back to the palace.

They stopped the car in front of the entrance Mateo typically used. When the back door opened, he began to slide out, but she stayed where she was.

When he glanced over his shoulder at her, she said, "I'm going to the cottage tonight."

He nodded. "Okay. I think we can actually work tomorrow morning. We'll do breakfast then go to the office and handle the things that can't wait so we can go to the hospital in the afternoon."

She smiled slightly. "Have you forgotten Arthur will be back tomorrow?"

He paused. The air changed. This was it. The end. Worse, it felt anticlimactic. The end of the most wonderful love affair of his life was his beloved telling him his old assistant would be returning.

His emotions rebelled, but in all the weeks they'd been together, he hadn't been able to divine a way they could have forever. If anything, his thoughts always hit roadblocks. And the roadblocks weren't nuisances, or inconveniences or even problems that could be solved. They were futures. Both Jessica and her daughter had rebuilt their lives from the ground up. He couldn't destroy that or ask them to roll the dice and take a risk that having Jessica marry into a royal family wouldn't bring a shower of press down upon them. After Sabrina's post that gave away Jessica's identity, there'd be no way.

"Does this mean you'll be in the assistant pool tomorrow?"

"I guess. I'll have to see HR."

"Maybe come to breakfast first? Fill Arthur in on what's been happening?"

She hesitated. "If you feel we need the transition?"

Relief filled him. "I do."

"Okay. See you at breakfast tomorrow."

CHAPTER SIXTEEN

MATEO'S SECURITY DETAIL drove her to the door of the cottage, and she thanked them before she ambled into the little house. Someone had lit a fire to take the chill out of the air. She suspected Mateo had instructed his security detail to handle it, but her chest tightened.

She'd never been so in sync with anyone...or so in love that she'd happily be the woman by his side forever, give up her simple existence to be his queen, if it were possible. But it wasn't. Monday, with Arthur returning, her final breakfast would be all about handing over her duties.

The thought of it broke her heart and filled her eyes with tears. Especially since Arthur probably didn't need to be brought up to speed. He'd done this job forever.

She'd be a redundancy—

She would no longer be Mateo's assistant. She would be a nameless, faceless employee in the assistant pool again.

Her head filled with images and ideas of how the following week would be. She wouldn't even see Mateo in passing. There would be no sneaking around because if they were caught there was no built-in excuse.

When Sabrina had outed her to the press, she'd agreed to stay in the palace and then the little cottage because her job kept her protected by palace security. Now...she would be an ordinary employee. No specific duties. Only requests from executive staff. Arbitrary jobs. No continuity. No position. Just jobs—

No one would miss her if she didn't show up the next morning. Technically, she could go home.

She took a breath.

She could go home.

She could go anywhere.

And maybe that was the thing to do.

Go. For real.

Get on with the rest of her life.

Not tomorrow. Not the next day. Right now.

Deep down inside she'd always known this was their breaking off point and a wise woman would accept that. She wouldn't hang around and pine over someone she couldn't have. She wouldn't spin fantasies about how things "might" work out.

She would recognize truth and move on.

She walked back to the bedroom to repack her suitcase with the clothes she'd brought with her the day security had scooped her up. She also had a lot of things at her apartment that she would want to retrieve. Technically, her rent was paid for a month. The smart play would be to leave now, find a new home—probably in another country—and return to pack for real and have everything shipped to her new apartment.

It seemed like such a good plan that she didn't consider that she'd been through a difficult weekend with Mateo and Sabrina and she might not be thinking clearly. She didn't consider the emotions connected to losing him. She simply acted. She finished packing her bag and called security. In less than an hour, she had made flight arrangements, and a guard was driving her to the airport.

Mateo arrived in the dining room the next morning finally feeling refreshed. The only way he could have felt better would have been if he had slept with Jessica, but knowing Arthur was returning she'd already drawn the dividing line.

So, he'd stayed up a good bit of the night, fighting the urge to call her until he had the answer to how they could have a relationship. For real. Forever. As always, he couldn't think of one, but he wasn't done trying. He'd fallen asleep out of exhaustion and slept surprisingly well. This morning, he would update Arthur on his duties and the clamoring staff who would want to see him, and he would text Jessica and tell her that he refused to believe they couldn't work this out.

He would text her every twenty minutes until she agreed with him.

He felt so good about his plan that he ordered blueberry pancakes.

Arthur arrived, electronic tablet in hand. "Good morning, Your Majesty."

"Good morning, Arthur. It's good to have you back."

Josh entered. "Arthur! You're back."

"Yes. It's good to see you, Prince Josh."

Josh took his seat. "Are we able to visit Sabrina yet?"

"She was very good yesterday. Still a little loopy from drugs, but I think you and Olivia can go any time you want. Together or separately."

Olivia arrived and took her seat. "We can finally visit?" She glanced across the table. "Hey! Arthur!"

"Good morning, Princess Olivia. I trust you slept well."

"Very well." She looked at her dad. "And I'm eager to see Sabrina. You and Jessica were all the company she had since the accident. She's probably ready for a good conversation."

"You wouldn't have been able to talk anyway. She slept on and off all day Saturday. Yesterday was better." He zeroed his gaze on his daughter. "Do not overtire her."

Olivia smiled demurely. "I'll be fine." She looked around. "Speaking of Jessica…where is she? Does she just go back to the assistant pool? I mean, now that she's trained in our inner workings, it might be good to keep her in the executive suite. I could use a good assistant."

"You have an assistant."

"Meh. I think I'd like Jessica better."

It twisted in Mateo's gut that they were talking about Jessica as if she were a commodity instead of a person. To his family, she was only an employee when to him she was everything. But he couldn't say anything. He needed to talk to Jessica, get her to admit she would stay. Then he'd talk to his kids...

Then...

Well, he didn't know what. But he could not believe his relationship with her had to end.

"Shall I read today's schedule?" Arthur asked.

Mateo's blueberry pancakes arrived. "Let's wait for Jessica."

Arthur frowned. "Security's docket from last night indicates that she was driven to the airport around midnight."

Mateo stopped cutting his pancakes. "What?"

"She left, Your Majesty. I thought perhaps she'd needed a small holiday after her stint as your assistant and that she'd given you a date she'd be returning."

He set his fork down. "No. She did not mention that to me. But I'll look into it."

"*I'll* look into it," Arthur corrected. He shifted his gaze to the tablet. "Your first call this morning will be to the hospital to check on Sabrina. Then you have two meetings you can't miss. But after that I'm canceling everything so that you can spend the afternoon at the hospital."

And just like that Mateo's world returned to the one he'd had before Jessica. When breakfast was eaten and they entered the office, Arthur immediately went to his desk to get the hospital nurse's station on the line, and confusion shimmied through Mateo. He felt like he'd fallen off a cliff and landed back in time. His weeks with Jessica became a weird memory, something so good he must have imagined it.

As if she didn't exist.

* * *

Jessica arrived in London late that morning. She'd basically slept on hard plastic airport chairs and on her flight. Having visited London, she knew a good, reasonably priced hotel and got a room. As soon as she was settled, she took out the burner phone she'd used to call Ellie when she'd first moved to Brazil and dialed her daughter.

"Mom? Why are you calling on the burner?"

"Are you kidding? After that mess with Sabrina, I wasn't going to risk the press tracing my calls."

"What mess… Are you talking about Princess Sabrina? I didn't think your work at the palace involved her."

Remembering that she hadn't told her daughter about her promotion to Mateo's assistant, she sat on the bed and slipped off her shoes.

"Get ready for a long story."

She told her daughter about the promotion and Sabrina's obvious dislike of her as the king's assistant, then the mess with her hiring hackers to dig into Jessica's past and the social media post telling the world she was Eleanore Smith's mother.

Ellie gasped in horror. "Are you kidding me?"

"No. The king held a press conference and more or less shamed the reporters for even wanting a ten-year-old story."

"That must be why there was nothing about it in the press here." She paused. "I also didn't see anything on social media."

Jessica eased up to the headboard of the bed and curled against it. "Maybe Mateo really did shame them into letting the story die."

"Mateo?"

She took a breath. "You don't work as someone's *personal* assistant for eight weeks without getting a little personal."

Eleanore laughed. "Oh, really?"

"Stop. I will admit it was fun having a handsome king interested in me—"

Ellie's gasp came through the phone. "He was *interested* in you?"

"We were interested in each other."

"Mom! You…you… I don't even know what to say."

The thought of her weeks with Mateo filled her with warmth and she laughed. "It was yummy. He was…is…so handsome and thoughtful and his first marriage had been arranged so I felt like I was his first love, and he felt like mine…"

"Mom! You scamp! You seduced a king!"

Jessica said, "Stop!" through her laughter. "The thing of it was our relationship would have been nothing but trouble. Royal families are always objects of the press. Your story would be magnified if I'd added a royal romance."

"Magnified?"

"Anybody who gets involved with someone in a royal family can expect to have their life dissected. That's actually why I called. I left my job and my apartment. I'm in London. I think I'll live here for a while. You know…maybe until I retire. Then I can get that little cottage in the woods." The sense of boredom about the cottage hit her like an avalanche. She'd somehow let go of that dream to include Mateo in her life and could even see herself as his queen. Now she was back to being the crone in the garden, who did nothing but read and knit. The shift almost gave her a headache.

Not ready to think about that, she ignored it. "Anyway, let's use the burners for a while, then we'll see where we stand."

"Okay." Ellie drew a deep breath. "But something feels off about using the burners. Wrong. I mean, when I first moved to Brazil these phones were like a lifeline. And moving around was almost normal. Now, everything feels off. Especially you leaving Pocetak."

Surprised, Jessica said, "You're just feeling that because we haven't had to move or hide for a while. Neither one of us has."

"You might have moved but you never left Pocetak. You never really hid the way I had to and—I don't know—Today

it all feels wrong." She took a breath. "Why did you leave Pocetak?"

"Because of Sabrina's social media post. She outed me. I
couldn't stay."

She didn't have the heart to admit she also couldn't bear to
see Mateo on the news, in the papers. Even now, the thought
of never seeing him again made her chest hurt.

Still, she was strong. Smart. She would get through the
pain of losing him.

"Okay. I guess I understand."

Ellie might understand but Jessica heard confusion in her
daughter's voice.

But this wasn't the time to talk about it. They could sort it
out once she was settled. "I'll be apartment hunting tomorrow and once I find a place I'll make one more trip back to my
old apartment to box things up and have them shipped there.
I'll get a new phone and send you both that number and my
new address."

Ellie quietly said, "Okay."

Jessica's heart splintered. She knew it had to be difficult to
move to a different country, stay away from friends… Only
talk to her mother by phone.

But there wasn't another way.

"Right now, I'm going out for some food then I'll take a
long shower and get some sleep."

"Okay. Goodbye, Mom."

"Goodbye, sweetie."

Her day went exactly as she told Ellie it would. She got
food and a shower and then went to bed. But when she woke
the next morning, and opened her phone to apartment hunt,
she didn't have the sense of urgency or excitement she'd had
the other times she'd moved. She'd been with the palace for
years. Been in her apartment for years. Without Sabrina's interference, she could have stayed there forever.

Thoughts of Sabrina became thoughts of Mateo, and her

breathing slowed. They'd been together ten or twelve hours a day for eight weeks. They'd flirted, danced, made love, ate breakfasts together. And now he was just gone from her life, as if a magician had snapped her fingers and made him disappear—

She stopped those thoughts. She would get beyond this. She always did.

But memories bombarded her. Especially dancing with him at the ball, in a dress he'd bought for her because he listened when she talked. But their quiet, private moments had been better. Right from the beginning she'd realized she could confide in him, and he could confide in her.

And today, his daughter was in the hospital. There was no doubt she'd recover, but he was alone. In a way, he was always alone.

She squeezed her eyes shut, absorbing the pain of knowing in her heart of hearts that she was supposed to be his mate. His helper. His lover. As he was supposed to be hers. She believed she was the answer to some silent prayer he'd made— maybe even decades ago.

But she couldn't be. Their stars did not align. Her being with him would expose Ellie.

Friday, Mateo went to the hospital at one o'clock in the afternoon as had been his practice all week. Sabrina was awake but grouchy. Which was how he knew she was coming back to normal. He found her doctor and spoke with him about letting her go home and what preparations would be necessary.

The list wasn't long, but it was specific and not for the first time that week, he'd wished Jessica was still his assistant.

But deep down he knew he didn't want her around to be his assistant. He wanted her in his life as his partner. And that couldn't be.

He asked the doctor to have the nurses print the instructions for his staff, then he walked back to Sabrina's room.

"I just made arrangements for you to come home."

She sat up awkwardly, trying not to move the leg in traction. "You did?"

"Yes. But there will be rules. There will be a nurse in your quarters at all times to make sure you're not doing anything physical beyond what you are allowed to do."

"Okay."

"And I will allow visits from friends but one at a time."

She swallowed as if preventing herself from saying something, but ultimately she agreed. "Okay."

"For someone who was grouchy when I came in, you're being very accommodating."

"I'm beginning to realize I was more than a little self-centered. That you were a really great dad and I took advantage of you."

He laughed. "Really? And you're going to change?"

"Jessica sort of told me I had to."

His heart twisted at the mention of her name, and he realized that was part of his sorrow. No one even said her name anymore. She was gone in a puff of smoke, and he seemed to be the only one who remembered her.

"What did she say?"

Sabrina shrugged. "Just something like I pushed you or pushed your boundaries or something." She shrugged again. "The part I remember was that she asked me if I ever told you I was sorry for things I did. And that's when I started to see things from your perspective. I didn't stop to realize I always made trouble for you."

He could almost see Jessica speaking to Sabrina honestly, firmly, but not yelling. Just throwing out breadcrumbs that his daughter clearly followed to a good conclusion.

"If you mean that, I might let you have two visitors at a time."

She laughed. The sound was like music to his ears. Jessica had done that. Put her on the right path.

His heart broke all over again.

"I know you liked her."

His head snapped up.

"She liked you too. What I can't figure out is why you let her go."

"It's complicated."

She snorted. "That's what people say when they don't want to be honest."

"I can be perfectly honest, but you might not like it. You're the one who brought attention to her daughter through your shenanigans with the video."

She sighed. "I was just mad."

"Yeah, well, your outburst had consequences. Her daughter who is hidden probably got harassed—"

He paused. He didn't really know what had happened.

Sabrina said, "Did the press come after her?"

He thought about that for a second. Weeks had passed between the video and his press conference and the ball. No one had shown him any repercussion articles. No one had even mentioned it again.

It was as if it was irrelevant.

Of course, he'd never asked Jessica. Lots could have been going on behind the scenes—

No. She would have told him. That was the kind of relationship they had.

"I think you should go after her."

He sniffed. "You? *You* think I should go after your nemesis?"

"I might have been a bit hasty. She's pretty nice."

"She's very nice. Very kind."

Sabrina grinned. "Very pretty." She sobered. "Go after her, Dad. I'd never seen you act the way you did with her. I'm going to feel really awful if you go back to being all stuffy like Arthur."

He laughed. They spent the rest of the afternoon talking

about her schoolwork and her potential place in the kingdom. This time, he didn't act as if it was a done deal. This time he made her understand that she was young, that neither her sister nor her brother had taken their place. They were both in training and it might be decades before Olivia was crowned queen and decades before Sabrina would be experienced enough to head up a department.

The sun had set by the time he summoned his detail and returned to the palace. Tired, missing Jessica, he ambled into the entry foyer. Marty Goodwin manned the main station just inside the door.

"Good evening, Your Majesty."

He stopped. Since the employee ball, things were a lot more personal between him and staff. "Good evening, Marty."

"The updates I'm getting from the guards at the hospital indicate that Sabrina's doing well."

"We're bringing her home tomorrow, getting nurses, a hospital bed...that kind of thing."

"We'll be on top of it."

"I know you will..." He turned to go but stopped and faced Marty again. "I know security took Ms. Smith to the airport, but did anybody by any chance find out where she was going?"

Marty gave Mateo a strange look. "She was a member of the palace staff. We always keep track of staff for a few months after anyone leaves just to make sure they aren't selling state secrets."

Mateo frowned. "Stealing secrets?"

"No one's ever done it, but it's protocol. We follow up on everybody. Anyway, we checked flight manifests and discovered she went to London."

"London?"

He shrugged. "We'll follow her employment history, learn where she's living...until we're satisfied that she didn't leave with confidential documents." This time, he laughed when he said it and Mateo laughed too.

"I know you're not kidding but I can also tell you think it might be going overboard to keep tabs on her."

Marty shook his head. "I have a sixth sense about these things. She's a good person. She won't be writing a tell-all book and she didn't take documents. But it's protocol to follow through. Better safe than sorry."

He nodded. "Good night, Marty."

"Good night, Your Majesty."

Mateo walked to the back stairway, his heart pounding in his chest. She'd gone to London. He loved London. He'd love to be in London with her.

Who was he kidding? He'd love to be anywhere with her.

Sabrina's questions about Jessica's daughter and the press popped into his brain and he turned and went back down the stairs.

"Marty, Sabrina asked me today if there were any repercussions to the stunt she pulled with the video, outing Jessica. I know your team is always doing threat assessments. Was there a problem?"

Marty hit a few keys on his laptop. "There was chatter on social media. There always is. A few podcasters brought it up." He scanned his screen. "It looks like the security people who listened to the podcasts reported that comments ran in Jessica's daughter's favor."

"Really?"

Marty laughed. "There was a general theme that people should just let her alone." He glanced up at Mateo. "I wouldn't say there would never again be interest in the story or that she'd never be hounded again, but if there was ever a time for someone to come out of hiding and give an interview, this might be her daughter's."

Ridiculous hope grew inside Mateo. Given Marty's background, if anyone knew how to navigate these waters, it would be him. And if he was right about Ellie not hiding anymore, there was a chance for him and Jessica.

Marty said, "When we look at something like this situation from a public relations perspective, there are two ways to handle it. The first is to hide, which is what Eleanore Smith has been doing. But the second is to confront the situation outright. To dare anyone to challenge or disagree with you. That's actually how a security team can bring a lot of enemies out of the woodwork. It's how we identify the real problems."

Mateo frowned, thinking that through. Having Ellie do a press conference that challenged her enemies would be the risk of all risks and not something Jessica and her daughter would agree to. Not after this many years of relative peace.

"Of course, you don't hold a press conference just to say I dare you to confront me to my face. There has to be some substance behind your motivation. A message."

Mateo said, "Such as?"

"If Jessica's daughter did an interview that said her situation was the worst time in her life but it's over and everyone could learn a lesson about trusting the wrong person from her story…she'd probably earn a lot of respect."

That sounded empty and insubstantial. "And that's it?"

Marty bobbed his head. "A lot of people can bring victory out of a bad situation by starting a nonprofit to help people who have been in a situation similar to theirs. In Eleanore Smith's case, I think the focus of the group could be a legal fund to help victims get justice." Marty caught his gaze. "To start and run a nonprofit like that, she'd have to have money though. Lots of it."

Mateo's heart stopped. A nonprofit could more than give meaning to Jessica's daughter's heartbreak. It could start her on a new path. Bring her out of the shadows and give her back her life.

"What she needs is a backer." He stepped away from the security desk. "Jessica told me Eleanore works in real estate in Brazil, but she was trained in PR."

"PR is a very good thing to know when you're running

a nonprofit. She could be the voice of the company. Then I think she'd have to hire lawyers, therapists, social workers, counselors."

"Exactly. Now, we just have to see if she's interested. Ready to come home and take the lead on this."

"If she's half as strong as her mother, I'm guessing she'll jump at the chance."

Mateo headed for the stairway again. "Call my pilots. I want to be in London first thing tomorrow morning."

CHAPTER SEVENTEEN

JESSICA HAD BREAKFAST in the hotel, then spent the morning looking at apartment listings, making notes. Everything was so expensive, she had decided to expand her search farther away from the city when a knock sounded on her door.

Thinking it was probably someone from housekeeping, she walked over and said, "Who is it?"

"It's me."

Mateo's voice sent unexpected happiness careening through her, then confusion, then fear. He couldn't stand in the ordinary hall of an ordinary hotel in a huge city where half the population could recognize him on sight!

She yanked open the door and dragged him inside. "Is your security team about ready to throttle you yet?"

He laughed, but he also kissed her quickly, then ambled into her room. "This is nice. A little simple, but nice."

"This is what normal people can afford."

"So, you're back to normal?"

Her face scrunched. "I've always been normal."

He laughed. "Sort of. After you left, Sabrina and I had a talk about her video."

She winced.

"She's extremely repentant and she actually asked if there had been any repercussions, and I realized I hadn't heard anything about her video. Security tells me Ellie was mentioned on a few podcasts and there was some social media chatter... but nothing serious. Almost as if no one cared."

"Ellie said she never heard anything about it either." Confused, she followed him to the small table in her room and offered him one of the two chairs. "Actually, Ellie hadn't even heard about the video at all."

He didn't sit. He stood a few feet away, looking tall and handsome and also normal. In his baseball cap and jeans, he wasn't a king. He was just the guy who made her heart melt.

"No news outlet reported it?"

She told her melting heart to settle down, that he'd clearly come to discuss Ellie's situation, maybe even to help her. No smart person turned down an offer of help from a man with genuine power.

"Not in Brazil."

"So, maybe what made it newsworthy in Pocetak was the fact that you were working for me?"

She thought for a second. "Yes. I think so."

"Which means, it was your connection to *me* that made it newsworthy."

Not sure what he was getting at, she nodded. "Yes."

"Which also means that anyone who has a relationship with me…whether it's a business association or a personal relationship is going to endure some scrutiny."

Now truly confused about where he was going with this, she was ready for him to explain himself. She crossed her arms on her chest. "What's your point?"

"I miss you."

She hadn't been expecting the conversation to become personal. He'd shifted gears so quickly that she didn't have time to stop the swell of longing that rode through her. Still, it was pointless for them to pine for each other, and they both knew it. "It's only been a few days."

"Six. And six days is a long time to miss someone."

She didn't know whether to laugh or commiserate. It almost seemed as if he didn't know how to handle the loss.

"It *is* a long time. But we both knew this was coming."

"What? Arthur returning to his job or you stealing out in the middle of the night?"

She winced. "It seemed like a good idea at the time. Everything happened so fast that leaving felt like a clean break."

"It was a horrible thing to do." He sighed. "Arthur was the one who told me that your drive to the airport had been on Sunday night's security docket. No one at the breakfast table seemed to be concerned. Everyone took it as you needing a few days away after spending two months as my assistant and you'd gone to London for a little break." He sighed. "So, there I was, upset because you'd left and not able to show it let alone process it."

The sadness in his eyes touched her heart. Duty had kept him from focusing anywhere but on his role as king. But he'd never been in love. Never had his heart broken. It was no wonder he couldn't process it. "This really is all new to you, isn't it?"

"It's not all new to you? You weren't upset?"

"Of course, I was upset."

"Then why did you leave?"

"Because we don't work as a couple. I can't be in your life. You can't be in mine."

"Two months ago, I agreed with you. Especially as our relationship potentially affected your daughter—brought her back in the spotlight. But with the lack of response after Sabrina's video, I'm not so sure anymore."

"You're telling me I should take what I want and to hell with my daughter?"

"I'm saying maybe it's time to stand up for yourself."

"Stand up for myself?"

"And for Ellie to stand up for herself. The two of you needed some time to pass quietly after her assault and the trial that was more like a circus. Now ten years have gone by. You're stronger. She's stronger. Maybe it's time to look the reporters in the eye and tell them that that's all behind you now."

She wanted to be indignant, but he'd told her as much before their press conference and Ellie had almost come to that conclusion in their conversation. Still, right now, it wasn't so much what he was saying that made her heart speed up and her stomach tighten. It was why he was saying it. He hadn't come to London, dressed down and sneaked into her hotel room to give her advice about her daughter.

He'd missed her so much he'd been thinking about her situation, trying to find a way to make it all work out. The magnitude of it didn't escape her.

"I do not want to lose you." He took a breath. "I do not want to live without you."

She licked her lips, not sure if she was afraid or overjoyed by what he was about to say.

"I want you in my life forever and if that means we have to address this once word gets out that we are romantically involved, it seems like a small price to pay. Maybe even time for Ellie to have a normal life."

Fear and longing collided. "Oh, my God. You want me in your life for real and you think that's a normal life?"

"It is for me."

She squeezed her eyes shut. Hope and happiness begged her to just say yes. She'd thought about this the whole time they were lovers. Longed for it. But she was older, wiser and experienced enough to know bringing Ellie out of hiding meant real trouble.

Yet, she wanted him. So desperately wanted him in her life forever, that she wished his optimism had merit.

"This isn't going to be as easy as you seem to think."

"I don't care." He sucked in a breath. "I love you. I have never felt this way before. I don't want to feel it with another woman. I want you."

"Is this a royal command?"

He snorted. "I could make it one. But I'd rather have you just be a woman with me. Not a royal. Not a subject. Not even someone who sees me as her king. Just a woman who loves me as a man. A woman who would share my public life but who would want me for myself…a guy with kids and an exercise regimen, who loves to ride horses and sometimes gets headaches and longs for the day he can sleep until noon. I've never felt like a king with you. Just a man. I never knew how good that could feel or how important it was until I met you and now, suddenly, I can't live without it." He caught her gaze. "My life, my needs have changed since I met you."

"You should be me. I wanted a quiet cottage in the woods. I wanted my daughter to be happy. That's all I wanted. Now, I want to sleep with you every night. I want to talk about our kids as if they are *our* kids. I want to be the person you tell your secrets to, the person who is by your side when you rule. I want to wake up to the sound of your voice."

"You love me too?"

She nodded.

He caught her hands. "It would not hurt if you said it."

She laughed through her tears. "I love you."

"Then we are going to make this work."

He kissed her then and she let herself melt with happiness and also the sense of destiny that always lived on the fringes of their time together.

He pulled back. "There is one more thing."

She winced. "I hope it's not another warning about what life with a king will be like."

He laughed. "No. I had a conversation with Marty and we got to discussing your daughter's situation from a security/public relations standpoint. He thinks if we start a nonprofit that's a legal fund to help victims it would bring Ellie into the spotlight but as a leader. Not a victim, but someone changing the world."

She thought for a second. "Oh, my goodness. She would love that."

"She definitely loves it. I called her last night. Midnight our time is only seven o'clock in Brazil."

Her eyes bulged. "You called Ellie!"

"I couldn't ask you to come back unless we had a real plan. The real plan involved her changing her life. So I called her." He smiled briefly. "Plus, I wanted to ask for your hand."

She laughed. "Did you freak her out?"

"At first she was a bit shell-shocked, but when we got to talking about her future, she could see it."

She studied his face. "I almost can't believe this."

"Believe it. We've got some hurdles, and your daughter has some work to do. But we're going to make it."

She rose to her tiptoes and kissed him. "Yes. We are. Thank you."

He pulled her to him for a proper kiss, then he hugged her tightly and whispered in her ear, "Guess who's going to be Ellie's right-hand person?"

She pulled back so she could see his face.

"Sabrina."

She laughed. "What?"

"I've been saying she needed time and experience, and she wasn't getting it just traveling to charity events with me. I think she needs to see a nonprofit working from the inside out. We'll give her the summer off, and while she's at university for the next four years, her part-time job will be working for Ellie."

"Wow. This sort of works on a lot of levels, doesn't it?"

"Took me awhile to figure this one out, but I got it." He kissed her. "And I got the girl too."

She laughed.

He took a relieved breath. "Let's go home. I have an entire country I need to introduce you to."

EPILOGUE:
THEIR ROYAL WEDDING

THEY MARRIED TWO years later in Pocetak's huge, ornate cathedral. Serving as bridesmaids, Olivia, Sabrina and Ellie walked down the aisle.

In the two years of starting her nonprofit and easing herself into the public eye, the story of Ellie's assault had come and gone in the press. But the story of her nonprofit spread like wildfire. Especially that she was a strong, competent leader.

Ellie had her life back.

She easily walked down the aisle behind her two stepsisters in her beautiful peach dress. Not caring if anyone took her picture, smiling like the happy woman she had become.

Holding onto Josh's arm in the vestibule of the huge cathedral, Jessica took a quiet breath.

Josh put his hand over hers. "Nervous?"

"I shouldn't be. A lot of time and soul-searching went into this decision."

Josh snorted. "I knew from the first time I saw you two together that you were meant for each other. That soul-searching was just a formality."

She laughed. "Maybe. Your dad *is* irresistible."

"And the funny thing is he never knew it. He was so wrapped up in his work that I don't think any woman ever caught his attention beyond a physical attraction."

"He's dedicated to your people, your country. I liked that

about him immediately. That, Josh, is the kind of thing you look for when choosing a mate. Sexual attraction is good, but virtue is better."

Josh bent down and kissed her cheek. "You're such a mom. Luckily, I have years before I have to be that serious."

Trumpets sounded the first notes of the "Wedding March." Jessica looked down the aisle toward the altar where Mateo stood, looking wonderful in his military uniform, flanked by Arthur and Pete.

Life at the palace was different now that Mateo held a yearly ball thanking the employees and venturing out into the other offices to say hello and into the kitchen to compliment the chef.

Even though it felt like they were miles away from each other, she smiled at Mateo and he smiled back.

She and Josh started down the aisle. The closer she got the more her nervousness subsided. Who would have even thought that she'd be marrying a king or that that king would have been able to talk her and Ellie into coming out in public, starting a nonprofit and becoming heroes rather than victims.

They reached the altar. Josh kissed her cheek and handed her off to Mateo. She didn't have a veil. She hadn't worn a traditional wedding dress. She'd worn what she'd wanted: a big ball gown with a skirt that would flare out when they danced.

They said their vows, kissed to seal the deal and started down the aisle again, followed by their four kids. One who would be a queen. One who would run parliament. One who now was a victim's advocate. And one who was Ellie's assistant but who at twenty, still hadn't figured out her life.

But Jessica knew Sabrina would come up with something, a cause to champion or a business venture to run, and when she did she'd set the world on fire. She had too much of her dad in her not to.

For two people who'd had questionable first marriages, they

had finally formed a real family where Ellie now had a dad and Mateo's kids now had a mom.

And everything really was right in their world.

* * * * *

*If you enjoyed this story, check out these
other great reads from Susan Meier*

One-Night Baby with the Best Man
Mother of the Bride's Second Chance
It Started with a Proposal
Fling with the Reclusive Billionaire

All available now!

HIS STRICTLY OFF-LIMITS BALLERINA

KATE HARDY

MILLS & BOON

For my Friday ballet classmates and teachers.

Thank you for the joy you bring to my week.

CHAPTER ONE

HE WAS THE most beautiful man Pippa had ever seen. Tall, with dark hair that flopped endearingly over his forehead and eyes the colour of cornflowers, he reminded her of an actor she'd had a huge crush on when she was a teenager. Despite the fact that it was the middle of the afternoon, he was wearing formal evening dress: a dinner jacket with a shawl lapel, a bow tie that matched his eyes as well as the silk handkerchief in his pocket, and a wing-tip shirt. She couldn't see his shoes, but she'd just bet they were handmade and highly polished.

She hadn't seen him around at the Fitzroy Theatre—she would *definitely* have noticed him—but clearly he was involved with organising today's fundraiser rather than just having a ticket to the garden party, because he was carrying what looked like a cashbox and a book of cloakroom tickets.

Prince Charming, come to help save the ballet company?

Or, rather, their roof. The Fitzroy Theatre was a Georgian building, literally creaking at the rafters. And work on listed buildings took for ever—arguing what work needed to be done, and how, was only the first stage. Finally Nathalie, the head of the Fitzroy Ballet Company, had lost her temper and pointed out that the longer it was dragged out, the worse the damage would become, and she wasn't taking risks with a single member of her team or their audience. Not to mention how much longer it would take to fix—and how much more expensive it would be. And if enough work wasn't done over the summer and they were forced to cancel performances, was the surveyor planning to reimburse them for lost takings? Or was *monsieur* going to use his common sense? She wanted his report in her email by the end of the day, or *heads would roll*—just as they had in the Place de la Concorde. She'd finished with a tirade of French invective, using her hand to illustrate a guillotine blade.

Despite towering over the diminutive Frenchwoman, the surveyor had stammered an apology—and emailed his initial report to her as instructed. Nathalie had immediately swung into action, contacting their season ticket holders to ask for their help raising money for the repairs.

One of their patrons had offered something even better than money: the use of their garden for a party to raise funds. The ballet company had pooled all their contacts to get prizes for the raffle: everything from spa treatments to afternoon teas, tickets to shows and cases of wine, signed books and backstage passes.

The garden was absolutely stunning. Wisteria draped lushly over the back of the eighteenth-century rectory, filling the air with a heady scent. The herbaceous borders bloomed with flowers in soft shades of cream, lilac, pink and blue, and the wall at the back of the garden held espaliered apple trees that were still studded with blossoms. It was the sort of garden you could laze in and dream in, with a wildflower patch in one corner and a rectangle of soft, lush grass that made Pippa want to pirouette across it towards Prince Charming. Particularly as a string quartet and pianist from the Fitzroy's orchestra were currently playing the 'Dance of the Sugar Plum Fairy' in the draw-ing room that opened out onto the terrace.

Pippa had been the understudy for the Sugar Plum Fairy last year and knew the routine by heart. Though, much as she was tempted, she'd never take the risk of dancing on an unknown surface. A trip on a small, hid-den bump could cause the kind of damage to her foot that would take her out of action for weeks. So she'd be sen-sible and stick to the role she and the rest of the dancers were playing this afternoon, alternating between meet-and-greets and carrying round silver platters of canapés. The bite-sized scone halves topped with strawberry con-serve and clotted cream on her own tray looked absolutely delicious, and she fully intended to eat one after she'd handed them over to a colleague.

Tickets to the garden party had sold out rapidly. And hopefully people were buying extra glasses of champagne and lots of tickets for the raffle, from the gorgeous guy with the blue eyes—who'd just caught her eye and smiled at her, raising goosebumps on her skin. She smiled back, and he started walking towards her. All of a sudden it felt as if there wasn't enough air for her to breathe. Which was crazy, because they were outside and the air was limitless.

Nothing could beat an English walled garden on a sunny Sunday afternoon in May, Rory thought. The flowers were at peak prettiness; everyone seemed to be chatting and laughing and enjoying the ballet music played by a string quartet, which he presumed was part of the ballet company's orchestra.

His role this afternoon was to charm people into buy-ing tickets for the raffle. He didn't mind giving up a Sunday to help, knowing how much his godmother adored ballet and that raising funds to help fix the Fitzroy's roof was important to her. Though he had to admit that he wasn't being *entirely* altruistic. The arts-based magazine show he hosted on a small commercial television channel had quietly gained a decent following, and he'd just pitched an idea for a series to his boss. He was pretty sure she'd agree to it; today would give him the opportunity to chat to the head of the Fitzroy Ballet Company and float the suggestion that one of their senior ballet dancers could appear in the series. In return, the publicity would help with the campaign for their roof, so it'd be a win for everyone.

He smiled, extolled the amazing prizes on the raffle table, talked to people, sold tickets and happily accepted donations. All was absolutely fine until he caught the eye of one of the waitresses. He'd noticed her earlier that afternoon and felt a jolt of recognition. Which was ridiculous, because he knew they'd never met. He would definitely have remembered her. But something about her drew him in, and it wasn't just that she was seriously pretty. There was something about her. She had *presence*.

Walking that gracefully with her tray, she had to be one of the dancers rather than one of the backstage team. She'd be perfect for his documentary. And snaffling one of the bite-sized scones would be a great excuse to talk to her.

When he caught her eye, he smiled at her. She smiled back. And it felt like more than just a polite gesture to a stranger; it felt like the beginning of something. Something unexpected. Something irresistible. He couldn't help making his way across the garden to her.

But then, when he was standing next to her and looking into eyes the colour of a stormy sky, all words went out of his head.

This was crazy. He made a living from talking, for pity's sake. He was *good* with words. He was known for putting people at ease. Why was he suddenly so inarticulate and clumsy with her?

'I...um... Are you enjoying the party?' he asked.

Oh, way to go, Rory.

She was obviously working, not a guest.

But she smiled again, and it felt as if the whole garden had lit up. Dazzling. Which was crazy, because they were outside in a sunny garden, not in a dim room where someone had just switched on a light.

'Yes, I am.' She proffered the tray. 'Hello. I'm Pippa. Can I tempt you?'

Yes. She definitely could tempt him. Which really unsettled Rory, because he'd sworn off relationships a year ago, when he'd realised that his latest girlfriend was yet another in the line of partners who didn't see him for himself. He was tired of discovering his girlfriends only wanted to date him because they thought he was on his way to being really famous and would take them with him, or because he was the younger son of the Earl of Riverford and they'd get into the society pages. So he'd taken himself off the market, to avoid the disappointment and hurt of realising that yet again he was invisible, and the surface glitter that he thought was unimportant was the thing that mattered most to his dates.

'Thank you,' he said, and took one of the mini scones.

He was about to take a bite when a shockingly unexpected white-hot pain lanced into his neck.

'Ow!' he said, putting his hand up to the sore spot. What the hell had that been?

Except now he was feeling a bit dizzy. Strange. And he didn't understand why. He hadn't had so much as a sip of champagne because he'd been busy circulating.

Her expression changed to concern. 'Are you all right?'

'No, I don't think I am,' he said, but his words sounded as if he was talking through a mouthful of sand, and he wasn't altogether sure she'd understood him. He shook his head. At least, he hoped he had, because everything was closing in on him. 'Need h...' He tried swallowing, to clear his throat, but he couldn't—and it was hard to breathe. Even though the sun was warm, he felt cold and clammy. He took a step, staggered—and then everything went black.

Something was very badly wrong. His sudden pallor, slurring his words, and then the way he'd staggered before falling to the ground in a dead faint...

The last time Pippa had seen something like this was ten years ago at a dance rehearsal, when her best friend had accidentally eaten something containing almonds and had an anaphylactic reaction. Thankfully Pippa had known where Sasha kept her adrenaline kit and how to administer it, so her friend had been just fine; and Pippa had gone on a first-aid training course that she'd kept up to date ever since.

If, as she suspected, this was an anaphylactic reaction, time was of the essence.

Ambulance, first. She set the tray on the floor, fished her phone from her pocket, unlocked it and handed it to the woman next to her. 'Can you call 999 for me, please?' she asked. 'Tell them it's an anaphylactic reaction and we don't have adrenaline. We need them here *now*.'

'Got it,' the woman said, and tapped the number into the phone.

Next, Pippa knelt beside the prostrate man and patted his pockets. No sign of an adrenaline kit. Time for Plan B. She scooped the mini scones off the tray, then stood up again and banged it with her fist like a gong. The string quartet stopped playing, and there was a hush.

'If there's a doctor here, or anyone with allergies who has an adrenaline pen with them, please can you come over here right now?' she called loudly.

There was a murmur and some movement among the crowd, but no offers of adrenaline were forthcoming. No doctor, either.

Then, to Pippa's relief, one person came over to help: a middle-aged woman in a beautiful dress. 'I'm not a doctor, and I'm afraid I haven't kept my first aid training up since I retired from teaching five years ago,' she said, 'but anything's better than nothing. I'm Carolyn.'

'Pippa,' Pippa said.

'What do you need me to do?'

'We need to check him over, and we might need to do CPR,' she said, turning the unconscious man onto his back. Hopefully he hadn't hit his head in the wrong place when he'd fallen. It was really worrying that he still hadn't woken up.

'Hello,' she said loudly, tapping his shoulder in an attempt to wake him. 'Can you hear me?'

When he didn't respond, she undid his bow tie and loosened the collar of his shirt. There was a large red patch on his neck. She remembered him saying, *'Ow!'* Had he been stung? Was he allergic to venom?

She checked his airway was clear, then she and Carolyn began to do CPR, swapping every couple of cycles to give their arms a break.

'Oh, my God—Rory!' said Rosemary, the woman who owned the house, rushing over as Pippa and Carolyn swapped again. 'What happened?'

'He collapsed out of nowhere, but there's a red mark on his neck. Do you know if he's allergic to bees or wasps?' Pippa asked, continuing to do the compressions to Carolyn's count.

'I've no idea. There aren't any allergies on his mother's side—I'm his godmother,' Rosemary said. 'He offered to help here today.'

'The ambulance is on its way,' Pippa reassured her. 'I…um—he was selling tickets.' She gestured to the cashbox and tickets he'd dropped.

Rosemary scooped them up. 'Thank you. I'll give them to one of the team, then go and wait outside for the ambulance.'

Pippa wasn't sure how often she and Carolyn swapped as they kept the chest compressions going, because time seemed to simply stop until finally the ambulance crew arrived. She was relieved to see one of the paramedics was carrying a defibrillator, and she kept going with the chest compressions while she filled them in on what had happened.

'It was a good call on your part,' the first paramedic said. 'And good work with the CPR. We'll take over now. Can you make sure everyone gives us some space?'

'Of course,' Pippa said; between them, she, Carolyn and Rosemary shepherded everyone out of the area, promising to update them as soon as there was news.

It took two attempts with the defibrillator, but at last Rory's heart was beating again. One of them administered the injection of adrenaline into Rory's thigh; then they lifted him onto the stretcher and put an oxygen mask over his face.

Rory still wasn't conscious, but at least he was breathing. And he was in the right hands, now, too, Pippa thought.

'Did you want to come in with him?' the paramedic asked.

'Me? We only met a few seconds before he collapsed,' Pippa said. 'He probably won't even remember me. Maybe his godmother?' She squeezed Rosemary's hand in reassurance. 'I'll make sure everything's sorted here, and someone from the Fitzroy will stay until you get back.'

'Thank you, my dear,' Rosemary said. 'For everything you've done.'

'Anyone here would've done the same,' Pippa said.

CHAPTER TWO

AFTER THE PARAMEDICS had taken Rory and Rosemary to hospital, people started coming over to Pippa, praising her quick actions.

She smiled and moved the conversation on. 'I only just met Rory, but this place belongs to his godmother, so I'm sure he'd want everyone to carry on enjoying the garden party. And, as he was selling raffle tickets, I'm sure he'd want people to keep buying them or donate to the roof fund.'

She cleared up the scones she'd scooped off the metal tray, then washed her hands, refilled her tray in the kitchen, and went to do the next bit of meet-and-greet.

Rosemary came back two hours later, when the garden party was winding down and people were helping to clear away tables and chairs. 'You saved Rory's life,' she said to Pippa. 'His parents are at the hospital with him now, and he's awake and talking again. He asked me to pass on his thanks, and ask whether you would mind giving me your details so he can say thank you himself?'

'It wasn't just me. Carolyn did the CPR with me—though I think she already left,' Pippa said. 'I'm sorry—I didn't think to take her details.'

'I'm so grateful to you both,' Rosemary said. 'I'm very

fond of my godson.' Her face was still drawn with worry. 'The thought of how nearly we lost him…'

'He's in the right place,' Pippa said gently. 'The hospital will look after him. Let me know if there's anything else I can do.'

'Thank you.' Rosemary took down Pippa's number and gave her a hug.

The next morning, Rory lay in the hospital bed, still feeling a bit groggy and very much out of sorts. According to the medics, it was possible to have a second severe allergic reaction, almost like an aftershock, so it made sense for him to stay in the hospital for a bit longer. But he would rather be somewhere much quieter and more relaxed, and not hooked up to monitors that beeped all the time.

He'd seen the panic in his mother's eyes when she'd arrived at his bedside, and the fear that she'd lose him. The love mixed with the worry. And he'd felt horribly guilty for scaring her, even though it hadn't been intentional.

Coming to terms with your own mortality wasn't easy, either. The doctor had told him that he'd need to carry around two auto-injectors of adrenaline all the time, in case he was ever stung again. Not only was he likely to react badly the next time he was stung by a wasp, the odds were that his reaction would be even more severe.

How could a creature so tiny—a centimetre and a half long, less than a hundredth of his height—have the power to kill him?

He could have *died*.

If it hadn't been for the quick thinking of the woman he'd been talking to, he wouldn't be here now. He owed her everything.

Rosemary, his godmother, had promised to find out his rescuer's name and get her details so he could thank her personally. At the very least, she deserved an armful of flowers.

Flowers that, ironically, he would need to avoid, in future, in case there was a hidden wasp. Ditto walking barefoot on a lawn, along with other delights he'd taken for granted in the summer. Enjoying a cool drink was out of the question, in case a wasp crawled into the can or bottle of beer he was drinking. Picnics were an equally bad idea, in case a wasp was attracted by the sweet scent of fruit. And no flapping the wasps away, because a panicking wasp emitted alarm pheromones which would summon other members of the colony to come to their rescue.

Just one teeny, tiny sting could pack one hell of a punch. In his case, not just the brief sharp, burning pain, or the minor swelling that normal people experienced for a few hours. His reaction had been systemic, affecting his breathing and stopping his heart.

Even now, the morning after, despite the prompt medical treatment he'd received, Rory still didn't feel great. Though he had to admit part of that feeling was mental rather than physical. His parents were insisting on picking him up from hospital tomorrow afternoon and taking him back to their London townhouse for a few days' rest. He loved his parents dearly, but he knew they'd spend the whole time wrapping him in cotton wool—and he wanted his life to go back to normal. Right back to how it had been Before Wasp. The life he'd planned and really, really loved.

Trying to distract himself, he flicked onto the internet on his phone and looked up the Fitzroy Ballet Company.

His rescuer had walked like a dancer, so the chances were high that he'd find her somewhere on their website.

And there she was, listed under First Soloists.

Pippa Barnes.

He clicked on the thumbnail of her face, and was rewarded with another picture, this time with her dressed as the Sugar Plum Fairy and executing a perfect pirouette. Her biography wasn't quite what he'd expected, though. Like him, she was the youngest of three. Her parents were both doctors, as were her two sisters; maybe that explained how she'd known what to do when he'd collapsed.

But Pippa hadn't gone to ballet school from the age of eleven, as the preliminary research for his series had led him to expect a high-level ballerina would've done. She'd taken ballet classes and exams, but she'd gone to a normal school and done her GCSEs and A levels. Then, at the age of eighteen, she'd swapped medical school for a place at a well-known ballet school, before joining the Fitzroy Ballet Company as an artist. Her rise through the ranks had been rapid: promoted to First Artist at the age of twenty-one, Soloist at twenty-two and First Soloist at twenty-three.

Rory read various articles and discovered that Pippa was widely tipped to be promoted to Principal Dancer this year—when she turned twenty-five. She was a real rising star in the world of ballet. She'd be perfect for his TV show. And maybe including her in the series would help her career, too; if she didn't make Principal Dancer with the Fitzroy this year, another company might spot the opportunity and snap her up.

He managed to shower and dress, which made him feel a bit more human, and was sitting normally in a chair, making notes, when his mother arrived.

'What are you doing?' Helena asked, frowning. 'You're supposed to be resting and letting yourself get better.'

'Sitting still and doing nothing is my idea of a nightmare,' Rory said.

Plus he'd spent too much time brooding already. At least when he was working he was too busy to ponder on his personal life—on the loneliness that had started to creep in, during quiet moments. But being alone was better than wasting his time with yet another girlfriend who only wanted him for what he could give her. He already had a family who loved him. He didn't need to find Ms Right and follow in his brother's and sister's footsteps. He was doing just fine on his own; and work helped him ignore any of the niggles about his love life.

'Besides, I have a series to plan. My boss gave me the green light for my documentary, this morning.'

Her eyes widened. 'Surely you're not intending to go back to work so soon?'

'Mum, I'm fine,' he reassured her. 'Luckily I've got a few pieces in hand, but I still need to do the live interview segment on Friday. I don't want to let anyone down.'

'Rory, you nearly *died* yesterday.'

Helena Fanshawe, the Countess of Riverford, was famous for being unflappable. When the King was still the Prince of Wales, she'd hosted him for afternoon tea with next to no notice. The fact that his mother was making a fuss now was a huge red flag for Rory.

'Mum, I know, but I've worked hard to get where I am now and I don't want to slip back,' he said, as gently as he could. 'I'm planning to spend a couple of minutes on the show warning people about wasp allergies. I was incredibly lucky because Pippa Barnes knew what to do and she saved my life. I want to pay that forward and give my audience the same knowledge.'

'That's a fair point,' Helena agreed. 'Though you do need to rest. Remember, they had to restart your heart.'

'Mmm.' Thankfully he didn't remember anything other than his throat feeling full of sand and then passing out, but he still had a sore patch of skin on his chest from the defibrillator pad. The nurse had suggested using aloe vera gel to cool the burn. Maybe he could distract his mother with that; or maybe such a visible reminder would worry her even more. He decided to keep it to himself.

'Why don't you let yourself get over it this week,' Helena continued, 'and go back to doing the show next week? Let someone else step in, just this once?'

'No. I won't take any stupid risks, Mum,' Rory promised. 'But I don't want to live the rest of my life holding myself back because I'm scared of encountering another wasp.'

She didn't say a word, but the worry was all there in her eyes.

What if he was *stung by another wasp? Would he die, next time?*

That was a question he didn't want to think about.

'Mum, please stop worrying. I'll carry the two adrenaline pens with me all the time, and I've got a diary note of their expiry date on my phone so I can make sure I always have medication with me that's in date. I have a card in my wallet right in front of my driving licence, telling people that I'm severely allergic to wasp stings and how to use the adrenaline.' He stood up and gave her a hug. 'Remember, I learned how to deal with any situation from the amazingly capable and calm woman who brought me up. And, before you say it, that's not flattery. It's a fact.'

Helena rested her forehead against his shoulder. 'I want you to keep your independence, Rory. Of course I do. And I know you're sensible. But we came so close to losing you yesterday. I've never felt fear like that before. Or such helplessness,' she admitted. 'I'm your mother, and I'm supposed to be able to protect you from everything. Yesterday, I couldn't, and I'm finding that hard to handle.' Her voice cracked. 'So forgive me if I wrap you in cotton wool a little too much, because right now I'm terrified that you might...' A single tear brimmed over her lashes, and she brushed it away. 'Sorry.'

'Oh, Mum.' His own voice was croaky, now. 'It isn't your fault, or Dad's. An allergy to wasps isn't hereditary. It can happen out of nowhere, even if you've been stung before and not reacted.'

'Rory...' She shook her head. 'I'm trying very hard not to fuss over you. But I really want you to stay with us for the rest of the week. Just so...'

'...you know I'm safe,' he finished. 'I get that, and I don't want you to worry. Let's compromise. I'll stay with you, but I'll be in the studio as usual on Friday.'

She gave him her best mum glare, clearly trying to make him back down and take the rest of the week off.

He stared back just as stubbornly, because he was absolutely going to do the job he loved. The job he *needed*. Without his job, who was he?

She sighed. 'All right. We'll compromise. But I'll drive you to the studio and your father will pick you up afterwards.'

He'd made his point. Time to give a little. 'You can stay in the audience, if you promise not to heckle.'

She gave him a rueful smile. 'All right. And, while

we're waiting for the doctor to see if he'll discharge you tomorrow, you can tell me all about this new series.'

Around lunchtime on Wednesday—when he hoped that Pippa wouldn't be busy in rehearsals—Rory called her mobile. As it started to ring, the butterflies in his stomach seemed to do a stampede.

This was utterly ridiculous.

He interviewed famous people for a living. People who'd won big awards, actors and musicians who were household names and had been at the top of their field for decades. Talking to a rising star in the ballet world shouldn't make him feel this nervous. Plus he'd already practised what to say.

But the first time he'd actually spoken to Pippa—the only time, he amended wryly—all the words had gone out of his head. And then he'd collapsed.

No wasps. There were no wasps. It wasn't going to happen this time, he reminded himself.

The line stopped ringing. 'Hello?'

'Pippa? It's Rory Fanshawe. You kindly gave my godmother your number.' Oh, and now he was gabbling like a teenager. He forced himself to slow down. 'I wanted to thank you for saving my life.'

'You're very welcome.'

She had a really nice voice, he thought. Kind. Sweet. Calm. 'I wondered if I could take you to lunch or something? To say thank you in person, I mean,' he added hastily. He didn't want her to think he was trying to hit on her. Because he wasn't. This was a combination of good manners and work.

'That's lovely of you to offer, but there's no need. Besides, I wasn't the only one who helped,' she pointed out. 'Carolyn did the CPR with me.'

Pippa wasn't taking the sole credit for saving his life; he liked that even more. And he was pleased that he was one step ahead on that front. 'I've already managed to get hold of Carolyn,' he said. 'I'm taking her to lunch next week.'

'Oh.' Pippa sounded surprised.

'It's the least I can do.' He paused. 'Are you free for lunch any time this week? Or next week?' he added, considering that it was already Wednesday.

'I only get a half an hour break between my class and rehearsal,' she warned.

'You still take classes?' He hadn't expected that.

'Every dancer takes classes, even the Principal Dancers. Whatever the stage of your career, you never stop learning,' she said.

The more he listened to Pippa talk, the more Rory was sure that she'd be perfect for his show. She was clear, articulate and could tell people who were interested in a career in dance exactly what to expect. He ignored the little voice in his head saying that the real reason he wanted to see her was because he'd felt more attracted to her at the garden party than he had been to anyone in months. This was an opportunity to get the perfect expert for his documentary. And that would keep the flare of attraction nicely damped down, because working with her would make her off-limits. He wasn't risking his series for a couple of dates that would no doubt turn out to be as disappointing as his last few. Even though she didn't seem like the last few women he'd dated, he'd been burned once too often to want to take a chance. 'Would you be free tomorrow?' he asked.

'Yes.'

'I assume your class is held somewhere near the Fitzroy?'

'All our classes are held at the Fitzroy,' she said.

'Tell me what time to meet you,' he said, 'and either let me know the name of a place you like nearby so I can book a table—and we can preorder lunch so we don't have to spend all your time waiting for food—or I can bring us an indoor picnic.' That way, they could avoid wasps. 'Do you have any allergies or dietary requirements?'

'No allergies and I eat almost anything,' she said. 'Your picnic idea sounds really good. The theatre restaurant isn't open at lunchtime, so we can use one of the tables there. Classes end at half-past twelve.'

'Wonderful. Thank you,' he said. 'I'll see you tomorrow at half-past twelve.' He'd been to the ballet before with his godmother, so he remembered the layout of the theatre. 'In the foyer next to the box office?'

'That'd be perfect,' she said.

Rory was smiling as he ended the call. Next, he'd call Nathalie Charrier, the founder of the Fitzroy Ballet Company, and run his ideas past her—just as he'd originally planned to do at the garden party, before a wasp had turned his life into chaos.

And, even though he told himself that the thrill he felt was simply the buzz he always had when he was working on a new idea, part of him had to admit the truth: he was really looking forward to seeing Pippa Barnes again tomorrow. And it wasn't strictly work.

CHAPTER THREE

PIPPA WAS DEFINITELY guilty of using muscle memory to
get through the warm-up in class on Thursday morning
rather than listening to the teacher. Demi-pliés, slow ten-
dus, port de bras…

Because her head was full of Rory Fanshawe, and the
fact that she was having lunch with him today.

She shook herself, knowing how ridiculous she was
being. It wasn't anything like a date. He'd told her that
he wanted to thank her in person for saving his life, and
he was having lunch with Carolyn next week for exactly
the same reason. It was more than likely that he was already involved with someone else. And, even if he *was*
single, she didn't have time for any kind of relationship.
Not if she wanted to make Principal Dancer this year.
And she really, really wanted that promotion. Getting
to the top position would prove once and for all that she
was good enough. That all the hard work and sacrifice
had been worth it. That she'd made the right decision
when she'd chosen ballet over a career in medicine, disappointing her family.

'Pippa, did you hear what I said?'

Jeanne, their artistic director, sounded sharp. Given
that Jeanne was one of the people Pippa needed to im-

press, letting herself daydream in class was a very stupid thing to do.

'I'm so sorry,' Pippa said. 'Would you mind repeating that?'

Jeanne rapped out instructions, and Pippa forced her mind off Rory and on to what she was supposed to be doing. She was careful to give the class her full attention after that, but even so Jeanne had a quiet word with her at the end.

'My advice is, keep your focus,' Jeanne said, her eyes glinting a warning. 'I'd hate to see you waste your opportunities.'

Wasting her chances because she was dreaming of someone unsuitable. Not that Jeanne had any idea who she was dreaming about, but losing her focus was unprofessional. Unacceptable.

Pippa felt the heat flood through her cheeks. 'I'm sorry. It won't happen again.'

'Good.' Jeanne strode off.

Pippa changed swiftly. She didn't have time to worry about whether her T-shirt and leggings were suitable; besides, this was an indoor picnic, so it really didn't matter what she wore, did it? As a concession to being outside work hours, she released her dark hair from the tight bun she wore for classes and rehearsals, and hurried out into the foyer.

Rory was standing next to the box office, as they'd arranged. He was carrying a woven willow picnic basket in one hand and a stunning bouquet in the other: stocks, roses, chrysanthemum and freesia, all in shades of pink and pale cream.

'Thank you for saving my life, Pippa,' he said, handing her the flowers.

She buried her nose in them, inhaling the sweet scents. 'You're very welcome. I'm glad you're OK.' Though he still looked tired; no doubt he hadn't had much rest in hospital. 'And thank you very much for these. You really didn't have to, but they're absolutely gorgeous.'

'They have their own water so you don't need to find a vase for them until you can get them home,' he added. 'I have to admit, I did have the odd twinge of nerves between the florist's and here, in case a stray wasp spotted them and sideswiped me on the way. But fortunately there were no vespine encounters.'

His smile was incredibly cute. And it was a nice change to meet a man who admitted his vulnerabilities instead of putting on a performance. In his shoes, having almost died from a sting, she'd be terrified of doing anything that might attract a wasp. But he'd used an odd word. 'Vespine?' she queried.

'Waspy,' he said. 'From *vespa*, the Latin for wasp.'

Given that his accent was slightly on the posh side, she wasn't surprised he knew Latin. He'd probably studied it at school. She smiled back. 'Shall we go and sit down?'

She led the way to the restaurant space. Some of the other dancers were sitting in the area, scrolling on their phones as they ate; normally she would've joined them, but today she found a quiet table.

Rory undid the picnic basket, shook out a red-and-white-checked tablecloth, then deftly unpacked two enamel plates, bamboo cutlery, glasses, a bottle of spring water in what looked like an ice jacket, and an array of food in reusable tubs.

She blinked. 'Wow. I was expecting maybe a sandwich, some fruit and a coffee from the shop round the corner. This is amazing.' A real picnic. A *posh* picnic. The sort that people would take to Glyndebourne.

'I looked up the best nutrition for ballet dancers, and based it on that,' he said. 'You said you were working this afternoon; the website recommended lean protein, veggies and wholegrains. I hope you like something here.'

Cold poached salmon, slices of chicken breast, chunks of avocado, a salad of quinoa with edamame beans and tenderstem broccoli, cold roasted Mediterranean vegetables, baby plum tomatoes and watercress—all beautifully presented. Pippa wasn't sure whether he'd bought it all at a deli or whether he'd prepared some of it himself at home, but he'd obviously put a lot of thought into the menu and she appreciated the effort.

'There are strawberries, blueberries and Greek yogurt for pudding,' he added.

'This is perfect. Thank you so much,' she said. 'This is a real treat.'

'Please, help yourself,' he said. 'Water?'

'Thank you.' She filled her plate while he filled her glass. 'How are you feeling?'

'Fine.'

But it was said a little too breezily. And those beautiful blue eyes didn't meet her gaze. 'Really?' she asked.

He sighed. 'I'm a little bit twitchy because of what happened, but I need to get back to normal sooner rather than later. The longer I leave it, the bigger the gap will be between BW and AW.'

'Before wasp and after wasp?' she guessed.

He gave her a wry smile. 'Exactly. And it doesn't help that my mother's wrapping me in a ton of cotton wool. We had a deal—if I stay with her and Dad this week, she won't give me a hard time about working tomorrow night. I thought we'd muddle through OK, but she's driving me mad, constantly worrying about me and checking on me. I'm carrying adrenaline pens and an instruction card, and I'm not going to do anything to risk...' He wrinkled his nose. 'Well.'

'Vespine encounters,' she said.

'Exactly. I've been trying to convince her that I'm not going to walk barefoot in Rosemary's garden, especially near the fruit trees when the apples have fallen, or sit anywhere near a wastebin on a summer day. And I won't be drinking anything in a can that's *remotely* attractive to wasps.'

'But you did carry these gorgeous flowers here,' she pointed out. 'Wasps like flowers. Especially ones that smell as lovely as stocks.'

He groaned. 'The florist is a three-minute walk away from the theatre. And I can't live in a sterile bubble for the rest of my life, Pippa. It's about being practical. Minimising the risks and living my life as normally as I can.'

She could understand that. 'You said you were going to work tomorrow night. What do you do?' She'd meant to look him up on the internet, but she'd been so busy at work that she hadn't had time.

'I'm a broadcast journalist.'

Working with words would also explain why he was comfortable using terms like 'vespine'. 'Broadcast. Does that mean radio rather than newspapers or magazines?' she asked.

'TV,' he said, but his tone was matter-of-fact rather than boasting.

So was he famous? How embarrassing that she didn't

know who he was. 'Sorry. I'm usually working in the evening, and I don't watch much TV,' she explained.

He smiled ruefully. 'I wasn't trying to show off or do the whole "dear girl, don't you know who I *am*?" thing,' he said, hamming up the quote in a way that made her laugh.

He didn't come across as an entitled celeb; he didn't have that hard, arrogant edge. She found him easy to talk to; he made her feel that he was listening to what she was saying.

'Though if you ever watch programmes about the arts in your free time, you *might* have heard of me,' he said.

'Sorry,' she said again.

'Don't apologise. You're busy making art rather than talking about it or watching it,' he said.

'So how did you become a broadcast journalist?' she asked.

'I did some work with university radio as a student, then started my own podcast,' he said. 'I got a job as a researcher in TV when I graduated, then had the chance to do some interviews myself. Then I worked my way up to being the lead on a show on an arts channel. It goes out at nine p.m. on a Friday night, though it's not live—we film the chat bit in the studio in the afternoon.'

'Tell me about your show,' she invited, intrigued.

'The first half is a round-up—snippets from new exhibitions or shows and brief interviews with the people involved. Actually, I love that bit of it,' he said, warming to his theme, 'because I get to talk to everyone from musicians and artists to writers and curators and there's always something new and fresh. The second half is more of a chat show, with guests in the studio.'

'Nine p.m. If it's a show night, I'm on stage; if it's not a show night, I'm most probably asleep,' she confessed.

He smiled. 'I'm not trying to impress you. It's just what I do. I know I'm very privileged because I can share people's joy in their jobs, as well as my own love of the arts.'

'Loving what you do is important,' she said. 'And I'm lucky in that way, too.'

'I wasn't stalking you,' he said, 'but I wanted to know a bit more about the person who saved my life, so I read your bio on the Fitzroy website, and a couple of articles. Your path to ballet looks a little bit different to everyone else's.'

She felt herself tense, and hoped he hadn't noticed. She *was* different. It was part of the reason why she had to work so hard. 'My parents are doctors,' she said carefully. 'So are my sisters. I'm the baby of the family. Everyone thought I'd be a doctor, too.' More than thought it. *Expected* it.

'You had a place at medical school, but you swapped it for ballet,' he said. 'Why?'

Because it was her dream. She'd tried to make herself do what her parents wanted, but she hadn't been able to give up on that. 'I fell in love with dance, right from my first ballet class as a four-year-old,' she said simply. 'The music and the movements, how they fit together and the way it makes me feel…it's all I've ever wanted to do. Even though I knew it wouldn't be an easy career, with lots of people all chasing the same parts, that didn't put me off. I don't mind the long hours rehearsing and honing my craft outside performances, or the unsociable working hours.' All the downsides of the job that her parents had pointed out in great detail. She gave him her best professional smile, not wanting him to know how hard the choice had been: disappoint her family, or spend her life doing something she didn't love. Whichever way she decided, she'd lose something.

'Getting that first break—no matter how hard you work—always involves a bit of luck,' she continued. 'My parents wanted me to have proper academic qualifications to fall back on; they said dance school would limit my options too much. Eventually we compromised. I did the academic stuff they wanted, and they let me have private lessons to make up for what I was missing at ballet school. I applied to university, but we agreed if I was accepted to ballet school they'd give me three years after my training to make it work. If I couldn't, then I'd go to university and train as a doctor instead.' Hopefully she'd made it sound a lot less painful than it had been. Her parents hadn't shouted or screamed or slammed doors; but the quiet disappointment in their eyes every time they looked at her had pierced a lot, lot deeper. And it had hardened her resolve to let nothing distract her until she got to the very top of her profession.

'Three science A levels *and* intensive ballet classes? It sounds as if you had to do twice the work,' he said.

She had. It had really polished her time-management skills. 'It was worth it,' she said. 'Now, I get to do what I love every single day. When I eventually become Principal Dancer, I know I'll only have a few years at my peak before I'll need to switch to directing, choreography or teaching, but right now I'm really living the dream.' She smiled. 'And that's without the rose-tinted specs. You?'

'Massively privileged,' he said. 'I could've joined the family business, but I'm the spoiled baby and, unlike yours, my parents let me do what I loved. For me, it was words. And I had some lucky breaks.' He smiled at her.

'Actually, speaking of work, I wanted to run a couple of things by you.'

She frowned. 'What sort of things?'

'Are you working tomorrow night?' he asked.

'Yes. Why?'

'Because I'd like to do a piece about the hidden danger of the summer arts season,' he said. 'This is the time of year when people go to outdoor concerts and performances—the Proms, Glyndebourne, garden parties at stately homes. Did you know that nearly three in a hundred people have a severe reaction to wasp stings?'

'No.'

'Neither did I,' he said, 'until it happened to me. I want to do a piece to camera about it. From my point of view as someone felled by a wasp; from a doctor about what to do if someone collapses in front of you; and from yours about how it feels to rescue someone. Plus,' he added, as if to head off her immediate refusal, 'you can mention the Fitzroy fundraiser in passing, because that was what you were doing when you rescued me.'

'Me, on TV?'

'I think you'd be a natural. You have a good voice for broadcasting,' he said. 'As you're working tomorrow night, maybe I could film you during your lunchbreak?'

'I'd need to think about it,' she said. 'And to talk to Nathalie, our director. I need her permission before I do anything.'

'Actually, I spoke to Nathalie earlier,' he said. 'Because that was only one of my proposals. The other is that my boss has given me the green light to make a small series about dance.'

'Dance is a big subject,' she said.

'Which is why I get to do a series rather than a single

show,' he said. 'I'm looking at the history of certain dance types, one per episode, talking a bit about famous dancers in history and the present, and there'll be a section where a professional dancer teaches me a routine over the course of a week.'

'What types of dance are you covering?' she asked.

'Ballet—which is where I'd like you to help—ballroom, tango, and disco.' He grinned. 'My mum says if I can get John Travolta to teach me disco and I let her be my runner so he dances just once with her, she'll be my PA for an entire year.'

Pippa chuckled. 'My mum loved *Grease*.'

'Mine watches the film when she's had a bad day.' He smiled back. 'It's like what you were saying earlier—my show's going to look at the work that goes into a performance and what happens behind the scenes. I want to show a dancer's journey from complete novice to reaching performance standard. A bit like *Strictly*, but without the knockout competition.'

'Isn't that the point of *Strictly*? The competition bit, I mean?' she asked.

'It's not the only point,' he said. 'My theory is that what the audience loves best is seeing the dancer's journey. Obviously the audience has their favourites, but have you noticed that they always root for the underdog? And they're always more excited about the dancers who don't have a clue to start with, rather than the ones who already have dance experience.'

She thought about it. 'That's true. But you said you want a professional to teach you a routine. Do you have any dance experience?'

'Not really,' he said. 'I learned to do the waltz when I was younger, but apart from that I've never done any formal dance training. If I went clubbing at uni I just did what everyone else did.' He looked at her. 'I was planning a video diary showing my progress, all the highs and lows. The audience will see me go from someone who's never even tried to do a pirouette to someone who's confident enough to dance a whole piece, and hopefully they'll see the moment when I'm close to giving up and then it clicks.' He paused. 'What do you think? Would you be up for being part of the show and teaching me a routine?'

Being on TV.

It would really boost her profile as a dancer.

'I'd need to clear it with Nathalie before I could even start to think about it,' she said.

'Actually, she gave me permission to ask you,' Rory said, 'but of course you'll want to talk it over with her before you make a decision. And I'm not going to pressure you for an answer within the next five minutes. We have plenty of time.'

'What kind of routine are you looking for? Something traditional, or something modern?' Pippa had always thought that choreography was a potential option for her in the future after she'd finished her performance career, but she hadn't taken it further than thinking about it. This was a chance to learn something new, open another door.

'I'm happy to hear suggestions,' he said. 'From *Strictly*, I know that the male contestants have a slightly harder job because they have to learn to lead.'

'It's not quite like that in ballet,' she said. 'In a pas de deux, the male dancer tends to support the female dancer and the attention's on her rather than on him. So a traditional pas de deux won't really work for your purposes.

I could teach you a simplified version of a variation—a solo,' she clarified. 'Something where your audience would recognise the music. Maybe something a ballerina would normally do en pointe, but we can adapt the footwork to suit you. Not because you're male,' she added, 'but because you need years of strength and mobility training first. Otherwise you risk really damaging your feet and ankles. I could adapt something to demi-point—tiptoes,' she explained. She thought about it for a moment. 'Maybe the "Dying Swan". Actually, that'd be a good one because it'll show how a dancer tells a story.'

He shook his head. 'Not a solo. The other thing about *Strictly* is that the audience likes to see the celebrity and the professional dance together.'

Something sensual, like a rumba; or something romantic, like a waltz. *A choreographed love story...*

The idea sent an unexpected ripple through her, which she suppressed instantly.

Absolutely not.

Rory Fanshawe might look like a fairytale prince and have excellent manners, but Pippa wasn't looking to fall in love with anyone. She didn't have the time or the space for romance in her life. Getting distracted by a relationship would mean not giving her all to her job—and then she'd be less likely to get the promotion she was working so hard for. She'd come so far; she didn't want to lose her chances now.

Guilt twinged somewhere underneath her ribcage. She wouldn't be able to give enough time to a relationship, either. She knew she didn't give enough to her family as it was. She was rubbish at staying in touch with her sisters, rubbish at being a dutiful daughter—and she'd be just as inadequate as a girlfriend, with her unsociable working hours and the fact that all her energies went into dancing.

'If you want a duet, then maybe I can teach your partner to dance, too,' she suggested.

And then she wished she hadn't opened her mouth, because that sounded as if she was fishing.

Which she wasn't. Was she?

'No partner,' he said after a beat. And then he looked her straight in the eye. 'Would your partner have a problem with me taking up your time between rehearsals and classes?'

Well, she deserved that one. She'd asked him a personal question first. 'No partner,' she said, echoing his words. Though Rory had just given her the perfect out. She didn't have time to teach him. No way could she take an entire week off work to teach him and be filmed.

But, before she could refuse, another thought slid into her head. In a month's time, the company would start their summer break. It would be the perfect time for her to work on Rory's project. And hadn't he said that they had plenty of time?

'I'll talk to Nathalie,' she said. Then her phone started playing three long rings—the sound to signal the end of an interval in the theatre, which she'd used as the ringtone for her alarm. 'That's lunch over,' she said regretfully. 'Sorry. I need to get back.'

'No problem. You did tell me you only had half an hour. I appreciate you giving up the time.'

She smiled. 'Thank you for lunch and the flowers.'

'My pleasure. I'm not pressuring you for an answer about the series,' he said, 'but if you could let me know later today about the two minutes or so to camera I'd need from you tomorrow about your experience saving a life when you were supposed to be saving a roof, that'd be great.'

'All right,' she said. 'I'll message you.'

Rory watched Pippa walk gracefully out of the restaurant area before he packed up the remains of their picnic. He really hoped she'd agree to do the show; she was articulate, passionate about her subject, dedicated to her career, and he thought he could learn a lot from her.

And she was single…

He pushed the thought away. The last couple of years, his social life had been a complete mess, with the women he'd dated interested in either Rory the up-and-coming TV presenter, or Rory the youngest son of the Earl of Riverford. None of them had seemed interested in who he was behind that, and he'd felt so let down. Was it so much to ask, to be seen for who he really was instead of his public persona? And every time he realised someone was only with him because of what he could give her, it had disappointed him more. It had made him miserable, to the point where it was easier just to focus on his job and enjoy spending his free time with his family instead.

Though the wasp incident had stirred up a few other things in his head, when he'd been stuck in hospital with too much time to think. What did he really want from life? Did he want to become a national treasure, with his own chat show on prime-time Saturday night TV? Did he want to take the more serious route and produce documentaries? Should he go back to the family business he'd sidestepped discussing with Pippa? Or did he want to settle down, the way his brother and sister had, and start a family of his own?

Though making decisions when he was feeling so out

of sorts would only lead to making the wrong one. Maybe he just needed a little time for things to settle again. Time to have fun. To remind himself how good it felt to be alive—without letting himself give in to the fear that it could all vanish in a second.

CHAPTER FOUR

AT THE END of rehearsal, Pippa headed for Nathalie's office and rapped on the door.

'Come in!'

Pippa ignored her boss's slightly fierce tone, guessing that Nathalie had been dealing with builders, and walked in with a smile. 'Do you have a couple of minutes, please, Nathalie?'

'As it's you, yes. What's it about?'

Typical Nathalie, not bothering with small talk. 'I wanted some advice,' Pippa said.

'Would that have anything to do with Rory Fanshawe?'

Pippa nodded. 'He said he'd already run things past you and you'd given him the go-ahead to talk to me. And I wanted to double-check you'd be happy for him to interview me about what happened at the garden party. He wants to do that tomorrow so it can go on his show tomorrow night.'

Nathalie nodded. 'It's a good opportunity to raise your profile. The figures on his show are very respectable. He suggested interviewing you in front of the Fitzroy, and he'll mention our roof.'

'I feel a bit of a fraud, though. Plenty of people know how to do CPR,' Pippa said.

'And plenty don't,' Nathalie reminded her. 'Or know

what an anaphylactic reaction looks like. He was very lucky you were there.'

'OK. I'll tell him I'll do it.'

'Good.' Nathalie rested her elbows on her desk and steepled her fingers. 'Did he mention his other project to you?'

Pippa nodded. 'It sounds fun. But I can hardly ask you for a week off to do it.'

'Of course you can ask, *chérie*,' Nathalie said silkily. 'But the answer would be no.' She paused. 'Just as it would be for Yuki.'

Yuki Ito was the other candidate for promotion to Principal Dancer; although they were friends, rather than deadly rivals, they were both very aware that there was only one slot. Pippa liked the other ballerina and rated her talent, but she really wanted to be the one who got the top job. It would validate the choice she'd made. And maybe then she'd finally stop feeling that she'd let her family down by not following in their footsteps.

As Nathalie's words sank in, the situation became horribly clear. 'He's asking Yuki as well?'

'He's asking you first, because you saved his life. If you don't want to do it, then Yuki would be the obvious next choice,' Nathalie said.

Pippa shook herself. The promotion was something she couldn't influence. All she could do was work hard, dance to the best of her ability, and hope that the Fitzroy's management team thought she was good enough. But doing the show… She'd liked what Rory had told her; she knew she'd enjoy the challenge of choreographing a piece and teaching a complete novice how to do it well.

Would it be a distraction, working with Rory—the way she'd let thoughts of him distract her in class this morn-

ing? Or would it give her the edge and show the team
that she was capable of being a good ambassador for the
Fitzroy and was ready to be promoted?

'What do you think about it?' Pippa asked carefully.

'I think,' Nathalie said, 'it needs to be your decision.'

Which didn't help in the slightest. She didn't have a
clue what was going on in her boss's head. A snap decision would be the wrong one. 'I think,' Pippa said, 'I'll
sleep on it. Make a list of the pros and cons.' And right
at that moment she wasn't sure which column Rory Fanshawe would fit in. Possibly both.

She thought about it all the way home. A nap and a
shower didn't make her thoughts any clearer. In the end,
she grabbed her phone. Her sisters were both working
part-time and this was the sweet spot between them getting home and settling the children down for dinner. Plus
talking to Rory had made her think more about her family. It would be good to connect with her sisters. She was
horribly aware that all too often they were the ones calling her, and she put off returning the calls on the grounds
that it was too late to ring them, or she had a rehearsal.
And then that made her feel she'd let them down, and it
was easier just to bottle out of it and send a quick text
instead of hearing the disappointment in their voices.

'Pips? Is everything all right?' Holly asked the second
she answered the video call, looking concerned.

'Yes—are you all right?' Laura asked, joining them.

'Ye-es. I just wanted a bit of advice,' Pippa said.

'Now you're really worrying us. What's happened?'
Holly asked.

'Nothing. Well, not *nothing*,' Pippa said. 'At the garden
party fundraiser, one of the helpers was stung by a wasp.

Anaphylaxis, nobody around with an adrenalin pen, so I had to do CPR. The paramedics had to shock him.'

'That's a tough situation,' Laura said. 'And well done, you. I assume he's OK?'

'Yes.' She paused. 'It turns out he has a TV show. He's doing a piece about wasps and what to do if someone reacts badly to a sting. And he's, um, interviewing me.'

'You're going to be on TV? That's fantastic! Which channel and when?' Holly asked.

'Tomorrow night, nine p.m.' She told them the channel.

'Hang on—that's Rory Fanshawe's show, isn't it?' Laura asked.

'You've seen his show?' Pippa was surprised; her oldest sister had never mentioned it before. Then again, she knew she hadn't really given Laura the chance to mention it. She kept most of their conversations light and easy, so she wouldn't have to face how she let her sisters down, too, by being so unavailable.

'I watch his show every week,' Laura said. 'I love the way he interviews people and gets the best out of them.'

'Me, too,' Holly said. 'Have you told Mum and Dad?'

'Not yet.' Pippa knew she ought to, but she also knew they'd focus on the fact that she was on TV because of medicine, not because of dance. And that would feel like another slap in the face.

'They won't want to miss seeing your first time on TV,' Laura said gently.

And now Pippa felt even guiltier. 'Sorry. Just… I know they wanted me to be a doctor. So did Gran and Gramps.'

'They all know how hard a career in the arts is,' Holly said. 'Mum and Dad just wanted you to have a safety net, in case it didn't work out. That's not the same as not believing in you, Pip.'

Pippa wasn't so sure. She'd really felt the pressure of her parents wanting her to make a different choice, and she still felt bad about not making the one that would've made them happy. 'Mmm.'

Laura came to her rescue. 'So what's the advice you wanted?'

'Rory's making a series about different dances—how they started, famous dancers, that sort of thing. And as part of it he needs a professional to teach him a routine. He asked me to do the ballet one,' Pippa explained.

'That's great! It'd look really good on your CV, too,' Holly said. 'Our little sister, the TV star.'

'It's only one programme,' Pippa reminded her.

'What does Nathalie think?' Holly asked.

'She says it's my decision.' Pippa grimaced. 'That's just it, Hol. If I do it, will I lose my focus? That could cost me the promotion. On the other hand, if I don't do it, will Nathalie think I don't have what it takes to make it to the very top?'

'You're the most focused person I've ever met,' Laura said. 'What makes you think doing the show will distract you?'

Pippa's face grew hot, and she hoped it wasn't as red as it felt.

But Holly was good at noticing things left unsaid. It was one of the reasons she was such a good doctor. 'You think Rory will distract you?' Holly asked. 'Mmm. He's very easy on the eye. I can see how he might…let's say, hold your attention.'

Pippa's face felt even hotter. 'I'm not in the market for a relationship.'

'We're not necessarily saying you need to date someone, but you do need a better work-life balance, Pip,' Laura said.

'More fun,' Holly added. 'Not just work, work and more work.'

'I love what I do. It's not like work,' Pippa protested.

'It's relentless, your schedule. I couldn't do it,' Laura said. 'You know you're always welcome here on your days off.'

'And mine. It's chaos, half the time, but it'll give you a break,' Holly suggested.

'I know. And I appreciate it,' Pippa said.

'But you're not going to take either of us up on the offer, because you want that promotion and you think working fifteen-hour days is the way to get it—which really *isn't* good for you, and I'm saying that both as your middle sister and with my GP hat on,' Holly said. 'I reckon you should do Rory's show. If Nathalie doesn't give you that promotion, then other ballet company directors will see the show and it could open some doors for you.'

'Agreed,' Laura said. 'Though I still think you need a proper break over the summer. Don't spend your entire break practising. Come to France with us. There's plenty of room in the villa.'

Her sisters, their husbands and children went away with her parents every summer for a fortnight, hiring a villa in Provence. They always invited Pippa, and she always turned them down because she was working or taking an extra class.

'All you have to do is sit in a garden, eating lovely French bread and cheese and strawberries, sip sparkling rosé, read a bit to the kids, and chill out with us,' Holly coaxed. 'We'll run interference if Mum or Dad try to talk you into keeping ballet as just a hobby. We get that ballet's your life.'

A life where she worked so hard to prove herself. 'We'll see,' Pippa said, not wanting to reject her sisters outright. She loved them, she really did. So why was it so hard to tell them that?

'If you won't come to France, then at least say yes to Rory,' Laura said.

'What if…?' Pippa stopped, not knowing how to frame the question.

'Do the coin test,' Holly said gently. 'Heads you do it, tails you don't. As soon as you see that head or tail on the back of your hand, you'll either be pleased or wish it had been the other one—and that will tell you what you *really* wanted to do.'

'I'll do that,' Pippa promised. 'Thank you both for listening.'

'That's what sisters are for,' Laura reassured her.

She lingered a bit longer, asking about her nieces and nephews and brothers-in-law, and she was thoughtful when she finally ended the call. Strange how they'd both assumed that something was wrong when she'd called. Did she really neglect her family so much?

Guilt throbbed through her. She was so focused on proving she'd made the right career decision that, yes, when she looked at it, she *did* neglect her family. Maybe she should change her mind about France. But then again, a dance career was so short. If she took time out now, she'd miss chances she couldn't afford to pass her by. She needed to be utterly dedicated to her job—and she had to hope that at some point in the future she could make it up to her sisters.

Holly's coin test was a good idea, though.

'Heads I'll do the show; tails I won't,' she said aloud, tossed the coin, and caught it on the back of her hand.

When she took the top hand off to reveal the coin showing tails, she discovered that her sister had been spot on. It really did tell her what she wanted...

Rory's phone pinged and Pippa's name flashed up on the screen at the top of the message.

Spoke to Nathalie. Happy to do piece about wasp. Twelve-thirty OK? What's the dress code? Pippa

He smiled and typed back.

Thank you. Twelve-thirty at the box office is fine. Dress code's whatever you feel comfortable wearing. Rory

He'd just sent the message when he remembered that she hadn't watched his show. He added swiftly:

Most people I interview wear whatever they normally wear at work.

She texted back.

Thank you. That's helpful. I'll bring lunch. Any (non-vespine) allergies or dietary stuff?

Oh, he liked those brackets. He liked *her*. And he was really looking forward to that interview.

He replied:

I eat anything.

And then he found himself typing:

Big weakness for brownies and scones.

No. That was steering into flirting territory.

Except, instead of hitting the delete key, he accidentally hit the enter key. And it was too late to recall the message because she'd already read it.

Oh, great. How to make himself look foolish in her eyes.

He was about to type an apology when his phone pinged.

Noted.

And she'd added an emoji to tell him he'd just made her cry with laughter.

Ah, well. At least it'd make her relax with him instead of being nervous about being filmed. Then again, her job meant walking out onto a stage and performing in front of a sea of strangers; the chances were, she'd find filming an absolute breeze.

And that was another thing. He'd been so focused on seeing Pippa again that he'd completely forgotten about Kenise, his camerawoman. He texted Pippa again.

My camerawoman's vegetarian—I'll bring wraps for all of us.

Pippa replied.

OK. Then I'm in charge of pudding.

* * *

On Friday, Rory woke feeling as if life was getting back to normal again. He had interviews for his wasp piece scheduled during the day, his guests had all confirmed they would be there for the chat show section in the studio at five, and he'd sorted out the order of the other pieces he was going to use in the round-up. Busy, busy, busy—just how he liked it.

His mother was lying in wait in the kitchen. 'Eat some breakfast before you go,' she said. 'And if you're tired, you'll stop. Promise?'

There wasn't a way to stop her worrying—or was there? 'Thank you for looking after me, this week,' he said, giving her a hug. 'And nagging. You were right—I needed these few days off.' That wasn't strictly true, from his point of view, but he knew it would make his mother feel better. 'And now I'm ready to do the job I love again,' he said.

'And you'll let your father drive you to the studio?'

'No need. I'm going there after my last interview to do the voiceover and put the wasp piece together, then run through the first half of the show to check timings,' he said. 'I'm not going to make him turn out in rush-hour traffic. I was planning to get a taxi back afterwards—unless you wanted to come and sit in the audience for the live section, in which case I'll take you both out to dinner and we'll get a cab home afterwards.'

'That'd be nice,' Helena said.

'All right. I'll put your names on the list with security, and I'll see you after the show,' he said.

He met Kenise, his camerawoman, at his GP's surgery for the interview; then they went to his godmother's house, where Kenise took various shots of the garden while he stayed in the kitchen, safely away from any wasps; he planned to add the voiceover in the studio. It was slightly unnerving to be back in the place where his heart had actually stopped beating; but at the same time he needed to face it and reassure Rosemary that he was absolutely fine.

Finally he headed to the Fitzroy Theatre. His first interview was with Nathalie Charrier to talk about the Fitzroy's upcoming gala show and the roof repairs; although he would've liked to get up on the roof to take a few shots, he thought that might be a step too far.

And then, at last, it was time to meet Pippa by the box office.

She was wearing leggings and a pretty T-shirt, as she had been yesterday, but today her hair was up in a bun and she definitely looked like an off-duty ballerina.

'Lovely to see you again, Pippa,' he said, shaking her hand and hoping it came across as professional. 'Pippa, this is Kenise, who does all my camerawork; Kenise, this is Pippa, the person who saved my life.'

'Good to meet you,' Kenise said, smiling broadly. 'Thank you for saving his life—and my job.'

'We all know you would've been snapped up within seconds,' Rory said, rolling his eyes and laughing.

'You said it would be about ten minutes of filming?' Pippa checked.

'Yes, though I won't use all of it on screen. I'll ask different questions, and you answer as if we're just having a chat. If you stop or mix your words up, that's fine. We can reshoot anything. I might stop and take a different angle, depending on what you say. Then I'll edit it together.'

'All right,' she said.

They went outside the theatre; Kenise took panning

shots of the exterior of the theatre, then came to join them on the steps.

'I had no idea I was severely allergic to wasp stings until I was talking to ballerina Pippa Barnes at the garden party, while we were raising funds for the Fitzroy's roof,' Rory said. 'And I was incredibly lucky to be stung in front of someone who knew exactly how to save my life. Pippa, how did you know something was wrong and what to do next?'

'At ballet classes, one of my friends was severely allergic to almonds and accidentally ate some,' Pippa said. 'She collapsed in front of me, the same way that you did, so I realised you must be severely allergic to something.' She ran through what happened.

'Thanks to you, I'm here to tell the tale,' Rory said. 'What was going through your head when you did the CPR?'

'That I wanted to keep the blood pumping round your system until the paramedics came,' she answered honestly. 'It was pure instinct.'

He ran through the procedure again, this time asking slightly different questions and with Kenise taking a different camera angle.

'And that's everything I need,' he said at the end. 'Thank you.' He smiled. 'Shall we have lunch?'

'Sure. If you'd like to find a table, I'll get pudding from my locker,' Pippa said.

'She's lovely,' Kenise said as he ushered her into the restaurant area. 'I can see why you're smitten.'

'I'm not in the least bit smitten, Ken,' Rory protested. 'As I said to you earlier, she's articulate and she loves her subject. I'd really like her to do the show—but only if she's happy to do it.'

'I think she likes you, too,' Kenise said.

Rory sighed. 'I'm not looking for a relationship. She's busy with her career, and I'm busy with mine.'

'You picked a few girls who weren't right for you,' Kenise said. 'She's not like them—she doesn't treat you as a TV star or as royalty. She treats you as an equal.'

'You've worked with me for four years,' Rory said, 'and I love you dearly. But please don't try to matchmake. This is business.'

'If you say so,' Kenise said, hamming up her Jamaican accent and making it sound more like *I don't believe a word of it*.

Pippa joined them a couple of moments later, carrying a patisserie box. 'This is from the bakery round the corner from my flat,' she said.

'And these are from the deli round the corner from my parents,' Rory said, bringing out plain paper bags.

'What, no posh picnic hamper today?' Pippa teased.

'My first interview was at eight, this morning,' Rory said. 'So there wasn't time to pretty it up. Today there are chicken salad wraps—that's hummus and falafel for you, Ken, in a separate paper bag.'

'Gotta love a boss who pays attention to his team,' Kenise said with a grin.

'Have you two worked together very long?' Pippa asked.

'Long enough to finish—' Kenise began.

'—each other's sentences,' Rory said, laughing. 'What Ken doesn't know about film isn't worth knowing. She's taught me a lot.'

'You already knew a lot before I met you,' Kenise said. 'And he doesn't mansplain, so I can put up with him.'

'Sounds good,' Pippa said with a smile.

'I interviewed Nathalie this morning,' he said. 'About the Fitzroy's roof, and the gala.'

'Will that be going on tonight's show?' she asked.

'Yes. And she also gave us permission to do some filming in the dress rehearsal this afternoon,' he said. 'The one for the gala show, with you as the Sugar Plum Fairy. I'd like to film the whole piece, then pick a few seconds of footage to include in my introduction to you.'

She looked surprised. 'I—well, if Nathalie's said yes, then it's fine with me.'

'I have to cut the show together and do the guest spots this afternoon,' he said, 'so Nathalie's changing the order just for today—you'll do your piece first, so Kenise can film and we'll leave before the next performer comes on.'

'Then I'll be skipping pudding,' she said lightly, 'and you and Kenise can finish that box between you.'

'If you're sure, then thank you,' Rory said.

'No, *really* thank you,' Kenise said. 'I love brownies.'

'My pleasure,' Pippa said. Her phone alarm rang. 'My cue for work,' she said.

'See you on stage,' Rory said. 'And I'll talk to you next week about the series.'

'Sure. Nice to meet you, Kenise,' she said.

'She's really lovely,' Kenise said. 'Your parents would like her. And your sister. And your sister-in-law.'

'It's business,' Rory said, even though he agreed with her privately. But Pippa had made it clear that she was focused on her career; nothing was going to happen between them. Plus he wasn't taking the risk of messing up his documentary, by getting involved with the person he wanted to star in it. She was strictly off limits.

Nathalie came over to them. 'Ready to film?'

'Ready,' Rory said.

She led them into the auditorium; Kenise checked the lights and then got into the right position.

Rory had seen *The Nutcracker* several times over the years, and was very familiar with the music and the traditional routine; but even so he found himself spellbound when Pippa walked out onto the stage.

He'd last seen her wearing leggings and a pretty T-shirt. It had only been a few minutes ago—and yet here she was, completely transformed into the Queen of the Land of Sweets, a gilded crown on her head. Her dress was of the palest pink, and it seemed to shimmer underneath the lights; there were tiny star-shaped sequins sewn on the bodice, and the tutu was overlaid with gauze. And the way she moved, light as thistledown, gliding effortlessly across the stage in perfect timing with the eerie sound of the celestina...

Rory was completely transfixed.

He'd never seen the piece danced so beautifully—so perfectly.

Right at that very second he really could believe that she was a fairy. That last chain of pirouettes, the complicated footwork, the delicate movement of her tutu, the smile on her face...

As the final note died away, he stood up and clapped, unable to help himself. 'Brava,' he called.

She smiled, blew him a kiss, then walked gracefully off the stage—a fairy queen to the last.

CHAPTER FIVE

PIPPA HAD BEEN so aware of Rory sitting in the front row as she'd danced. She'd felt as if she'd been dancing just for him. And she'd loved every second of it, channelling the character of the fairy queen, her movements light and precise and in perfect timing with the music.

At the end, Rory had given her a standing ovation. He'd looked stunned, as if he hadn't expected her to dance quite like that. And he'd looked as if the magic of the piece had sprinkled its fairy dust on him, too. She hadn't been able to resist blowing him that kiss. And then, being a coward, she'd left the stage without looking to see his reaction.

If she was honest with herself, yes, she was attracted to him.

Which made the 'tails' bit of the coin test the sensible choice: she shouldn't do his show, because there was a huge risk that she might let him distract her from her goals. What if Rory became too much of a temptation? If she didn't get that promotion, then she'd be failing her parents all over again. She'd already disappointed them by choosing dance over medicine. Being a flop at her career wasn't an option. Doing Rory's show would be too much of a risk.

The problem was, she'd *wanted* that coin to land heads-up.

So did she follow her heart and do the show, or did she follow her common sense and turn him down?

The more she thought about it, the less she could answer.

Maybe she needed to let things settle in the back of her head for a bit longer.

Between rehearsals and the evening performance, Pippa texted her parents to let them know that she was going to be on Rory's show that evening, giving them the time and channel in case they wanted to see it. After chatting in the restroom with some of the other dancers, then a snack of a banana and an energy bar, she had her hair and make-up done, got changed into her costume and warmed up her muscles again, preparing to dance.

As always, the second that the curtain went up, the familiar adrenalin kicked in. Pippa loved the challenge of dancing the twin roles of heroine and villainess in the same show, portraying the emotional vulnerability of Odette and the seductive deception of Odile. And she hoped that just maybe she might inspire one young dancer in the audience, the way she'd been inspired at her own first visit to see *Swan Lake*.

On her way home after the show, she checked her phone; there were messages from her sisters and both her parents saying they'd seen her piece on Rory's show. Her sisters had said she looked as if she were flying when she danced, so light and delicate; her parents said how proud they were of her for saving Rory's life.

Well, of course her parents would focus on the medical side of things, she thought wryly. The life they still felt she should've had.

But then her mother had added, *'You dance so beautifully.'* Which made Pippa feel as if her mother, at least, was finally starting to understand how much her career meant to her. Maybe one day she would stop feeling that she'd let them down. Though, that didn't mean she had room in her life for a relationship. How could she prioritise romance over the thing that made her who she was? She'd only end up letting a partner down as much as she'd let her family down.

Back at her flat, she made herself a mug of camomile tea, heated up the pasta dish she'd prepped earlier, and found Rory's show on the catch-up section of the arts channel. She curled up on the sofa and ate dinner while she watched. His piece about the wasp stings was excellent, but she really enjoyed the piece on the Fitzroy, with Nathalie talking about the gala and how they'd be dancing favourite ballet pieces, from traditional classical works through to more modern choreography.

She could see how Rory had edited the bits he'd filmed with her to help tell the story effectively. He'd used several short clips of her dancing, and ended the section about the Fitzroy gala with Pippa's last few pirouettes in the 'Dance of the Sugar Plum Fairy'. She was used to practising in a studio with a mirror, so she could check she was happy with any particular pose or move, but seeing herself dancing on screen felt very different—almost as if she was watching someone else. She was relieved to note that the clip was technically flawless.

The final section was the chat show, and she loved the way Rory drew his guests out. He had a real knack for putting people at their ease, and it was more like watching old friends having a good chat than a formal interview.

At the end, she messaged him.

I enjoyed your show.

A moment later, her phone pinged with a return message.

Thank you. I enjoyed your Sugar Plum Fairy.

Thank you. I'll be watching your show in future.

I'm definitely getting a ticket for the Fitzroy gala show. What did you dance tonight?

Swan Lake. Though dancers don't necessarily play the same part every night.

Why not?

That message was rapidly followed by:

Can I call you?

Sure.

Her phone rang.

'Hey. I know you're working tomorrow, so I won't keep you long,' Rory promised. 'Tell me about *Swan Lake*.'

'Tonight I danced Odette/Odile,' she said, 'but some nights I dance as one of the Two Swans in Acts Two and Four, and other nights I dance as one of the Prince's sisters.'

'Why don't you dance the same part every night?' he asked.

'Because some parts—like Odette/Odile—really take it out of you,' she explained. 'A dancer risks burnout if they dance a major part every single night. Plus you need several people in every performance who can cover different parts, in case someone's taken ill at the last minute or has a family crisis and can't make a show. Besides, it's good for dancers to learn a mix of parts, so they can extend their range and repertoire.' She paused, realising that he hadn't said a thing. 'Sorry. I can get a bit boring about dance.'

'You're not boring,' he said. 'I'm being quiet because I'm making notes. These are the kinds of points I'd like to cover in the series—which isn't me pressuring you to say yes, it's just you've given me something really interesting to think about, and probably a ton of questions.'

'Oh.' He wasn't bored, then. Funny how that made her feel warm inside.

'Do you dance every night?' he asked.

'It depends on the cast. Sometimes I have a night off during the week, though I normally come in and watch the performance from the wings.' Then it occurred to her that it might not be what he'd meant. 'We don't have shows on Sunday or Monday, so that's the equivalent of the weekend for me.'

'I hadn't really thought about that, but you work Friday and Saturday nights,' he mused. 'Of course your "weekend" wouldn't be the same as it is for someone in an office job.'

'It's all part of working in the arts,' she said. 'Musicians on tour have a lot of travelling in between shows, and they might be working ten or fourteen days in a row, depending on what their promoters book. And you probably work unusual hours.'

'Well, yes,' he said. 'But it doesn't matter, because I love my job.'

'Me, too,' she said.

'Well, I'm glad you enjoyed my show,' he said. 'No pressure, but I'll wait to hear from you about whether you'll do the ballet documentary with me. I've already got a yes from the tango expert.'

'And John Travolta for the disco?' she couldn't help teasing.

'Sadly, my mum's going to miss out on that one. But, yes, I have a disco dancer arranged.' She could practically hear the smile in his voice. 'Plus a tango expert and a ballroom specialist.'

'OK. Speak to you soon,' she said.

The next morning, in the middle of the conditioning class, it occurred to Pippa that Rory could shadow her for a few days. If he took part in the warm-up, he could experience the exercises for himself; and although he wouldn't be doing any actual dancing, he could at least see how rehearsals worked. Maybe the wardrobe team could fit him for a costume and do stage hair and make-up, too. Obviously he'd be used to make-up for the chat show segment of his TV show, but stage make-up was very different and it could be fun.

At the break between class and rehearsals, she went to find Nathalie. 'I was thinking—could Rory maybe shadow me at work for a few days?' she asked. 'Not all the time, obviously, but enough so he gets an idea of how things fit together to make a performance and what goes on behind the scenes?'

'You've decided to do the show, then?' Nathalie asked.

'*Nearly* decided.' She just needed to banish those last

niggling doubts. 'But it would be useful background for him, even if I don't do the show.'

'He'll only be observing, not filming?' Nathalie checked.

'Observing, and maybe doing the conditioning class, if Kenzo doesn't mind. It wouldn't be fair to anyone to put him in a rehearsal class, when he doesn't have a clue what a tendu is or what "fifth position arms" means,' Pippa said, 'because either we'd have to stop and show him what to do, or he'd try to follow us and get in a muddle.'

'I'll talk to Kenzo about it,' Nathalie said. 'If Rory gets to a point where he wants to film anyone other than you, then everyone needs to agree to it. And they need credits on the programme.'

'Of course,' Pippa said. 'Thank you, Nathalie.'

Before the rehearsals started, she texted Rory.

Talked to Nathalie. She says you can shadow me here, watch the classes and rehearsals, and maybe take the conditioning class.

Her phone rang almost immediately. 'Is now a good time for you to talk?'

'I've got about three minutes,' she said.

'OK. Are you busy on Sunday?' he asked.

Why? Was he going to ask her out? All her nerve-ends started to tingle. If he did…what if she gave in to the temptation to say yes?

'Just catching up with chores,' she said carefully.

'Maybe we could meet up, if you have time. I can answer any questions you might have about the dance show.'

He hadn't been asking her on a date, then: this was work. And how ridiculous that she felt disappointed.

After all, hadn't she been telling herself that she didn't want him to distract her? And she had nothing to offer him anyway. Dance always came first, even before her family. How could she even consider committing to a relationship, when it was obvious that her partner would have to take second place to her career? She'd end up letting him down, the same way she'd let her family down.

Even if she could get past that, there was the fact that they'd be working together. It really wouldn't be appropriate to have a relationship with him. He was off limits.

'I haven't quite made my decision, yet,' she said. Which wasn't strictly true; she'd made the decision, but she was having an uncharacteristic wobble about it. Normally, she knew exactly what her next move would be, where her career was concerned, but something about Rory raised all the doubts she'd suppressed over the years.

'Or we could just meet up for a coffee,' he said. 'I would suggest going for a walk in the park, but I'd hate for you to have to save my life all over again.'

She ought to tell him she was too busy to see him. But her mouth seemed to have other ideas. 'We could go for an indoor walk,' she said. 'Maybe in a museum or a gallery?'

'That would be great. Where would you like to go?'

She'd done it, now. 'Somewhere easy to get to—how about the National Gallery?'

'OK. I'll meet you by the entrance at…when's good for you?'

She usually slept in a little later on Sundays. 'Eleven?'

'Eleven it is. I'll see you then.'

The warmth in Rory's voice made her feel warm all over, too. But she made herself concentrate and not think of him at all during rehearsals.

On her lunch break, she looked him up properly—telling herself it was just because she wanted to know more about him if she was going to work with him. There seemed to be a lot of pictures of him on social media, at parties with gorgeous actresses and models; clearly he lived a glamorous life.

She skimmed over the words, then stopped dead and backtracked. The *Honourable* Rory Fanshawe? Hang on… Did that mean he was minor royalty or something?

A couple more clicks, and she discovered that Rory was the youngest son of the Earl and Countess of Riverford.

But he'd introduced himself to her as Rory Fanshawe, not as Lord Whatever-He-Was. Though being blue-blooded would explain his accent and his knowledge of Latin, which tended to be taught more in private schools than state schools.

A little more research told her that he'd gone to Eton, as had his older brother; his sister had gone to a private day school.

They were from totally different worlds. Worlds that she didn't think would fit well together. How would his family ever think her enough for him? Surely they'd expect him to end up with someone born into the aristocracy—someone who understood that way of life? She wasn't enough for her parents because she hadn't gone into medicine; she wasn't a good enough sister because she let dancing get in the way of keeping in touch; and if she wasn't good enough to make Principal Dancer it would all have been for nothing. Risking a relationship with Rory and failing that, too—that was one step too far.

So the ridiculous thoughts that had been starting to form in her brain would just have to be ignored. There was no chance of anything romantic developing between them. She and Rory might become friends, but no more than that.

In a way, she thought, finding out the truth about his background had done her a favour. Knowing that nothing would happen between them meant that she could do the show without being distracted by him.

On Sunday, Pippa headed out to meet Rory in Trafalgar Square. The area was already busy with people snapping pictures of Nelson's column and the lions, and children watching the fountains.

Rory was waiting for her by the entrance to the National Gallery, as they'd arranged, and together they went into the main hall.

'Shall we start with the oldest ones and work forwards?' he asked. 'Or can I take you to see my favourite painting here?'

What would the son of an earl like most? she wondered. Something very traditional? Or something that kicked against the traces?

'Show me your favourite,' she said.

It turned out to be one of the more modern pieces in the gallery: a woman in a room, with her back to the artist.

'*Interior*, by Vilhelm Hammershøi,' she said, reading the notes next to the painting. 'I'm sorry, I've never heard of him.'

'He's one of the Danish Symbolists,' he said. 'This is a painting of his wife in their house in Copenhagen. I like it because we only see her back, so whatever she's thinking or doing is a complete mystery to whoever's looking at the painting—and that means whatever you think the painting means.'

She looked at him. 'And *that* never occurred to me, either. Did you study History of Art at uni?'

'English Literature,' he said with a smile. 'I've learned a bit about art from the curators I've talked to over the years. I wrote an article for an internet magazine about Hammershøi's work, a couple of years back. *Dust Motes with Sunbeams* is the painting I really fell in love with.' He took his phone from his pocket, tapped on the screen and brought up a painting to show her. Winter sunlight shone diagonally through a window in the centre of a room, illuminating particles of dust and throwing patterns of light and shade on the floor. 'The light's the connection between the inside and the outside,' he said.

'I can see why you like it,' she said. 'It's lovely. Almost like a photograph.'

'And this one,' he said, shepherding her over to a painting of a lake among mountains, the water whipped into zigzags by the wind. 'Again, it's the light and the colour palette that draws me in.'

'Basically you like Scandi art?' she asked, peering at the description by the painting and discovering that the artist, Akseli Gallen-Kallela, was Finnish.

'I do,' he said with a grin. 'Lottie—my sister—teases me about *hygge* all the time. But I really like the clean lines and the lightness of Scandinavian style.'

Which was a million miles away from the huge dark paintings found in stately homes—or the acres of gilding. 'I kind of expected you to be a big fan of Reynolds and all the royal portrait painters,' she said.

He frowned. 'Why?'

'I looked you up,' she said. 'You never said your dad was an earl.'

At least he had the grace to wince. 'Ah. That.'

'Should I be calling you Lord Fanshawe?' she asked.

'No. I'm the younger son so I'm plain Mr. Though I get a courtesy title to use on paper,' he added.

'That's the "honourable" bit?'

'Yes, though I don't use it at work. My brother Jamie is the heir apparent, so he gets one of Dad's other titles. He's Viscount Allingham.' He sighed. 'I *did* tell you I had a privileged upbringing.'

She remembered; she'd misinterpreted it at the time. Though he hadn't enlightened her, either. 'I didn't realise you meant you were part of the aristocracy.'

For a moment, he tensed. Then he said, 'It's honestly not that big a deal.'

She wasn't so sure. Why was he sensitive about her asking about his upbringing? Maybe she should be kind and back off; but she was curious. Really curious. 'Isn't it? I mean—you must know the royal family.'

'I do, but only in the same way that say a teacher would have a lot of teacher friends, or you have a lot of dancer friends. It's only part of my life. That's why I didn't mention it before,' he explained. 'It honestly isn't a big deal. This isn't the Regency era; my parents aren't snobs who look down on people who haven't been born into privilege. Neither of my in-laws come from the aristocracy.'

She bit her lip. 'Sorry. I didn't mean to accuse your family of being snobbish.' And her earlier thought about her social class being a barrier between them—well, it wasn't.

'I'm probably being oversensitive,' he said. 'Because I hate it when people see me as a posh boy trading on my dad's connections. I did think about using a stage name for my broadcasting work, but then I realised it'd be a bit pointless because it'd only take a couple of clicks on a search engine to find out who my dad is. But I got my job because of what I can do, not because of my name.'

It sounded as if people had accused him of that before. She wasn't surprised that rankled, because from what she'd seen he put a lot of work into his show. In his shoes, she'd be a bit sensitive about it, too.

'I just want to be seen for who I am—as a person,' he said.

'I can understand that,' she said. 'I suppose it's like the children of rock stars or actors—they might want to follow in their parents' footsteps because they love music or acting. But, however hard they work, people will still think they only got their first break because of who their parents are.'

'Exactly,' he said. 'The society rags call me a prime catch because I'm the son of the Earl of Riverford, and I loathe it. Marriage shouldn't be about seeing someone as a fish to be reeled in—it should be because you're attracted to someone and you like spending time with them.' His face darkened. 'And I hate it when women flirt with me because they think I can get into them into TV.'

Pippa was shocked. 'You think that's why women date you—because you could be a good connection for them?'

'Put it this way, I don't seem to be very good at picking someone who sees me for myself,' he said.

And she'd pretty much asked him questions that made it sound as if she was just like his exes, interested in his connections rather than in him. 'I'm sorry,' she said. 'I didn't mean to trample on a sore spot.'

'It's fine.' He blew out a breath. 'Just sometimes it gets to me. I mean—I'm twenty-nine. My brother and sister were both married by the time they were my age.

They both had children. They were *settled*. And here I am, racketing around.'

'Is that what you're looking for? A life partner and children?' she asked carefully.

If that was what he really wanted, it was something she couldn't give him. Not without giving up her career, which she wasn't prepared to do; or asking him to wait for so many years that her fertility would be on the wane, which wouldn't be fair to him.

'No. Yes. I don't know.' He shook his head. 'Everything was a lot clearer before the wasp issue. I was taking a year or so out of dating to concentrate on my career and get a bit closer to where I want to go next,' he said. 'But, this past week, my family's wrapped me in cotton wool and I've had nothing to do except think.' He grimaced. 'I felt as if I was sleepwalking, in hospital. Stuck behind a wall and I couldn't get out.'

'To be fair, they did need to keep an eye on you, in case you had another reaction,' Pippa said.

'I know,' he said. 'But living in my head hasn't been good for me. I thought I knew where my life was going, but now it feels as if I'm lost in a maze full of briars. I've been reassessing everything and it's made me wonder: am I letting my family down?'

Oh, she knew that one well. *Really* well. He had her complete sympathies.

'I feel like the spoiled, selfish baby who doesn't seem to stick to anything and always dates Ms Wrong,' he finished.

'You don't come across as a spoiled baby,' she said. 'I wouldn't presume to lecture you about your love life, but you've clearly stuck to your career. If you couldn't do your job well, you wouldn't get decent ratings and you would've been replaced by now, with someone who'd bring in the viewers and more advertising money.'

'I wasn't fishing for compliments,' he said, 'but thank you. Looking at it that way helps.'

'What you said about feeling that you've let your family down?' She gave him a wry smile. 'That makes two of us.' She grimaced. 'And I know we're supposed to be talking about your dance series, but that bit's not for public consumption and I'd rather you didn't include it in your show.'

'Noted. And you can trust me,' he said. 'Apart from the fact that I keep my word, if you said anything to the press about what I just told you, they'd have a field day.'

He had a point: he was as vulnerable to gossip as she was. Maybe more so, because television had a much wider reach than a ballet stage. 'This stays between you and me,' she said. Which felt strangely intimate. She'd just told him things she hadn't told anyone else; and she had the feeling that he'd confided in her in just the same way. They were almost strangers; yet there was a connection between them. Maybe it was because he'd been so close to death and she'd been so instrumental in saving his life, but she felt oddly close to him.

'Why do you think you've let your family down?' he asked. 'You're doing really well in your career.'

'I'm the only one in three generations of my family not to be a doctor,' she said. 'I chose ballet over medical school.'

'If you have a talent, surely it's a waste to ignore it and do something else just because everyone else in your family does?' Rory asked.

'Maybe,' she said. 'But, because I didn't take a conventional route into ballet, I always feel that I have to work twice as hard as everyone else, even to prove that I have the same kind of commitment.'

'That's why you're so focused on getting promoted?'

She nodded. 'It'll show everyone that I made the right career choice.' Including herself: maybe then she'd feel that she was good enough to do her job, not an imposter.

'You're doing what you love,' he said. 'That tells me you've made the right choice. Would you be happy, being a doctor?'

'I don't know,' she said. 'But sometimes I think maybe I should've followed the career path my parents planned for me. At least as a doctor I'd be doing something important. Helping people.'

'As a dancer, you're helping people,' Rory said. 'The arts are food for the soul. A world without music, without paintings, without theatre and dance—where's the joy?'

'That's what your programme's about, isn't it?' she asked. 'Sharing the joy.'

He nodded. 'I know what you mean, though. Sometimes I feel as if I'm frivolous. Not the showbiz parties—there aren't anywhere near as many of those as the press likes to make out, and they're not my idea of a good time anyway—but the arts are so often seen as a luxury. They're the first thing to go when money's tight and bills need to be paid.'

'Except maybe they're more than a luxury,' she said. 'The arts are about your mental health. Like you said—it's about the joy. And maybe seeing something on your show will persuade the audience to try doing it themselves. Dancing's so good for taking you out of a tough place. When you're counting steps and you have to concentrate on what your arms and legs are doing, you don't have the headspace to think about your worries. Even if it's only for half an hour, that tiny break from worrying can give you the strength to carry on.'

'It's the same when you're watching a film, or reading, or wandering round an art gallery and telling yourself the story behind the picture—it's like a step out of your real life that helps you put a bit of space between you and your worries, and it means you can cope.' He paused. 'We're on the same side, Pippa.'

'I think we are,' she agreed.

'Let's walk and look at some more paintings,' he said, and she walked with him towards the Impressionists' room. 'I know I said I wasn't going to pressure you—but I think you'd be perfect for my series. You love your job and you're good at explaining what you do.' He paused. 'So what's holding you back from saying yes?'

CHAPTER SIX

FOR A MOMENT, Pippa looked haunted, and Rory was about to back off when she said, 'If you really want to know, I worry that doing your show is going to distract me. I can't allow *anything* to sidetrack me. My parents don't understand why I never date, and my sisters are always nagging me not to work so hard—but I *have* to. I don't have *time* to date. If I lose my focus at work, I'll lose my chance of being promoted. And that promotion's really important to me.'

She'd said it would prove to her parents that she'd made the right career choice. Perhaps, he thought, she needed that proof for herself, too. To show her that all the sacrifices she'd made were worth it.

'Or maybe you could see the documentary as a safety net,' he said. 'There's a pretty good chance that the management team of other ballet companies will be watching it. They'll see you dancing, but more importantly they'll see how you come across on screen. If Nathalie doesn't give you the promotion, I reckon you'll get calls from people interested in you joining their companies as a Principal Dancer.'

'Maybe,' she said. 'Though I like working at the Fitzroy. It's the first company that gave me a chance—and it feels like home. I don't want to leave.'

Rory understood exactly what she meant. If he wanted to climb the ladder, eventually he'd need to move on from the company that had given him the chance to hone his skills; he'd still miss his team and their camaraderie. 'You won't get distracted,' he said.

She didn't look as if she believed him.

And then the penny dropped. That pull he'd felt towards her—did she feel it, too? His mouth went dry. Was *he* the reason she was holding back?

The words slipped out before he could stop them. 'Do you think *I'm* going to distract you?'

Her face coloured. 'Yes,' she muttered.

Now he got it. And, now he thought about it, he had a feeling that she could distract him, too. 'Don't worry. You're perfectly safe with me,' he said, 'I'm not looking for a relationship.' At least, he didn't want the kind of relationship he'd fallen into for the last three or four years, where his girlfriends hadn't seen him for who he was inside. 'The same way that I'm safe with you, because you're obviously not looking for a relationship, either— plus you see past me being the youngest son of the Earl of Riverford or being a TV presenter.'

She frowned. 'But you just told me your series could help my career.'

'As a ballerina, or at least give you options elsewhere if Nathalie doesn't promote you,' he said. 'That isn't the same thing as helping you get a start in TV.' She wouldn't be using him for his connections, the way his exes had; but dating her would be a mistake. She'd been very clear that she didn't have the time or space in her life for a relationship. Which meant anything that might happen between them had no future. What was the point in setting himself up for more hurt?

'I suppose—'

But, before she could continue, a middle-aged woman came over to them, and asked, 'Rory Fanshawe? It *is* you, isn't it?'

'Yes,' he said.

She beamed at him. 'I told my husband it was you. He said I was being a silly old fool.' She turned to Pippa. 'I'm so sorry to interrupt your date, my dear. But I wanted to tell Rory how much I enjoyed his show. I watch it every week without fail.' She turned back to Rory and smiled again. 'If it wasn't for you telling us about it, I would've missed that wonderful exhibition of the Pre-Raphaelites the other month.'

'That's good to hear. I hope you enjoyed it,' Rory said, smiling back at her.

'I did—very much. I just wanted to thank you,' she said. 'I'll let you get on with your day.'

'Thank you. And it was lovely to meet you,' Rory said, shaking her hand.

'Does that happen very often?' Pippa asked quietly when the woman was out of earshot. 'People coming up to you when you're out?'

'It's becoming more frequent,' Rory admitted. 'But, actually, that's the best bit of my job—hearing from a viewer that I've shared something they've really enjoyed. That my work's made a difference. I'm always happy to talk to fans. Without them, I wouldn't have a job.' He looked at her. 'Don't people come up to you?'

'Outside the Fitzroy? Not really. Apart from ballet-goers, most people wouldn't know who I am,' she said. 'Though that isn't an issue. I'm just happy being able to do what I love.' She paused. 'So what's your game plan?'

'I'm still working that out,' Rory said. 'I love the format of my show. I like meeting new people, and I think one of my strengths is getting people to open up to me. What I do in the arts round-up is halfway between commercial television and the more formal documentaries that the critics like. I'd like to think there's a way I can keep doing both. I enjoy the commercial stuff with a broader audience that persuades people to look at something they might otherwise miss, but I want to do serious arts documentaries as well—to go into more depth with things than I can in my show right now.'

'Your dance series is the first step towards that—pun not intended,' she added.

He chuckled. 'But it works very nicely.' He looked at her. 'You're the first person I've told about any of this.'

'Even though we're practically strangers.'

'Maybe that makes it easier,' Rory said. 'We don't have any expectations of how each other will react.' He paused. 'What's your game plan, then? Apart from becoming Principal Dancer?'

'I've got maybe ten years left dancing on stage in a lead role,' Pippa said. 'After that, it's either playing character roles—say, Juliet's nurse in *Romeo and Juliet* or Carabosse in *The Sleeping Beauty*—or teaching. Or maybe choreography. But Principal Dancer is at least my five-year plan.'

Even though she didn't quite believe in herself, she'd planned her career and she'd work hard enough to get where she wanted, Rory thought. 'That sounds good,' he said.

His hand brushed against hers accidentally as they walked through the gallery, and it felt as if he'd been galvanised. He didn't dare look at her to gauge her reaction, and instead pretended it hadn't happened. He kept the conversation light and focused on the art, and discovered that she liked paintings full of sunshine—and, of course, Degas' ballet dancers.

But, as they moved through the rooms, he found himself really aware of her; sometimes, when they stood looking at a painting and talking, they were close enough that he could feel the warmth of her skin and smell the sweet vanilla scent of her perfume. Even though he was trying to concentrate on being professional, he found himself wondering what it would be like if this was a real date. What it would be like to hold her hand. How it would feel to hold her close. How her mouth would feel against his...

It had been a while since he'd felt a pull like this towards someone. And he knew he needed to suppress it: she'd already said she didn't want to get distracted from her career. Despite his good intentions to say goodbye and leave her to think about whether she would do his show, his mouth had other ideas, because he said, 'Can I buy you lunch? Not with strings—just because it's my turn.' And because he really wasn't ready to say goodbye to her just yet.

'Thank you. That'd be nice.' Her smile was open and honest, and it made him feel as if his heart had just done a backflip. Which was crazy. He wasn't supposed to be thinking about her in those terms.

They queued up in the café; she chose a goat's cheese, spinach and red pepper quiche with a green superfood salad.

'That looks so good. I think I'll have the same,' he said.

'So what's your favourite ballet?' he asked when they'd found a table, wanting to keep her talking to him, and guessing that her job was her favourite subject.

'To dance or to watch?' she asked.

'Both,' he said.

'*Swan Lake* to watch,' she said promptly. 'Whether it's the version with the scary all-male swans, or the absolute precision of a traditional version with the cygnets in tiaras and tutus. I love the music and the routines—and it always, always makes me cry.'

'Ballets are always tragedies, aren't they?' he asked. '*Swan Lake*, they both die; *Romeo and Juliet*, they both die; *Giselle*, they both die.'

'Actually,' she said,' there's a version of *Swan Lake* with a happy ending, where Prince Siegfried fights Rothbart and pulls off his wing, and that takes the enchantment off the swans, and he marries Odette.'

'It's nice to know that a happy ending's possible,' he said, 'but then how would it work with the music?'

'I don't have an answer for that one, because I've never seen that version,' she admitted. 'But tragedies aren't just in ballet. It's in opera, too—*Madame Butterfly, Tosca, La Traviata*. And everyone dies in Shakespeare's tragedies.'

'But there's comic opera—things like *The Marriage of Figaro*,' he said. 'And Shakespeare also wrote comedies.'

'There's a ballet version of *A Midsummer Night's Dream*,' she said. 'And there are other ballets with happy endings: *Sleeping Beauty* and the *Nutcracker*.'

'OK. I'll give you that,' he said. 'What about your favourite ballet to dance?'

'To be fair, it's whatever we're doing right now. I always find something new in a performance, even when it's a role I've danced before,' she said. 'I really loved doing *Cinderella*, last year. We had a different perspective—Cinderella was loved by the stepmother, but the stepsisters teased her by throwing her scarf around and she got upset about it being lost. When her dad went back to find it, he was accidentally killed by hunters. The stepmother was lost in grief and couldn't bear to have Cinderella around as a reminder of why her husband died.'

'That's definitely a different take on the fairy tale,' he said. 'And I like that. A motive that's stronger than just money.' He rolled his eyes. 'And yes, I know, that's rich coming from my background.'

'A double pun—very clever,' she said.

He inclined her head in acknowledgement. 'Which role did you dance?'

'Cinderella,' she said. 'And the bit I loved was my transformational dress.'

'What's that, in layman's terms?'

'It's a little bit of stage magic. In the first act, I wear a peasant dress. About half an hour into the show, I'm offstage for three minutes, and that's when I change into the transformational dress—it looks like the peasant dress on the outside, but there's a ballgown underneath,' she explained.

'You can change a costume in less than three minutes?' He could feel his eyes widening. He hadn't known that was possible.

'The wardrobe, hair and make-up department are extraordinary,' she said. 'It happens in opera and plays, too—they all work together at the same time, at amazing speeds.'

'So how does the dress work?' he asked. 'Don't the audience notice there are two dresses?'

'No. As I said, Wardrobe's amazing. It's all about the material they use and how they roll it to hide one dress under the other, sort of in a pocket. I pull a secret ring to unravel the stitching, then do some pirouettes,' she told him. 'The movement makes the peasant dress drop down and act as the underskirt to the ballgown—which unfurls and swishes round me. The coach takes me to the ball, and that's when I change out of the transformational dress into the proper ballgown.'

'That's really clever.' And he liked the fact that he learned new things, with her. 'Though have you just broken a rule—you know, like magicians are supposed not to tell anyone how they do their tricks?'

'No, because even when you know how it's done it still looks amazing and you can believe in the magic,' she said. 'On the nights I wasn't dancing, I'd sit and watch it from the wings because it's just astonishing. There's probably a video about it on YouTube, if you wanted to look it up.'

'I think I need to include the make-up and wardrobe departments in the show,' he said. 'And I love the sound of that transformation scene. Do you think Nathalie would agree to let me film you dancing that piece?'

'You'd have to ask her,' Pippa said.

'So what happens in a normal day, as a ballet dancer?' he asked.

'Classes—stretching and conditioning, then technical—followed by rehearsals. Nathalie's agreed that you can observe and I was thinking, it might be useful for you to do the stretching class, to get a feel for what it's like. I talked to Kenzo, our physical development lead, and he said you can come along.'

'Thanks. Let me check my diary,' Rory said, and took out his phone. 'You have Mondays off, so I'm assuming the next class is Tuesday. What time?'

'Nine, and Kenzo's very hot on punctuality,' she said.

'Got it,' he said. 'What happens in technical classes?'

'Barre work to start, then combinations in the centre, then the big jumps.'

'The ones where I wonder if they've secretly got a trampoline in the floor, because how can you humanly jump that high and move your legs so fast?' he checked.

She chuckled, and he noticed how her eyes crinkled at the corners. Almost like rays of sun, he thought.

'It takes a lot of practice,' she said. 'People dip in and out of rehearsals, depending on what their role is. After lunch, it's more rehearsals, maybe a break, and then the show.'

'So basically you're at the theatre from nine in the morning until after the show at night, either rehearsing or dancing? Those are seriously long days,' he said.

'But it's my choice to do it.' She shrugged. 'It's just how it is. I love what I do. I catch up with family and friends on the phone, and I get to see them on Sundays, if they're free—as doctors, my family all work unsociable hours, too.'

Guilt flooded through him. 'Sorry. I didn't mean to take up so much of your free time today—especially now I know it's so limited.'

'I didn't have anything planned today,' she said, 'or I would've said I was busy and suggested talking to you another time.'

'I appreciate you making time for me.'

'No problem.' She smiled. 'Now you know what my day-to-day life is like as a dancer, tell me about life as a television star.'

'It's probably easier to show you,' he said. 'Maybe you could shadow me when I do an interview, so you get an idea of what happens and the sort of thing I'd ask you, if you want to be part of the series,' he added hastily. 'And then I can show you how I edit the footage—how I decide what to include and what to leave out.'

'I take it you plan your questions before you do the interview?' she asked.

He nodded. 'I try to get a feel for my subject's background so I've got an idea of the kind of questions I want to ask, but they're more of a guide than something rigid. I try to let my subject lead and tell me things in their own words, because they're the expert,' he said. 'I'm looking forward to tomorrow's interview, because it's with a film score composer, Judith Parrish. She's only in her mid-twenties, and it's still quite rare to have a woman composing for films. Which is crazy,' he added, 'when you look at female pop stars and how many of them write their own songs.'

'What kind of films does she write for?' Pippa asked.

'She's written the score for a new version of *Persuasion*. I want to talk to her about that—what inspires her, how she approaches developing a score, what kind of research she does before she starts composing and how she structures it,' he said, He looked thoughtfully at her. 'If you decide to choreograph, later, maybe she'd be a good contact for you. Say, in developing a brand-new ballet.'

'I hadn't thought about that before,' she said. 'Developing something completely new. A new story, to new music and new routines, instead of reworking the classics.'

'Is that what you'd want to do in the future?' he asked.

'Maybe. That could be my plan for years ten to fifteen,' she said. And there was a light behind her eyes he hadn't seen before. Something new, something magical—perhaps even a dream so new she hadn't shared it with anyone else.

'Maybe she could write some pieces for your dance series, if you wanted new choreography,' she said.

Rory loved the idea of working with Pippa to create something completely new—and he told himself it was nothing to do with wanting to spend more time with her, and everything to do with developing his career towards producing critically acclaimed documentaries. 'Maybe. How long does it take to choreograph a new piece?' he asked.

'It depends on how long you want the piece to be, and whether it's a solo or for several dancers,' Pippa said. 'Choreographing's the quick bit. Teaching it to the dancers takes longer.'

Something was buzzing in his brain, something that felt like the light he'd seen in her eyes. Was it the excitement of new possibilities—or was it *her*, making him feel so different?

'If you're not doing anything else, you could come to Camden with me tomorrow and meet Judith,' he said impulsively.

'Won't she mind?'

'I'll call her this evening and check. But I'll tell her you're shadowing me because I'm hoping to work with you on another project. Plus, you work in the arts so you understand the importance of confidentiality.'

'All right,' she said, and it felt as if the sun had lit up the whole room—which, he thought, was totally crazy, considering that they were indoors and it was raining outside.

'Thank you. And I guess I've taken up enough of your Sunday,' he said.

'I do have a pile of laundry waiting for me,' she admitted. 'Though I've enjoyed today.'

'Me, too.' He wanted to linger, but he didn't want to scare her away.

'I'll see you tomorrow.'

'I'll check with Judith and text you the details later this evening,' he said. 'If she says yes, then I'll meet you at Camden Tube station at half-past nine.'

'OK. I'll wait to hear from you.'

He resisted the impulse to kiss her goodbye—it wasn't appropriate, and he wasn't supposed to be thinking about her in those terms—and instead watched her walk through the crowd. The way she moved, so graceful and sure, drew him. And he'd enjoyed talking with her; instead of sticking to social small talk, he'd been able to talk to her about something deeper, the kind of things he didn't usually share.

Pippa Barnes intrigued him. Maybe spending more time with her would help him shake off this weird sense of being hemmed in, which he'd been feeling ever since he'd got out of hospital. And maybe he could return the favour by making her see that she'd made the right choice in becoming a ballet dancer.

CHAPTER SEVEN

ON MONDAY MORNING, Rory was waiting outside the Tube station at Camden—making sure that he was well away from litter bins, the florist's stall, and anything else likely to attract wasps.

'Morning, sunshine,' Kenise said, walking up to him. 'Ready to go?'

'No. We need to wait for Pippa,' Rory said.

'Pippa?' Kenise raised her eyebrows. 'Why?'

'She's shadowing me today,' Rory explained. 'Just as I'm shadowing her tomorrow, though we're not actually filming—it's preliminary research.'

'Ri-i-i-ight,' Kenise said, sounding completely unconvinced.

'If she sees how I work, it might make her more relaxed about agreeing to do the show—and shadowing her will be helpful background for me,' Rory said.

'You're not doing this with any of the other dancers,' Kenise pointed out.

'Of course I am,' he said. 'I'm using the same structure for all the episodes: looking at the history of dance, famous dancers of the past, and then a day in the life of a modern dancer. We're filming them performing, and doing a video diary of them teaching me a routine.'

'But Pippa's the only one shadowing you,' Kenise said.

'She saved my life. I owe her.'

Kenise scoffed. 'Sounds to me like you're trying to find a good excuse. You really like her, don't you?'

Yes. And it was all a mess in his head. She'd made it clear she didn't want to get involved with anyone. How stupid would it be to let himself fall for someone who was unavailable? Almost as stupid as it had been to let himself fall for women who didn't see who he really was inside.

Except he thought Pippa *did* see him for exactly who he was. And that made her even more tempting.

'It's irrelevant,' he said. 'She's not looking for a relationship and neither am I.'

'You're protesting a bit too much, sweetie,' Kenise said.

He knew that. And he rather thought he was trying to convince himself as much as he was trying to convince Kenise. 'We're probably going to be colleagues. Which puts her completely off limits, because I don't want to risk making a mess of this documentary. Writing, presenting and producing: it's my chance to take the next step in my career, build myself up as someone people take seriously. Open some doors for me.'

'But you still like her.'

The worry must've shown on his face, because Kenise patted his shoulder. 'Don't worry. I'm not going to say anything in front of her.'

'Thank you,' he said.

'But if you're serious about the documentary, you need to focus on that and put your feelings for her to the side— at least for now,' Kenise said.

Which was pretty much how Pippa was approaching her chance for promotion, Rory thought. Work came first, second and last. Until last week, he wouldn't have had a problem with that, either. But then he'd nearly died, and it had changed him. Made him determined to live life to its fullest—to want everything. That made it hard for him to ignore the attraction he felt towards Pippa, even though he could come up with plenty of reasons why he should keep her at a distance. And he wasn't used to feeling so conflicted. 'Yeah,' he said. 'Let me take your camera.'

'I appreciate your gentlemanly concern, but I can manage,' Kenise said.

'I know you can, but it's heavy. I don't mind carrying it for a bit.'

She smiled at him. 'Right now you sound like my baby brother.'

'I guess,' he said, 'that's a step up from being like your ten-year-old.'

'Oh, you remind me of him as well,' she said, laughing.

Pippa wished she'd thought to ask Rory about the dress code. Did he wear a suit to do interviews, or would he opt for something more smart-casual? She'd chosen navy Capri pants, a navy top with stylised white daisies, flat shoes, and her hair was pulled back in a low ponytail, tied with a navy chiffon scarf. Hopefully it would be smart enough, but not over-formal.

When she came out of the Tube station, she looked round to find Rory. He was standing by the wall, a few paces away, with his camerawoman; clearly they had a good relationship, because they were laughing and Kenise was patting his shoulder. To her relief, he was wearing a white shirt, chinos and no tie: smart casual, then. Kenise was dressed all in black, which didn't surprise her; in her experience, photographers tended to wear black so they'd blend into the background and make their subjects relax, and she assumed that it was the same for video camerawork.

Today she'd get to see him at work, learn more about what made him tick—and she was really looking forward to it. Because they might be working together, she reminded herself; not because it meant a chance to spend more time with him.

Though she'd really enjoyed talking with him in the art gallery.

'Good morning,' she said brightly as she joined them.

'Ready to go? It's about a ten-minute walk,' Rory said.

Judith Parrish's flat was on the bottom floor of a Victorian house. Judith herself was a slight woman about the same height as Pippa, dressed in black trousers and a black T-shirt, her dark hair in a pixie cut.

'Lovely to meet you, Judith,' Rory said warmly, shaking her hand. 'This is Kenise, my camerawoman; and Pippa Barnes, the ballet dancer from the Fitzroy we spoke about yesterday.'

'Lovely to meet you, all,' Judith said. 'Come in.'

She ushered them into a living room which had gorgeous parquet flooring and a rug in the centre; an upright piano was set against one wall, with a cello case next to it; there was a sofa under the window, two tub chairs and a coffee table, and bookshelves in the alcove either side of the fireplace, which looked full of music scores.

'Would you mind if we moved the furniture a little?' Kenise asked. 'I'd like you and Rory to sit opposite each other in the tub chairs for the interview, but I could do with some room to move round you for extra shots.'

'Help yourself,' Judith said. 'Though I'd prefer the piano and cello to stay where they are.'

'Of course,' Rory said.

Judith smiled. 'I'll make some coffee.'

'Can I do anything to help?' Pippa asked.

'It's fine,' Judith said. Once she'd checked how everyone took their drinks, she headed for the kitchen while Rory and Kenise checked lighting and moved the chairs where they wanted them; Pippa sat on the sofa, out of the way.

When Judith came back and the drinks had been handed round, Rory said to her, 'I do have a list of questions, but basically we're going to chat and Kenise is going to film our conversation. I might stop you and ask you to repeat something, or ask you something in a different way—it doesn't mean you've done anything wrong, just that I'm keeping my options open when I come to edit the piece. Anything you don't want to answer, that's fine, and we can edit the question out without making it look awkward. If you can include my question in your answer, that'd be helpful, but it doesn't matter if you forget.'

Pippa listened, fascinated, as he got Judith to talk about her experience with music and how she developed a score.

Discovering that Judith had gone to a costumed Regency ball in Bath fanned the flames of the idea she'd had the previous day about creating something new for Rory's series.

Clearly he'd thought about it again, too, because he asked, 'The way Judith develops a score: is that how you develop choreography, Pippa?'

'It's a very similar process,' Pippa said. 'Just as Judith watches a film and works out the mood and the music to suit, I listen to music and work out the phrasing and which movements fit.'

'How long would it take to compose a two-minute piece and choreograph it?' Rory asked.

'Working out the choreography and writing it down might take an hour, maybe two,' Pippa said. 'Then I need to learn it so it's automatic, in my muscle memory. If I'm teaching someone else, I'd break it down into smaller phrases, and keep repeating them until the dancers know them.' She smiled. 'As you'll find out when you learn the dances for your series.'

'I could write something fairly quickly,' Judith said. 'I'd talk to the choreographer about the themes and the story we want to tell, and between us we'd come up with ideas we could work up. So if you wanted something set on a frosty winter night, say, I'd come up with staccato, glittery phrases.' She grinned. 'I'm cheating massively here because obviously this isn't mine, but winter, for me...' She walked over to the piano, sat down, and played the beginning of the 'Dance of the Sugar Plum Fairy'.

'You need quick, light movements in the choreography to match that,' Pippa said. She looked at the centre of room then at Judith. 'Would it be all right if I roll the rug back, take off my shoes and show him?'

'Of course,' Judith said.

'You don't necessarily need ballet shoes to dance. Obviously I don't have my pointe shoes with me so I'll do everything on demi—that's tiptoes, to you,' she said to Rory with a smile. 'Judith, please could you play something wintry?'

'How about this?' Judith played the middle section of the first movement of Vivaldi's 'Winter' from *Four Seasons*.

'Perfect—give me a minute or two to warm up,' Pippa said.

'I'll play from the start and you come in when you're ready?' Judith suggested.

Pippa did a very quick warm-up, then executed some light, quick but graceful movements when Judith got to the middle section. She finished with a pose and smiled at Rory. 'See? A frosty morning.'

'You just did that off the top of your head?' Rory asked.

'No. It's the "Fred Step"—the signature piece of the choreographer Frederick Ashton,' Pippa explained. 'It's a series of steps and you can repeat them however you like.'

'In a lot of music there's a short phrase which is repeated, inverted, then repeated again,' Judith said. She turned to Rory. 'What's your series about?

Rory explained it to her. 'Though I'm beginning to think it'd be good to ask the dancers to develop a new piece, too—say, two or three minutes.' He looked at Judith. 'Would you consider composing something for me?'

'I'd be happy to talk to your choreographers,' Judith said. She looked at Pippa. 'If that includes you, would you be happy to work with me on a piece?'

'I haven't actually agreed to do the series, yet,' Pippa said, 'but I'm leaning that way—and I love the idea of doing something fresh. Maybe you could include a bit about choreography for all of them, Rory,' she suggested.

'We could maybe do something wintry,' Judith said thoughtfully.

'Or maybe a year in a garden: spring with everything growing, summer all lush and in bloom, autumn with leaves coming down, and a frosty winter morning,' Pippa suggested.

'With you wearing a glittery tutu?' Judith asked.

'Or a chiffon skirt, one colour for each season,' Pippa said. 'At the end of each "movement" I could go offstage, where Wardrobe would be waiting to swap my skirt.'

'While you're changing costume, we'd have a short musical transition between the seasons,' Judith said.

'I wish we'd been recording that,' Rory said ruefully. 'It would've been perfect to include in the dance series.'

'Actually, I did record it,' Kenise said. 'Including Pippa dancing. I just need some noddies from you now, Rory.'

'What are noddies?' Pippa asked.

'Shots of Rory nodding his head with his listening face on—we use them in editing. You'll see it in TV interviews all the time,' Kenise explained.

She'd need to learn new jargon, then; though Rory would also need to learn new things. The more Pippa thought about it, the more she was tempted to do his show. And, if she was honest with herself, the more she was tempted by Rory himself...

Later that day, Rory took Pippa to the TV offices to review the footage from the interview. He showed her what he would cut, where he was going to splice in a section of an old home video Judith had sent, and where the film trailer with Judith's music would fit in.

'It's like putting together a gala show—making sure you balance each section and mix up the tender and the dramatic pieces, the solos and the ensembles,' Pippa said. 'And I get why Kenise filmed your noddies.'

'I ought to let you get back,' he said.

She smiled. 'I'd appreciate a reminder on how to get to the front door. All those corridors look the same.'

'I'll walk you out,' he said. 'I need to give your visitor's pass back, too.' He paused. 'What do I need to wear for the conditioning class tomorrow?'

'Whatever you'd normally wear to the gym,' she said.

'If you've got close-fitting tracksuit bottoms, that'd be good. And bring water.'

'Got it,' he said. 'Thank you for coming with me to see Judith today. And for your ideas—I never thought about getting everyone to do new choreography to original music.'

'I think it'd give the show an edge,' she said. 'But it's your show—and your call.'

'It's a collaboration,' he said, 'because we all have to work as a team for it to come together.'

'I guess,' she said.

She handed her badge in at the reception area and was signed out.

Rory walked outside with her. 'See you tomorrow.' He leaned forward as if to kiss her on the cheek. Except somehow his lips connected with the corner of her mouth.

'Sorry,' he mumbled.

Pippa's face felt hot, and she didn't dare look him in the eye. 'It's OK.'

'I...um...' His voice faded, as if he didn't know what to say.

'See you tomorrow,' she said, and headed in the direction of the Tube station. She could still feel the touch of his lips at the corner of her mouth, and it sent a shiver of pure desire through her. Far from being a friendly peck on the cheek, it had turned into something else entirely.

She was going to have to be very, very careful...

Rory headed for the Fitzroy Theatre on Tuesday morning, really hoping that he hadn't messed everything up yesterday. How could he have been so clumsy? He'd felt so at ease with Pippa that it had been natural to kiss her cheek—except he hadn't.

He'd kissed the corner of her mouth.

And although he'd apologised immediately and she'd said everything was fine, he knew it wasn't. She'd really blushed. Luckily she hadn't returned his gaze, because his face had felt as hot as hers had looked.

The worst thing was, he hadn't been able to stop thinking about it since. Being that close to her. What would it be like to kiss her properly? What would it be like if she kissed him back?

Had her blush been purely from embarrassment, or had she felt the same spark of desire that he had? Had she been thinking about their kiss, too, and wondering what it would be like if they really connected?

Even the thought of it made his mouth tingle with need.

He was going to have to be really careful today. Act all cool and calm and collected, even though inside he wasn't. He could focus on work...couldn't he?

Just as he walked up the steps, Pippa was there.

'Good morning. Ready for class?'

'Yes,' he fibbed. She was acting all brisk and breezy and professional, as if nothing had happened yesterday, so he'd follow her lead.

'Good. We're going through the stage door,' she said, shepherding him round to the back of the building and letting him in through an unobtrusive entrance. 'Here's the changing area, and this is the key for one of the guest lockers,' she said, giving him a key with a number on the fob. 'I'll meet you back here in five minutes and take you through to Kenzo's class.'

He changed in record time, put his things in the numbered locker and was ready when she came back to collect him.

The room she took him to was similar to his gym, with

mirrors on one long side. The only difference was that there were barres fixed to three of the walls.

A man who looked to be in his mid-thirties, with an incredibly athletic physique, was setting out hand weights and resistance bands. He looked up as they walked in. 'Morning, Pippa,' he said.

'Morning, Kenzo.' She smiled at him. 'Rory, this is Kenzo, our physical development lead,' she said. 'Kenzo, this is Rory. He's making a programme about ballet— Nathalie's spoken to you about it.'

He nodded. 'It's a good idea to come and do a class so you get an insight into what it takes to be a dancer, Rory. Do you have any gym experience?'

'I do weights twice a week,' Rory said. 'I used to enjoy walking but that'll have to be strictly outside wasp season for me now; I'm planning to go to the gym for cardio instead.'

'Sensible,' Kenzo said. 'I'll just check anyway—you know how to engage your core?'

Rory nodded.

'Good. Any injuries or health conditions I need to know about—apart from the wasp allergy, obviously?'

'No, and I've got my adrenaline pens with me,' Rory said.

'Glad to hear it,' Kenzo said. 'You'll probably know some of the exercises we do, but some might feel a little bit different because you'll use a dancer's position. Have you done glute bridges and calf raises before?'

'Yes,' Rory said.

'Good. It's all about strength and flexibility,' Kenzo said. 'The ones you probably won't know—Pippa, can you demonstrate plié squats?'

'Sure,' she said. 'This is second position feet.' She

stood with her feet apart, her toes turned out to the sides. 'Then you need second position arms.' She talked him through it. 'Start with bas bras—that's lowered arms— lift them up to first, as if you're holding a beach ball, then stretch your arms out to second, keeping them curved. Don't let your elbows drop.'

Realising she was expecting him to copy her moves, Rory did so. He looked down at his feet. 'I can't get my feet to go out the way yours are.'

'I wouldn't expect it,' Kenzo said. 'Work within the limits of what's comfortable for you, and do the turnout as far as you can.'

'Then you do the plié—bend your knees as you lower your body until your thighs are parallel with the floor. Back straight, chest lifted.' Pippa looked at him criti- cally as he copied her. '*Nearly.* Can I move your arms?'

'Sure,' he said, hoping he sounded much more cool, calm and collected than he actually felt. Even though it was an impersonal contact, his skin still tingled where she touched him to move his arms into the right position. What would it be like to feel her fingertips skating across his skin if they were alone, in a private space?

'Then push through your heels and straighten your legs,' she said. 'That's good.'

Next, she demonstrated arabesque lifts.

'There's no *way* my leg's going to go up that far be- hind me,' Rory said ruefully.

'Not the first time, but gradually your flexibility will improve. Do this every day for a month—you'll really see the difference in your movements,' Kenzo said.

'The same as with a relevé—a rise,' Pippa said. 'Face the wall and use the barre to get your balance—you can do this with the back of a chair at home. Feet together in parallel, then rise onto the balls of your feet.'

He followed her instructions.

'When you're ready, lift your hand from the barre and balance,' she said.

He lasted for three seconds before he started wobbling.

She smiled, but she wasn't laughing at him or pitying him. It was more like fellow feeling—encouragement, and it made him feel warm inside.

'Do that four or five times every day,' she said, 'and I guarantee you'll be able to hold the position for ages and move both arms into a variety of positions without your feet wobbling by the end of the month.'

'It's really good for balance and stability,' Kenzo said.

The final movement Pippa showed him was a port de bras, involving light hand weights and moving his arms in a similar way to the first exercise, plus lifting them over his head in what he always thought of as the 'classic' ballerina arms.

'Try to lift from your back, not your shoulders,' Kenzo said. 'Stand at the barre next to Pippa; you can follow her if you need to because she knows the routine. And we can have a chat after the class. Pippa said you wanted to know the science behind the training. I can show you what we do here, and you can let me know what you'd want to film—or what you'd want to try.'

'Thank you,' Rory said. 'That's really helpful.'

The rest of the class filed in. All the female dancers were wearing leotards and leggings with a cardigan, while the male dancers wore form-fitting tracksuit bottoms, shirts and hoodies.

'Everyone, this is Rory,' Pippa said. 'He presents an

arts show on TV. He's joining us for today's class with
Kenzo, then observing rehearsals and class with Nathalie's agreement.'

'Are you the one whose life Pippa saved at the garden
party?' one of the other dancers asked.

'Yes, and I'm very grateful,' Rory said.

Kenzo started music for the warm up, then gave instructions for the moves. Thanks to the quick introduction
Pippa had given him, Rory didn't feel completely useless.

His chat with Kenzo afterwards meant that he missed
seeing Pippa's class, but he was able to watch the first
set of rehearsals. He stayed for lunch—she'd brought an
extra wrap for him—then watched the full rehearsal in
the afternoon. It was a dress rehearsal for *Swan Lake*,
and Pippa was dancing the role of Odile/Odette. He'd
seen the ballet several times, over the years, but Pippa's
performance really stood out for him. Not just the per-
fection of the technical stuff, which was impressive in
its own right, but the way she made him *feel* the story.
He could really believe she'd been enchanted and turned
into a swan, and only the love of the handsome Prince
could break the spell. It had made him want to rush onto
the stage, hold her close, and tell her that he'd fight the
wicked sorcerer for her.

Which would be the worst thing he could do, and it
would make her run a mile.

Why was he even letting himself think about her in
those terms?

He really needed to get a grip.

'I don't know what they're called,' he said when she
walked off the stage and joined him in the auditorium,
'but that bit when you're Odile and you do all those pirouettes at the end—that was absolutely amazing.'

'The famous thirty-two fouettés,' she said. 'That piece is notorious, technically, because you're supposed to stay in one place and it's very easy to travel a little bit.'

'You looked to me as if you stayed in one place. But how did you not get dizzy?' he asked.

'Spotting,' she said. 'You look at one place in the room and watch it for as long as you can before you turn your head, and bring your head back as quickly as possible.'

'I'd better let you rest before tonight's show,' he said, 'but thank you for arranging today with Nathalie and Kenzo.'

'You're very welcome,' she said. 'Are you coming to do the class tomorrow?'

'If you don't mind,' he said, 'and maybe I can watch your class afterwards, as I missed it today?'

'No problem,' she said.

He collected his things from the locker, and she walked out through the foyer with him.

'I hope the show goes—' he began.

'"Break a leg" is what you say,' she cut in swiftly. 'Dancers are a superstitious lot, and that includes me.'

'Break a leg,' he said.

Not wanting to make the same mistake he'd made the previous evening, he contented himself with shaking her hand. His fingers tingled where his skin touched hers. He was going to have to learn to deal with this, and fast, because he didn't want to put her off doing the show with him.

Though it wasn't the only reason he needed to keep himself at a distance. She'd made it clear that she wanted her involvement with him to remain on a purely professional level.

'See you for breakfast tomorrow in the café round the corner?' he asked.

'Ten past eight at the latest,' she said. 'We need enough time to digest breakfast before class.'

'All right. Ten past eight,' he said.

Though he couldn't stop thinking about her all the way home. That evening, when he was doing some research, he found himself doodling her name in the margins of his notes. It felt horribly like being a teenager all over again, and he was beginning to see what she meant about him distracting her; she was certainly distracting him. Even though he knew there was no sense to it, he *wanted* her. And it wasn't going to happen.

'For pity's sake, Rory, stop whining and get on with your work,' he told himself loudly, and tried to focus on the book he'd picked up from the library.

It didn't work.

A cold shower didn't help, either.

All he could think about was her. Seizing the day. Making the most of every minute.

In the end, he made himself a mug of tea and thought about it. There was definitely something between them; her reaction when he'd accidentally kissed the corner of her mouth told him that she felt the same kind of pull.

She didn't want a relationship.

He didn't want a relationship.

So was there a compromise? Could they, perhaps, have a mad fling? Knowing that there wasn't the pressure of a future and anyone else's expectations, maybe they could simply enjoy their physical reaction to each other. No strings, no pressure, no distraction: just mutual pleasure.

He'd have to work out a way of asking her without making it sound demanding or sleazy.

But maybe if they could get it out of both their systems, they'd be able to concentrate.

* * *

On Wednesday morning, Rory walked into the café at five past eight. He thought he might beat her to it, but Pippa was already there, sitting at a table with a coffee. She waved to him and smiled, and his heart felt as if it had done a backflip.

'Morning. I haven't ordered food yet, but I needed a coffee,' she said as he slid into the seat opposite her.

'What do you recommend?' he asked.

'Everything's good, here—but I'm having scrambled eggs on seeded toast,' she said. 'And then Greek yogurt with blueberries and chia seeds.'

'Scrambled eggs sounds good,' he said. 'Though I could be tempted by a blueberry muffin.'

Once the waitress had taken their order, she asked, 'How do you feel, this morning?'

Better for seeing her. Not that he could tell her that. 'A tiny bit stiff,' he admitted.

'You need to do some stretching in the evening if your muscles are tight. Stretching's the thing that everyone forgets in the gym because they're in a rush,' she said.

'I'm definitely guilty of that,' he said. 'I know I need to warm up before a workout, but I'm not always good at remembering to cool down afterwards.'

'It only takes five minutes, and it'll make a difference,' she said. 'So what's your schedule looking like, this week?'

'Research for the dance show, talking to some experts, seeing a curator about an exhibition of commonplace books, and I've got an interview tomorrow morning with a stained-glass restorer working on some of the oldest stained-glass in England,' he said. 'I'm going to Norfolk for that one.'

'Sounds interesting,' she said.

'I'd offer to let you come with me,' he said, 'but I assume you're working?'

'I am,' she said, 'though I'm not dancing tomorrow night. If you're free tomorrow evening and you're back from Norfolk, you could come and watch the show in the wings with me.'

'I'd like that very much,' he said.

When they did Kenzo's class, he was aware that everyone else was much more graceful than he was, and had a much wider range of movements; but he could also balance a little more easily than he had, the previous day.

On Thursday, he found he actually missed doing the conditioning class. But the interview went well, and when he met Pippa at the Fitzroy that evening he thoroughly enjoyed watching *Swan Lake* from a very privileged position in the wings, seeing how things worked backstage. He remembered what she'd told him about how slickly the wardrobe, make-up and hair team worked, and he could see it in action for himself.

And, best of all, Pippa reached for his hand when Odile was pretending to be Odette and seducing Siegfried into marrying him. She kept holding his hand during the whole of the last act, when Siegfried realised his mistake and tried to find Odette. He realised she was crying, and moved closer to her, releasing her hand and sliding his arm round her shoulders to comfort her; and he was surprised to realise that his own lashes were wet, too.

'Sorry about that,' Pippa said at the end of the curtain calls, mopping her eyes with a tissue and moving slightly so Rory dropped his arm from round her shoulders.

'Though I did warn you that *Swan Lake* makes me cry, every single time.'

'It's very emotional,' he agreed. 'The music, the dance, all together…it's quite a spectacle.'

They walked back to the Tube station together; his hand brushed against hers once, twice, making little sparks rush through her. And then his fingers caught hers lightly.

Maybe it was the emotion left over from the show, and remembering how good it had felt to have his arm round her, holding her close through the final dramatic act, but she didn't pull her hand away.

And they were still loosely holding hands when they got to the station.

She wasn't ready to let go.

His expression told her it was the same for him.

Common sense. That was what she needed. A neutral conversation. Small talk. Don't look at his lips or start to wonder how they'd feel. He'd made it clear he wasn't looking for a relationship. She wasn't, either.

So why couldn't she untangle her fingers from his? Why couldn't she stop looking at his mouth?

'Did you enjoy the view from the wings?' she asked— and hoped he didn't hear the rustiness in her voice.

'Stunning,' he said. 'You were right about the magic of the performance—even when you know how things work, it doesn't stop you enjoying the spectacle.'

'I love watching from the wings. You can feel the buzz from the audience as well as the energy from the stage,' she said.

'I think I get that, now,' he said.

He was definitely looking at her mouth, before glancing up at her eyes.

And she knew she was doing the same. Wondering. Thinking about it.

She wasn't sure which of the two of them moved first, but then her arms were round his neck and his were round her waist, and they were kissing. Tiny, tentative brushes of their lips against each other, teasing and tempting, building the heat, until she felt as if she were burning up from the inside.

She broke the kiss, but she couldn't take her arms from round his neck.

'That wasn't supposed to happen,' he said, and she was gratified to hear that he sounded as shaken as she felt.

'We shouldn't be doing this,' she said, trying to talk herself into moving away from him, even while she yearned to be closer.

Except he was clearly listening to the words she was saying and didn't realise how much he tempted her, because he said, 'You're right, it's a bad idea,' and disentangled himself gently from her.

Hearing him agree with her common sense so easily and so rapidly made her wish that he'd raised at least a token protest. How stupid she'd been, virtually throwing herself at him.

Her misery must have shown on her face, because he said quietly, 'I admit—I wanted to kiss you, and half of me doesn't regret doing it.'

Which meant that half of him *did* regret it. So he was as torn as she was, between the common sense that said 'don't take the risk', and the longing that said 'forget the world and do it now'.

He stroked her face. 'We can't get involved with each other. Even if we—' his voice cracked slightly '—want to. You're focused on your career. I'm focused on my documentary, and hoping it opens doors for my future. Neither of us has the space in our lives for any kind of relationship.'

He was talking complete sense.

But.

Was it her imagination, or did his eyes hold a very different message? He'd said half of him *didn't* regret it. That he'd wanted to kiss her, too.

'And I want you to be in my documentary. I don't want to ruin our working relationship,' he finished.

'I don't want to ruin that, either,' she said. 'I don't want to get distracted and lose my promotion. Or to have to choose between ballet and a relationship, because I can't give enough to both of them at the same time.'

'I've given up dating. I've been there, done that, made all the wrong choices,' he said. And then he moistened his lower lip. 'But.'

Oh, God. She wanted to kiss him again. Right here, right now, until they were both dizzy. Suddenly it was hard to breathe. 'But?'

'This *thing*—this pull between us…it's not just me, is it?' he checked.

The vulnerability in his expression made her tell the truth. 'No.'

'I could walk away from you now,' he said. 'Put you back at arm's length. Except I know how much I'd regret it.'

So would she. Because she'd never felt this kind of attraction to anyone else. She'd always been too focused on her job to even *notice* anyone else.

'What are you suggesting?' she asked.

'Maybe,' he said, 'we need to do the crazy thing. Get it out of our systems. And then, once we've done that, we can go back to being sensible.'

'You think that would work?' Because she wasn't convinced that a fling would actually get him out of her system. 'What if we…?'

'Fall in love? We won't,' he said. 'Neither of us want a relationship. Both of us want to chase our dreams. So that makes a fling safe for us. We're on the same page. No strings, no promises, no holding each other back. And because we know it's temporary, right from the start, neither of us will get hurt. Neither of us will be let down. Neither of us will get distracted from our dreams.'

'Uh-huh.' It sounded perfect. But what if…?

Clearly her doubts showed, because he sighed. 'If I'm being honest, I'm not entirely sure it'll work. But right now we're both distracted anyway. We might as well be distracted and enjoy it, than distracted and…well…' He groaned. 'See, that's proof. Before I met you, I was never incoherent. But, the first time I met you, I made next to no sense when I spoke.'

'To be fair, you'd just been stung by a wasp and were having a massive anaphylactic reaction,' she said.

He nodded. 'That's the thing. Nearly dying has made me realise how precious life is—how I should make the most of every minute. That's why I don't want to walk away from you—from whatever this is.'

She raised her eyebrows at him. 'You sound like a seventeenth-century poet telling me to seize the day.'

He raised his eyebrows back at her. 'You did A level sciences. I didn't think you'd know Herrick and Marvell.'

'Some of my fellow dancers did English—and they love sharing poetry,' she said. '"Gather ye rosebuds while ye may."'

'As long as there aren't any wasps in the roses,' he said wryly.

'So what do we do now?' she asked.

'I want you, Pippa,' he said simply. 'I know you're busy at work. I know you're driven and you want that promotion more than anything else. I respect that, and I'm not looking to change you. I want you to do my show, because I love the way you dance and I think you'd be fabulous on screen. I think my viewers are going to fall in love with you. If you want to keep things between us strictly work, that's fine. We'll both be sensible and do that. But if you want to be with me, too—keeping everything low key, no pressure, no demands—that's also fine.' His eyes held hers. 'It's your choice.'

She could keep herself strictly focused on her work; or she could give in to the attraction and see what happened. He had the same reservations that she did; and he was right. They were on the same page. This would be safe.

'You're busy at work, too,' she said. 'Your documentary series could lead to all sorts of things—maybe opportunities to work abroad. Paris, America, Australia. And I'm based here. It'd be sensible to…well, not start something we can't finish.'

'I know. But I don't want to be sensible,' he said. 'I want to make the most of every second.'

And maybe they could do that without making promises. Or *almost* no promises. 'It's exclusive, while it lasts?'

'Neither of us has the time for a fling with each other, let alone a fling with someone else as well.' He brushed the pad of his thumb against her lower lip. 'But, yes, it would be exclusive.'

'All right,' she said. 'I'll do the show.' She paused. 'And…'

'And?' he asked, his voice rough with need.

'Carpe diem,' she said, and kissed him.

CHAPTER EIGHT

On Friday, Rory was busy at the studio all day but couldn't stop thinking about Pippa. He still couldn't quite believe that he'd asked her to have a fling with him—or that she'd agreed to it. He went hot all over at the memory of the way she'd kissed him last night. How long had it been since someone had made him feel like a teenager?

But he managed to focus on his guests for the show, and made sure they all enjoyed the experience. Showbiz was a small world, and he wanted to keep his reputation of being a pleasure to work with rather than risk people thinking that he was just dialling it in.

Later that evening, his phone pinged with a text from Pippa.

Loved the show. Want to have breakfast tomorrow?

He knew she was due at the Fitzroy at nine-fifteen sharp for Kenzo's class. He texted back.

Our café, five past eight?

Works for me. Come to class after?

Sure. How did Swan Lake go tonight?

Fine. Thirty minutes of curtain calls!

Deserved, he thought. Watching her dance was a joy.

When he woke, the next morning, even though it was raining it felt like a beautiful day—because he was going to be seeing Pippa.

He was sitting in the café at eight o'clock, literally a minute before she walked through the door. How beautiful she was, he thought, how graceful and lovely; she made the day feel brighter just by walking into a room.

'Hey,' she said and sat opposite him.

'Hey, you,' he said, smiling back. 'I missed not seeing you yesterday.'

'I missed not seeing you, too,' she admitted.

When the waitress came over, she ordered coffee and eggs Florentine; he ordered the same.

'What are you dancing tonight?' he asked.

'One of the Two Swans,' she said.

'You look so cute in a tutu,' he said.

She dipped her head in acknowledgement. 'Thank you.'

'Cute, full stop,' he added.

Her grin widened. 'I know someone very cute, too. Though I don't think I'd put him in a tutu.'

'How would you dress me for ballet?' he asked, suddenly curious.

'As the Stranger, in Matthew Bourne's *Swan Lake*. All in black. That dance in Act Three is *incredibly* sexy. Or Oberon in *The Dream*, with a spiky crown and fairy wings and an outfit that looks as if you're part of the forest, wreathed in ivy and berries.' She took her phone out and found him a photograph. 'Like this. All wild and elemental.'

He looked at the photo. 'Very Green Man.' And not at all how he saw himself.

'As a character, I think Oberon needs his comeuppance. But he's very pretty to look at,' she said.

'I'll take that as a compliment,' he said. 'For the record, I agree with you. I don't know the ballet, but I know the play—and Oberon is an arse. In his shoes, I wouldn't have tried to steal the child from Titania or tried to humiliate her.'

'I know.' She blew him a kiss, and he went hot all over.

To the point where he just blurted it out. 'I was thinking—as tomorrow's Sunday, you don't have to be at the Fitzroy in the morning. Can I make you dinner tonight after the show?'

'That's very kind of you to offer,' she said.

Wanting to circumvent the 'but' that he could see so obviously in her face, he said, 'I can drive you home from my place after dinner.' He paused. 'Or—if you want to— you could stay over. I have a spare toothbrush. Maybe we can do something tomorrow, if you're free.'

'Sorry. I'm going to see my sisters tomorrow,' she said.

They'd only agreed on their fling last night. It was just between the two of them. It was ridiculous—more than that, it was unreasonable, he told himself sharply—to feel disappointed that she didn't want to introduce him to her family. 'Have fun,' he said.

'My sisters think I'm a horrible workaholic who needs a social life. If they met you, they'd drive me crackers with a ton of questions.'

'To be fair, you *are* a workaholic who needs a social life,' he said. 'But I rather like being a workaholic, too. And I don't want a social life like the one I had a few months ago.'

'Are you saying it takes one to know one?' she teased, her gorgeous eyes crinkling at the corners.

'Yes. So can I cook you dinner tonight?' he asked.

'I'd like that—and you're welcome to come and watch the show in the wings, if you're not busy,' she said.

He was, but he'd catch up with work later. 'I'd love that,' he said.

'Come to the stage door for quarter to seven,' she said, 'and I'll take you through.'

After breakfast, they did the conditioning class. This time round, Rory found it easier.

Kenzo came over to him at the end of the class. 'Well done. I can see the improvement in your balance already.'

'Thank you,' Rory said, feeling as if he'd achieved something.

'Told you so,' Pippa said with a cheeky wink. 'See you later.'

Later. When he needed to impress her with his cooking—no, he corrected mentally, he needed to be *himself*. This wasn't about him. She'd be hungry after the performance and wouldn't want to wait hours for him to fuss about in the kitchen. He could cheat and buy something from the chiller section at the supermarket, but he wanted to make a bit more of an effort. Something that he could make this morning, leave in the fridge, and reheat quickly tonight. For pudding, he played it safe, buying a selection of summer berries and a tub of really good vanilla ice cream.

Back in his kitchen, he roasted chunks of aubergine on a tray with tomatoes and garlic, and made a batch of gnocchi. Once the vegetables were done, he finished making the Norma sauce; the flavours would develop nicely in the fridge during the day, and when he and Pippa got back here after the show it would take about five minutes to boil the kettle, cook the gnocchi and reheat the sauce.

Satisfied that dinner would be fine, he spent the afternoon researching for his documentary and making notes.

After the final close of the curtain, Pippa showered and changed, then met Rory in the auditorium.

'I've called a taxi,' he said, 'because it's quicker at this time of night. We'll be home in ten minutes.'

She knew Notting Hill was pretty, but she couldn't help being charmed when the taxi dropped them on one of the cobbled streets. The mews houses in Rory's street were all painted pretty pastel ice-cream colours; his house was cream, and there were bay trees in terracotta pots either side of the grey front door. Other houses had pots of tulips underneath the window; one had an old tin bath full of herbs; and one had a beautiful canopy of wisteria.

'What a gorgeous neighbourhood,' she said.

'Thank you.' He smiled at her. 'I love it, here—and I'm lucky because all my neighbours are nice, too.' He unlocked the front door and ushered her inside. 'The bathroom's here on the left,' he said gesturing to a door; the other side of the hallway appeared to be cupboards.

Inside, the entire ground floor had been opened up into one room, with a stripped pale wooden floor and cream walls. There was a pale grey kitchen in an alcove at one end of the room. The dining area was in the middle of the room, next to a cast-iron fireplace; the table was already set for two. At the far end was a comfortable living room area with a large sofa, bookshelves and a state-of-the-art TV.

There were exquisite framed paintings on the walls, and an open staircase leading up to the next floor. One of the paintings looked familiar. 'Isn't that the picture you showed me in the National?' Pippa asked.

'It's a good-quality print,' he said. 'Though the oils are all originals. When I was interviewing the curator of the Hammershøi exhibition, she told me about a group of modern painters who were influenced by him. I went to their studios and bought the ones that caught my eye.'

'I'm sure I've heard someone say that when it comes to art it's better to buy something you love, rather than something you think will turn out to be an investment,' she said.

'That's a good rule,' he agreed.

'They're lovely. It's all about the light, isn't it?'

He nodded. 'Dinner will be literally five minutes. Can I get you a glass of wine?'

'Thank you for the offer, but it'd send me straight to sleep,' she said. 'Some water would be lovely, though, please.'

He went over to the kitchen area and fetched her a glass.

'Thank you. Is there anything I can do to help?' she asked.

'It's just a question of boiling the kettle for the gnocchi and heating the sauce through,' he said. 'Please, make yourself at home.' He lit the candle in the middle of the dining table and headed back to the kitchen area.

Pippa browsed the books on his shelves, glass in hand. As she'd expected, knowing that his degree was in English, there was lots of classic literature, plus a shelf of art books. The mantelpiece was covered with framed family photographs, very similar to her own collection: weddings, christenings, his graduation and what she assumed were the latest photographs of his nieces and nephews. Rory was clearly very close to his family.

He'd switched on a smart speaker, and a gentle Einaudi

piece flooded into the room. It was the perfect music to chill to, she thought.

'Dinner is served, madam,' he said, a couple of minutes later, placing two bowls on the table. He turned the overhead light down so the candlelight flickered.

'This smells delicious,' she said as she sat opposite him.

'And it's properly home-made, not shop bought,' he said. 'Gnocchi with sauce *alla* Norma.'

She blinked. 'You made your own gnocchi?'

'It's pretty simple,' he said. 'And quick.'

'I appreciate it,' she said, and took a bite. 'Ooh, that's fabulous.'

'Thank you.' He looked pleased. 'Mum always said she didn't want to raise men who were domestically incompetent. She taught all of us to cook, and Jamie and I did just as many chores as Lottie when we were growing up.'

'But your dad's an earl. Surely you had…' She tried to think of a less inflammatory word than *servants*. 'People to help with the domestic stuff?'

'We do,' he said. 'The hall would be a bit much to handle without staff to help us, inside and out. But Mum wanted the three of us to have a normal-ish upbringing, so we'd grow up appreciating our privilege rather than becoming like those entitled twerps who treat people with contempt.'

'I like the sound of your mum,' Pippa said approvingly.

He smiled. 'Everyone gets on with my mum. She can be a bit bossy in a crisis, but that's probably a good thing—she doesn't panic or flap.' He wrinkled his nose. 'Apart from last week. That drove me bananas. Though, to be fair, the wasp thing gave her a bit of a scare.'

'It would have freaked everyone in my family, too, even though they're all doctors,' Pippa said. She looked at him. 'They all saw me on your show. And I felt there was a bit of "told you so" from them.'

'That you'd done the CPR well? To be fair, you did. You saved my life. And my family appreciate that, too.' He spread his hands. 'They also noticed the dancing and they're all getting tickets for the gala show.'

'I bought tickets for my family,' Pippa said.

He frowned. 'Surely they bought their own?' And then he must've remembered the little she'd told him, because he said, 'Or is that the only way you think they'll come to see you dance?'

'My sisters and brothers-in-law would. But my parents…it's awkward,' she said. 'Even giving them tickets felt as if I'm rubbing it in that I chose something they didn't want for me.'

'And when they do see you dance, you feel as if you have to do twice as well as you've ever done before?' he asked gently. 'Pippa—you do *know* you dance like an angel?'

'Thank you but, I wasn't fishing for compliments,' she said.

'I know that,' he said. 'A career in the arts is hard enough, without the added pressure of feeling you've let people down by not doing what they wanted. Have you ever considered that they might be the ones letting *you* down, by not supporting you to follow your dreams?'

'Yes, but I'm the baby. I'm kind of meant to follow in their footsteps.' She sighed. 'I found a way to follow my dream. But that's why I have to get the promotion. Otherwise all the disappointment I've caused them, the way I've put dance as a priority over my family—that'd be for nothing.'

He reached across the table and squeezed her hands. 'You're good enough to get that promotion. And plenty of people prioritise their career, especially in the early years.'

'I don't do as much as I should to stay in touch,' she said. 'I feel guilty about that.'

'It goes both ways,' Rory said. 'If you're the one who always makes the phone calls, or always messages first—that's not fair.'

'They call me and message me,' Pippa said. 'But I don't make enough effort. I find excuses for why I can't drop in and see them. Usually work-related.'

'Once you've got the promotion, you'll have time to look at your work-life balance,' Rory said. 'But I get what you mean. My family try hard not to ask me if I've met someone or when I'm going to settle down—but that's more pressure than if they asked me straight out, because I can see what they're thinking. Whenever they ask me to some social event, I'm always wondering if they've invited someone to introduce me to.'

'Maybe you need to invent a partner,' she said.

'Maybe,' he said.

'But what I don't get,' she said. 'Is why you haven't already been snapped up?'

'Because I'm rubbish at picking dates,' he said. 'The last half a dozen—they've only wanted me because of who my family is, or because they think I can get them into celebrity parties, their photo in *Celebrity Life!* magazine, or I'd be a useful stepping stone in their own TV career. And I'm at the point where I think that being *myself* just isn't enough for anyone. I'm so tired of it. That's why I stopped dating.'

Not being enough.

She definitely knew how that felt.

Maybe she could help him; or maybe they could help

each other. 'Just to be clear: I don't want you for your family,' Pippa said. 'And me doing the documentary—that's a win for both of us.' She spread her hands. 'As for this thing... I'm see you exactly for who you are. Someone I like. Someone I find attractive. Someone who makes me see things in a slightly different way. So I guess in my eyes, you're enough just as you are.'

He took her hand, dropped a kiss on her palm and folded her fingers round it. 'That's a lovely thing to say.'

'I meant it,' she said.

His eyes were very, very blue. 'I appreciate it. Now, would you like coffee?'

Which was a very nice way of changing the subject, she thought. 'Not for me, thanks—though if you have any camomile tea, that'd be lovely.'

'Sorry.' He shook his head. 'Though my sister Lottie was on a health kick earlier this year and I bought green tea for her. Would that be OK?'

'No, it's fine. I'll stick with water,' she said. 'Can I do the washing up?'

'Absolutely not.' He looked at her. 'Would you like me to drive you home now? Or can I persuade you to stay a little longer and dance with me?'

Stay or go. He'd made it clear that it was her choice. They'd agreed: no strings, no pressure.

'What sort of dance?' she checked.

'A slow dance,' he said. 'Nothing formal or structured. Just you and me, and the kind of Saturday night radio station that plays all the old smoochy stuff without too much chatting in between.'

She couldn't remember the last time she'd done anything like that. 'That sounds good,' she said.

He switched the music to a digital radio station that

was playing an old song she loved, Paul Weller's 'You Do Something to Me'; then he drew her into his arms. As they swayed softly together, he dipped his head so his cheek was right next to hers.

This wasn't the kind of dancing she did very often, but she loved the feeling of being so close to Rory: the soft music, the candlelight, the scent of the bergamot candles... When was the last time someone had done something this romantic with her? She had no idea, but right at that moment she felt *cherished*.

Giving in to temptation, she moved her head slightly, and the corners of their mouths touched.

And it was as if she'd just lit touchpaper, because all of a sudden they were kissing, really kissing, hot and urgent and needy.

When he broke the kiss, his pupils were huge in the candlelight, and she had no idea how long they'd been kissing. She just knew that her whole body was quivering with need.

'I can drive you home now,' he said. 'Or I can drive you home tomorrow morning, in time for you to meet your sisters.'

He'd really paid attention to what she'd said, she thought. And he wasn't demanding anything: he was giving her the choice.

'Tomorrow morning,' she said.

'I was hoping you'd say that,' he said. He kissed her again, scooped her up, blew out the candle, and carried her up the stairs.

CHAPTER NINE

THE NEXT MORNING, Pippa woke early; for a moment, the unfamiliar light in the room threw her, but then she remembered where she was. Rory was sprawled on the bed beside her; he looked very cute asleep. Sleeping Beauty, she thought, and she couldn't resist waking him with a kiss.

'Well, good morning,' he said, stroking her hair back from her face. 'And you've just made it that little bit better.'

Just as he'd promised, the previous night, he had a new toothbrush for her, and he'd put fresh towels in the bathroom, urging her to use whatever she wanted.

After a breakfast of toast and peanut butter, along with excellent coffee, he drove her back to Hackney. 'Have fun with your sisters,' he said.

'You have a lovely day, too,' she said.

'I'll spend it being nagged about wasps,' he said. 'Everyone's coming up to London for lunch with my parents.'

She leaned over to kiss him. 'I'm sure they won't nag. They just want to see for themselves that you've recovered.'

'Maybe,' he said. 'At least I get the fun of playing cards with my nieces and nephews.' He laughed. 'Those angelic little faces hide the souls of pure card sharps.'

He looked the picture of a doting uncle as he talked about them, and a little warning bell rang in the back of her head. Did this mean Rory wanted children?

Not that it was a real issue. They were having a fling, which meant keeping it light and not serious. But maybe she needed to remember not to get carried away: not to get used to having him in her life, because she couldn't give him what he wanted and she didn't want to add him to the long, long list of people she'd already let down.

'That sounds familiar,' she said, forcing herself to smile brightly. 'With us it's Monopoly, and my youngest niece always seems to end up with all the green and purple sets. You should see the glee on her face when she collects the rent on multiple hotels.'

He chuckled, and kissed her back. 'Speak to you soon.'

The second he got to his parents' house he was wrapped in fierce hugs. Firstly by his mother, which he'd expected; secondly by his elder brother, which—given that Jamie really wasn't the demonstrative sort—he hadn't.

'I don't care if you're not the spare any more, since Phin was born—you're way more important to me than the estate is. You stay away from wasps, you hear?' Jamie asked, his eyes narrowing.

'Absolutely,' Lottie, his sister, agreed. 'And you need to wear this.'

Rory dubiously eyed the box she handed him. 'What is it?'

'Open it and put it on,' she said, putting her hands on her hips and fixing him with her bossiest stare.

He opened it to see a bracelet made from black plaited leather, with a silver tag embellished with a red medical alert symbol and engraved with the words *Anaphylaxis—info inside*.

'Wear it,' Lottie said. 'Then if anything happens and you can't get to your adrenaline pen in time, whoever comes to the rescue will see the bracelet and know to open this panel to get all your medical information.'

'It looks like a manacle,' he said.

'I don't care. It'll keep you safe.' Lottie added his third fierce hug of the morning. 'I don't want my baby brother at risk.'

'I won't be taking any risks,' he assured her.

'Just wear the bracelet,' Lottie said. 'Please. So I can sleep at night.'

He gave in and fastened it round his wrist. 'Happy, now?'

'Better,' Lottie said. 'But oh, dear God, when Mum rang us last weekend...'

'You rushed up to see me for yourself. You've spoken to me every day since, both of you. You know I'm absolutely fine,' Rory said. '*Really*. You two are the first people I'd come to if something was wrong, I promise. Just as I hope you know I'm there for you.'

She ruffled his hair. 'We do.'

Jamie gave him the gentlest punch. 'Yes. We do. But we still worry about you.'

'Don't,' Rory said. 'I might be the baby, but I'm sensible.'

'You're a TV star. Sensible and celeb don't go together,' Lottie teased.

He laughed. 'They do in my case.'

'Not when you keep dating unsuitable women,' she said. 'You need to find someone nice.'

He had—but he wasn't ready to talk about that, yet.

'Jamie and I could find you someone,' Lottie persisted.

'That's kind, but no. Consider me off the market. I'm concentrating on my career for now.' As for Pippa... He liked her. A lot. But they'd agreed to nothing more serious than a fling. Looking to the future would put too much pressure on their relationship. No promises meant no disappointments—for both of them.

After lunch, the children all asked to go to the park.

'I'll stay here,' Rory said. 'The park's prime wasp territory. Much as I like playing football with you, I don't want to make it one-nil to the wasps.'

'We'll be on guard for you, Uncle Rory,' Phin, his oldest nephew, said immediately.

'We can flap at them so they fly away,' added seven-year-old Bertie, not to be outdone.

'Thanks for the offer, boys, but firstly you *never* flap at a wasp—it makes them panic and send out "help" signals, so the rest of their mates come to back them up. And, secondly, wasps can fly faster than you can run,' Rory said.

Phin scoffed. 'No *way*.'

'Yes, way,' Rory insisted. 'The average speed of a wasp is seven miles an hour.'

'But they wouldn't be able to fly very far,' Bertie said. 'They'd get tired and have to stop.'

'*Average* speed,' Rory said. 'If the wind's right, and it's really annoyed, a wasp can fly at speeds of up to thirty miles an hour.' He mimicked a wasp speeding over to them. 'Zzzzz...'

'Now you're really teasing us,' Phin said.

'Am I? As a journalist, I always do my research before I use facts and figures. Look it up, my young sceptic,' Rory said, handing over his phone.

Phin put the question into a search engine and narrowed his eyes as he read the answer. 'That's amazing!' he said at last.

'Wasps are amazing,' Rory said. 'Look up pictures of

their nests. They're works of art—and it's incredible to think they're all made with wood-shavings and wasp spit.'

'Wasp spit? Yuck!' said Sarah, his oldest niece.

'It's clever stuff,' Rory said. 'Off to the park with you. I'm staying put. And, while you're out, I'll raid Granny's kitchen and make cake.'

'I want to make cakes with you, Uncle Rory! I don't want to play football,' Lydia, Lottie's three-year-old, said. 'We could make fairy cakes. Granny bought sparkles to go on the top.'

'OK to leave her with me, Lottie?' Rory asked.

'Just don't let her get completely covered in flour,' Lottie said, with a weary nod.

'We'll borrow one of Granny's tea towels and use it as an apron,' Rory said. 'And I like the sound of those sparkles. Come on, Lyds. Let's go and make cake.'

The rest of the adults headed off to the park with the children, leaving Rory with Lydia. He got his niece to count out the paper cases as she put them in the bun tin, helped her crack the eggs and fished out bits of shell when her back was turned, and helped her spoon the mixture into the cases. He thoroughly enjoyed making pink buttercream icing with her, letting her smear it all over the top of the fairy cakes; sprinkling tiny silver stars and pink edible glitter on top was huge fun.

By the time they'd finished baking—and Rory had managed to clear up the glitter, which had spread over a surprisingly large area of his mother's kitchen—all felt right again with his world. He was in the middle of a family he loved dearly, and who loved him all the way back. Though, weirdly, a little part of him was starting to wonder if his siblings were right. If he needed to start dating someone who'd fit in with their family, just by being herself. As for Pippa… Well, she had her own pressures to deal with. She didn't need to deal with his issues, too. He liked her. And that would have to be enough for now.

Later that evening, Pippa texted him.

Good day?

He typed back.

Excellent. You?

Pretty good. Want to come here for breakfast tomorrow?

Love to. Though I have an interview at ten.

She called him. 'Where's the interview?'

'The TV studios,' he said. 'King's Cross.'

'King's Cross is…let me check… Maybe forty-five minutes from here. Say you left here at nine. We'd still have time to have breakfast together.'

'I'll be there at eight,' he said. 'Anything you want me to bring?'

'Just you,' she said, and he could hear the smile in her voice.

All the same, the next morning, he took her something special in a sealed plastic tub.

'Made yesterday afternoon by Lydia, my youngest niece, and me, while the rest of them went to the park,' he said.

She opened the tub and smiled. 'How fabulous! I've never seen so much glitter on a fairy cake before. I'll save it for my afternoon snack. Please say thank you to her for me.'

'I will,' he promised.

'Though you took a risk, bringing that here, with all that sugar,' she said.

'No, I didn't. It was in a sealed tub. I assure you that not a single wasp twigged what I was carrying or tried to mug me for it,' he said. 'Besides, Lottie's making me wear a manacle. Look.' He held up his wrist in disgust. 'The joys of big sisters.'

'I have two,' she reminded him. 'Actually, a medical alert bracelet is quite a good idea.'

'It still looks like a manacle,' he grumbled.

'Never mind. You'll just have to tell everyone you're Spartacus,' she teased. 'The coffee's brewed. Come in and sit down.'

Her flat was a small one-bedroomed place on the first floor of a purpose-built modern block in Hackney. Like his house, it had wooden floors and cream-painted walls, though the art in her living room was all either floral or ballet-related. There was a framed print of Degas' dancers; another of a stylised tulip with a line drawing of a ballerina that turned the tulip into a skirt; a publicity poster for *The Nutcracker* from four years ago which he guessed had been one of her shows; and an amazing black and white photograph of a ballet dancer seeming to fly through the air while doing the splits...and then he realised that the ballerina was *her*.

'That's an amazing photo of you,' he said.

'Press photo from earlier this year,' she said. 'My sisters had it enlarged and framed for me. They've each got one, too.'

She didn't mention her parents, he noticed, so he wouldn't mention them, either.

There were more framed photographs on a shelf, similar to his own collection—weddings, christenings, her sisters' graduation days, her nieces and nephews. The flowers he'd bought her earlier in the week were in a large vase on the coffee table, beautifully arranged. There was no TV, though. And no books.

She must've noticed him noticing, because she said, 'I tend to read eBooks rather than paperbacks; it's easier, because I read on the Tube or during my breaks at work.'

'I'm not judging you,' he said. 'I just have a lot of books from my student days. And a TV because—well, work.'

'I'm not judging you, either,' she said with a smile, and handed him the mug of coffee. 'Take a seat.'

The table was laid for two; she'd set out a jug of freshly squeezed orange juice, a bowl of berries and a tub of Greek yogurt. A couple of minutes later, she came to join him, carrying a basket of warmed brioche buns and a plate of bacon. 'Help yourself,' she said. 'Sorry, I don't have any ketchup.'

'That's fine. This is all lovely,' he said. 'I like your flat.'

'It's small,' she said, 'but it's home.' She slotted some bacon into a brioche bun. 'What's the subject of your interview, this morning?'

'It's for the dance series. I'm talking to a ballroom dance teacher,' he said. 'She won some pretty big competitions, in her professional days. Nowadays she teaches in community halls, and hosts professional tea dances—people can just turn up for a cup of tea, a slice of cake and a dance, and there's no bar on age or ability. She's talking to me this morning about the benefits of dance and ageing.'

'Co-ordination, balance, and keeping you mentally

sharp because you have to think about the music and the movement, which in turn makes connections in your brain,' she said. 'I've read some good articles on that. Plus there's the social aspect. I have friends who teach classes for beginners or older adults, and there's always a coffee after class. I'm guessing her students usually go off somewhere for a drink and a chat afterwards.'

He nodded. 'She says she has a band with a singer for the tea dances, but she uses taped music for her classes. She's going to teach me for two hours a day, to fit in between her classes and my work.'

'Sounds good,' she said. 'I assume all your teachers are going to take you through the basic steps, then teach you a routine. Which ballroom dance are you doing?'

'She said she wanted to teach me something new, so not the waltz—she says the quickstep's fun. And we're going to demo it at one of her tea dances.' He smiled. 'I did think it would be fun to do it at Blackpool Tower, given it's the most famous ballroom in the country, but we can't make the schedule or the budget work.'

'That's a shame,' she said. 'But a tea dance demo sounds fun. I was wondering where you planned to do the dances you've learned—I think you definitely need a proper audience, after all that hard work, not just a TV camera.'

'I'll see what my experts suggest,' he said. 'What are you planning for me?'

'I'm still thinking about it,' she said. 'Actually, I'm seeing Judith Parrish later today, to discuss music and choreography. She might have some ideas.'

He'd finished his third bacon roll and a bowl of yogurt and berries when he realised he needed to leave, or he'd be late for his interview.

'Sorry. I should've stopped talking and done the washing up earlier,' he said.

She brushed it aside. 'It's fine. It'll take me two minutes. *Go.*'

'I'll call you later,' he promised.

It was late by the time Rory finished, that evening, and called Pippa. 'Sorry. I know you're back at work tomorrow, so I won't suggest going out for a drink,' he said.

'It's fine. How did you get on with your ballroom dance teacher?' she asked.

'The interview was great. And she's taught me the first few steps. Did you know it was originally called "the Quicktime Foxtrot and Charleston"?'

'What a mouthful!' She laughed. 'It'd take you nearly as long to say it as to dance it. Are you enjoying it?'

'It's fun,' he said. 'Though it really is quick. I'm not going to need cardio at the gym while I'm learning this.'

'Good,' she said.

'How did you get on with Judith?'

'We had a really good time. We've got some ideas for the new choreography. I don't really want to tell you anything about it, though, because I'd like it to be a surprise,' she said.

'I hate surprises,' he said.

She laughed. 'Tough. I'm still not telling you.'

Over the next couple of weeks, Pippa and Rory fell into a routine of snatching breakfast together in the café round the corner from the Fitzroy on the days she was working, and Rory went to three of Kenzo's classes a week. By tacit agreements, on Saturday nights, he cooked dinner and she stayed over at his; on Sundays, they did something together where wasps were unlikely to bother them; and on Sunday nights he stayed at hers.

Even though Rory kept telling himself this was a temporary fling, it was starting to feel like more than that. It felt like a real relationship. And it terrified him how easy and natural he found it to be with her—how quickly they'd adjusted to each other's quirks. How much he looked forward to seeing her. She was the highlight of his day.

Was it the same for her, too?

And did she, too, wonder how hard it would be to lose this from their lives when his documentary had finished, she'd got her promotion, and they'd gone their separate ways?

He wasn't going to ask her, because the answer was almost as scary as the question. So he kept their conversation light, that evening, when she asked him how the documentary was going.

'I'm doing the quickstep as a demo at a tea dance; a tango, as part of a show; and the disco routine in a competition.'

'That all sounds great.' She smiled. 'I hope I get to see the dancing live, and not just the filmed versions.'

'I'll see what I can do. Obviously it depends on whether it fits in with your performances,' he said. 'Have you decided what you want me to do with the ballet routine?'

'I think you need to do a show for ballet, too. And we'll up the stakes so it's a challenge for both of us.' She looked at him. 'Dance for the audience at the Fitzroy.'

He shook his head. 'Even if you put me in a really minor part, I'm not going to be up to the standard to join your company in *Swan Lake*.'

'You're not going to be dancing in *Swan Lake*,' she said

with a smile. 'We've got a month before the gala show. I know it means you'll be learning other routines with other dances at the same time, but I think you're capable of doing it without confusing your steps. And if we do thirty minutes every day you'll learn the routine better than if we concentrate your training over a whole day every week.'

'But Nathalie's already sorted out what's in the gala, hasn't she?' he asked.

'That's the thing about galas. We're performing favourite pieces from lots of ballets rather than staging one single ballet, so we can be flexible with what we're including and the running order.' She looked at him. 'If Judith's willing to come and play, that'd be another famous name as a draw for both the gala and your show. We'd be able to offer the world premiere of a new piece, and a famous TV presenter as a guest dancer; and if Kenise films it your show can use that as well as your performance.'

'I'm not *that* famous, he said. 'And I'm not a dancer.'

'Not a dancer *yet*,' she corrected. 'We're working on that. And you are famous,' she reminded him. 'You have a prime-time Friday night slot. OK, so it's on one of the smaller channels, but it's still prime time. People know who you are. Dancing at the Fitzroy is going to get publicity for your documentary, and people are going to tune in to find out what it's all about.'

'Supposing Nathalie says yes. What do I dance?' he asked.

'One of the big solos—maybe the Sugar Plum Prince variation,' she said, and found a video of it for him on her phone.

He watched it in horror. 'No way am I ever going to be able to do all those leaps and pirouettes, even if I did it on a trampoline.'

'I was going to simplify it for you,' she said. 'You can still get the feel of the piece and tell the story, at your own level. How about a male version of the "Dying Swan"?'

She found him another clip. And that one was even scarier.

'That's very…gymnastic,' he said, trying to be diplomatic. 'I'm nearly thirty—not as flexible as I was when I was a teenager. Besides, in all the other episodes, I'm dancing with the person who taught me, not doing a solo.'

She coughed. 'Well, it'd be a bit difficult to do a quickstep routine or a tango on your own.'

'I think I should dance with my ballet teacher,' he said.

Which sounded a bit better than *I want to dance with you*, which was what he really wanted to say.

'Let me think about a routine,' she said. 'We need something where you're not going to lift me. Which isn't me being fussy or saying you're a weakling—it's…' She drummed her fingers on the table, clearly trying to think of how to phrase it. 'If you put your partner down wrong, there's the risk of a potential fracture. I don't want to put that kind of pressure on either of us.'

'Then why do they allow the celebs to do lifts in shows like *Strictly*?' he asked.

'Lifts are only allowed in some dances,' she pointed out. 'And ballroom dance lifts aren't quite as high as the ones in ballet.'

'So no lifts.' And it was weird how disappointing that felt, to know that he couldn't dance ballet *properly* with her.

Maybe his disappointment showed in his voice, because she said, 'You can still dance something fabulous. I'll tweak things so it's lower risk for both of us, and it'll still be a challenge for you.'

* * *

They were curled up together on his sofa, the following Sunday afternoon, when the idea came to Pippa. *'Carmen.'*

'*Carmen*? I thought that was an opera?' Rory said, looking confused.

'It's a ballet as well. "Habanera" would be great. You'll know the music.' She hummed the tune and was pleased to see the recognition on his face.

'So what's the ballet about?' he asked.

'The same as the opera. Carmen's a free spirit; Don José, one of the soldiers, falls in love with her, but she falls in love with the bullfighter Escamillo. They end up in a love triangle; there are a few fights; and, at the end…' She wrinkled her nose. 'Don José kills Carmen.'

'So it's your typical ballet-cum-opera tragedy,' he said.

'Pretty much,' she said. 'But the "Habanera" bit isn't tragic. It's where you see Carmen all bright and sparkly. I like the version where she's in jail and Don José's trying to resist her but falls for her. The two dancers share the spotlight and there are no lifts, but you'll do some flashy-looking turns.' She grinned. 'And you'll get to look *very* sexy in a soldier's outfit.'

'What about you? What does Carmen wear?' he asked.

'A little black dress. Let me show you the clip,' she said. 'Though you need to see this on a big screen. I want you to really see what's happening and feel all the feels, as it were.'

'We can connect the phone to the TV,' he said. Between them, they sorted it out and he came to sit beside her on the sofa.

She pressed 'play', and the music spilled into the air. Carmen, in handcuffs, danced lightly in and out of the bars, while Don José tried to ignore her and do his duty as a brave soldier—but gradually he began to follow her lead, and finally she walked free while Don José remained behind bars, wearing her handcuffs and looking as if he didn't understand what had just happened.

'Oh, my God,' Rory said, his voice husky. 'That has to be one of the sexiest...'

'Want to dance it with me?' she asked.

'Definitely,' he said. 'But is it too...well, *hot*, for a gala show? I don't want to embarrass either of us.'

The way he kissed her then left her in no doubt of his feelings.

'You have a point,' she said. 'The other piece I was considering—well, it makes me a bit twitchy even suggesting it.'

His blue eyes glinted. 'Tell me anyway. I won't take offence.'

'There's a gorgeous version of the "Rose Adagio" in *Sleeping Beauty*,' Pippa said. 'Instead of the Princess dancing with the four different suitors—which is the traditional one—she finds someone she's really attracted to, and dances with him in the garden. He's pretty much forbidden to her, and they both know it, but they can't help their feelings. It's glorious. I know it's a bit longer than you originally wanted, but I think it's worth it. Let me show you the first half.' She found the clip, and they watched it together.

'I get exactly what you mean. The Princess falls in love with the gardener,' he said. 'I love how they're teasing each other with the roses. It's like the first time you fall in love with someone, all the fizziness and dizziness.'

Which was the way she was starting to think about Rory—and that was seriously scary.

'But it has all those lifts,' he said.

'We'll replace them with turns,' she reassured him.

'I don't get why you were twitchy about suggesting it,' he said.

'It's the second half.' She pressed 'play' again.

'Instead of pricking her finger on a spindle, she pricks her finger on a rose…and dies,' he realised at the end. 'Back at the time this was set, there were no antibiotics. You could die from pricking your finger on a rose.'

'That's what made me twitchy,' she said. 'You were stung by a wasp, and you almost…' She felt tears pricking her eyes at the idea of a world without Rory in it. 'It's a bit too close to the bone.'

'But there's a happy ending. Everyone knows that, in the end, Sleeping Beauty's woken by true love's kiss,' he said. 'And I woke up, too, thanks to you—because you gave me the kiss of life.'

'Mmm,' she said, not quite trusting herself to speak.

'You know what? That'd be a lovely story in my series as well as for the gala,' he said. 'And afterwards, after you "die" on stage, I can tell the story of how you saved my life. The audience will love it.'

'So we're going for the "Rose Adagio"?' she asked.

'The "Rose Adagio",' he confirmed. And then he gave her the wickedest grin she'd ever seen. 'As long as you do the "Habanera" with me privately.'

'I will.' She returned the grin. 'And that's a promise.'

CHAPTER TEN

PIPPA COULDN'T REMEMBER being this happy. She loved her job, she loved her life, and she loved seeing the way Rory was falling in love with all forms of dance. He was teaching her a different way of looking at things, too— something which she hoped was filtering through to the way she did her job, enriching it.

What she hadn't expected was to adore the challenge of adapting choreography for a beginner and teaching Rory to dance. Nathalie had agreed to let Pippa perform the premiere of her *Four Seasons* piece with Judith at the gala performance, as well as dancing the rechoreographed version of the 'Rose Adagio'—and, even better, she'd agreed to let Rory film both pieces for his documentary.

He'd said to Pippa that they were on the same side. More than that, she thought; they'd become a team. Trusting each other. Letting each other in, admitting their fears. Seeing each other for who they were, flaws and all. His job and his position as the son of an earl weren't important to her at all; it was the man himself she liked. The man who made her laugh with terrible jokes. She liked him. *Really* liked him. To the point where she was beginning to hope that their fling wasn't just going to fizzle out—that they could build on it and make it work.

She'd always thought that love wouldn't happen for her.

That there wasn't space in her life, because she couldn't risk letting someone distract her from getting to the top in her career. But Rory made her wonder if things could be different. There was no pressure. He didn't make her feel as if she was letting him down. And he wasn't distracting her—if anything, she was dancing better than she'd ever danced before.

Could they make something more from their fling?

With the right person, could she make space in her life and have ballet *and* a partner?

Could Rory be her Mr Right?

Before they started training, Pippa took Rory to her usual dance supplier and found him some black canvas ballet shoes, as well as a dance belt. He looked horrified when the assistant brought it out. 'It's like a G-string!'

'Which means it won't show through your dance tights,' she said. 'And yes, you do need to wear one— firstly to support your anatomy, and secondly to protect you from injury. You wouldn't play cricket without a box, would you?'

He rolled his eyes, but agreed and tried them on until he had the right fit.

She enjoyed teaching him the foot and arm positions followed by the basic steps, especially when his confidence grew enough that she could name a step and he could do it without needing her to remind him with a prompt. She was pleased to note that he was quick at picking up the combinations.

It probably helped that they practised every day; on days when Pippa wasn't dancing Odile/Odette, they used one of the practice rooms at the Fitzroy to run through their tweaked version of the Rose Adagio, polishing each section before moving to the next and then recapping everything they'd done so far. And at weekends they pushed the furniture back in his living room, rolled up the rug and danced there.

She hadn't seen as much as she would've liked to of Rory's dance diaries, but luckily the afternoon of the tea dance had been on a day when she hadn't been needed for rehearsals and actually had some free time, so she'd seen his quickstep routine performed live. Plus she'd been able to attend the dress rehearsal of his tango—a gorgeous, sensual dance that he'd then re-enacted with her in his flat on the Saturday night. The disco competition hadn't worked out with her schedules, but he'd promised to let her see what they'd filmed. And they'd come second, which had thrilled him.

Teaching Rory had made Pippa more aware of the way she danced, and in the middle of their third week Nathalie took her to one side. 'Whatever you're doing,' she said, 'I approve. Because you're taking dance to the next level. Your Odile was always technically flawless, but now you're putting more of your heart into the performance.'

Because of Rory. Not that she could say that.

'I think it's teaching, and maybe the choreography, because it's given me a different view of how routines work,' Pippa said. 'There are a couple of bits I haven't quite sorted out yet, but I've switched most of the lifts to a turn.'

'Show me what you've got so far, and I'll see if I can help,' Nathalie said.

Rory was less keen when he arrived for practice and Pippa told him Nathalie was going to watch them. 'I'm not ready for an audience yet. What if I mess it up?'

'You smile and keep going,' Nathalie said. 'I'm sure there are times in front of a camera where you say "um" or the wrong word. You don't stop then, do you?'

'Actually, we do. We stop and redo a few sentences, and then I splice the right bits together afterwards,' Rory said.

'What about when you do live interviews?' Nathalie asked.

'You don't have a choice, then. You have to smile and keep going,' he admitted.

'*Exactement*. This is the same. Don't worry if you get a few steps wrong. It won't matter. I need to see the soul of the piece.' She flapped a dismissive hand. 'Now show me.'

'Breathe. *Smile*. You've got this,' Pippa said. 'You're the gardener, you've fallen in love with the Princess, and she dazzles you. The only thing you can see is her—just as you dazzle her and the only thing she can see is you.'

'Got it,' he said. 'We dazzle each other.' Then he grinned. 'I've been thinking about my ballet stage name. That could be it—Dazzle.'

'No,' she said.

'Or maybe that should be my disco name,' he mused, 'and I could be Rory Fan-Nureyev.'

She groaned. 'That's worse.'

'Wait until you hear the rest. Rory Fanstaire dances ballroom.' His grin broadened. 'And Rory Fandango dances the tango.'

She could see he was cracking terrible jokes to cover his nerves, and she really wanted to kiss him better—but at the same time they'd agreed to keep their fling just to themselves. Kissing him in front of Nathalie would be a really bad idea. She didn't want her boss realising that things were changing between her and Rory, and assuming that Pippa's commitment to her work would start to slip.

'You're not Rory any more. You're the gardener,' she reminded him. And she was the Princess, falling in love with the gardener—except she was still Pippa. And, even though she was still keeping it to herself, she knew she was falling in love with Rory. 'Go sit on the bench.' She connected her phone up to the room's sound system, then went to sit on the bench with him. As the music started, she rested her head against his shoulder, and then they began the dance.

They ran through the routine with only a couple of stumbles.

'And here's my sticking point,' Pippa said. 'We're about three minutes in. This is where we're taking shelter in the greenhouse and the rain stops, and everyone comes back into the garden.' She frowned. 'It'd be too complicated to make it an ensemble piece.'

'There's a natural break in the music, so you could stop there,' Nathalie said.

'But then we've only told part of the story,' Rory said. 'We've got that extra minute and a half, where they're still happy and madly in love—but then she pricks her finger on the rose and it all goes horribly wrong.'

'And the problem's that tiny bit in the middle,' Nathalie said. 'You're right—we can't bring in half a dozen dancers just for a few seconds. But maybe,' she added thoughtfully, 'you could use a projector to show people coming into the garden while the Princess and the gardener are in the greenhouse. Then the projection fades out again, and you dance the second part.'

'I guess it depends on the mood we want to create,' Pippa said. 'Do we stop with them both having just fallen in love, or do we go on to the moment tragedy seems to strike?'

'Everyone knows *Sleeping Beauty* has a happy ending—she doesn't die, and he wakes her,' Nathalie said. 'If you leave it in the middle, you're ending on an anticlimax. It's pretty, but nothing happens to make you want to know what comes next. I think you should go for the drama.'

'What do you think, Rory?' Pippa asked, wanting him to be part of the decision. 'It means a fair bit of work, learning another two minutes.'

'Let's do it,' he said.

'Good choice,' Nathalie said, smiling. 'I like what I've seen. I'm not going to comment on the bits that need polishing, because you know that for yourselves. You're doing all right, Rory.'

From the plain-speaking chief executive, that was a high compliment.

'I'll talk to Marcos in Lighting about a projector,' Nathalie continued. 'Decide what you want the crowd to do, Pippa, block it through, and we'll film it.'

'Thank you,' Pippa and Rory said at the same time.

'I think you've simplified it well, Pippa—even without the lifts you've got that sense of falling in love,' Nathalie said. 'Though I noticed that one lift you left in.'

The straddle over the back. Pippa knew her boss's feelings about taking risks, because Nathalie always hammered it home to the team. 'It's a tiny, tiny, *tiny* lift. And it's an easy one,' Pippa said. 'I'm confident about it because I've seen the lift Rory does in his tango.'

'All right, then. Though you're sensible to leave it at one,' Nathalie said.

'I'm not taking risks with either of us,' Pippa reassured her. 'That's why we're doing turns rather than lifts.'

Nathalie nodded. 'When do I get to see the piece you're doing with Judith Parrish?'

'End of the week. Rory's banned,' Pippa added. 'Judith and I have been doing a video diary with a bit of help from Kenise. But he doesn't get to see the files until after the gala.'

'Considering it's *my* documentary,' Rory said, 'I'm not very happy about that.'

'If you analyse it all the way through development, then the final piece won't have as much impact on you,' Pippa argued. 'My way, you already know the concept, but you see the final as a brand-new audience would, and *then* you can take it to pieces and look at the development.'

'That's a good approach,' Nathalie said.

'You're biased because you're her boss,' Rory grumbled.

'I'm her boss because I saw her potential and I hired her,' Nathalie retorted. 'Get on with your practising. I need this room in fifteen minutes.'

'Oui, madame,' Pippa said with a smile.

Rory had never been this happy. His whole life seemed to have changed since Pippa had saved it. Her working hours were as unsocial as you could get, but they'd managed to work their dates around it—meeting for breakfast instead of dinner, doing Kenzo's classes together, spending weekends catching up with his family and friends on Saturday, and doing normal 'couply' things with Pippa on Sundays. She liked art galleries and museums as much as he did; and he quickly found that he could talk to her about anything.

Because they'd agreed up front this was just a fling, with no expectations, he found himself relaxing instead of wondering when it was all going to go wrong, the way his relationships had in the past. And she seemed to be relaxed in his company, too.

The dizzy, fizzy feel to the *Sleeping Beauty* piece was how he was feeling about Pippa, too, but he wasn't going to say anything yet. He was starting to hope that maybe the bond they were building was one that could actually last; but what if he'd still got it wrong? What if she didn't feel the same? Would she walk away? He didn't want to risk jinxing it by admitting how he felt.

The following Sunday, they were having a lazy morning at his place when his doorbell rang.

Odd. He wasn't expecting visitors or a courier.

He opened the door to see Jamie, Lottie, their partners and all four children.

Oh, no.

Much as he loved his family, if he invited them in, he'd have to introduce them to Pippa. But if he didn't invite them in, they'd assume something was wrong.

Why were they all here, anyway? Hadn't he reassured them enough that he was perfectly fine and wasn't going to take any risks?

'We just called round to see if you'd like to come out to lunch with us. A new café just opened and apparently they do the most amazing pancakes,' Jamie said.

'I…um…' *Come on, think.* But the words were stuck in his head.

'Too many cocktails last night?' Lottie teased.

'No, I…' He rubbed a hand across his eyes. There wasn't a choice. They'd have to meet her. 'Come in.'

'Sorry. I didn't realise you already had company,' Lottie said when she saw Pippa sitting on the sofa.

'We were just…uh—' Then he saw the cafetiere on the coffee table and the panic in his head eased. 'Catching up over coffee. Pippa, this is my brother Jamie and my sister-in-law Miranda, my sister Lottie and my brother-in-law Martyn, and my nieces and nephews—Phin's ten, Albert's seven, Sarah's five and Lydia's three.'

'Lydia—you're the baker with fabulous glitter, right?' Pippa asked, and the little girl nodded shyly.

'Everyone, this is Pippa Barnes. My friend,' he said.

'Don't be shy, Rory,' Pippa said, and for one brief, hope-filled moment he thought she was actually going to tell them they were dating.

'I'm becoming Rory's friend,' she said, 'but I'm teaching him a ballet routine for his TV series. See, I've got my pointe shoes with me.' She nodded to the shoes on top of their box, and Rory was really glad they'd done some practising earlier. 'We're practising here because Rory's house has enough room if we move the furniture.'

Of course she wasn't going to out them. She was telling the truth—just not the whole truth. Although he wasn't a fan of untruths, he knew this white lie would stop anyone getting hurt; it meant there was a good chance they'd get away with this and wouldn't be grilled over their relationship until they were ready to share. Most of him was relieved, but an irrational bit of him was disappointed that she'd dismissed their deeper connection so easily. That didn't bode well for the future.

Lottie frowned. 'Don't you have a studio where you teach him?'

'It's at the theatre, which isn't open on Sundays,' Pippa said. Rory knew this wasn't strictly true because she had a key and there was a rota where the dancers could book the studio rooms for practice.

'Hang on. Aren't you the one who saved Rory's life?' Jamie asked.

Pippa flapped a hand. 'That's all done and dusted. I'm busy teaching him how to be a ballet dancer, which is a lot harder.'

Neither Jamie nor Lottie looked convinced.

'Thank you for saving him,' Jamie said. 'I can't tell you how grateful we all are.'

'You don't need to,' Pippa said. 'And I wasn't the only one. There was Carolyn, who did the CPR with me, and the paramedics. It's honestly not a big deal.'

'It is to us,' Lottie said quietly.

'He's fine,' Pippa said. 'And when he's not, he can practise ballet—which is the best thing I know to help you chill out.' She smiled at Lydia. 'Now, young lady. Your uncle gave me one of your cupcakes—because it's always nice to give your teacher a little present—and it was awesome. I've danced in a tutu that colour and it had tiny silver star sequins, just like your sprinkles.'

'You were a fairy ballerina?' Lydia asked.

'The Sugar Plum fairy,' Pippa said with a smile.

'I want to dance like the Sugar Plum fairy,' Sarah said.

'Do you have lessons?' Pippa asked.

'No.' Sarah looked disappointed.

'I can teach you all a bit now,' Pippa offered, 'if you like and if your mums say it's OK.'

'It's fine,' Lottie said, 'as long as it's no trouble to you.'

'Fine by me, too,' Miranda said.

'But boys don't dance ballet,' Phin said, narrowing his eyes.

'Oh, yes, they do,' Pippa said. 'There are some productions of Swan Lake where all the swans are boys. They wear feathery trousers and they hiss, so they're scary. Dance isn't all about tutus and fairy wands—it's about telling a story. Sometimes it's a happy one and sometimes it's a sad one.'

'Do they really hiss?' Albert asked.

'Just like real swans do,' Pippa said. 'Do you want to try?'

Lydia, Sarah and Albert all started hissing.

'That's brilliant,' she said, smiling. 'Now, have a think about how little swans move. What do you think they do? Do they glide, like their mum and dad—' she demonstrated '—or are they still a bit wobbly because they're babies?'

'Wobbly!' Lydia cried, and did her best to waddle. Her sister and Albert followed suit.

'That's perfect,' Pippa said. 'Phin, you're older. How would a swan who's nearly old enough for the swan equivalent of big school move?'

Phin shrugged.

'I think,' she said, 'he tries to be all sensible and quiet because he thinks he's supposed to be like the grown-ups—but then he sees what fun his brother and cousins are having, hopping about. Do you think he'd just sit and watch with the adults, or do you think he'd join in with the little ones?'

Phin looked at her, saying nothing.

All the other adults were silent, wondering where this was going and if Phin was about to throw a pre-teenage hissy fit.

Pippa did a quick move Rory recognised as a pas de chat, then winked broadly. 'It's a lot more fun doing ballet than watching. Me, I'd rather be here being a wobbly cygnet—' she demonstrated '—than sitting still and sipping a cup of tea.' She mimed drinking from a porcelain cup with her little finger extended.

Phin was clearly thinking about it; finally, he nodded and went to join the others.

Rory almost sagged in relief. Pippa had managed to connect with his nephew. Then again, why had he doubted her? 'I'll make some coffee.'

'I'll help,' Martyn said.

'Right, gang. We're swans,' Pippa said. 'How do our heads move?'

They bobbed their heads, and even Phin joined in.

'Now, arms—they're wings. We can do big moves when we're flying through the sky—' she demonstrated dramatic arm movements '—or we can do little moves when we're gliding along the water.' She showed them little rippling movements with her arms.

Rory glanced at his siblings and their partners and saw they were all spellbound by Pippa. He knew this was going to be reported back to his mum and she'd start asking difficult questions, but right at that moment he didn't care; he just wanted them all to see Pippa the same way he did.

The children copied the swan arms, following Pippa's direction.

'There's a really famous dance about little swans. Can I teach you?' Pippa asked.

They all nodded enthusiastically, this time including Phin.

'Rory, can we have the carpet rolled back?' Pippa asked.

'Sure. We were going to do that anyway. And we'll move the tables,' he said, roping Jamie and his brother-in-law Martyn into helping him.

'Roll your socks down to the middle of your foot,' she said to the children. 'I want you to be able to glide, in some places, but I don't want you to slip, so you need to keep your heels bare to give you some grip on the floor.'

Rory loved how clear she was with her instructions, and the children were paying very close attention.

'We'll do the legs first, and when we've got that right we'll do the arms,' she said. 'Listen to the music and tap the beat with me with your right foot. One and two and three four five, and...' she counted.

'Semiquavers and rests,' Phin said laconically.

'Great—you're a musician!' Pippa said. 'What do you play?'

'Piano.'

'I love piano music,' Pippa said. 'Maybe you can play for me sometime.'

He blushed and nodded.

'What's your favourite piece?'

'I just did Grade Two,' he said. 'My teacher let me choose my favourite piece from each list. I did "Haggis Hunt", and "Hedwig's Theme".'

'I don't know "Haggis Hunt",' she said, 'but we sometimes use "Hedwig's Theme" as part of our warm-ups, and that's lovely.'

'I liked them a lot,' Phin said, 'but my favourite was Einaudi's "Snow Prelude"—it's like you're standing outside, looking up at the sky and seeing all the snowflakes swirl down around you.'

'It sounds like music for you is like dance is for me,' Pippa said. 'We're going to have some real fun now.'

She got the children to warm up their feet, then looked at Lottie and Miranda. 'You can come and join us, if you like.'

'No, no—we'll watch,' Miranda said, but she sounded wistful.

'If you want to stay in the audience, go and sit down. But any of you can hop up and join in at any time, and that's fine,' Pippa said. 'Just warm your feet up, first—like we're going to do.'

She took the children through some warm-up exercises, then taught them the basic footwork.

'Bravo,' she said, clapping. 'And now we add the arms. You're going to cross arms to do this, just like the little swans do on stage when we dance *Swan Lake*.'

The children immediately crossed their arms in the style of 'Auld Lang Syne'.

'That's good,' Pippa said, 'but ballet gives you a bit more movement, so you need a little bit more of a gap between you all. There's a trick to that—instead of holding the hand of the person next to you, you hold the hand of the person next to them. And then we tuck in nicely at each end.'

Within ten minutes, she had the children dancing up and down Rory's living room, then rising onto tiptoe and lowering back to flat feet, all in perfect time with the music.

'And that's it!' she said when the music ended. 'Take a bow—or a curtsey, and remember to smile at the audience,' she said to the children, clapping.

The adults all dutifully clapped.

'Well done, my little swans. You were excellent,' Pippa said. 'I'd better go now and let you have time with your family, Rory. We'll catch up with ballet practice tomorrow.'

'Don't go, Pippa,' Lottie said. 'Come for lunch with us.'

'I...' Pippa looked awkward.

Rory was about to step in with an excuse when Lottie asked, 'Unless you're busy?'

'Nothing that can't wait until tomorrow,' Pippa said. 'If you're sure—if you're not just being polite.'

'Very sure.'

When they went out to the café Jamie had mentioned, Rory noticed that Pippa ended up being sandwiched between Lottie and Miranda. And they were chatting as if they'd known each other for years.

'Stop worrying. Lottie's not going to grill her,' Jamie said, nudging Rory in the ribs.

'No need. Miranda will do that,' Martyn added, chuckling.

'Not funny,' Rory said. 'Pippa's my new colleague. Sort of. She really *is* teaching me to dance for the show.'

'The way you look at each other,' Jamie said softly, 'I think she's a lot more than that.'

Rory sighed. He should've known he couldn't quite get away with this. 'It's really early days. I don't want Mum putting any pressure on. As soon as you or Lottie tell her, she'll be planning a wedding.'

'We'll tell her,' Jamie said, 'but we'll also tell her to back off.'

Rory scoffed. 'As if that's going to work.'

'Oh, it will,' Martyn said. 'Lottie has other news to distract her.'

Rory felt his eyes widen as he guessed what Martyn meant. 'Seriously?'

'Shh,' Martyn said. 'Don't tell Lottie I told you. We're not supposed to be telling anyone until twelve weeks.'

'Congratulations,' Rory said.

And how weird was it that he felt wistful about his sister having another baby? He didn't do wistful. He enjoyed his nieces and nephews hugely, but he'd never thought about having children of his own. Probably because he'd never dated anyone he wanted to start a family with. And it worried him that Pippa was different—that, since being with her, he was starting to want different things from life.

'She's lovely,' Jamie said. 'She's not like the usual women you date. And she's brilliant with the kids. Phin's heading towards being a teenager, and I thought he was going to be in a sulk—but she made him feel part of everything. She really got him.'

'Yeah. She's special,' Rory said.

Jamie raised his eyebrows. 'That's what I said about Miranda,' he said gently. 'She wasn't like the women who looked at me and immediately saw themselves as the future Countess of Riverford. I take it Pippa knows who Mum and Dad are?'

'She does,' Rory said. 'And obviously she knows about my job.'

'We'll make sure Mum backs off,' Jamie said. 'Because, when you're ready to give us a sister-in-law, I think Pippa might be the one.'

CHAPTER ELEVEN

BROODY.

Rory had never, ever expected to feel broody.

The way he'd planned things, he was going to take a break from dating and concentrate on moving his career to the next level. Once he'd done that, he'd think about what he wanted in a partner and try to find someone who saw him for himself, not for his job or his background. All neat and tidy and sensible.

But then the wasp had happened, and his close brush with dying had made him question his choices. It had made him question *everything*.

He'd gone back to Plan A, but that surge of attraction towards Pippa had seriously got in the way. Their fling was supposed to be all about getting it out of their systems so they could be sensible again—but somehow it had turned into something else. Falling in love with her particular art form had gradually changed to falling in love with *her*.

Seeing Pippa with his nieces and nephews at the weekend and that unexpected conversation with his brother had crystallised something in his head. Now, he knew exactly what he wanted. Not just his career, but a family of his own. Children. And he wanted more than a short, intense fling with Pippa. He wanted her *permanently*. He wanted to plight his troth to her in front of all their family and friends. To love, honour and cherish her for the rest of their days. To watch her walk gracefully down the aisle to him, smiling behind her veil. To make a family with her. Cuddle their babies—and he'd do his fair share of changing nappies. Read their toddlers stories together, doing all the voices between them.

The problem was, how did that fit in with what *she* wanted from life?

He knew how much Pippa wanted this promotion. Even though he thought she'd made the right career choice, she still doubted herself and thought she'd let her family down. Reaching the peak of a dance career would prove to them, and her, that she'd been right not to become a doctor.

But promotion to principal dancer meant she might need to travel a lot more, touring and guest-starring with other ballet companies. None of that fitted with marriage and babies. Did she even want children in the future? Then again, the way she'd been with his nieces and nephews, warm and inclusive…it made him hope that she did. Though they'd need to talk about it, and he definitely didn't want her to feel that she had to choose between her career and him. Ballet was a huge part of her life, and he wanted her to be happy.

So how could he convince her that they could find a compromise? That she could still do the job she loved, while having the family he wanted?

Rory tried to tamp down the feelings, not wanting to have the conversation before the gala and mess everything up, but the more he tried to suppress his feelings the more the longing seeped through.

Either he was doing a good job of hiding what was

in his head, or she was so focused on the gala that she hadn't noticed how antsy he was. And then a really horrible thought struck him: maybe she *had* noticed. Maybe she'd worked it out. Maybe she didn't feel the same way he did, and was trying to work out how to let him down gently...

At last, it was Saturday night and the Fitzroy's Gala Show.

Rory and Pippa were dancing third.

The first piece was Yuki dancing the Sugar Plum Fairy; she was exquisite, and the audience clearly loved it.

The second piece was the 'Dance of the Little Swans'— another popular choice, but Rory found himself unable to focus. He was too aware of what was coming next.

Nathalie walked onto the stage with the microphone. 'I'm sure many of you know Pippa Barnes from her performances here. Tonight she'll be dancing with a television star I'm sure many of you know well too: Rory Fanshawe. Since she saved his life when a wasp sting nearly killed him, she's been teaching him to dance for a documentary he's working on. Tonight, they're going to perform a special version of the "Rose Adagio" from *Sleeping Beauty*.'

Rory was so full of nerves that he couldn't even stand still.

The worst thing was, he knew that both his family and Pippa's were in the audience. He hadn't introduced her to his parents yet, and she hadn't introduced him to hers— or to her sisters. What if he messed this up? What if he let her down? What if this was such a dreadful performance that it made Nathalie decide to give the promotion to Yuki rather than to Pippa?

He'd been so cavalier about this, so sure that his documentary would get her noticed and help with her promotion. How would he live with himself if the opposite happened? Because he wasn't a knight on a white charger, riding up to save the day and rescue the damsel. Pippa didn't need rescuing: she was doing perfectly fine on her own. He'd behaved like every other entitled, clueless male.

And she was so cool and calm and collected, it was unreal.

'Break a leg,' she said, and winked at him. 'You can do this, Rory Fan-Nureyev.'

Even the nickname—the one *he'd* made up to tease her—couldn't make him smile. Because now he had to go out on that stage and give the best performance of his life—a performance he wasn't entirely sure he could do.

'Ignore the audience. I'm the Princess. Dance with me. *Dazzle* me,' she whispered.

How did he do that? How? He'd forgotten every single step she'd taught him. Which leg was meant to go in front when he did the first turn? Where did the arms go? What if he tripped over his own feet—or, worse, tripped over hers and broke her ankle?

He was shaking as he walked across the stage. It was utterly ridiculous. He'd spent years in broadcasting and he was perfectly used to talking in front of an audience. He could've compered the show for Nathalie without the slightest hesitation, and he would've done it well, charming the audience and showcasing the dancers.

But it was one thing knowing that more than a million viewers would be tuning in to watch his Friday night programme, and quite another knowing that two thousand ballet fans were going to watch him dance right here and now *on this stage*.

With his show, he knew what he was doing. He knew he was good enough. With this, the stakes were higher—it was Pippa, not him, who'd lose out if he made a mistake.

The seconds dragged on and on as they walked to the bench. Every step felt like lead. Why had he talked her into dancing with him? Why hadn't he just done the really simple version of the 'Dying Swan'? Why had he had to show off?

Why was he the one facing the audience, when she was the professional dancer?

But then the harp signalling the beginning of the adagio rang out into the auditorium. The stage lights went up. She leaned across and rested her head on his shoulder. He tipped his to one side and rested it against hers. Breathe, breathe, port de bras—then she was lying on the bench with her head in his lap, and suddenly he was the gardener and she was the Princess. The audience faded away. The spotlight was simply the sun coming out in the garden after the rainstorm. And they danced, flirted, came together for a hug and for him to offer her a red rose he'd magicked from nowhere, dipped away again...

They'd practised little and often, because she said he'd remember it better that way. And he discovered that she was right. They'd done this so often that he didn't actually have to think about it. All he had to do was let his muscles remember what happened along with each note in the music, let the Princess dazzle the gardener, and dazzle the Princess in return.

Every note of the music was full of yearning and sweetness. Rory loved every second of being with her in that pretty dress, with its frothy petticoats that spun as they turned. He loved running with her to shelter in the 'greenhouse'. Nathalie's projection idea worked perfectly with people strolling in the garden—and Carabosse was there, too, holding a black rose and bringing the hint of danger to come.

The projection faded, and he and Pippa went back to the bench. Pippa 'found' Carabosse's black rose they'd hidden in the bench earlier, and for a moment Rory heard the audience gasp in horror as they realised its significance.

One last fleeting dance of joy, of knowing they loved each other and thinking it was all going to be perfect, and then the Princess picked up the rose again, pricked her finger, and 'died' in the horrified gardener's arms.

The stage lights went out—and then he heard the applause. Way, way more applause than he'd had from an audience before. People calling, 'Bravo!' People cheering. People whistling and stamping their feet.

And when the lights came up again and he and Pippa stood in the middle of the stage, holding hands, he blinked into the lights and he could see the audience giving him a standing ovation.

She did the most graceful curtsey, and the applause was deafening.

And then she stepped to the side. 'Bow,' she whispered, and gestured with her hands to showcase him.

He bowed, and somehow the applause got even louder. Which was utterly insane, because he wasn't the ballet star.

He tried to remember what they'd practised. *Smile, wave and walk off the stage.*

He was smiling so widely that his face almost hurt.

'Well done. You were brilliant,' she whispered when they got into the wings.

'It was all you,' he said. 'I was so scared I was going to mess everything up for you...' And then, because he really couldn't help himself, he kissed her. Not as if she was the Princess and he was the gardener, but because Pippa Barnes dazzled him more than anyone he'd ever met and he'd really fallen in love with her. He kissed her as if his entire life depended on it.

The rest of the show passed in a blur after that; Rory watched from the wings, but he couldn't take any of it in, beautiful as the music and the dancing were.

And then it was time for Pippa's world première. The piece he hadn't seen or heard. He slipped out of the wings and went to stand in the side aisle, just behind Kenise and her camera, out of the way of the audience.

The stage crew moved the piano onstage, and Nathalie introduced Judith.

'Tonight I have the pleasure of giving you the world première of Pippa Barnes' ballet *Four Seasons*, with an original score by award-winning composer Judith Parrish—who will be performing the music for us herself, tonight.' Clearly the audience knew exactly who Judith was, too, because there were whistles and cheers and loud applause.

The lights dimmed as Nathalie walked off, then brightened to show Pippa crouched in the centre of the stage, wearing a pale green calf-length chiffon overdress on top of a skin-tone leotard. She was slowly unfurling, like a spring flower; the solo piano sounded like dappled sunlight on a forest floor, quiet at first and then becoming louder as the flower grew. The music was beautiful, reminiscent of Einaudi. Even though he knew the concept of the piece, she'd refused to let him see her dance it or even see the costume until tonight, wanting him to get the full impact.

And wow.

This was a bravura performance. She gave everything to the dance, and she was spellbinding, drawing pictures in his head. Spring flowers all fresh and new, like the beginning of a love affair; the drowsy sensuality of a rose in full bloom; leaves falling in an autumn storm, like an argument; and finally winter frost in the morning sun, showing him that even at the end it was bright and sparkling.

It clarified for him what she brought to his life. Warmth, brightness, beauty. Letting her slip through his fingers would be a huge mistake, bringing nothing but regret. So he needed to be as brave as she was on the stage: he needed to tell her how he really felt. Maybe not tonight—there was too much going on—but he'd make sure they found the time during the week. And he'd open his heart to her.

The piece ended with Judith crashing the piano like thunder and Pippa with her arms up like a bolt of lightning, spinning round in a triple pirouette before gracefully ending.

The stage went dark for a moment, and when the lights came back up the audience gave her a rapturous reception. Including Rory, who went to the edge of the stage and handed her the huge sheaf of roses he'd arranged for Kenise to bring. 'You were *amazing*,' he said.

The rest of the company and the guests all came back on stage, to a standing ovation. Rory lost count of how many curtain calls there were.

Finally, Nathalie walked onto the stage again with her microphone. 'I'd like to thank you all for coming tonight,' she said. 'To thank our guest stars, our dancers, our wardrobe and stage crew, the lighting and sound technicians—all of you came together and made this a night to remember. And, between the ticket sales, donations tonight and the fundraiser, I'm delighted to say that we've raised enough money to fix the roof.'

The cheers, Rory thought, were enough to *raise* the roof.

'We have one last week of performances, and then we'll be back in the autumn,' Nathalie said. 'I hope we can welcome as many of you as possible—hopefully here, but if we have to work on another stage I'll let you all know where we are. We're the Fitzroy Ballet Company, and we appreciate every one of you. I wish you goodnight and a safe journey home.'

The lights went up in the auditorium, and the safety curtain rolled down.

CHAPTER TWELVE

ON WEDNESDAY MORNING, Nathalie called Yuki and Pippa into her office between class and rehearsals. 'We've made a decision about the promotion to Principal Dancer,' she said. 'We've been talking about it, and we think you equally deserve the position.'

Pippa tensed. Nathalie wouldn't tell them both at the same time, would she? Surely she'd tell them separately? They both wanted the position, and it was going to be really hard for the one who didn't get it.

'We're promoting you both,' Nathalie said. 'Congratulations.'

It took a moment to sink in.

Yuki had got the promotion.

And so had she.

Yuki looked as stunned as she felt. For a moment, neither of them moved, as if moving would break the dream and wake them; then Pippa flung her arms round Yuki, and then they both hugged Nathalie.

'Thank you,' Pippa said. 'You have no idea how much this means.'

'Me, too,' Yuki said. 'I think this is the happiest day of my life.'

'We'll make the formal announcement on Saturday

night, at the end of the show,' Nathalie said. 'I trust both of you can keep it secret until then?'

'Can I tell my mum?' Yuki asked. 'She'll keep it to herself. But she's supported me all the way through my career—I feel she's worked for this as much as I have.'

'Of course you can tell your closest family—both of you,' Nathalie said. 'But not a word to anyone else until Saturday night. And make sure they know they have to keep it quiet, too.'

'Of course,' Pippa said, and left Nathalie's office, looking as insouciant as she could.

She'd done it.

She'd made it to the top of the tree. Principal Dancer, at the age of twenty-five and with a non-conventional route into her career.

All the hours she'd put in—they'd been worth every single second.

And there was one person who'd really get how she felt, who'd feel the same delight that she did in her news. Especially because he'd admitted after the Gala Show how scared he'd been of failing and messing up her chances. He hadn't failed, and neither had she. She couldn't wait to share this with him.

Pippa grabbed her phone, opened the text app to bring up Rory's name—and then it hit her.

She couldn't tell him yet.

Enough people had witnessed their kiss in the wings at the Gala Show for everyone in the company to know now that they were an item; but she was pretty sure that Nathalie wouldn't class Rory as family. Plus he was a journalist. What if he accidentally let it slip to his editor, who insisted on him breaking the news on his show on Friday night—the day before Nathalie made the announcement? Even though Pippa trusted him, she knew Nathalie was right; the more people who knew, the more likely it was that the news would leak.

Instead, she texted her sisters and her mum.

TOP SECRET—will be announced Saturday after the show. Am not allowed to tell anyone except closest family. You're not allowed to tell anyone either. I GOT THE PROMOTION!!!!

It didn't feel quite the same. But they'd be pleased for her—wouldn't they?

Rory made the last adjustments to the ballet episode, then settled back to watch the whole thing again and double-check he was happy.

He was pretty sure he had the balance right. After the show, Kenise had given him the tapes she'd taken of Pippa and Judith's collaboration—which Pippa had insisted needed to be top secret—and he'd spliced the relevant bits in after the footage from the Gala Show. Because Pippa was right: it had much more impact if he saw the whole piece and then analysed it.

He paused after the Sleeping Beauty section, rewound, and watched it again.

They'd definitely caught the feeling of falling in love, the excitement and the way nothing else mattered except being together. Even without the lifts, her choreography had been clever enough to bring out all the emotion. And she was right—this dance wasn't just showcasing the Princess, it was both of them together.

This was something to be proud of. Something that one day, if they were lucky, they could show their children. Well, he didn't actually know if Pippa wanted children, and she'd been clear that her career was her priority for the next few years. He was getting ahead of himself. But at the same time he couldn't help wanting everything with her.

Acting was part of dance; but he didn't think that Pippa was simply telling the Princess's story, here. That dance had been about them, too. About the way they'd fallen in love. Although they hadn't discussed it, he was sure she felt the same way he did: that their fling had moved on, turned into something deeper and much more real. Something that could last.

Even though they hadn't scheduled meeting tonight, he couldn't wait until breakfast tomorrow. He needed to see her. Needed to tell her how he felt. Needed to ask her to take a chance on him.

He managed to get a last-minute ticket for *Swan Lake*; even though it was up in the gods and his view wasn't great, he didn't mind because it meant he got to see her dancing. Tonight she was dancing Odile/Odette, and he loved every second she was on stage.

At the end of the show, he made his way down to the stage door. From his time working with Pippa at the theatre, everyone at the Fitzroy knew him, and the security team just smiled and waved him in.

A few minutes later, Pippa came out of the dressing room with several of her colleagues, chatting and laughing. 'Rory! Hello. I wasn't expecting to see you tonight,' she said, smiling at him. 'We were just heading off for pizza. Guys—do you mind if Rory comes, too?'

'Of course not,' Livvy, one of the other dancers, said. 'He's practically one of us, now he's danced on our stage.'

'And you did so well on Saturday night. Give us a

year, and we could get you doing lifts,' Teodoro, one of the other dancers, said.

'I wouldn't dare. I'd be terrified of dropping someone,' Rory said. 'Guys, can we catch up with you in a second? I just wanted a quick word with Pippa. About the filming,' he improvised.

'Sure. We'll go ahead and grab our table. Come when you're ready. Shall we order your usual for both of you, Pippa?' Livvy asked.

'Is *funghi di bosco* pizza OK with you?' Pippa checked.

'Sure,' he said.

Once the others had gone on, Pippa asked, 'Is there a problem with the film?'

Her expression added, *Something so terrible that you needed to tell me tonight instead of waiting until breakfast tomorrow morning?*

'No. I really enjoyed the video diary you did with Judith and Kenise,' he said. 'And you were absolutely right about making me wait to see the première first.'

'Then what did you want to talk about?' she asked.

'I've watched our performance from the Gala Show,' he said.

'Ye-es,' she said. 'You let me come into the studios to watch it with you on Monday.'

'I've watched it several times since then,' he said. 'And I think it works because it isn't just the gardener and the Princess falling in love.' This was the biggest risk he'd ever taken in his life. And he hadn't scripted it. He just hoped she'd know that the words were coming straight from his heart. 'It's me falling in love with you, for real.'

She stared at him, those storm-grey eyes huge.

'I know we said we were just going to have a fling and get it out of our systems, but that hasn't happened for me. I love you, Pippa. I never expected this to happen, but I really love you. The more I see you, the more I want to be with you. I'd kind of got lost in my head, after the wasp thing, questioning everything—but being with you changed that. I know what I want, especially after seeing the way you were with my nieces and nephews. I want *you*. And children, if we're lucky.' He dropped to one knee. 'I haven't bought a ring. Partly because I think we should choose it together, and partly because I just couldn't wait a second longer to ask you. That's why I came here tonight. Will you marry me, Pippa? Be my love, my wife, the heart of my family?'

Pippa stared at him in shock.

Marry him.

Have children.

But…she couldn't. Not now. She hadn't had the chance to tell him yet about her promotion—but now was completely the wrong time for her to get married, have a career break and have babies. The next five or ten years were the peak time for her career.

And even if she did manage to juggle babies and her career, what about Rory? His career was taking off, too. His documentary series would bring him to the attention of arts editors on other channels. He'd have opportunities he'd want to take. If they both focused on their careers, they'd be letting their children down. If she focused on her career, she'd be letting him down.

He wanted a family. He wanted children.

She'd seen how close he was with his nephews and nieces. He'd definitely be a hands-on father; but did he want children enough to be the parent who took the career break, the parent who worked from home and put their job second?

She'd spent years feeling that she'd let her parents down. Today, when Nathalie had called her into the office, was the first time she'd really felt validated—and even that was a bit wobbly, because her mum still hadn't replied to the text she'd sent about her promotion. Her sisters had both replied, messages full of emojis and exclamation marks, along with plans to celebrate at the weekend with champagne. But her parents clearly still felt she'd let them down, to the point where they were having to force themselves to congratulate her.

She didn't want to spend the rest of her life feeling she'd let Rory down, too—either making him wait years for the children he wanted, or making him put his career on hold so she could progress hers.

She had a choice to make: love, or her career.

Whichever one she chose, she'd lose the other.

If she told him her worries, he'd tell her they could work it out. But Rory was a wordsmith, and he was from a privileged background. He'd never really had to struggle for anything. He hadn't exactly been handed his career on a platter—he'd worked hard and he was good at his job—but with a career in media you needed a lucky break as well as talent. He'd had the contacts to give him that first break. He'd tell her that everything was fine…

But how could it be?

In ballet, if you took a break you'd be forgotten. She needed a good couple of years as Principal Dancer to make her name before she could take a break. She'd be doing guest spots with other companies, as well as dancing at the Fitzroy—and that would mean long hours and lots of travelling. That didn't fit well with babies and young children—she'd hardly get to see them, or Rory. She'd be a failure both as a partner and as a parent.

On the other hand, if she gave up her career, would she start to regret all the might-have-beens? Would she even start to resent Rory and the children, blame them for the choice she'd made?

'Pippa?' He looked up anxiously at her. 'Will you marry me?'

Her throat dried.

Whatever she said would hurt him. Asking for time to think about it would only prolong the agony.

To be fair to both of them, there was only one answer she could give.

'I'm sorry,' she said. 'No.'

No.

She'd said no.

And it felt as if all the air had been sucked out of the room.

Rory stared at her. 'No?'

'No,' she said. 'I can't marry you.'

Couldn't, or *wouldn't*? Though that was splitting hairs. The end result was the same. She'd said no.

And it hurt.

It felt worse than that white-hot throbbing pain when the wasp had stung him, the wooziness and everything going black.

At least that had only been temporary. The sore spot on his neck and the burn mark on his chest from the defibrillator had become less painful, with regular application of aloe vera. They'd faded, leaving nothing more than a memory.

But there was a big difference between a physical pain

and this, the feeling that something had just crushed his ribs and everything underneath them had turned into rubble. This was the kind of pain he didn't think would ever go away.

He'd made the most stupid mistake of his life: thinking that this time it would be different, because she saw him for who he was. But in the end it had been the same old, same old: he'd been the one who'd invested in the relationship, and his partner hadn't. Yet again he'd fallen for someone who didn't love him back. Someone who didn't want him. He'd opened his heart, bared his feelings—and she'd said no.

'I'm sorry,' she said again.

This wasn't how it was supposed to happen. In his head, she'd said yes, he'd picked her up and spun her round and made sure he set her back gently on her feet, and they'd kissed until they were dizzy, and it was all going to be the happiest ever after.

In real life, she'd said no, and he was down on one knee, feeling like the biggest fool in the world.

'I'm sorry, too,' he said quietly. He wasn't going to make even more of a fool of himself by asking why she'd turned him down. She'd made it very clear she didn't want him. What was the point in dragging it out? The simple facts were that he'd changed his mind about their fling, and she hadn't.

He got to his feet. 'I'll…um…'

No. He wouldn't see her around. *Have a nice life* sounded too bitter. All his skill with words seemed to have drained away, along with what was left of his heart.

In the end, he said lamely, 'Bye, then.'

'Rory,' she said as he turned to leave. 'Rory.'

But there was nothing she could say to make this better. He didn't want to hear it, so he didn't stop to listen. He put one foot in front of the other, mentally gritted his teeth, and walked away.

CHAPTER THIRTEEN

PIPPA WATCHED RORY LEAVE, feeling as if she'd been soaked in a downpour, wrung out, and left in a heap on the floor.

Though it was her choice.

She'd picked her career, not love. She'd been the one to turn him down, so she was just going to have to make the best of it.

But tonight she couldn't face being in anyone else's company.

She texted Livvy, the colleague who'd offered to order the pizzas for her and Rory.

Sorry to back out at last minute. Have awful headache. If too late to cancel our pizzas will settle up with you tomorrow, P xx

And then she slipped out of the stage door.

Today should've been the best day of her life—well, second-best day, because Saturday was the day that made her promotion official. But she couldn't ever remember feeling this miserable and hopeless before.

But what other choice could she have made?

If she'd said yes—become Rory's wife, his equal partner, the mother of his children—she would've had to give up everything she'd worked for. And her sisters were right about her being a horrible workaholic; it was simply who she was. She couldn't change. She would've resented Rory for holding her back—or, if she'd made him wait for years before they started the family he wanted, she would've felt that she'd let him down. And she was so *tired* of feeling that she'd let people down.

She slept badly, claimed she'd been fighting off a headache when everyone expressed concern at how awful she looked, the next morning, gritted her teeth and just got on with her job.

But even when the card from her parents arrived—a beautiful line drawing of a ballerina on the front, and the words she'd longed to hear for so many years, written in her mother's tiny difficult-to-read doctor's handwriting, inside—it didn't lift her heart.

Congratulations on being promoted to Principal Dancer. What an achievement, and very much deserved. We're both so proud of you.

But I'm not proud of me, she thought. *I hurt Rory. He didn't deserve that.*

No matter which way she looked at it, she couldn't see another way. Whatever she'd done, he would've ended up hurt. Better to end it now than slowly and more soul-destroyingly. If that was even a word. Oh, for pity's sake, she couldn't even string a sentence together. He would've known what to say. Rory, who always finished her crosswords, who knew a poem or a Shakespeare quote for every eventuality under the sun, who could charm the moon with his words.

He'd charmed her.

The brightness he brought with him, the way he showed her to look at paintings in a different way, the way he'd become captivated by ballet. In their practice sessions, he'd worked and worked and worked until he got it right. He'd listened to her. He'd done everything she'd asked of him. He'd stepped out of his comfort zone for her. He'd walked out on that stage, and she'd seen how nervous he was, but he'd danced. For *her*.

She'd fallen in love with him, too.

And part of her had wanted so desperately to say yes to his proposal. To be with him. Her husband, her life, the heart of her family.

The way she'd been with his nieces and nephews, drawing out Phin's love of music and Lydia's love of putting sprinkles on cake, teaching all of them to dance like little swans: that morning had put a dream in her head, too. Of teaching her own children to dance, with Rory there, joining in or directing with his broadcast journalist hat on.

But she couldn't have it all. Nobody could. You had to make sacrifices along the way. She'd learn to cope with the collateral damage to her own heart; she just wished she hadn't damaged his.

The rest of the week was hideous. Even Saturday, when Pippa knew Nathalie was going to make the big announcement after the show, felt as flat and stale as champagne left out in a glass overnight.

And she couldn't stop thinking about Rory. Feeling guilty for hurting him, and missing him at the same time.

'The show must go on,' she reminded herself fiercely. One last performance as Odette/Odile, and then she'd have a break over the summer. Maybe she'd take her sisters up on their offer of going to France with them. Getting out of London, where there were way too many memories of Rory, might help.

At least she was dancing *Swan Lake*, not *Sleeping Beauty*.

Rory had been spot-on in that. It had worked so well precisely because it was real, not just acting. She'd gloried in dancing with the man she'd fallen in love with, knowing that he loved her too, even though neither of them had declared their feelings. If she ever had to dance that with anyone else, it would break her.

Though it distracted her to the point where in Act Three, at the very end of Odile's triumphant dance, she felt herself slip.

Felt the wrench on her ankle.

Heard the pop.

Knew she'd done something serious.

She stayed in pose, as required; then managed to walk off stage through the pain. But the second she was in the wings, out of sight off the audience, she stopped and unlaced her pointe shoe.

Her ankle was definitely swelling. And it really hurt to put weight on it.

'Are you all right? What happened?' Yuki asked, hurrying over to her.

'I don't know.' Pippa blinked back the tears. 'I'm not sure if it's a sprain.'

'Can you walk?' Yuki asked.

Pippa tried again, and was shocked by how much more painful it was this time to put weight on her ankle. 'I can walk, but I'm not sure I can dance,' she said bleakly.

'Pippa?' Nathalie bustled over. 'What happened?'

'I slipped. I...' She couldn't bail out of the last act. She had to do this for the good of the company. She took a deep breath. 'I'll be OK. I'll take ibuprofen and ice my ankle while I'm in the wings.'

Nathalie examined her ankle. 'I'm not a medic, but I don't think you've broken your ankle. Though I've seen enough ligament tears to recognise one—if you dance on this, you're risking permanent damage. And that's not happening in my company.' She snapped her fingers. 'Yuki, you're taking over now as Odette. Livvy, I need you to dance Yuki's part in the "Two Swans". Go and get changed!' She looked at Pippa. 'And *you* are going straight to the hospital.'

So she wouldn't even be here when her promotion was announced. *If* it was still announced. If Nathalie was right and she'd torn a ligament, it could be months and months before she was fit enough to dance again.

'I—' she began.

'No arguments,' Nathalie said firmly. 'Your health is important. Go, *petite*.'

'I'll go with you,' Aeris, one of the junior dancers who was watching from the wings, offered.

It was a long, long wait. Aeris did her best to keep Pippa chatting and distracted as they waited for a doctor to see her, but all Pippa could think about was what damage the doctors would find and how long she'd be out of dance.

And the MRI scan gave the worst news.

'It's a grade three ligament tear,' the doctor said.

'Does that mean surgery?' Pippa asked.

'For people who aren't elite athletes or dancers, it's an injury that would heal without surgery,' the doctor said. 'But, given your job, you'll want to be back at peak fitness like yesterday. I think you'd be better off with surgery, a cast, and physio. But you'll need to be careful in rehab—don't try to be brave and work through the pain, because you'll do more damage and slow your recovery down.'

'How much time are we looking at until I can dance properly again?' Pippa asked, needing to know the worst.

'Six months.'

Six months?

It sounded like a lifetime.

There was no way she'd keep her promotion, now. Not only that, she'd lose ground, and this meant six months out of the most crucial years of her career. Everything she'd worked for was slipping away, and there wasn't a thing she could do about it.

'We'll immobilise your foot for now,' the doctor said, 'and we'll operate in the morning. Provided there aren't any complications, you can go home tomorrow afternoon.'

Even though it was late, the theatre director had said she wanted to know as soon as there was any news, so Pippa phoned her.

'That's not as bad as it sounds,' Nathalie said. 'We're having two months off for the summer, while the roof's being fixed. You're only missing four months.'

Only.

'And I'm sure Rory can distract you for those four months,' Nathalie added.

Ri-i-i-ight. Rory distracting her was why she was in this mess in the first place.

Pippa closed her eyes. No, that wasn't fair. It wasn't his fault. It was all on her. And it was her fault she'd let the Fitzroy down. 'He won't be distracting me,' she said. 'We won't be seeing each other again.'

'That,' Nathalie said, her voice carefully neutral, 'is a shame. I liked him.'

The lack of judgement, the kindness, was almost Pippa's undoing. 'I'll be back to work in six months,' she said. 'I assume you didn't announce my promotion. I mean, you can hardly promote someone who can't even do the job right now.'

'It's my company,' Nathalie reminded her, 'so I can do what I like. As a matter of fact, I announced Yuki's promotion *and* yours at the end of the show. And if it takes more than six months for you to be back to full fitness on my stage, then it takes more than six months.'

'You're not sacking me?' The words spilled out before Pippa could stop them.

'You can't sack someone for illness,' Nathalie said. 'Though, even if it was legally allowed, it would be totally amoral and I wouldn't do it.'

'What if I...?' Pippa forced herself to say the words, to face the issue. 'What if I never get back to full fitness?'

'Don't overthink it,' Nathalie said sternly. 'Focus on the positives. You'll have the surgery, we have an excellent physio who can help you with rehab exercises, and...' She paused. *'Qui vivra, verra.'*

But what if the damage was too much? Pippa wondered. What if she couldn't dance any more?

She'd chosen her career over Rory. If she lost her dancing, too, then she'd lost everything.

Unable to face any further conversations, she told her sisters the news by text. Telling her parents was too much to handle; she'd do it after the operation, she decided. So she was truly shocked when, at seven o'clock the next morning, her mother walked onto the ward.

'Mum! I— What are you doing here?'

'Supporting you,' her mother said. 'I assume you're nil by mouth?'

Pippa nodded.

'Right. If you give your permission for your doctors to talk to me, I can make sure they're taking the best approach for you. I've been reading papers on ligament tears and dancers all night.'

Pippa's eyes filled with tears. 'Oh, Mum. I…'

Amelia gave her a hug. 'I know. This probably feels like the end of everything, but it's not. It's just a little bump in the road. Six months is nothing. This time next year, Principal Dancer Pippa Barnes will be getting rave reviews on the stage of the Fitzroy again. And you'll do the first two weeks of rehab with me—either I'll come and stay with you, or you can come back home for a couple of weeks, whichever you'd prefer.'

'But you can't! You've got work,' Pippa said.

'I've already organised a locum to cover me. You're more important,' Amelia said. 'And I'm not leaving you to struggle alone with crutches.' She smiled. 'Besides, it'll be a lot easier for me to nag you to keep your foot raised above the level of your heart if we're actually in the same house.'

'I never expected…' Pippa shuddered. 'I mean, I know I disappointed you and Dad. The first in three generations of our family not to be a doctor.'

'Dancing,' Amelia said, 'is a very uncertain career. We only wanted the best for you. Yes, we had huge doubts. But I apologise, because I can see now we were wrong to hold you back. And, just so you know, you're not a disappointment. You're a very bright shining star, and I've always thought you're more than capable of doing absolutely anything you put your mind to.'

Pippa rubbed the tears from her eyes. 'Don't. I'm trying to be brave.'

'Of course you're brave. You get on stage six nights a week and bare your soul under the spotlight,' Amelia said. 'You're going to get through this. I've got your back. So have your sisters and your dad.'

And this time Pippa let the tears fall freely.

The surgery was successful, and Pippa went to stay with her parents. Her father shocked her even more than her mother had, by spending time playing cards with her and chatting, keeping her mind busy.

She missed dancing more than she could have believed possible.

And she missed Rory even more.

But she'd been the one to end it. And she'd taken his number off her phone so she wouldn't be tempted to call him.

The following week, Amelia checked a text message at the breakfast table. 'That television programme you were doing bits of—Holly says it's being screened tonight.'

Oh, no. Pippa didn't think she could bear to watch it.

But it seemed she didn't have a choice.

And it was all there. The history, the clips of famous ballet dancers, her teaching him to dance. Rory grumbling, 'Even when I'm cleaning my teeth, I hear your voice saying, "Straight knees!" or "Shoulders down!" and find myself checking my posture.' And the two of them dancing the 'Rose Adagio' on the Fitzroy's stage, the glorious music and their faces shining with love as they spun round the stage… She had to clench her fists to stop herself weeping.

'You really do have a special talent,' her father re-marked.

The praise she'd so desperately longed for. And it wasn't enough, any more. Nothing was enough, with-out Rory.

'And he's such a nice young man,' Amelia added. 'You must have enjoyed working with him.'

'I did.' And how she ached for him now. How she missed him. But she was doing the right thing for both of them, keeping her distance, she reminded herself. He wanted a family. She'd given him the freedom to find someone who'd give him what he needed.

She became aware that both her parents were looking at her expectantly.

'I'll have to send him—well, it can't be flowers. Not with his wasp allergy. Champagne,' she said.

Because it would only be polite to congratulate him on his series, wouldn't it?

'Delivery for me?' Rory was surprised, but accepted the box the runner brought in from reception. 'Thanks.'

He opened the box to find a card.

Congratulations on the series. Pippa.

Beneath the card was a moulded pulp bottle protector, and inside that was a bottle of champagne.

So she'd watched the show last night? He hadn't been able to watch it—seeing them dancing the 'Rose Ada-gio' together would've just been too hard, since she'd turned him down.

But if she'd watched it and she'd sent him champagne on same-day delivery, that had to mean something? You wouldn't go to that much trouble if it didn't really matter to you.

Did she miss him as much as he missed her? he wondered. Or was he just trying to convince himself that he hadn't got her completely wrong? Maybe he should just be sensible and keep his distance. At least that way he wouldn't get hurt again. He'd be foolish to jump to the conclusion that champagne meant she missed him. That it was some kind of coded message: fizzy, dizzy, just like their dance...

'Ooh, bubbles! Very nice,' Kenise said, walking into the office. 'Who are they from?'

'Pippa.'

'Uh-huh.' She raised her eyebrows. 'Are you going to call her?'

He shook his head. 'I'll text her.'

'I'm not going to pry,' Kenise said, 'but it's very obvious that something's happened between you. You've been miserable for days. I bet it's been the same for her.' She sighed. 'I like her and I think she's good for you. So whatever the row was about...'

Pippa had turned down his proposal of marriage. Flatly. Completely.

And he didn't want to talk about it.

Kenise shook her head. 'Sweetie, you can't sort out a fight by text, or even a phone call. Go and see her. Talk to her, face to face.'

He wasn't sure that Pippa would want to talk to him. He fell back on an excuse, even though it sounded utterly lame. It *was* utterly lame. 'I don't know where she is.'

Kenise scoffed. 'She's like you. If anything upsets her, I reckon she'll bury herself in work.'

Just as he did. He pushed the thought away that he and

Pippa were two halves of the same whole. 'She can't. The ballet company's on their summer break, and the roof's being fixed.'

'The roof isn't going to affect the studio. And dancers are paranoid about keeping themselves dance-fit. You know exactly where she'll be,' Kenise said. 'Just go. I'll field anything that comes in.'

Was sending him champagne Pippa's way of reaching out to him? After all, she could've ignored the show completely. Or just sent him a congratulations card.

The more he thought about it, the more he wondered.

But the bottom line was that he *missed* her.

To hell with his pride. He'd take the risk and talk to her.

So he went to the Fitzroy.

Pippa wasn't there, but Nathalie Charrier was in her office. 'Pippa won't be here for weeks,' she said.

'Why?' Rory asked.

'Why did you want to see her?' Nathalie countered.

'She sent me champagne. I wanted to say thank you in person.'

'You'll have to text her instead,' Nathalie said, offhand.

Rory sighed. 'All right. Saying thank you in person was just a feeble excuse. I...miss her.'

Nathalie folded her arms. 'What did you do to upset her?'

'I'll tell you,' he bargained, 'if you tell me why she's not in the studio with everyone else.'

'Agreed,' Nathalie said. 'You first.'

He told her.

Her mouth thinned, and she told him what had happened at the end of Act Three.

Pippa had rescued him. Now it was his turn to rescue

her from the devastation she must feel after her injury. 'I need to see her,' he said. 'Where is she?'

'I'd be breaking every Data Protection Act rule in the book if I told you,' Nathalie said, standing up and going to a filing cabinet. 'But perhaps,' she continued, fishing out a file and leaving it on her desk, 'the address of her next of kin might be a *petit* clue.' She muttered something Rory didn't quite catch, particularly as it was in French; knowing how acerbic Pippa's boss could be, he assumed it was something along the lines of '*petit*, just like your masculine brain'. It wasn't strictly fair; Pippa had been the one to call a halt. Then again, maybe he'd rushed her. Now he'd had time to think about it, hadn't she admitted to him that she didn't think she had space for both love and ballet in her life? Had he pushed her too fast, so she'd thought she had to choose?

If they talked it through, were completely honest with each other, he could show her that he was prepared to wait. To support her dreams. To compromise. And then maybe she'd be prepared to take a chance on him.

'Excuse me a moment,' Nathalie said. 'I'll just fetch a glass of water.'

Rory smiled, and the second she'd left her office he picked up the file. The one containing Pippa's personal details, including her next of kin.

He blinked as he read it. She was staying with her *parents*?

Well, OK.

He noted the address on his phone.

'You might also like to know,' Nathalie said, coming back into the office, 'that she's been promoted to Principal Dancer.'

He hadn't known that, either. 'Did that happen before

or after her injury?' he asked, replacing the file on her desk and keeping his tone casual.

'I told her on the Wednesday morning.'

The day he'd proposed to her. She'd known about her promotion, but she hadn't told him she'd met her goals. Hurt flared, but he damped it down. This wasn't about him; it was about *her*.

'I also made her promise to keep it confidential because I'd announced it at the end of the Saturday show,' Nathalie said.

There were times when Pippa would play completely by the rules. An embargo was definitely one of them. So maybe she'd wanted to tell him, but felt she couldn't break her promise to her boss.

'Which I did,' Nathalie added with a sigh. '*After* I'd sent her to hospital.'

'Hang on.' Rory was shocked. 'Are you telling me she didn't even get to be there for her big moment?'

'I'll redo the announcement just before her next performance on my stage,' Nathalie said. 'However long it takes until then. I value her.' She folded her arms again and fixed him with a stare. 'Hurt her, and you'll be dealing with me.'

'I won't,' Rory said, 'I'll keep you posted. And thank you.'

'Don't let me down,' Nathalie said. 'Make her shine again.'

Rory wasn't taking any chances. He'd also noted Amelia Barnes' mobile phone number. He texted her to introduce himself—on the grounds that most people wouldn't answer a number they didn't recognise, but might read a text—and asked her to call him. Five minutes later his phone shrilled.

It was an illuminating conversation, on both sides.

He went home via the florist's, picked up his car and drove to Pippa's parents' house. Amelia answered the doorbell.

'You've got ten minutes,' she said. 'But if you hurt—'

'I'm not going to,' he interrupted gently. 'And besides, you'd have to fight for your place in the queue. I'm not sure of your chances against Nathalie Charrier—or my own mother, come to that, despite the fact that she hasn't met Pippa yet.'

To his surprise, Amelia grinned—and he could really see where Pippa got her smile. 'You'll do,' she said. 'She's in the living room. First door on the right. I'll be in the kitchen if you need anything.' She looked pointedly at his feet.

'Shoes off,' he said. 'Got it.'

Pippa looked up as the door opened. 'Mum—oh!' she said, shocked to see Rory.

'Wait—I need to do this properly,' he said, and did a couple of the turns she'd taught him for the 'Rose Adagio' routine before presenting her the bouquet with a flourish.

'Oh, Rory,' she said, her voice catching.

'Don't cry,' he warned, 'because Nathalie is terrifying, your mum's roughly on the same level, and so is mine. If there's a single teardrop from you, between the three of them, I'll be in fear of my life.'

'Don't be ridiculous,' she said, but she couldn't help smiling.

'I didn't know about your ankle until a couple of hours ago,' he said. 'I'm sorry. That's hard.'

'It's character-forming,' she said. 'And in a way it kind of did me a favour. Because now I know I'm not a—' her voice wobbled '—disappointment to my family.'

'I could've told you that, even though I haven't met them. Well, I had a short but very useful conversation with your mother, when I left Nathalie,' he said. 'By the way, congratulations on making Principal Dancer.'

'Nathalie told you that, too?'

He nodded. 'She said she'd given you the news unofficially on Wednesday.'

So he knew she'd kept it from him. 'I wanted to tell you, but Nathalie swore me and Yuki to secrecy,' she said.

'She told me,' he said. 'I've been thinking. Being Principal Dancer means you're going to be travelling a bit more, at least for a few years. With a decent internet connection, any writing or researching I happen to do can take place anywhere. And it's up to me to arrange interviews. They might just turn out to be with people who live somewhere near wherever you're performing on tour.'

Was he telling her that he'd fit his career around hers? 'What are you saying?' she asked carefully.

'I'm saying that my feelings for you haven't changed. I love you, Pippa Barnes. It's nothing to do with the fact that you saved my life—it's you. The brightness in you that makes everything around you sparkle. I want *you*.'

She lifted her chin, knowing they needed to confront the big issues. 'But you want a family.'

'And you don't?'

That was the thing. 'I hadn't even thought about it before I met you. I was focused on becoming Principal Dancer.' And she'd got there.

'And now?'

'I want a family. *But...*' And this was the important thing. 'I'm not ready yet. Maybe I won't be ready for a couple of years—and by that I mean a couple of years after I can dance again. It might be six months from now until I've healed well enough to do that.' She dragged in a breath. 'I don't want to disappoint you, Rory, the way I've disappointed my family.'

'The thing is—and you've told me you know this now,' he said, 'your family *weren't* actually disappointed in you. They're just not very good at articulating their feelings.'

That stung. 'And you are?'

'I make my living from words. I'm articulate. I can use words of one beat, if you want me to,' he said, and grinned. 'Or we can have polysyllabic conversations, if that's your preference.'

'OK. You've made your point,' she said.

'Yes, I want children,' he said. 'With you. But I'm happy to wait until you're ready. And I'd also like you to know that I don't expect you to give up your career for me. You've put in years of hard work to get where you are, and I understand that—I've done the same. So we'll work it out together. We might need a bit of help to run the house, and maybe a nanny and a personal assistant—but we'll be a team and we can make it work the way we want it to.'

She was silent, thinking about it. A team. Making it work, together.

'You turned me down when I asked you to marry me,' he said. 'And maybe I rushed you, because when I realised what I felt about you I wanted everything, right then, all at once. But I can be patient. Because I love you,' he said. 'I want to be with you. Life without you is like trudging through murky slush, the day after it snows. And I'm prepared to wait until you're ready—because you're worth it.'

'You love me,' she said, almost in wonder. She'd pushed him away, and he still loved her.

'And you're killing me here,' he said. 'Was I wrong about our 'Rose Adagio'?'

'No. You weren't,' she said. 'It worked because I'd fallen in love with you, and it showed.'

'So you do actually love me back?'

'Yes,' she said. Knowing that words were important to him, she added, 'I love you, too.'

'And the only reason you turned me down is because you're not ready to have children, and you didn't think I wanted to wait? When you could have talked to me about it, and I would've told you that I would?' he checked.

She squirmed. 'Yes. And I've learned from that: next time I make an assumption, I'll talk to you.'

'Good,' he said. 'I think we're on the road to being safe from Nathalie and our mums combined. Almost, but not quite.' He paused. 'Pippa Barnes, I know we've only known each other for a couple of months, but it's enough for me to be sure of what I want. I love you. Will you marry me?'

And this time, she smiled and said, 'Yes.'

EPILOGUE

Five years later

RORY SAT IN the auditorium of the Fitzroy Theatre, his toddler daughter Aurora on his lap, while the dress rehearsal of *Sleeping Beauty* unfolded on the stage in front of them. It was the traditional version, where the 'Rose Adagio' was danced with her four suitors. Though he would always love the version he'd danced with Pippa on this stage.

'Mummy dance,' Aurora informed him solemnly.

'Yes.'

'Mummy princess.'

'Yes,' he agreed. 'She's dancing as someone called Princess Aurora.'

Aurora frowned. '*Me* Rora.'

He nodded. 'You were named after her. She's our favourite princess.'

'Rora dance with Mummy?' Aurora asked.

'Later,' he promised.

She looked pleased. 'Daddy dance baby swans too?'

He chuckled. Practically as soon as Aurora could walk unaided, she'd started to dance—and she loved it when the three of them did the 'Dance of the Little Swans' together.

'We'll do the baby swans,' he said. 'When we get home.'

Aurora clapped, then settled back on his lap to watch her mother dance across the stage.

And life, Rory thought, couldn't get any more perfect.

* * * * *

If you enjoyed this story,
check out these other great reads
from Kate Hardy

A Fake Bride's Guide to Forever
Wedding Deal with Her Rival
Tempted by Her Fake Fiancé
Crowning His Secret Princess

All available now!

MILLS & BOON®

Coming next month

HOW TO WIN BACK A ROYAL
Justine Lewis

It was a face she knew well. One that was tattooed on her heart.

She recognised the frown, the narrowing of his light brown eyes and the sudden tenseness in his shoulders. But there were differences as well. The beard for starters. Auburn, like the rest of his hair, thick and well established. It was clipped neatly and well groomed. Not the result of neglect, but purposeful.

He *wanted* to look different.

She didn't blame him one bit. She'd often toyed with the idea of dying her own light brown hair to see if she'd be able to go unrecognised.

Beard or no beard, she'd recognise this man anywhere.

Why here? Why now? Why him? This was her 'get out there and forget Rowan James' weekend. This was *not* meant to be her 'run into your ex unexpectedly' weekend.

They were separated by two metres but an ocean of grief and pain. She stepped towards him, half wondering if he would simply turn and flee. She wouldn't blame him if he did. Her instincts told her to do the same.

Continue reading

HOW TO WIN BACK A ROYAL
Justine Lewis

Available next month
millsandboon.co.uk

COMING SOON!

We really hope you enjoyed reading this book.
If you're looking for more romance
be sure to head to the shops when
new books are available on

Thursday 24th
April

To see which titles are coming soon, please visit

millsandboon.co.uk/nextmonth

MILLS & BOON

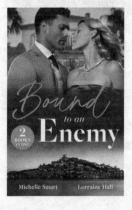
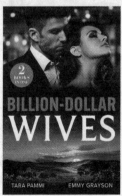

Afterglow Books is a trend-led, trope-filled list of books with diverse, authentic and relatable characters, a wide array of voices and representations, plus real world trials and tribulations. Featuring all the tropes you could possibly want (think small-town settings, fake relationships, grumpy vs sunshine, enemies to lovers) and all with a generous dose of spice in every story.

♪ @millsandboonuk
◎ @millsandboonuk
afterglowbooks.co.uk

#AfterglowBooks

For all the latest book news, exclusive content and giveaways scan the QR code below to sign up to the Afterglow newsletter:

SCAN ME

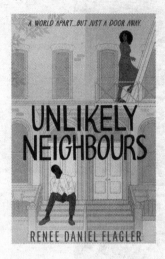
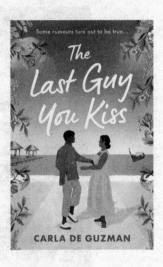
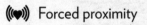
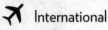

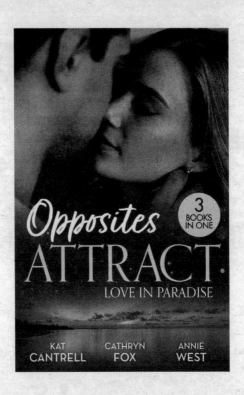

OUT NOW!

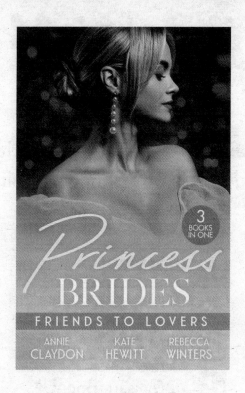

LET'S TALK

Romance

For exclusive extracts, competitions and special offers, find us online:

f MillsandBoon

X @MillsandBoon

O @MillsandBoonUK

J @MillsandBoonUK

Get in touch on 01413 063 232